To Grace,

Thank you for your support!
Enjoy & Uphold Your Honor!!

Honour

T.R. Michaud
10/26/19

authorHOUSE

AuthorHouse™
1663 Liberty Drive
Bloomington, IN 47403
www.authorhouse.com
Phone: 1 (800) 839-8640

© 2019 T.R. Michaud. All rights reserved.

No part of this book may be reproduced, stored in a retrieval system, or transmitted by any means without the written permission of the author.

Published by AuthorHouse 07/22/2019

ISBN: 978-1-7283-1740-3 (sc)
ISBN: 978-1-7283-1739-7 (hc)
ISBN: 978-1-7283-1738-0 (e)

Library of Congress Control Number: 2019908738

Print information available on the last page.

Any people depicted in stock imagery provided by Getty Images are models, and such images are being used for illustrative purposes only.
Certain stock imagery © Getty Images.

This book is printed on acid-free paper.

Because of the dynamic nature of the Internet, any web addresses or links contained in this book may have changed since publication and may no longer be valid. The views expressed in this work are solely those of the author and do not necessarily reflect the views of the publisher, and the publisher hereby disclaims any responsibility for them.

Acknowledgments

I would like to take a page to acknowledge those responsible for giving their aid and making this book a reality. Karen Alves, entrepreneur and owner of Design Principles, Inc. for the cover sleeve. Karen is a very close and personal friend of mine. Her talents and enthusiasm, along with her tireless devotion and support, have once again captured the artwork that I wished for. Thank you for creating the magic that only you can!

Cheryl Sisson for transcribing my written words into type. Your support is unmeasurable. Cheryl also attends "Meet & Greets" with me and double duties it as my photographer so I can capture photos with those of you interested in my tales. Thanks for putting up with all my craziness!

Finally, to those few who took the time to read and comment on this story before it was shared with you, the reader. Thank you; Charles, Auntie Pat, Joel, and my little sister, Cherie.

For Jennifer "JLo" Lopez

Ms. Lopez has not only been one of my favorite performers both singing and acting, but my desire to act alongside her inspired this story.

Prologue

Hamilton, England 1422

The summer night was both clear and cool with stars filling the sky above. Their light shining down illuminating the small, stone cottage along with its surrounding farmland and countryside. The field's grass waved from north to south due to a lite breeze blowing across the English land. Outside the rock structure tranquility filled the night's air while inside the compacted house unrest robbed the peace from its three occupants. The grunts and cries of childbirth consumed the shack's serenity.

"I can see the baby's crown," calmly informed Mary despite the chaos surrounding her. "Just another push or two Liz and the child should breach," she added.

Sweat ran like streams down Elizabeth's face and her long, brown hair was matted against her head. The woman's brown eyes shifting between the village's midwife seated at the end of the table between her spread legs and her husband, Robert, standing beside her.

"Breath my dear," he instructed using one hand to push her wet hair towards the back of her head and out of her face. His other locked in Elizabeth's grasp as she squeezed it trying desperately to rid herself of the accompanying pain.

The laboring woman only nodding in acknowledgment as she prepared for another push. A look of determination reflecting in her eyes.

Bracing her heels against the edge of the wooden table that she laid upon, Elizabeth balled up her empty hand and squeezed her husband's with the other. The woman tucked her chin into her chest while the veins in her neck began to swell and bulge as she put her all into another push. What started out as a low, straining grunt through clenched teeth slowly turned into a triumphant scream when the unborn's crowning head and shoulders finally made their way out. Within the brief seconds that followed, the newborn's feet along with the placenta ended the tiring journey for both mother and child.

"It's a boy, Liz!", excitedly revealed Mary, as the little fellow began to cry from the sudden change in temperature from his mother's warm womb to the coolness of the air surrounding him now. "He's so beautiful," the midwife cooed.

"Let me see him," Elizabeth tiredly requested reaching down towards the seated woman. A weary smile dressed her face.

"Hold on Honey. Let me take care of the afterbirth first before wrapping him up."

"You did it my love," appraised a smiling Robert while stroking her hair backwards a couple more times before bending over and planting a kiss on his wife's forehead. "I love you," he softly added straightening up.

"And I you," she replied with a smile that mirrored his. Elizabeth followed her statement up with a small peck on the back of his hand that she had been holding.

"Here you are Liz. Your son," came the midwife handing the new mother her wrapped up newborn.

Both Elizabeth and Robert gazed down at the baby bundled in a small blanket. Love and pride reflecting from the flickering candlelight in their eyes met their son's small, brown orbs looking up in the direction of his parent's voices.

"You have done good work," complimented Robert.

"No, we have done good work Master Daniels," corrected his wife offering Robert her lips. Her husband more than happy to oblige her request.

"Your father is impressed with you already," she softly said to their son.

'What will be his name?", interrupted Mary rising from her stool holding a clay bowl filled with bloody water and the afterbirth. She had just finished cleaning and bandaging her latest patient.

"His name shall be Russell," softly informed the new mother. "Russell Daniels."

"That's a good, strong name for a boy," approvingly smiled Mary. "I shall bury that," offered Robert taking the bowl and starting for the doorway. "You stay and sit with my wife for a time."

Opening the wooden portal, he turned back to the midwife, "My many thanks Mary. I know not what we would've done without your help."

Mary just smiled. "You would've had a baby Master Daniels."

Robert returned her smile with one of his own before turning and walking out into the night. The new father shutting the door behind him.

Standing outside and feeling the lite breeze blow both relief and happiness washed over him. Gazing up and into the night's sky, Robert was about to offer a prayer of thanks to the Almighty when he took notice of a shooting star above. The sight causing him to delay his verbal donation. The new father watched it fly through the heavens for a couple of moments before giving his thanks to God for the blessing bestowed on him and his wife.

"Your Majesty!", excitedly came one of the castle's servants as she entered the royal's master bedroom from the balcony. The girl, not yet a young woman, had just stepped outside to get some fresh air only moments ago after assisting the castle's midwife in delivering the queen's first child. "I just witnessed a star shooting across the night's sky!", she informed Hamilton's Lord and Lady. "Do you know what that means?", the servant added the inquiry.

Before either the king or the queen could answer, the excited girl still caught up in the rapture of the arrival of the kingdom's new heir responded to her own query. "It's a favorable sign from our Heavenly Father!"

Both Queen Margaret, who was lying in the royal bed cradling her newborn son, and King Stephen, who was standing nearby looked at one another before they both broke out in laughter at the servant's joyful excitement.

"It is true!", the castle's help said glancing between the two.

"It is indeed," happily offered the king beginning to contain himself. "It is indeed," he repeated.

Switching her gaze from her chuckling king to the queen, the servant girl slightly bowed her head. "My lady," -she respectfully addressed- "What shall you name the prince?"

Queen Margaret looked over to her smiling husband and then back to the girl. "We have decided Joan to name him Matthew." Her eyes falling on the sleeping newborn in her arms. "Prince Matthew," she softly added the heirs title.

Chapter 1

Hamilton, England 1432
(10 years later)

The plump, small bird with its brown back along with its rusty orange face and breast bounced to and fro on the three foot high stone wall. The solid barricade made from the independent rocks collected mostly from the tilling of the farm's field and piled together stretched in both directions from the spot of the avian. The little, winged creature always seeming to keep one of its eyes on the boy no matter in what direction it ended up facing after each of its small springs. The robin giving the impression that it watched Russell as much as it itself was being watched. The bird chirped several times like it was trying to communicate with the boy sitting on the ground located roughly five feet away. His back resting against a small tree. An occasional bleat offered by one of the sheep from the flock Russell tended while the animals grazed in the background.

"What are you pondering over Sir Robin?", he asked while gazing at the neck-jerking bird. "Or do you have a nest somewhere in the wall's many nooks and crannies?"

The little, winged creature seemed to answer with a melodious chirp.

Russell stood up slowly as not to frighten the bird and began to turn his back on the wall's occupant. "As you wish Sir Robin. I shall honour your request for secrecy," he informed the avian before beginning to walk towards the huddled up flock preparing to shepherd them back to the barn and their pens.

As the farm's animals escorted by Russell began to leave, the boy glanced back to the now empty stone wall. "I shall see you tomorrow Sir Robin provided it be in God's will," he claimed to the vacant barricade.

Turning back, the shepherd led his flock back home.

⇌

Elizabeth Daniels along with her eight year old daughter, Nicole, were in the middle of washing the household's laundry outside the rear of their stone cottage when the long, brown-haired child, whose looks favored her mother's, noticed her brother leading the flock of sheep towards the barn. Just the mere sight of her older sibling, Russell, seemed to bring joy to the little girl.

"Mother, look!", she excitedly pointed in the direction of the shepherd. "It's Russell!"

Elizabeth looked up from the circular, wooden tub used to scrub one of her husband's dirty shirts and smiled at the appearance of her returning ten year old son ushering the fluffy-coated animals.

Dropping her gaze back towards her daughter, she acknowledged the child's hidden message. "Well go ahead Nicole. I know you wish to go see your brother. There will still be dirty clothes left and I will require your help when you return," she informed her youngest child accompanied with a smile.

Returning the facial expression, Nicole took off running in the direction of her brother. "Russell! Russell!", she yelled.

The mother grinned from ear-to-ear as she thought about the closeness between her only two children before returning her attention back to her duties. The woman's heart filling with pride.

⇌

Robert peeked out of the doorway to the small, stone barn where he had been bedding the only horse's stall along with the pen used to house the sheep as soon as he had heard his daughter call to his only son. The man relieved that he had just finished throwing down the new hay when Robert took in the sight of Russell herding the flock towards the building.

"I do not think that boy is ever late," he thought to himself before disappearing from the structure's entrance.

Grabbing the pitchfork that he had leaned against the wall, Robert used the tool to straighten out any bunched up hay. The family's only horse watching the preparations from its newly cleaned stable.

Russell heard his name being called a couple of times before he saw Nicole running towards him and the sheep. When he did notice her though, a smile instantly spread across his face and he began to leave the flock behind as he walked to meet his sister. Russell knew that Nicole's excitement along with the fact that she currently rushed at him would end up startling the meek farm animals causing them to scatter in every direction. Both he and his father could most likely spend the rest of the afternoon and into the night searching across the whole of England for the lost members of the flock.

"Russell you're back!", excitedly stated Nicole as she hugged the boy.

Her brother laughing as the two embraced. "Well where else could I have gone and received a hug like this?", he queried. "Everyone else in the village would have probably said, it be that Daniels boy and his sheep again coming. Pay em no mind and they shall go away from here," he added jokingly.

"That's not true," she responded. "Everyone in the village likes you."

"Where did you hear that rumor?", the boy inquired while holding his sister out at arm's length and masking his face with a serious look.

Nicole glanced up into his eyes searching them for any hint of playfulness before slapping her brother lightly on his chest when she noticed Russell fighting to hold back a smile.

"It's true you know! Wait and see when we go to church tomorrow," she remarked catching him in the tease.

The boy finally letting his smile win out as he pulled his younger sister back into his embrace. "It does not matter if no one liked me as long as you find fondness with me. That is all that counts," he informed her.

This time Nicole pushed herself back to arm's length. Looking slightly up at Russell she said in a tone as serious as a heart's beat, "I do like you Russell and the others do too."

"Why thanks pixie," he smiled. "Let's bring these sheep to the barn."

"Okay."

"After you my lady," offered Russell while taking a step back with his right foot and giving Nicole a sweep with his hand followed by a slight bow. His younger sister giggled, "You're just like father. Always full of chivally."

"Chivalry," he corrected with a smile.

"That be it," she agreed as both siblings led the flock to the barn.

Later that evening the family of four sat around the only wooden table in their compacted cottage sharing in conversation over the day's last meal. Their small house only consisted of three rooms with the largest being the area the four sat in presently. It contained a small fireplace with a black cauldron off to its left. Cabinets and shelves lined one wall holding not only jarred food products that were not susceptible to spoiling at the end of the day but also plates, bowls, and cups. The only piece of furniture in the room was the wooden dinner table and its four chairs. A couple of black spikes had been hammered into the three thick, wood posts supporting the cottage's roof with two lit lanterns hanging from the large nails. The place's floor was made from lumber.

Nicole slept in one of the other rooms and the third one belonged to her parents; Elizabeth and Robert. A small loft only large enough to accommodate a sleeping pallet and a small wardrobe chest was recently built by Russell's father. It was where the boy rested his head at night. A ladder led up to the platform.

"Everyone's clothes should be ready for church on the morrow," shared Elizabeth before taking a sip of a spoonful of chicken and potato soup. Her eyes closing as the broth's seasoning danced across her palate. "Mmm. Tastes almost as good as my mother's," she openly confessed.

Glancing over to her smiling husband, Elizabeth added, "Almost I said." Robert only letting out a soft chuckle.

"I saw him again today father," Russell announced after swallowing a piece of bread he'd been chewing.

"Saw who son?"

"Sir Robin," replied the boy expressing surprise at his father's inquiry.

"Oh him!", came Robert feigning his own surprised expression while all the time tossing a wink to his wife. "What was he doing?", he continued to query.

"He was bouncing all over this part of the stone wall looking at me and chirping up a storm."

"Sounds like he was talking to you," broke in Nicole.

"Do you ponder?", questioned her father leaning over and rustling her long, brown hair. A giggle escaping the little girl.

"I think Sir Robin wanted me to leave so I wouldn't see where his nest was," the boy offering his opinion on the matter.

"In that case Russell, what did you do?", his mother inquired.

"I did what father had told me mother," he replied. "He said every one of God's creatures deserves to be treated like we want to be treated, so I honoured Sir Robin's wishes for privacy and turned around before heading back here with the sheep. When I looked back to the wall, he was nowhere in sight."

Russell's gaze turning back to his father seeking not only his answer but also his approval of the boy's actions. "I believed he returned to the place where his nest hid."

Wearing a smile full of pride on his face, Robert praised the boy's actions. "Remember son, honour owns several more qualities."

"I know father," acknowledged the boy nodding.

"But with that being said," -continued Robert- "that was an honorable thing you did for Sir Robin. I am proud of you."

A grin instantly grew on the little boy's face causing his younger sister and mother to smile as they shared in Russell's joy.

After the family had finished eating supper, both Russell and his father headed out to the small, stone barn where the horse along with the flock of sheep were housed for the night. Robert wanted to make certain that the animals would be fine before he and his family turned in. Both father and son double-checked the locks to the pens making sure none of the animals would get free and wander off in the darkness. The two secured the structure before heading around back towards the farm's only cart.

The two-wheeled, wooden, mode of transportation was big enough to carry both children in its bed along with a couple of items depending on what they were and their size. The driver's seat was a bench wide enough across for Robert and Elizabeth to sit. The buggy had two poles protruding from its front that were used to hitch up the horse although at the present time their ends rested on top of two flat stones. One of the wheels was locked in place due to a brake that was applied by the operation of a long-handled hand lever.

Robert helped Russell climb onto the driver's seat. When the boy settled into a spot, his father began to address the lad.

"I am proud of you Russell and your grandfather would be also," he stated pleased with his son.

Again like at the supper table, a smile began to spread on the boy's face.

"You are a good son and no father could be more blessed with such a fine lad as you. The way you carry yourself, respect other folk, and treat those around you especially your mother and Nicole just goes to prove that one day you will make a good man," sincerely proclaimed Robert.

"It is as you have taught me father."

Now it was Robert's turn to smile. His grin caused not by pride in himself but rather one by a father fully impressed in the way his child was growing up. The man knowing that the boy was heading down the right path in life, and he could see that someday later his son would be one who lived a life of righteousness.

"The morrow is the Sabbath and since the Lord has decreed that it be a day of rest, I have decided you are now of age to learn how to shoot a bow."

Russell felt a wave of excitement wash over him from his father's sudden revelation and almost jumped clear off the cart. "It is time father?!", the excited boy asked.

"It is time,..." -he slightly smiled- "...but only after you have taken the sheep out to feed. I shall teach you what my father had taught me. That is my word," nodded Robert. "And what is it they say about a person's word?"

"A man's word is everything and speaks of his integrity if upheld," confidently replied the ten year old. "If a man has nothing else, he still has his word and that in itself should adhere to a code of values. For without it, it means less than a grain of salt and his integrity is close to nothing at all."

"Very good my son," appraised Robert with a smile.

Helping the boy off the cart, both father and son started back to the cottage.

The sun had been taking its leave from the sky and within a short time nightfall would replace the pinkish hue that now hung above. Elizabeth and her daughter were just finishing up washing the supper's dishes near the farm's well when Robert and Russell approached.

"Let me my dear," her husband offered taken the two wash pails filled now with only clean dishes from his wife and daughter.

"Always a gentleman my love," added Elizabeth as the Daniels family made their way into the cottage.

"Mother guess what?", queried Russell trying to contain his excitement.

I ponder not the slightest of notions."

"Father is going to teach me to use a bow after church tomorrow!", her son rushing out his answer.

"He is, is he?" she smiled.

"Yes. Father said so himself."

Later that night in the darkness of their sleeping quarters, Elizabeth broke the room's silence while her and her husband lie next to one another. "You are a very good father and a wonderful husband, Robert. I believe there not to be a better man than you throughout the whole of England."

Robert turned over to his side facing his wife's silhouette. "It is you my love that brings out the best in me."

"No Robert. It is you all alone," she corrected. "Did you see our son's face when he told me about you teaching him how to shoot a bow? It is because of you that our son is a fine boy. Not anyone else!"

Elizabeth leaned forward in the darkness and covered her husband's lips with her own before he could say anything else. Her arms pulling him on top of her as their tongues found the familiarity of each other's mouths. Soon soft moans of pleasure escaped from between her lips.

Chapter 2

Russell, along with the other of the cart's occupants, bounced up and down as the wooden buggy followed the dirt road towards the fortified city. Its wheels both falling into and jumping out of small ruts in the earthen way. The singing of robins and other woodland birds dying out the closer they came to the hustling and bustling town. All the Daniels wearing their Sunday's best to church on this morning.

"It always smells so horrible the closer we get father," stated the grimacing Nicole getting a good whiff of the rotten stench in the air.

"That is why I favor the countryside," admitted the girl's mother over her shoulder. "The air is cleaner and pleasant to breathe."

"Lets go folks!", shouted one of the city's guards. "Keep it moving!"

Ahead, a filthy man dawning tattered robes stood near the fortified wall's entrance begging for hand-me-outs. His fortune of acquiring anything from those passing through the opening was not in his favor.

"Something for a poor man who knows only misfortune these days!", he pleaded while stumbling up towards the Daniels cart. "You look to be a fine fellow blessed with a beautiful wife and children my lord," he added.

"And you need to come up with a new line David. This one has appeared to have run its course," smiled Robert looking down from his seat. He and his family had heard the same compliment every Sunday morning offered from this one particular unfortunate for the past several years.

A brief chuckle escaped the poor beggar. "You may be right sir," he admitted before casting his own grin.

"Russell, hand the man that small bundle," directed Elizabeth.

Reaching down and picking up the small package wrapped in a piece of cloth, the boy handed it to the poor man.

"It be a small bowl of chicken and potato soup with two rolls," informed the woman seated on the other side of her husband.

"Thank you and bless your soul kind lady," appreciatively came the dirty-robed man giving a slight bow of his head. "May the Almighty bestow blessings upon you and your family."

"And you also," wished Elizabeth accompanied with a smile.

"Lets go folks! Keep er moving!", shouted the guardsman again.

Robert gave David the beggar a nod as the poor man stepped back from the cart. When he thought the man was at a safe distance away, Robert flipped the reins signaling his horse to continue into the city. The Daniels disappearing through the wall's opening.

"Now go in peace children and may the Lord be with you," wished the priest ending the day's sermon.

"And also with you," the congregation replied.

The chapel returned back from its peaceful life as folk said their farewells to one another or headed for the room's double oak doors. Two members of the church swung both portals open sending the exiting followers spilling out into the crowded and noisy city streets. The busy fairways bringing the congregation back down to earth. The four members of the Daniels family leaving with their neighbors and friends; the Bradfords.

"Are you bringing Gwenyth and the girls over?", queried Robert walking and speaking to the head of the Bradford's house.

"If you will have us," responded Charles. "Unless both you and Elizabeth desire to spend some time at our place?"

"No. No. Please come over," answered Robert before explaining his inquiry to his longtime friend. "I promised Russell that after the sheep have been fed than I shall begin teaching him the use of a bow. I had the notion that you would like to join us while our wives speak of women things and the girls play."

"In that case, I am happy to accept," smiled Charles. "We shall need to briefly stop at our place on the way to your house so I can retrieve my bow and quiver. Lynn and Anne can also change into their play clothes."

"Very well," agreed Robert. "I shall follow you."

After a brief stop at the Bradford's cottage, the two horse drawn carts continued down the dirt road for roughly a couple more miles until they arrived at the Daniel's place. Robert and Charles stopped the carts and applied the wooden brakes that held one of the two wheels stationary. Both men jumped from their seats to aid their wives and children off of the wagons.

"Go and change out of your church clothes first before you take the flock out to the pasture. I will meet you at the tree near the stone wall when I am done unhitching the horse," Robert explained to Russell.

The boy nodding his head in acknowledgment before darting into the cottage.

"I would say the boy's excited," laughed Charles. "He just took off like his britches were on fire."

Robert couldn't help but share in the laugh with his longtime friend.

Within minutes, which actually seemed like forever to Russell, his mother along with Gwenyth watched the boy run past the two sitting at the table and out the house's door.

"I love you mother!", trailed out the entryway behind him.

The two women only laughed.

Lynn Bradford, who was the same age and had the same petite build as Russell's younger sister Nicole, played in an open field with her best friend. Her hair was also long and straight brown just like the Daniel's girl, and from behind it would be easy for someone to mistake one for the other.

Lynn's sister Anne was three years younger, and even though the child had still retained some of her baby fat, there was no doubting the siblings' relation to one another. She accompanied her older sister and Nicole in the grassy pasture between the stone cottage and the forest located on the perimeter of the open land.

The two, older girls were caught up in a game they called "cat's cradle" where they would run a long piece of string between both of their hands and take turns going either up and through or down and through the others. Pulling the string taunt it would be the other girl's turn to try. The game ended when the twisted threads bunched up and became tangled.

Caught up in one of the matches, neither Lynn nor Nicole witnessed Anne move off heading away from them. The youngest girl's attention captured by a butterfly.

Russell's tongue hung out of the side of his mouth as he drew the bow's string back past his right ear. Beads of sweat formed on the boy's forehead from the strain of the pull's fight against his shoulder and right arm.

"Remember son. Do not just let go and dry fire the weapon," advised his father. "Fight the resistance it has to spring back and return to its normal position."

Russell fighting past the bow's pressure point in the draw. "Why is it so hard at a certain spot but pulls with ease before and after that area?", he queried returning the weapon to its original position.

"Because son, at this point the weapon's string is causing the bow to stretch itself. This is what gives it its shooting power." Robert demonstrated exactly what he was speaking about before continuing. " At any place before this point there is no pull on the bow's shaft and after this area, the pull goes with the draw instead of against it due to the shape of the weapon," the boy's father running his hand over the curve of the shaft.

"Father, how long before I can fire an arrow?", desperately inquired the boy.

"You need to strengthen up your shoulder and arm making the draw both easy and fluid," Robert admitted, but before he could finish the rest of his answer his wife's screams interrupted the boy's lesson.

"Robert! Oh Robert!", shouted Elizabeth running towards him with a crying Gwenyth and two of the three girls in tow.

"What troubles you?", he asked concerned as she rushed up to him. Elizabeth's husband trying to eye the others for any telltale signs of the problem.

"Where is Lynn?", queried Charles glancing between his wife's eyes and those of his friend's spouse.

"Nicole said she ventured off into the woods in search for Anne," a panic-stricken Gwenyth replied.

"But the child is with you," stated the girl's father taken in the sight of his youngest daughter amongst them.

"Lynn and I couldn't find Anne so we went to the border of the trees and called for her," explained Nicole. "Father, we thought she had gone in there but when I ran back to the house to retrieve mother Anne was there."

"Go on child," instructed Robert when he noticed his daughter start to pause for a moment with tears beginning to fill up her eyes. Already fear had consumed the girl, but if the men had any chance of finding the lost child alive, time was of the essence.

"When I returned to tell Lynn that Anne was at the house, she had already gone into the forest," worried Nicole. "I yelled for her father but she never called back."

"You must find our baby Charles!", hysterically sobbed Gwenyth.

"We will," he proclaimed gazing into her eyes while grasping both of his wife's shoulders.

"Father, I can help!", Russell quickly blurted out. "You have taught me how to move in the forest and how to find my way home if ever I should get lost.

"Are you sure you want to chance the boy becoming lost himself?", questioned Charles.

"But I won't," pleaded Russell staring into his father's eyes.

Robert paused for a brief mental deliberation. "The boy is right. He does have the familiarity of the place and should be well off," admitted Russell's father. "He will join us and we will look for your girl my friend."

Turning to Elizabeth, Robert made a final request before their son and both men headed into the forest. "You ladies return to the house and wait there for are return. Take the flock back to their pen."

The two women along with Nicole and Anne watched as Charles, Robert, and Russell rushed into the woods.

Placing an arm around Gwenyth's lowered shoulders, Elizabeth ushered the heartbroken woman and the children back towards the cottage. "They will find Lynn. You will see Gwenyth, everything will be well."

The clear, summer day seemed to wear on and still there had been no sign of Lynn. The three rescuers had split up, and now the forest's air was filled with the shouts for the missing girl. While searching Russell had made his way down to a slow flowing stream.

"Lynn!" "Lynn!", he shouted.

The boy followed the stream for roughly half-a-mile when he noticed out of the corner of his eye a thistle located behind a log shake. Russell froze knowing that a wild pig could be the cause. Remaining still and making sure to stay quiet, he continued to watch the prickly plant. A faint sobbing carried on the air from its direction.

"Lynn, is that you?", softly the boy asked.

No one answered.

After several moments, Russell mustered every brave bone in his ten year old body and slowly began to make his way over to the plant and log. He noticed a two foot long stick laying on the ground and bent to pick it up. Looking it over and satisfied with its thickness, the boy stalked towards the area.

"Lynn, is that you?", he asked a little louder this time.

"Yes," came the response between sobs.

"It's me, Russell," identified the boy. "Are you alright?"

"I hurt my ankle and I'm scared," the hidden girl sobbed.

"I'm coming to help you," advised Russell still carrying the stick in his right hand.

Lynn looked up as Russell's head came into view over the log.

"Your father and my father are looking for you as well. Can you walk?"

"No. It hurts too much," the sobbing girl gazed at her savior through wet, puffy eyes. Tears had freely run down her cheeks.

"Father!", his son calling for aid.

Looking back to Lynn, Russell cast a reassuring smile. "I will get you back to your mother," he matter-of-factly declared.

"But I'm scared."

"Do not worry. I know my way home and besides we'll probably run into my father or yours before then," he reasoned.

"What if we run into one of those wild pigs though?", Lynn's voice cracked at the question.

"I shall not allow you to be hurt," Russell swore. "I will protect you," he added while reaching down and offering his hand to the scared, little girl.

Lynn reached back up and took hold of it. Russell was only two years older than her, but somehow she believed every word he said. Helping her up, Lynn wrapped an arm over Russell's shoulder and leaned against him for support.

"Are you ready?", he queried smiling at the girl whom had stopped sobbing.

Lynn nodded her acknowledgment before the two started their journey back.

"They found her!", excitedly cried Elizabeth when she took in the sight of her husband, her son, and Charles carrying Lynn coming towards the cottage. Relief lifted the pressure off of Gwenyth as she ran to her rescued daughter.

"Are you well child?", inquired her mother reaching her husband and Lynn.

"Besides injuring her ankle she is only shaken," replied Charles giving his oldest daughter in his arms a smile. "She'll be fine now."

Russell saved me mother," came Lynn. "I was afraid but he protected me."

"Thank you Russell. That was a brave thing you did," praised Gwenyth while rubbing Lynn's hair towards the back of her head.

"Father always says that the right thing to do is to protect others when for whatever the reason they cannot defend themselves," quoted Russell. "Besides it was Lynn who was brave, I had a stick," he smiled.

Robert also smiled and then rustled his son's hair.

Chapter 3

Prince Matthew sat on his grand-sized bed beside the young woman whom he had known all of his life so far listening intently to the ending of the story she had been telling him. The young royal's eyes transfixed upon the servant girl's face and lips as he focused not to miss a single word of the tale. It was a narrative that the prince had heard over a hundred times, but Matthew never minded hearing the story again due to it being his favorite. The other fact being that the woman always relayed the account with a renewed vigor causing the ten year old prince to never lose interest even though the boy knew what was about to come next.

"But before the assassin could slice the sleeping king's throat, the chamber's door flew open and William rushed into the room!", the servant narrated while swinging her arm giving the appearance of throwing open an imaginary door. The woman paused offering the boy the scene's full effect.

Prince Matthew's mouth slightly ajar in anticipation for what came next. His gaze locked on the storyteller's eyes.

"Reaching over his shoulder and quickly plucking an arrow, William nocked it and pulled the bowstring back aiming at the startled assassin, who had jumped back in his surprise."

"What did the king do?", inquired the royal caught up in the tale.

"Naturally he awoke startled and confused by the sudden noise," relayed Joan. "Sitting up in his bed, King John glanced between William and the armed would be murderer."

Again, the servant paused and she could make out the expectancy in the young prince.

"After a brief moment, the surprised assassin started for the defenseless king, but William let loose his arrow. It flew through the air missing King John by this much," -she emphasized holding a hand up with her two fingers spaced roughly two inches apart- "Striking the attempted murderer right between his eyes!", the storyteller using the index finger from the hand she had just held up displaying the amount of space to point at the exact spot on the boy's forehead. "Saving the king."

"Boy, that William sure was a good shot! Huh Joan?", impressible asked Matthew while wearing a smile.

"The best in the whole of England they would say."

"What did King John do?"

"Well as legend has it, the king indebted to William for saving his life, offered him a place at court along with granting his savior some land," replied Joan. "But the hero only accepted some land to start a farm."

"Why? His rescuer could have been a noble."

"King John was also perplexed by William's decision. When he queried as to why the rescuer only wanted a small piece of estate, the man gave one of the most noblest answers the king had ever heard. He said because he loved his grace and he was bound by both duty and loyalty to protect him if ever a threat should arise," smiled Joan.

Both of the chamber's occupants looked to the doorway of Prince Matthew's bedroom when Queen Margaret, who had stood there in silence listening to the servant tell the story began to clap.

"Mother!", excitedly came her son. "Were you standing there listening the whole time?"

"My Lady," greeted the servant rising from her seat on the prince's bed and bowing her head.

"Please Joan," came the queen as she entered the chamber. A humble elegance seemed to fill the room. "Sit down. I have known you since you were but a child, and you are like one of the family."

The young woman returning to her spot on the bed. "Thank you my lady."

"And yes my son. I had the pleasure of sharing in the ending of William the Brave's tale," smiled the boy's mother. "A very honorable act by no doubt an equally, honorable man."

"I apologize for breaking up your story time,…" Queen Margaret glanced amongst the two, "…but your father requests your presence in his private study."

Matthew turned to Joan. "Can we continue with the stories later?", he asked the woman.

"Of course my prince, but do not forget your lesson on proper mannerisms before we do," she replied.

The young boy dashing from his room heading for his father's study.

Joan stood and began to rub the bed where both her and the prince had been sitting. The wrinkled impressions in the cover disappearing as they worked their way out. Satisfied, the servant began to tidy up the chamber looking up as Margaret approached.

"My queen," she addressed the royal woman.

"You are aware that a place in my son's heart has your name inscribed on it," Margaret informed the young woman. Smiling, she continued, "He loves you Joan like that of a second mother."

"Thank you my lady," replied the servant. "He is a good boy and will make a great and loved king when the prince's time arrives," praised Joan.

Queen Margaret nodded her head in acknowledgment while the corners of her lips turned up. Stepping forward she reached out for Joan's hand taking it in her delicate grasp. "You are part of the reason why that boy is the way he is," she softly stated. "Your good nature and loving personality is an example to Matthew that will benefit him one day when both the king and I have left this life." Her majesty continued looking the servant woman in her eyes. "As a mother, I thank you."

"It is I who owe you and the king my thanks my lady," confessed Joan. "When my mother passed leaving me as a young child, the king could have cast me out to fend for myself but he didn't."

"That would not be just nor would it have been right," admitted the queen.

The servant offering a smile as she continued. "Instead, you both took me under your watchful eyes and made sure I was learned in the proper upbringing of life. The two of you always provided me with a place to lay my head, a full belly, and shelter from the cold. It was you who was at my side when I was taken with the night visions after my mother was gone.

How in this lifetime could I ever repay you and the king?", a tear rolled from the corner of Joan's eye.

The queen raised her free hand up to the young woman's cheek, wiping the single tear that rolled down her face. Staring into Joan's eyes, Margaret softly began to speak. "Remember child, it is never about paying a debt. People do because they want to do. In the Lord's kingdom even a lost sheep matters to the shepherd. King Stephen is not our Heavenly Father but he is the ruler of this kingdom here on earth. In his eyes, everyone he sits over matters especially a motherless child." The queen once again gave a smile before pulling the young woman to her breast in an embrace.

"Thank you my lady," replied a teary Joan. "You are the mother that I never had."

The phrase causing even the queen to shed a royal tear.

"Enter!", the curly, black-haired man with a face full of beard shouted over the top of a black, leather bound book from across the chamber. His eyes held on the slowly opening wooden door.

"Mother said you wished to see me father," came the young boy's voice.

"Yes Matthew. Please come in."

The prince closing the portal behind him after he had entered the room and then strolling over to his father.

"What is it you would like to see me about father?", inquired Matthew still slightly excited from Joan's tale of "William the Brave."

King Stephen recognizing a pent up energy in the prince's body language. "Matthew you seem quite stirred up about something. Where were you when your mother found you?"

"In my room father."

"And what is it exactly you were doing?", queried the king looking down his nose at his son, who had just sat down on a wooden, rocking chair.

"Joan was telling me about William the Brave and King John," Matthew hastily replied while beginning to rock back-n-forth. The young prince couldn't hold the story to himself and began to narrate the whole tale back to his father. The speed of the chair's movement becoming faster and faster towards the approaching assassination attempt.

Honour

The boy's father sat across from his only son giving him his undivided attention while remaining silent until Matthew had finally come to the tale's ending. The future heir breathing heavy from the lack of oxygen uptake during his hastily reciting of the whole legend.

"Mother said William was very honorable," the young prince added. "What do you think father?"

"I believe your mother is proper in her answer," confirmed King Stephen. "But most importantly what do you think?"

Prince Matthew rocked slowly for a minute as he pondered the question and answer in his mind. Looking up to the chamber's ceiling, the boy lowered his eyes until they met his father's waiting gaze. "I think William was honorable like mother said."

"Why?", questioned his father.

"Because he stuck to a certain code that he believed in," replied the boy. "I think King John ruled his kingdom showing fairness and just to the people causing the folk throughout the land to like him."

"Do you ponder King John respected others and that is why maybe they liked and respected him back?"

Prince Matthew nodded his head in approval. "Yes father."

"And do you believe that William the Brave saved the king because he was a good or bad ruler?"

"I believe he was definitely a good person!"

"So if King John is a good king and William performs a loyal act by rushing to his bedside to save him, then is it proper to say that through King John's actions toward the folk of his kingdom along with the actions performed by William to save his king that both men are honorable?", asked the boy's father waiting stoically in anticipation for his son's answer.

Again Matthew took a minute or two to reflect on his father's query and only when he felt he had the proper decision, the young prince addressed the bearded man. "I believe both men were honorable father because if you respect and treat others well than that is honorable. Also, if you live and stick to a certain belief of right and wrong and defend those beliefs than that is,..." -the prince's words trailing off as his mind searched for the one word his father used all of the time- "Integrit. Integity."

"Integrity?", queried Stephen.

"Yes father. Integrity. To stick to and defend your beliefs."

King Stephen chuckled briefly before once again addressing his son. "Very well done my son! You will make a good king one day just like King John."

A smile appeared and grew on Prince Matthew's face at the sign of his father's approval.

"You really like Joan don't you son?"

"Yes father. She is a very nice lady!", the boy beamed with excitement. "She is always telling me stories and legends."

King Stephen let out another chuckle before he spoke. "Remember son, she serves you because of your birthright to the throne, but she deserves your respect and well treatment because Joan is a person."

"I know father. When I take my place on the throne I want to rule this kingdom as you do," sincerely swore the prince. "I wish to be the leader that I hear spoken in the halls that you are. They say folk love you like mother and I do."

The king leaned forward giving the impression that he had a secret to share with his son. Matthew leaned towards his father. "To be a good leader son one must first learn how to be a better follower. For once he has learned the hardships of a good servant then and only then can one lead fairly and justly," -the boy's father adding as he sat back- "We go to church on the Sabbath so we can praise the Almighty with the townsfolk and listen to their voices."

A smile grew on the boy's face for Matthew always seemed to like meeting the people at the chapel.

"Now go son and find Joan before you are late for your lesson."

The smiling prince embracing his father in a loving hug. King Stephen laughing behind the boy sprinting out of the room for his favorite storyteller. For a moment, the excited Matthew forgetting all about his manners and closing the heavy, oak door with a loud **"THUMP!"**

Chapter 4

The church's congregation was quiet listening to their guest speaker reading from the dais' lectern that one could hear a pin drop. Their unblinking stares locked on King Stephen as he just finished reading the second of three scriptures for this day's service.

"This last one is my favorite Holy Writ from the Sacred Book of the Lord's Words," shared the king looking around at the chapel's folk. "It is from First Kings: chapter three; verses nine through fourteen. Our Heavenly Father is speaking to King Solomon," the king setting the upcoming scene before beginning to recite the good word.

"'So give your servant a discerning heart to govern your people and to distinguish between right and wrong. For who is able to govern this great people of yours?' The Lord was pleased that Solomon had asked for this. So God said to him, 'Since you have asked for this and not long life, or wealth for yourself, nor have asked for the death of your enemies, but for discernment in administering justice, I will do what you have asked. I will give you a wise and discerning heart, so that there will never have been anyone like you, nor will there ever be. Moreover, I will give you what you have not asked for-both riches and honor- so that in your lifetime you will have no equal among kings. And if you walk in my ways and obey my statutes and commands, as David your father did, I will give you a long life!"

King Stephen looked up from the open black, leather-bound Bible to the Heavens. "Amen."

The congregation following his lead expressing their appropriate closing to the literature as one. "Amen."

Glancing to the seated priest, the crownless royal met his nod with one of his own before turning back and addressing the other members of the church. "My brothers and sisters; as you can see I do not dawn my crown, nor does my wife, in this Holy Place." Stephen pointing over to a seat on the dais where Margaret, her crown absent from her brow, and Matthew sat. One on each side of an empty high-back chair. "This is because this is our Father's house and he is King of kings!"

Pausing for a brief moment to allow the effects of his last statement to sink in, the royal speaker continued. "I was just talking with my son on the days before coming here that for one to lead with fairness and justness like that of the wise King Solomon, than a good leader must before that be a better servant."

Stephen's eyes surveying the room as he paused a second time.

"My wife and I humbly request that after the service has come to an end you good folk of the land approach the dais allowing us to greet you one at a time. I also query that you accept our small gift of a roll with a spot of jam on the top."

A small murmur of both acceptance and excitement passed though the congregation of the packed temple. The king taking back their full attentions as he once again spoke. "Would all join me in speaking the Lord's Prayer?"

The royal bowing his head as he dropped to a knee facing a statue of the Christ crucified on a cross. The church following his actions. Soon all their separate voices becoming one.

When the prayer was finished, Stephen rose to his feet and started for the empty seat in between his wife and son.

The priest rising and taking his place back at the lectern. "May God be with you."

"And also with you," replied the unity of the church's members.

<hr>

The service had come to an end within the last half-an-hour or so, but a line of loyal subjects looking forward to greeting their beloved king and his family still formed winding its way through the church's chapel. Most folk seizing the opportunity during this occasion to speak freely to their royal leader. All the while the prince was more than happy handing out the delicious, baked treats.

"What happened to you child?", sweetly inquired the queen slightly bending over, as a woman with her limping daughter at her side stepped up to meet and greet Margaret.

The little girl quietly staring up at her.

"Go ahead Lynn. Tell our queen what happened to you," prodded the girl's mother.

Looking up to meet the royal woman's eyes, Lynn softly informed her of the recent incident. "Well my lady, I thought my sister Anne had wandered into the forest near Russell's house so I went looking for her and got lost along with hurting my ankle. Father believes it is twisted and says it will heal within a week's time."

"Who is Russell?"

"He is one of my friend's children," stated Gwenyth. "Her oldest my lady," the woman added.

"How old is the boy if I may inquire?", inquisitively asked Queen Margaret.

"Of course my lady," Gwenyth humbled. "He is ten years of age."

The queen stood straight with a hint of amazement glinting from the corners of her eyes. ""Ten you say. He must be a brave boy," she admitted.

"He is my lady!", Lynn confirmed. "But he said I was brave because he had a stick in hand."

Both Queen Margaret and the little girl's mother glanced at one another and smiled.

"I believe he was right," the royal woman agreed casting a smile at Lynn.

"Please take a couple of rolls from my son," -sweeping her hand towards the prince- "Compliments of the castle's baker."

"Thank you my lady," bowed Gwenyth. Lynn duplicating not only her mother's words but her actions as well. The two receiving a roll each as Matthew offered them.

"Is it true? Did you really get lost in the woods?", queried the young royal.

"For a time," replied Lynn.

"What happened to your sister? Is she well?"

"Oh yes. She never went into the forest, but was with mother instead," answered the girl before turning to point in the direction of her father and sister standing in the other line waiting to greet the king. "That is Anne and Father there."

Prince Matthew's eyes following the girl's finger in the direction of her sister in the arms of her father.

"That is relieving to hear," he stated. "But I would like to ask one more question of you if I may?"

"As you wish your grace," Lynn agreeing to the request.

"While you were in the woods, did you happen to see any wild boar?", the young prince's face taking on a look of seriousness.

"No," perplexed by the young royal's reason for the question, the girl followed her answer up with a query of her own. "Why?"

"Because I overheard the castle's hunters telling my father that they have not seen any signs of the animals in the royal forest as of late. Hence, if they are in those woods than I will surely inform them for I long for the delicious pig." His mouth even seemed to water, as visions of the cooked and prepared swine briefly locked in his mind's eye.

"Oh well," Prince Matthew added before glancing back to the roll Lynn held. "I hope you enjoy it."

"What the boar?", the girl puzzled.

"No, the roll!", he corrected with a smile.

"My many thanks my prince," came Gwenyth's appreciation as she began to usher her daughter out of the way, so the next person in line could greet the queen and her son and receive their own donations from the royal family. "Queen Margaret and Prince Matthew have others to see Lynn. Let us take our leave," she added.

As the girl along with her mother walked away, Gwenyth's daughter, still slightly puzzled by the young royal's query, glanced back at the boy.

Matthew's gaze locked on the forest adventurer.

"Mother," he called to Queen Margaret.

She looked down to her son eliciting a response.

"That girl reminds me of the story that Joan told me of the warrior heroine from France."

"Why do you say that Matthew?"

"Because it sounds to me like that girl is already beginning to take small journeys like the ones Joan of Arc took when she was a child."

"Is that what you believe?", inquired the boy's mother as she smiled at him.

"Maybe," the young prince responded after a couple of silent moments accompanied with the raising and lowering of his shoulders.

Matthew continued to hand out roll after roll until the church's congregation slowly cleared from the place. Two thoughts seemed to battle for his mind's attention; the adventurous girl from the countryside who reminded him of the French heroine and the disappointment of no end in sight to the drought of missing a royal, boar dinner. The latter seeming no doubt a dilemma to the would be one day king.

Chapter 5

Hamilton, England 1438
6 years later

Russell drew the bow's string back fully behind his ear and shut his right eye using his open left one to take aim for his upcoming shot. The weapon's strain from its pull no longer affecting him like it had first done when the boy began to learn how to use the missile-firing instrument. His years of practice and strengthening up had made Russell a very good shot with the bow.

Standing in the tree line, Russell used his one aiming eye to sight and lock on the wild boar making its way across the grassy bank of the slow, flowing stream. The pig's nose to the ground in search of a scent that led to food. Grunts and heavy, exhaling snorts following deep sniffs of the land escaped from the animal. The beast raising its large head displaying six inch tusks to the sky every now and then sniffing the air. The sixteen year old, a smart enough hunter to know now how to stay downwind from the boar.

Slowly and cautiously, Russell waited for the right time to let loose his nocked arrow. Only when he believed the swine was in the right spot, the shooter fired the bow. Its arrow flying from the trees and finding its mark in the pig's hairy body behind the animal's front leg. A high-pitched squeal erupted from the swine more from the surprising hit then from the actual piercing of its heart. The kill shot dropping the wild boar to the ground dead. Russell waited a brief time before running out of the tree's cover and exposing his position to the animal. The hunter wanted to make sure the pig was dead before he ended up having a wounded and angry animal regain its feet and charge him. The young man knew things could go bad quickly if he was careless.

"Father!", yelled Russell satisfied with the encounters outcome. "I have fallen one by the stream!"

Looking around the young man left the forest heading into the small clearing that ran the perimeter of the water. He jogged up to the dead beast to get a closer view.

"Father, I have got one!", he shouted a second time.

"I am coming Russell!", came a voice carrying on the air out of the surrounding forest.

Russell couldn't believe the size of the deceased as he got closer to it. The pig would definitely be enough to feed his family of four for at least a couple of days. "Got some pretty big tusks on it," he softly said as he examined one of the enlarged, protruding teeth.

Bushes and shrubs rustled in the background off in the distance and the young man knew his father had finally arrived to help him gut the pig and then bind it to a pole made from a thick tree branch. The three had brought it along on their hunt to carry a deer or a boar out of the woods and back home.

"Did you retrieve the pole and the rope?", he inquired while looking back in the direction of the noise. Russell's eyes grew to the size of gold coins when only twenty feet away stood another large, hairy, wild boar. Its own eyes set on the young man. Issuing a high-pitched squeal of anger, the ornery beast charged at the hunter kneeling next to the pig he had moments ago killed.

With the oncoming swine closing the distance between it and its prey, Russell had very little time to act. Still gripping the bow in his left hand, the young man moved with lightning speed as he reached for an arrow housed in the quiver on his back while propelling himself forward rolling over the dead boar. The hairy pig armed with at least five inch tusks of its own slashed at the hunter as it ran by. Russell's quick acrobatics allowing him to dodge out of the way of the animal's attack. The boar's momentum causing it to run right by the spot where Russell had been kneeling only seconds ago. Fortunately for the swine, one of its protruding bone weapons caught the young man's lower leg ripping his pants and causing Russell to suffer a superficial slice. Blood began to trickle from the shallow cut and the hunter now turned prey grimaced from the pain of the wound.

Russell had no time now to worry about the injury to his leg as he swiftly nocked the arrow he had retrieved and drew the bow's string back preparing a shot. Hitting the ground and landing on his lower back almost in a laid back position, the young man held the weapon across his body with the arrow's feathers drawn to his hip.

The ferocious animal spun quickly after its direct miss and came again at the elusive hunter. Rage in its eyes as it once again set its sight on Russell and charged. An angry squeal came forth from the boar.

Fighting through the burning pain in his leg, Russell took aim and concentrated waiting as long as he could making sure that his one shot would give him the best chance he so desperately needed to escape a mauling. The young man whispered a small prayer before letting loose the arrow. He watched as it flew towards the charging pig biting into the animal's head right above its eyes while at the same time a second arrow sunk into the middle of the beast's skull. The onrushing boar instantly dropped to the ground. Its momentum carried it forward plowing up the grassy terrain. Clumps of dirt shot skyward before it came to a rest only inches away from the original swine. The rage in its eyes now replaced with the unblinking stare of death.

Russell turned his head looking behind him to see his father rushing in his direction carrying his own bow and Lynn's father following carrying his bow along with the pole and ropes needed to carry the first dead boar home.

"Are you well son?", anxiously cried Robert.

The young hunter laid back on the grass and exhaled a breath of relief before he responded. "I am fine father." Gazing towards the sky, Russell softly added, "Thank you."

"I would be inclined to say we both got one," pointed out his savior looking down at his son.

The prone hunter cast a smile up at the two grinning faces looking down upon him before sharing in a brief laughter at the now relieved close call.

It had taken the three hunters twice as much time to carry the two kills out of the forest after finding another pole-like limb to lash the second boar to and dividing the rope out evenly securing both carcasses to them. Russell also required several minutes to clean and wrap a cloth around the bloody cut on his leg. The wound leaving him with a slight limp in his gait. There was no denying that all three men struggled with the loads of dead weight.

Once the hunters had returned to the Daniels' small farmstead, both Robert and Charles decided to hang the boars up in a stone slaughterhouse that would allow for the pigs' blood to drain from their bodies. The two had made the decision that at some point on the morrow they would skin the animals and start butchering the meat from the kills.

Meanwhile, Russell had limped into the cottage where he was welcomed by the sounds of a loud inhalation from not only his mother and sister but also the three women of the Bradfords' household. Elizabeth ran to his aid when she noticed his torn and bloody pants accompanying his limp.

"Oh my!", gasped his mother as she jumped up from her seat at the table. "What happened Russell?"

"It's nothing mother. Just a nick," her son brushing off the seriousness of the close call. "It appears worse than it really is."

"Come take a seat," she offered helping him to the chair she had just been sitting in. "Let me have a look at that."

Russell laid his bow on the table and removed the quiver from his back placing it near the weapon before dropping into the chair.

Lifting his leg and cradling his boot on her lap as she kneeled in front of him, Elizabeth rolled up the torn pant's leg revealing the wound caused from the animal's tusk. A makeshift bandage from a piece of the pant's material covered the cut. Slipping the field dressing down, a small trickle of blood ran from the shallow injury.

"See mother, I told you it's not bad," confirmed her son.

She looked up at Russell smiling and pat him on his foot's instep. "Okay son but I shall clean it and put a fresh bandage on it," she informed him. "How did this happen anyways?", she inquired rising up from her knees.

"A boar almost got me."

"From what I have witnessed already I would say he did."

"It is not that bad mother."

"Where was your father?", Elizabeth queried while filling a wash basin up with water from a pitcher.

"He saved me," Russell answered.

Returning to her seated son, his mother stared up into his face. "Tell me the whole of it Russell."

The young man spent the next ten minutes or so narrating the events that led up to his injury. Russell finished his story just before his father and Charles walked through the door.

Elizabeth was just rising from the floor finished with cleaning and bandaging the wound, but before she could say anything Russell addressed Robert. "Father, did you get them both up and hanging?"

"Yes son, but the query is how are you feeling?"

"What do you mean both?", Elizabeth puzzled. Her eyes glancing between her husband and son.

"The boy shot two of them today," advised Robert.

Turning her attention back to Russell, a small scowl began to make its way onto her face. "I thought you said there was only one boar!"

"Well I did not want you to worry mother so I left out a few details in my tale," came her son.

Before anyone else could say anything, Charles walked over and placed a hand on Russell's shoulder. "You should be proud of the lad Elizabeth for the boy's actions earlier this day are the only reason why he is still here. Most men I know, never mind a growing boy, would have been badly mauled or even dead right now." Charles glanced back-n-forth between the two Daniels' parents before returning his gaze back to Elizabeth. "Robert has taught this young man well," he proclaimed.

Russell's mother looked over at her husband. "But he said you killed one."

"No my dear. Russell killed both of the beasts," corrected her husband. "My shot was only to make sure that the animal would not be rising up anytime soon."

Walking over to Russell, his father patted him on his shoulder. "You did a fine job son," he praised. "You have come a long way with the bow."

"Thank you father," smiled the appreciative young man.

The next day the Bradfords made the trip back to the Daniels' farm so Charles could help Robert skin and butcher the two boars. With all the meat that they would both be getting from the wild pigs, the two had decided to give some of the pork to the neighbor who lived roughly a mile on the other side of Robert's small farm. Both Paul and Juliet were in their early fifties and would definitely appreciate the edible gift.

"I shall be right out father to help you and Mr. Bradford," informed Russell seated at the table while starting to slip on one of his boots.

"No son," corrected his father. "I think you should stay here and take care of your leg. You do not want anything to cause an infection and plague you."

"But father, I will be fine," he tried to plead.

"Your father is right," softly interjected Russell's mother who had also been sitting at the table along with Charles' wife, Gwenyth. "Stay and do your mother the honour of partaking in a hot cup of tea and shared conversation with both Mrs. Bradford and I."

Russell badly wished to go to the stone slaughterhouse but he had been raised to honour thy mother and father, so the young man accepted their wishes, placing them above his own desire. "Yes mother," he softly agreed.

Elizabeth gave her son a small grin while patting his knee twice. She then cast a smile at her husband along with Charles before finally glancing across the table to Gwenyth sitting down. "Very well. Let me heat some water for tea," she proclaimed rising from her seat and starting for a pot she used specifically to heat water.

"I know you would rather be out with us son but I want to make sure that your leg is well so we can continue with your sword lessons in a couple of days," remarked Robert before following Charles out of the cottage's door.

"How are your sword lessons coming along anyhow?", inquired Gwenyth looking over to Russell. Her face wearing a pleasant expression and her eyes shifting to Elizabeth, who met the glance with a smile of her own.

Even Gwenyth's oldest daughter Lynn, who was now fourteen years of age and only two winters younger than Russell, seemed to have her interest peaked by her mother's query. The girl was not into the same boyish stuff Russell liked, but after overhearing her father retell the events from the hunt to her mother in the cart on their way home yesterday and recalling the time from six years earlier when the boy rescued her from the forest, Lynn was slightly taken aback by Russell's bravery. She was still a girl by age's standard but mentally she was like that of a young adult. Even already Lynn knew that if her mother and father were to find a proper suitor for her that she would soon be of marriageable age in two more years.

The Bradford girl liked everything about Russell's character. He was both brave and honorable, and those two traits seemed to cause the girl to gravitate towards his personality. The fact that Russell never looked down on her and always treated others with respect was definitely a plus, but the one thing that had always stuck with her in Lynn's heart and mind was the fact that Russell had saved her. He, a ten year old boy, had come looking for her years ago and had promised to reunite her and her mother back together again. That boy had done what he had said he was going to do and upheld a promise to a scared, little girl. She never forgot that. Somehow Russell had taken root in Lynn's heart and a flower had begun to grow there.

Chapter 6

Lynn and her younger sister of three years, Anne, sat at one of the windows in their stone cottage watching large snowflakes drift down from the sky. The snowfall had already blanketed Hamilton leaving an eight inch cover of white on the ground along with anything else outside that lay at rest. The shower of ice crystals covered the leafless trees and gave the surrounding landscape a glittering appearance. A plume of smoke rose from the small house's chimney.

Inside, the place was warm and toasty thanks to the blaze burning in the fireplace. Both of the Bradford daughters sat on wooden chairs that they had pulled away from the shack's table and placed by one of the cottage's two windows. A yearning to play outside in the snow grew in their hearts the more they gazed upon the winter wonderland. Their mother and father sat peacefully at the table in the furniture sets other two seats. A cup of steaming hot tea rested in front of each one of them.

"Mother, may we please go outside and play in the snow?", pleaded Anne while turning halfway around in her chair. The girl wearing an expression rivaling that of a beggar.

"I am not sure if that be such a good idea," answered Gwenyth feigning her recognition to her youngest daughter's craving desire. "What if you got so caught up in the flakes and wandered away getting lost?", she inquired.

"That wouldn't happen mother," responded the girl with a seriousness in both her look and her tone. "Lynn would go with me to make sure of it."

"And how do you know your sister would wish to accompany you out and into the cold?"

Anne glanced to Lynn. Her older sister never taking her sight away from the falling snowflakes on the other side of the window. Now the youngest Bradford feeling cornered by both the question and Lynn's lack of acknowledgment to the inquiry quickly gave the only response that came to her mind. "Father will go with me!"

Gwenyth giggled as she watched Charles, who was right in the middle of taking a sip of his tea, almost spit out the small amount that he had in his mouth when he heard the child's statement. A moment later, he turned in his seat to ask a query of his own, but was cut off before he could even begin his question.

"Please father!", begged his youngest daughter. "It will be a nice time," she tried to convince him.

Charles watched her beg for a couple of seconds before turning back towards his wife. Taking another sip of his tea and swallowing, Gwenyth's husband placed his cup back on the table. "Alright. Since you whittled me down child, go and put on the proper wear," he advised.

That was all Anne needed to hear. Dashing from her seat at the window it wasn't long before she disappeared into the room that she shared with Lynn to prepare for her journey into the winter's snow.

Lynn snapped out of her daydreaming when she heard her mother call her name a couple of times. Turning in her seat, the girl looked towards the table where both of her parents sat. "Yes mother," she answered.

"Is all well with you?", puzzled Charles.

"Yes father," she assured him. "I was just lost in thought."

"Are you joining Anne and your father outdoors?", inquired Gwenyth.

"I am mother," replied Lynn stepping away from her seat at the window and starting for her room.

Gwenyth watched as her oldest daughter disappeared through the doorway. The woman thought to herself trying to figure out why Lynn seemed to drift in her own thoughts. Why her bouts of daydreaming or getting lost within her own mind had become a regular thing lately. It wasn't noticeable to neither Anne nor her father, but Gwenyth recognized it more frequently now. Was something wrong or not? She was actually so caught up in her own thoughts on the matter that she never noticed her husband rise from the seat and leave the table in order to dawn the proper attire he would need for his father-daughter date in the snowfall.

"Lynn honey. Your mother wishes to see you," announced the fourteen year old's father later that night while coming out of the bedroom him and his wife shared.

His daughter glancing up from her knitting as he entered the main room. "Yes father."

Lynn was cautious not to tangle up the yarn with its two needles as she carefully placed the interlaced fabric and its tools down on the chair. The girl starting for her mother and father's room. She rubbed any wrinkles out of her nightgown on her way.

"Mother," Lynn called when she got to the homemade blanket, her mother had knitted last summer, hanging from the door's jamb allowing some type of privacy for the chamber's occupants. The room's door needed to be left open during these cold months so the fireplace's heat could keep the whole cottage warm.

"Come in," softly welcomed her mother's voice.

Lynn pushed the soft partition to the side with a sweep of her hand and entered the lantern lit room. Two wooden, clothes chests, one on each side, sat at the head of her mother and father's sleeping pallet. The girl's mother sat on the poor man's bed.

"Father said you wished to see me," verified Lynn.

"Yes child," Gwenyth patted the pallet's covers inviting her daughter over. "Please come have a seat so we can speak on something."

Lynn walked right over to her mother and took a seat waiting for Gwenyth to start the conversation. Her eyes locked on her mother's face while the woman pushed the girl's long, straight, brown hair towards the back of her head.

"What troubles you my dear?", queried Gwenyth gazing into her daughter's brown eyes.

"Nothing mother."

"Please honey," she softly spoke all the while searching the girl's face for any telltales that stated different. "You can fool your father most of the time and Anne also, but I am your mother and I know when something troubles both of my children." Gwenyth's tone matching that of the soft radiance cast from the room's only lantern. She looped a piece of hair behind her daughter's ear while searching each of Lynn's eyes. "Speak with me."

Her oldest daughter's gaze went form her face to Lynn's own lap. "I am confused and worried mother," she admitted.

"About what child?"

The girl glanced back up to her mother's face before once again returning her gaze back to her own lap. Lynn's hands were together and she nervously fiddled with her fingers. "I am worried because I am approaching the age where men tend to start selecting women as their wives and mates. I am confused because I already have a fondness in my heart for a certain boy but I do not feel like my feelings are warranted." Lynn looked back up at her mother.

"My child, your feelings are never wrong nor unwarranted," softly advised Gwenyth. "They are exactly what they are; yours. You own those feelings not anyone else and they are kept here," the girl's mother pointing at Lynn's heart.

"But what if the boy does not like me or another asks for my hand in marriage?", a tear forming in the corner of Lynn's eye as she emotionally questioned her mother.

"Oh honey," Gwenyth pulled her daughter to her breast while rocking and stroking Lynn's hair consoling her worried child. "Sometimes we do not get what we want. Not because we are not worthy of another's love or because we live in a world that knows no love but because everything knows a reason. Our Lord has a purpose for us already written."

She slowly pushed the girl away from her close embrace so she could gaze into her daughter's eyes as she spoke. "Sometimes we pray to our Heavenly Father but our prayers seem to go unheard or unanswered and we think just that. The truth is that God already has a purpose for you that knows no existence with what it is that you want. Do you understand what I speak of?"

"Yes mother, but it seems so unfair," responded a sniffing Lynn.

"I know child, and this world is harsh, but that is why the priest at church always reminds us to keep looking up instead of casting our gazes fixed towards the ground."

Gwenyth reached under Lynn's sunken chin and lifted her daughter's head up investigating her watery eyes. "You can stay with your father and I for as long as need be. Do not rush what will one day be on your doorstep."

Lynn shook her head in acknowledgment.

"Never fear or be consumed with worry my dear," softly came her mother. "The Lord promised he would never allow you more hardship than you can handle. You only need ask Him and He shall grant you the strength needed to confront the problem as it arises," her words of advice confirmed with a smile. "Your father was not my first choice in a man," Gwenyth openly admitted. "He was not?", shockingly asked Lynn.

"No, but I could not have asked for a better man. He is a good father; a good husband; a hardworker and provider for our family. The Lord knew he was not what I wanted but rather who I needed. I love your father and no other can ever replace him when he is gone," proclaimed Gwenyth.

Lynn wiped her wet eyes with one of her sleeves as she followed up her last inquiry with another. "What happened to the man you wanted to be with?"

Her mother gazed over the girl's shoulder for an instant and exhaled heavily in a type of laughter with her mouth closed before answering. "He was hung two years after you were born for murdering his wife and infant son."

An expression of shock overtook Lynn's face.

Moments later Gwenyth changed the subject of their talk back to her daughter and threw out her next to last query. "Does this boy, whomever it may be, know that he has caught your eye?"

"I know not mother," confessed Lynn. "He is probably unaware that I exist."

"If he has seen you before than how can he not? You are beautiful," smiled her mother.

Lynn returned the smile and leaned forward to embrace her mother in a long hug. Gwenyth adding one more statement before the two parted. "Make sure that whomever this boy is he treats you with both honour and respect."

"Yes mother."

That night, Lynn lay awake staring into the darkness of the room with several thoughts running through her mind keeping her peaceful rest at bay. The girl's eyes searching the obscured ceiling for any kind of an answer to help solve her inner turmoil. Lynn's earlier conversation with her mother weighed heavy on her conscious awareness. Her sister's rhythmic breathing from slumber breaking the silence of the night.

"Our little girl is growing up," Gwenyth announced to her husband laying beside her in bed.

Charles turned his head in the direction of his wife. "What do you mean?", he inquisitively queried.

"I mean Charles, that a boy has caught her eye," replied Gwenyth looking to meet her husband's stare. "Have you not noticed Lynn's thoughts have been drifting being both quiet and distant at times?"

Her husband thought to himself for a moment before responding. "Yes at times, but I did not ponder over it enough I would imagine."

"Well I am telling you she has Charles!", driving her point home.

"Is that why you wished to speak with her earlier?", he asked.

"Yes."

"Did she happen to mention who this boy is?"

"No,..." -admitted Gwenyth- "...but I told her to make certain that whomever it is respects her and treats her honorable like you do with your family.

A smile creased Charles' face and within a second later came a smile reflected from Gwenyth. The look mirroring the happiness that her words brought with them.

"Do you really feel like I do?", he questioned.

Rolling over to face her husband, Gwenyth placed a hand on one of his cheeks and met his stare with a loving gaze of her own. "Well I needed to tell the child something," she offered as a smile broke through her loving expression.

"Evil woman!", chuckled Charles shaking his head.

"No. Of course I do," his wife informed her husband, who was presently feigning injury. She nuzzled back up to the man resting her head on his hairy chest.

"Do you ponder it be a boy at church?", Charles asked into her hair.

"No. I know who it is," she stated with confidence.

"Then who?"

"It would be no one else but Robert and Elizabeth's son."

"Who? Russell?"

"Why do the Daniels have other sons that I know nothing of?", replied Gwenyth while breaking another smile.

"That be two. Is someone feeling a tad frisky this night?", queried Charles while tickling his wife's side for a moment.

Gwenyth letting out a quick giggle and softly slapping her husband's chest. "Stop you brute!", she laughed.

"But how do you know it is Russell my dear?", Charles asking his final inquiry.

Resting her head back on her husband's chest, Gwenyth's answer was confident and to the point. "Because, I am the child's mother and I am certain he be the one."

That response alone was enough to end her husband's questioning.

Chapter 7

Russell skidded on his back across the white, blanket of snow that covered the ground. The cold and wet ice crystals invading his brown cloak, that his mother had made during the past summer, left him shivering for a brief second from their chilling touch. The young man's right hand still clutching his wooden, practice sword all the while keeping his sight locked onto his opponent. Russell starting to quickly rise as he watched his father rush at him holding his own practice sword's hilt at shoulder height.

Within moments, Robert was falling upon his son bringing his wooden blade down to cleave into the young man, but the student moved quicker and rolled forward passing his father on his right side away from the downward strike. At the end of Russell's evasive roll, the student kicked back making contact with the bend in his father's leg. The shot sending Robert forward and dropping him to a knee allowing his son to rise to his feet behind him and take a defensive stance. Now it was the young man's turn to be the aggressor.

Russell rushed at his kneeling father from behind, but the teacher was luring his opponent. As the pupil got within the right range for a surprise attack, Robert threw a handful of snow into the young attacker's face. Russell tried to quickly throw up an arm to block the launched powder but he wasn't fast enough and some of it got pass his defense and into his eyes. The temporarily blind student attempted to halt his charge but the slippery blanket of white, along with his momentum forward, caused his body to continue ahead into a side-thrusting kick from Robert's kneeling position. The strike catching the sliding out of control student in the stomach and launching him backwards off of his feet.

Russell came down hard on his back but his teaching had helped him to keep a grip on his wooden sword's hilt. The pupil knew that to lose a handle on it meant more trouble for him in a real fight in lieu of a mock one. The young man swiftly rubbed the sight back into his eyes but it was too late. Above him stood his father pointing his practice blade at his son's throat while using a foot to pin down Russell's wrist to his sword arm.

"Do you yield?", inquired Robert casting a small smile only at the edge to one side of his mouth.

"That is not fair father!", protested the shouting Russell.

The teacher mockingly laughing at his student's statement. "Their be nothing of fairness in a fight boy. So I shall only ask you one more time. Do you yield?"

"I yield," hesitantly replied his beaten son.

"Then release your sword and I shall let you up," sternly came Robert's statement. He watched as his pupil slowly relinquished his grip on the weapon's hilt. The teacher cautiously removing his foot from the boy's pinned wrist while still holding his sword's point at Russell's throat. "Come on son. Nice and slow," he ordered after kicking his student's practice blade several feet away from them.

"I said I yield father," the young man confirmed while rising from his prone position.

"I know, but you must always be both cautious and aware," warned Robert. "For not all men are honorable foes and their words mean nothing more than a dead man's breath."

"Oh, and blinding me by throwing snow in my eyes knows honour?"

"Son, honorable men would not be trying to steal your possessions. Honorable men would not misuse their skill by taking advantage of others," the lesson's teacher advised his student. "Not all men fight as you say 'fair', but instead will do whatever it takes to win the upper hand. Even if that means blinding you with snow, or dirt, or anything that will strengthen their chances of winning a fight."

Robert dropped the point of his practice sword towards the ground and placed a hand on Russell's shoulder. "You have learned a lesson that knows no value this day son. Better here with me in mock combat then in a real fight when life or death matters!"

"You are right again father," realized the young man. "I will be better the next time."

Robert's gaze met Russell's as the teacher used his index finger to point at the student's forehead. "Remember my son, this needs to be in control at all times over that..." -he dropped his digit to his son's heart- "...if you wish to out think your adversary and remain alive. But if you lose heart than you're dead already and you just know it not yet," he added with a slight nod.

The young man walked over to his practice sword and bent down retrieving it from the accumulating snow. Turning, he met with his approaching father before they started back in the direction of the cottage and out of the cold weather.

Robert laid his hand once more on his son's shoulder looking the young man in the face. "You get better at each lesson we have just as you did with the bow. I know not disappointment with you son and I want you to know that I am proud of you always."

Both father and son shared a smile before once again starting for their home. The snow beginning to fall heavier, as they walked away from the scattered footprints on the field of mock battle.

Chapter 8

Half-a-dozen multiple, candle-holding candelabrum illuminated the private, study chamber where a man with wavy, salt and peppered hair, along with matching facial hair, lounged comfortably on a burgundy-colored settee reading a brown, leather-bound book. The script's title in one inch, raised, gold lettering identifying it as "The Holy Bible'. The man's absorbed concentration stolen from the Holy Word, as a knock on the room's door broke the quietness of the chamber's only sound caused by the burning candles hissing.

"Enter!", he answered while peering over the top edge of the book.

The oak door opened and a young man of sixteen years of age walked through the entryway. His hair seemed to match that of the other room's occupant but instead it was completely black like that of a crow. He wore a full body robe of red color that concealed any signs of his feet, and even his stroll across the chamber had an air of royalty about it.

"You wish to see me father?", asked the newcomer after shutting the door behind himself and advancing towards the lounging, older man.

"Yes Matthew," replied King Stephen laying the Holy Book on a small table in front of him. "I would like to speak with you. Please, sit down son," he invited pointing to a matching colored chair on the other side of the table.

The prince taking the seat with a look of interests painted on his face as he waited for his father to proceed.

"Your mother has asked me to speak with you because she believes something troubles you. Is there anything that is bothering you?", inquired the young man's father.

"No father," the prince stoically replied.

The king sat for a moment in silence after the answer before deciding to try and probe a little more. "Are you sure lad?"

"No father. All is well," Matthew once again reassured retaining his emotionless tone.

"I see," admitted Stephen staring into the young man's eyes before he continued. "Out with it Matthew before this enigma haunts you as flies do a horse."

"But. But father. I said nothing brews inside of me!", his son pleaded while leaning forward in his seat.

"I am sorry Matthew. You may be able to fool others but not me. Remember son, I am your father and along with your mother we have known you your whole life," pointed out the king while offering a slight shake of his head. "I know by your face expression when something is troubling you."

"Father, my face wore no expression..." -he admitted- "...because nothing is causing me any type of bother!"

"That is exactly it Matthew. When something ails you son, you are without expression and both your mother and I know that the lack of any kind of facial or verbal manifestation is a sign of something beginning to torment you," revealed King Stephen keeping his gaze on the young man.

A frustration built in the prince due to the telltale exposing his facade.

"Out with it Matthew," sternly ordered his father as his stare met and held his son's for a moment.

After the brief interlude, the prince broke the silence between the two.

"It is just that I am already of the age that soon I will be expected to select a bride and produce an heir to sit on the throne one day." Matthew looked away for a second and then back to his father. "What if I feel nothing towards the woman that has been chosen for me or we do not have any children right away? Then what?"

King Stephen pondered on his son's query along with his answer for a time before he responded to the prince's worry. "Matthew, when you were born were you already able to run through the castle dashing this way and that way?", he asked while waving his hand to-and-fro.

"Of course not father. I had to learn how to walk before I could run."

"Then why is it now that you wish to rush to your future time in your life when you only need to walk in the present?", questioned Stephen. "Now is the time when you should be observing and experiencing the actions a king needs to rule on his throne."

"But father, the people of England are going to expect an heir when I am king," stated Matthew with a hint of worry in his tone.

"Then you must be speaking with a ghost," reasoned his father.

The prince stared at the king puzzled by his last statement. "What do you mean a ghost?"

"Well the last time I looked, I was still king of England and still dwelled amongst the living," Stephen gazed at the hand he held out in front of himself at eye level.

Prince Matthew lowered his head. "I am sorry father. I meant no disrespect to you or the crown."

"Of course not son, but do you understand what I am saying to you?", the young man's father reaching over the small table that separated the two and touching his son. "Do not bother yourself with worrying about an heir to sit on the throne. You will be allotted plenty of time to fill your days later regarding that matter when it presents itself. For now, learn how to be a fair and just ruler who governs his people with love and honour. If you give it to them they will return it," advised the king. "Hence, the people need and expect someone who can lead them before they will require from you an heir."

"You are right father. Not only a wise king but a wise man," praised Matthew as his father's words brought with them relief to his worries. "What about a bride? What if my feelings for her are absent?"

"I favor to believe that you have a long time before you require one so between this day and that maybe you will find one that suits your taste," Stephen reasoned.

"How do you know father?", inquired the young royal.

"I do not. Only our Almighty Father does, but I assure you I have not seen any signs from the dead's collector as of yet."

"Who?", puzzled his son. "The Reaper?"

"That would be him," cleared up King Stephen. "Hence, if you are in a rush to be married I can always find you a woman. I hear there are plenty of them about in search for a husband, although I cannot guarantee that she will have all of her teeth," he teased.

"Father! You would not!", the prince shockingly responded.

King Stephen chuckled at his son's expression.

"Look at mother," the young royal pointed out. "She has all her teeth."

"True son, but she chose me," informed his father before opening his mouth and pulling his cheek to one side exposing a couple of missing teeth. The king then removed his finger and chuckled. "I would be inclined to say the joke is on her."

Both father and son shared in a moment of laughter before the prince asked another query. "What do you mean mother chose you? I always thought the king chose his bride."

"A king does son,...." -replied Stephen- "...but your mother stole my heart when I first laid eyes on her. I could not remove her image from my mind and she was all I could think about." Gazing into the air above his son's shoulder, he reminisced as he thought about an earlier time in his life.

Returning his look back to Matthew, the young man's father openly admitted, "She chose me before I her."

"How will I know father when that certain one makes herself known to me?"

"You will know son here and here," the king pointing first to Matthew's heart and then to his forehead.

The room filled with silence again and only the hissing from the burning candles could be heard. Again it was the young royal to break the quietness between the two.

"Father,..." -Matthew started before dropping his gaze to his feet and continuing his words- "...I own these odd feelings towards girls now. Where at one time I thought all girls except mother and Joan were ehrr,..." -giving a look of disgust on his face- "...I now feel an attraction to women." The prince looked back up when his father rose from his place on the settee and approached him.

Patting his son on the shoulder, King Stephen smiled down at Matthew. "Those feeling are not odd son instead justified. They only mean that you are becoming a man. Do not fear them or attempt to lock them away but embrace them," consoled his father.

Prince Matthew rose from his chair and hugged his advisor. "Thank you father. I count myself lucky to be your son."

"No Matthew. It is I who thank God everyday for blessing your mother and I with the gift of you," humbly corrected the man. "You make the both of us happy and bring joy to a man's brow plagued with many concerns."

The embrace between the two tightened a bit and only a knock on the chamber's door broke their shared bond between father and son.

"Enter!", ordered King Stephen.

The serving girl, Joan, opened the wooden portal and stepped into the royal's private study. "Your majesty," she addressed the king. "There is a courier for you with a message from Scheffield in the castle's waiting chamber."

"Very well. I shall be right there."

The woman offered a slight bow accompanied with a nod before slipping back out of the room's entrance closing the door behind her.

"Shall we continue our discussion son?"

"I believe I am better now father. Thank you."

King Stephen smiled at Matthew and dropped his arm over his son's shoulder. "One more word of advice. Remember always use this and think," Stephen pointed at his own temple. "Do not lose your head in the heat of passion and always respect and honour the woman. You may be a king one day and with that title comes power, but men who know not honour take what is not offered freely to them!", the young man's father stressed his last words as they walked towards the study's wooden portal.

"Now let us go and see what words your cousin in Scheffield has for us," remarked the king as both royals strolled out of the room and into the hallway.

Chapter 9

The cracking and popping caused by the logs burning in the fireplace were the only audible sounds amongst the rest of the cottage's silence. Outside, snow fell again on this Eve of Christmas, but inside the place was warm and cozy especially up in the room's loft where Russell laid wide awake. The sixteen year old's thoughts actively running amok through his head.

Laying on his right side with his eyes open, Russell watched the shadows from the flickering fire down below shift and dance on the far wall along with part of the room's ceiling. The young man's hands, pressed between his cheek and his sleeping pallet, supported his resting head. The boy's eyes locked on one particular spot, as he reflected on his previous years of lessons with both the bow and the sword.

"How is it that an average commoner knows so much about both weapons?", he thought to himself. "I fully understand the bow because one would need to know how to hunt for food, but the blade seems more like something one in the king's army would be familiar with," he reasoned. "Was father ever in the service to the crown?"

Russell seemed perplexed by the self inquiry but should he broach the subject with his father. He had never questioned the man's word nor his actions in the past, so why should he start now. "What kind of farmer was as proficient with a blade as a knight?", the young man puzzled. "A farmer knight?", Russell silently chuckled. "On a crusade for the goose that laid the golden egg!", a smile creased the young man's lips as he jokingly thought about how humorous and farfetched his story sounded.

Rolling onto his back, Russell's grin faded as he mentally began to pick apart his latest tale. "Maybe father was a crusader, or more so his father who actually taught him. That would explain why he knows how to use a sword and fight so well." The ideas rapidly fired throughout Russell's tireless and active mind. "Maybe one of my ancestors protected England or its king and queen," his smile slowly returning. "Russell the Protector of England! The defender of the people and righteousness! The crusader of honour and dignity!", -throwing his right arm into the air as if the young man was thrusting a sword to the Heavens-, "High guardian of all under God's grace!"

Russell's thoughts raced and images flooded into his mind's eye of him protecting everyone from King Stephen and Queen Margaret to the common people like his father, mother and his sister. Even the memory from six years earlier when he had found Lynn and not only swore to protect her but also return the scared, lost girl to her mother, drifted into the young man's head. This time though, he had quickly altered the vision in his mind substituting their ages from then to now and replacing the stick he had held in his hand with the image of a sword. The same sword his father would hand down to the young man.

Slowly the self-proclaimed defender lowered his raised arm gripping the imaginary weapon of justice letting it fall to his side. Russell held onto the images of those pretty, brown orbs and dimpled cheeks of the family friend's daughter. Closing his eyes, he could even smell the berry-scented soap she used. Lynn's portrait was now locked into the young man's conscious replacing the notion that existed only moments ago of being England's protector. No matter how much he tried, and it wasn't that much at all, Russell couldn't stop thinking about Lynn. The young man growing fonder of the Bradfords' oldest daughter throughout the years.

Staring at the dimly lit ceiling of his sleeping loft, Russell's thoughts were of both him and her one day sharing each other's companionship and hoping a love could blossom. The only two questions that existed between his romantic ideas and the daily reality of life was; Would she feel the same way about him when and if Russell exposed his heart to her?,and most importantly, Was Lynn even aware of his existence as a mate, a partner, and a lover?

Closing his eyes while wearing a small grin, Russell began to drift off towards sleep. The young man was glad that on the morrow he would be seeing Lynn at mass before his family would be sharing in a small feast at the Bradfords' cottage celebrating the birth of Christ. Just partaking in the sight of the young woman and the thought of breaking bread with her left Russell both content and question free for now. Eventually slumber consumed the young man.

His soft slippers quietly padded down the stone, corridor's floor as he silently made his way down to the royal kitchen. Unlike that of his chamber, which was warm and comfortable, Prince Matthew was more than glad he had worn his night robe for this journey. The young royal had set out to retrieve a midnight snack in the castle's cold air. He had been awake reading when the city's watch bell tolled announcing the arrival of Christmas Day. Knowing that he would be up for at least another two or three hours, the prince decided to have a snack after he offered a birthday wish and prayer to the Christ.

Torches burned and hissed every dozen feet housed in their black, wrought iron sconces allowing Matthew's sight the advantage of being unhindered by the darkness. Their blazes causing shadows to dance and flicker on the upper part of the corridor's walls.

Taking a left turn, the sixteen year old prince followed an elegant staircase down a small, curving path to the palace's first floor. Two guards watched as Matthew stepped from the bottom run. The young royal delaying his quest for food to speak with both men.

"David. Andrew," greeted the prince. "How fair ye on this night?"

"My prince," replied both men at almost the same time. "All is well sire," informed David.

"Very well fine sirs," nodded Matthew. "I am off to retrieve a snack at this late hour. Would either of you wish for me to return with something for you?", inquired the royal.

"No your majesty," responded David with a slight shake of his head. "My thanks."

Matthew looked to Andrew, but he also shook his head. "No my prince," confirmed the guard. "Thank you for your query."

Prince Matthew nod his affirmation before starting for the hallway on the right of the staircase headed for the castle's kitchen. Before he got five feet away from the two men-at-arms, the young man turned to address both of them.

"Remember, my father is throwing a feast that shall last all of the day. Your presence as our guests at sometime throughout this holy celebration is humbly requested," he reminded David and Andrew in case they had forgotten. "Our family believes we are all one under God, and like the king of kings who welcomes all that are worthy into his kingdom and a seat at his table, my father welcomes all those responsible for the protection and upkeep of his family, this castle, and our city to come feast with us and Hamilton." The prince added one more statement before turning to resume his journey, "I hope I shall see you both there later this day. Good night fine sirs and Merry Yuletides."

"Many thanks my prince," gratitude filling David's voice.

"God Bless you, the king, and our queen," added Andrew as Prince Matthew vanished through the entryway and into the corridor leading towards the kitchen.

Following the hallway for at least another hundred or so feet and making a left and then a right turn during the trek, the young royal came up to a set of double-swinging, oak doors. Light was shining from the outline cracks of the wooden portal and the gap in between its bottom and the stone floor. He was aware that the cooks would be up beginning preparations for the large, yuletide feast but Matthew assumed that wouldn't be for another couple of hours from now. Stopping and putting an ear to one of the spaces in between the two oak doors, the prince heard the grunts of a man and a woman. The late night binger was preparing to leave the two caught in their lust undisturbed, but the young man suddenly realized that the grunts were not those of lovemaking but actually the sounds of a struggle.

The prince slightly pushed one of the swinging doors ajar just enough to peer into the room. His eyes took in the sight of a short, pot-bellied cook trying to force a woman forward over the counter. One of his meaty hands reaching under her pulled up dress as she tried desperately to push herself erect and out of his grasp. Matthew couldn't tell who the woman was but he had seen enough. Pushing the portal silently open, he snuck into the kitchen and headed for a cutting block of knives located on one of the counter tops.

The ripping sound of cloth joined the struggling grunts that filled the atmosphere. The noise seeming to have two different effects between the attempting rapist and the panic-filled victim. The tear causing an excitement in his voice accompanying his actions while the approaching violation brought louder pleads from the teary-eyed woman.

"Just a little more you tease!", enthusiastically announced the cook while trying to fidget with the ties of his pants. The rotund man's weight leaned against the woman's back allowing him to use both of his hands.

"No! Please!", pleaded the victim. The very air being squeezed from her lungs by her attacker's weight. "You need not do this!", she stated in between sniffles.

"Or should I say you're not going to do this swine!", declared Matthew while pulling the rapist's head back by his hair and holding a butchers blade up to the cook's throat. "Now get off of her you fat load of dung!", he ordered while yanking the attacker back away from the woman.

Feeling the pressure that had pinned her to the counter top relieved, the shoulder-length, brown-haired, petrified woman quickly stood up and rapidly moved away from her assailant along with her unseen rescuer's voice. When she was several feet away, the woman turned her watery eyes to her attacker and her hero.

"Joan!", surprisingly confirmed Matthew when his gaze finally met the woman's teary eyes. Taking in the sight of the almost victim, anger built up in his soul and then exploded as the prince kicked the bend in the cook's right leg with his own left foot and yanked back on the man's hair dropping him to the stone floor. Balling up his left fist, the royal struck out catching the falling assailant in his nose with a hammer strike. The hit driving the rotund man to the ground. Blood exploded and sprayed out of the one-time attacker's fat nose.

Hitting the ground hard, the cook gazed upon the one responsible for ruining the start to his merry morning. It was his turn now to plead when the realization of who had just stopped him looked back down at him. "My prince. I am sorry!", he apologized with a voice full of panic. "It is just that she,..." the bleeding man's words cut short by those from Matthew.

"Is a woman!", the royal shouted. "Do not beg for my forgiveness but rather hers!", advised Matthew while pointing the knifes back towards a trembling with fear, Joan. "Your transgressions are with her not I!"

"How could you, you pig?", cried the shaken woman.

"It is because you,..."

"Shut up swine!", ordered Matthew.

Turning to the woman her rescuer asked, "Are you well Joan?"

"I am now thanks to your aid my prince," the brown-haired woman replied through sniffles.

"Go to the stairs and retrieve the guards," he informed. "Bring them here." Matthew glanced over to Joan. "Can you do that?"

The woman's only response was a nod before rushing from the kitchen to get David and Andrew.

Prince Matthew closed the door to his chamber behind him after following the shaken Joan into the room.

"Here sit on the bed," he softly invited while strolling over to a wooden stand holding a small bowl and a pitcher filled with water. Taken them from their resting place, Matthew brought them over towards the spot where the woman sat. Leaving them on a night stand, he returned a moment later carrying a small cloth and a clean nightdress that the prince laid on the bed.

The royal poured some of the clear liquid from the pitcher into a bowl and then dunked the cloth into the water. Removing the wet fabric and ringing it out, the young man kneeled down and began to softly wipe and clean the dirt from Joan's teary-dried face. Gazing into her eyes he smiled at the woman, as she had already begun to calm.

"You are safe now," Matthew softly assured. "The guards have taken the man to the dungeon where he waits on my father's decision what to do with him."

"But you should not be doing this," admitted the woman while looking at the cloth the royal used to clean her face. "I am the servant and you are the prince," she pointed out.

"For not this night," Matthew softly added followed by a smile. "I am here to serve and protect a friend that I have sworn a duty to God to watch over." The young royal pushing a lock of hair behind Joan's ear before he continued. "So my lady, I ask that you allow me the honour of serving a friend this night?"

Joan stared down at the sixteen year old, royal protector meeting his smiling gaze. Leaning forward she embraced him, and he her, in a hug. A love that had already blossomed before this night strengthened the bond of friendship between the two. A short time later they separated.

Putting the wet cloth into the bowl, Matthew rose from his knees. "I shall be outside the door. Take your time preparing yourself for rest," he once again softly spoke to the woman. "The clean nightdress is for you to change into something more fitting for bed. When you are ready for my return just call and I shall enter."

The prince strolled to the door and opened it.

Joan watched him shut it behind him.

Matthew entered the room, shut the wooden portal behind him, and locked it. He looked over to the bed where Joan laid already under its covers meeting his gaze. The young prince approached the grand piece of furniture and sat on its edge still locked onto the woman's eyes.

"Are you well?", he smiled his inquiry.

"I am."

Leaning down, the young man planted a kiss on the woman's clean forehead. "You are safe Joan, so take some rest," he assured her before rising from his seat on the mattress' edge.

Turning, the prince walked over and blew out all the remaining candles still lit allowing only the blaze from the fireplace to be the room's only light.

"What of you Matthew?", Joan asked while propping herself up on her elbows and witnessing the young man take a seat in a cushioned chair. "Where will you slumber?"

"I shall be here watching over you while you sleep like a shepherd remains ever vigilant over his flock," stated the prince. "I will not slumber while you rest, and if you should wake feared by night visions than I will be here standing guard to chase them away sending them fleeing like hungry wolves."

Joan smiled at her protector. "Good night my shepherd," she bid before lowering herself and resting her head on the royal's pillow.

A short time later sleep seized hold of her and she remained content in her slumber all the while subconsciously knowing her guardian would keep the wolves at bay.

Chapter 10

Christmas morning was the first day since four days prior that the sporadic snow flurries had stopped and the sun shined brightly in the sky. Its radiance brilliantly illuminating the earth's blanket of white giving the impression of hundreds of diamonds shining embodied in the ice crystal covering. The light reflecting back towards the sky caused spots in the eyes if gazed upon it for too long. Even the trees were covered with the white powder and icicles hung scattered throughout their branches.

A small cloud flowed from Russell's mouth as the young man crossed the smooth, snow-covered field in just below calf-height powder. His steps slowed as his trudge brought him closer to the white, stone wall. Carrying his bow in his right hand and wearing his quiver in its usual place, strapped on his back, the bundled up farmer held a small, cloth-like sack in his left hand.

Arriving at the rock barricade, Russell used his bow to wipe away some of its blanket of ice crystals until he could almost make out the individual stones underneath. The young man took hold of the small sack with his right hand holding the cloth item near his weapon and polished off more of the snow with his now empty hand. When the farmer was satisfied that the spot would get no cleaner, he lowered the cloth-like sack onto the wall.

Russell untied the two knots and opened the piece of fabric revealing a quarter of a loaf of bread. Raising his head, the young man scanned both ways down the stone partition and past it into the leafless forest. Glancing behind him at the bare tree that he had spent so many days leaning up against while sitting on the ground, Russell searched but still could not find the one he was looking for.

A whistle, much like that of a sound produced by a bird, carried from his lips through the cold winter's air. Again, a plume of smoke escaped his mouth as he called for his childhood friend. "Sir Robin!" The young man waiting a brief moment before whistling and calling for the avian a second time. "Sir Robin!"

As if materializing out of thin air, the farmer watched as a small, not as plump as it was in the summer, brown back with a rusty, orange face and breast bird approached flying low over the white-covered wall. Russell smiled recognizing the series of chirps the avian gave as it drew closer. The young man breaking off little pieces of the bread for his friend's arrival.

Without any hesitation, Sir Robin landed on the wall near the baked offering all the while chirping up a storm as if the little creature was excitedly greeting a long-time companion. Following the brief introduction, the winged animal pecked at several of the pieces that the young man had broke apart.

Russell only smiled at the bird's excitement before addressing the little fellow. "Well met Sir Robin. I offer you Christmas wishes on this sunny day," he greeted.

Sir Robin gave a couple more chirps before digging back into the bread pieces. It was more than obvious that the little bird had grown both familiar and comfortable around his human friend over the years. As a young boy growing up, Russell had always treated Sir Robin with an utmost respect and accompanied by the fact that he had brought the avian food on numerous occasions throughout the last six years only caused the winged animal to allow the forming of a bond between the two.

"You would appear to be extra hungry this day," noticed Russell. "I would hope that you are not out here starving my friend."

Sir Robin only taking a second to eye the young man before returning to his feast.

"We have known each other for a time now and it would not do me well to know of your starving to death because you are bashful enough not to fly to my cottage," his human friend reprimanded. "I hope that is not the case."

The bird swallowing the crumb before issuing a series of chirps and whistles that barraged the young man.

"I yield," conceded Russell while raising his hands to a height around ear level. A smile creased his lips and a chuckle escaped him. "I yield," he mitigated a second time.

"Well Sir Robin like always it honours me to see you. I must take my leave for now, but as I go I bid you merry wishes for the remainder of the day," offered the young man. "I hope you enjoy mother's bread. Until we meet in a day or two, take care of yourself my little friend."

Turning and leaving the bird to its feast, Russell started back for the cottage. He knew he had to aid his father in hooking up the horse to the cart so they could be on their way to mass. The thought of speaking with him over his sword training seemed to weigh on his mind. The young man knowing the opportune time would arise so he brushed away the enigma. His attention also captured by a chirp from the wall.

Using his empty hand to shield the sun's brightness from his eyes, Russell watched as the avian took flight heading in his direction. For some odd reason, the farmer stuck out his hand in front of him with his arm still bent at the elbow. Sir Robin landed softly on one of his uncovered fingers. The bird's three, tiny toes wrapping around the exposed digit. Russell smiled watching his friend look at him with its head tilted sideways and its blinking eye. Sir Robin let out one more series of chirps before taking flight again accompanied with a whistle. The young man answered with a whistle all his own before turning and restarting home again. A grin crossed Russell's face and a warming filled his soul as he softly commented to himself, "He has never done that before."

Robert was just leading the horse out of the small, stone barn into the sunny Christmas day when he noticed Russell approaching him through the blanket of snow. His son looking towards where he stood by the large, hoofed animal displaying a smile on the young man's face.

"Well someone looks happy," observed Robert continuing to lead the horse towards the small cart.

"It is the work of Sir Robin father," admitted his son joining him in the walk. "He flew over to me and landed on my finger. The bird has never done that in all these years," continually smiled Russell.

"Sounds to me like the fellow knows ease with your company," confirmed his father. "Here, lend me your aid with this Russell, Friend to Sir Robin." It was now Robert's turn to smile.

Both father and son worked together hitching the horse to the cart as they prepared for the families travel to attend mass in the city. The two shared in very little conversation more focused on the work at hand. If there was any talk between them, it was based on the task they were performing at the time. With the snowy conditions hindering their upcoming trip, Robert made extra sure the hooking up went without a snag.

"Father. May we engage in serious talk?", queried Russell when the two were finally done.

Wiping his hands off by rubbing them together, Robert gazed over the horse's back to his son. "Of course Russell. There is always time to speak between a father and his son."

Clouds of smoke shot forth from the animal's nostrils as it loudly snorted.

Robert patted the beast of burden on its flank and softly spoke into its ear before crossing in front of the horse and walking up to his son. "Go ahead son. What be on your mind?"

Russell paused for a minute searching his thoughts for both the correct words along with the proper way to bring the issue that he had wondered about last night up to his father. "I am very grateful for the way you have chosen to raise me father, and I mean no lack of respect in my query," the young man briefly pausing and gazing over his father's shoulder before continuing.

Robert patiently waiting for the question.

"I know understanding for the reasoning behind your knowledge with a bow, but how is it you have come to know acquaintance and be so much learned with a sword?"

Again a moment of silence had found its way into the two's conversation, but now the break seemed to be caused more from Robert than Russell. The young man's eyes locked onto his father's face in an effort to try and read the man's expression.

"I am sorry father," apologized Russell breaking the quietness. "I lack not respect in my query!"

Taking another second, Robert asked his own question. "Why would you ponder your query to be one of disrespect?"

"Because, I should not be questioning you father."

"Russell, a man who does not question another's actions or motives is that equal to a puppet. He is controlled by another's thoughts along with his influences and is therefore no wiser than a fool," sternly reasoned Robert. "To be a man, one must think and act for himself. He must take a stance willing to defend his beliefs against any obstacle that he deems threatening towards his credence."

"But what if the person's word that differs from yours is a king?", the young man inquisitively asked.

"A king is still a man in his true form. He only wears a guise of what is right based on his beliefs," Robert addressed his son's query. "A king inherits a kingdom with his soul basis pertaining in birthright or his status, not in what the commoner views as fair and just. Do not let yourself be fooled Russell by the good King Stephen that we have adopted as our ruler. Where he is fair and just, there are others who sit on a throne and evil and wickedness run their land."

"I understand father," acknowledged the young man.

"So do not find yourself to be disrespecting to query another man. Only fools and puppets follow without question. A wise man who thinks for himself inquires when another's reason defies his beliefs," added Russell's father.

"It be your wish to know how I have been acquainted in the use of a blade. Is it not?"

"It is father," confirmed Russell.

With his son alongside of him, Robert walked towards the back of the braked cart. "I will try to explain it all to you, but hold any inquires you may have for now. Your mother and Nicole shall be coming out at anytime prepared to meet up with the Bradfords and be off to church."

Russell nodded his affirmation.

"The art of swordsmanship was handed down to me by my father, who in return received the weapon's knowledge from his father," stated Robert. "This went on one more time throughout our bloodline where it began from one of our ancestors whom was himself, a former knight."

Russell's eyes seemed to widen at the revelation. He couldn't believe what he was hearing. "What kind of a knight?", he automatically asked interrupting his father before remembering to hold all of his queries for later. The astonished, young man quickly apologized for the intrusion. "My apologies father."

Shaking off the interruption, Robert continued his tale. "A royal champion. One who was chosen by the Queen of England to not only protect her but to also uphold her honour. For many years he remained ever vigilant until one day the royal woman died a natural death. Her only son King Roland ascended to his seat on the throne.

"For many years to follow, he fought and warred in the feudal times of England until one day when he died on the field of battle. History has it that the knight was defending the royal carriage as it flee after an attempted ambush plot to kill the king and his queen with child had failed. Those who would return to the palace after the last of the attackers were killed say, the champion known as William fought to his death with the heart of a lion."

Russell sat captivated hanging on the words of his lineage. He hoped his mother and sister would not leave the cottage until after his father had finished.

"Years before William the Lion, that be what the scribes and scholars call him, met his end; the man had a child named after his namesake. He taught his son in the ways of the bow and the blade but more importantly instilled in him the path of honour. The boy grew into a man of integrity and reverence following in the footsteps of his father," recited Robert.

Again, an awestruck Russell lost his self-control and blurted out his excited query. "His son became a knight also?"

"No son," patiently answered the young man's father. "Remember, I told you earlier that the Lion had fought off an ambush attempt allowing the queen with child and King Roland to escape?'

"Yes."

"Well years later the queen would give birth to a son she named John, and after an early demise, King Roland would leave his throne for his heir to be crowned the new king. In time to come, King John would be saved from an assassin's knife in his own chambers. The savior was none other than William the Lion's own son," Robert gazed upon his ever aware son with a look of one preparing to let the cat out of the sack. "You know of who I speak," he informed the young man.

Russell's face took on a puzzled expression as he desperately tried to find the solution. "I know of him?", he perplexed.

"Yes. Your mother and I have told you the story about William many times when you were a child."

Still Russell squinted as he tried calling back into memory a time when he remembered hearing about the man William. Suddenly a notion rushed into his mind and pieces between the story his father told now and a child's tale fell into place. "You cannot be speaking on the story of 'William the Brave'?"

What started off as a grin turned into a smile when Robert heard his son ask the unbelievable question. "Yes Russell. William the Brave is my father's father. What you have knowledge of this day, the bow and the blade along with the path you take on how you carry yourself journeying through life, can all be traced back to the honorable champion, William the Lion."

Russell's mouth hung open in awe and he still couldn't comprehend the tale his father narrated explaining the young man's bloodline. Questions began to pop into his head and he wasn't sure which one he wished to ask first. Robert's son was about to ask his first query when his mother's voice broke the cold winter's air.

"We are ready to leave Robert," announced the man's wife from the cottage's doorway. "Can you come and lend aid to Nicole placing her in the cart?", she asked her husband.

Both Robert and Russell looked upon each other wearing two different expressions. The older man knowing that a bombardment of queries would be on their way in the upcoming future. His son appeared to wish that this astonishing confession had not taken an intermission for the time being.

"Son, bring that bow and its quiver here and place them in the house please," came Elizabeth. "I am sure the Bradfords will be awaiting our arrival."

The two left the cart; one to retrieve Nicole and the other to leave a family tradition behind, but for only the time being.

Chapter 11

A second knock resonated through the grogginess of Joan's subconscious waking her from her restful slumber. With her eyes still shut, the woman stretched her arms above her head while snuggling her body into the large, bed's mattress in an attempt to find more comfort. A deep, throaty groan escaped the servant as she reached out in the midst of the elongation. Waiting a brief moment, the woman opened her eyes and used the back of both her fists to wipe the sleep from them. She laid on her back staring up at the canopy of the royal furniture as her eyes tried to focus in the dimly lit room. From the corner of her left eye, Joan caught the gliding movement of a dark silhouette crossing the chamber's floor. The woman heard the door unlock and took in the sight of light from the hallway enter the room when the portal swung open.

"Yes mother," Joan heard the prince's voice.

"Matthew, you should be preparing to leave for church," the queen advised the young royal. "Are you just waking?", she asked her son while stepping into the dark room on her way to the double-curtained windows.

The prince closed the door and turned to address Queen Margaret's back. She was almost at the first window. "Mother, you mussant do that," he tried to reason, but the royal woman pulled open the first set of window covers bathing half the chamber in the bright, sunny light.

Joan quickly leaned up propping herself up and onto both of her elbows. The servant casting a worried glance to the prince.

Matthew returning the gaze all the while wearing a stoic expression on his face before shifting his stare back to his mother. He watched as the queen pulled open the other set of covers and turned around to address him.

"Matthew, I am aware that you enjoy slumbering late into the morning, but..." Queen Margaret's statement fading out halfway before she had finished as the woman noticed the occupant in her son's bed. "OH!", the queen's hand shooting up to her bosom in surprise.

"It is not what you ponder mother," her son started to reason.

"My lady, I beg you do not perceive the wrong notion!", Joan stammered while quickly pulling back the sheets and blanket and jumping out of Matthew's bed. "It is as the prince said! It is not what you think!"

Queen Margaret's face turned another shade of red when the fazed mother took in the sight of the servant standing wearing her son's nightdress.

He knew he had to take control of the awkward moment before things started to get further from the truth and out of hand if they weren't already. Strolling across the room to his mother, the prince attempted to explain the queen's uncomfortable discovery of an older woman in the sixteen years old's bed.

"Mother, it is not what you ponder," he explained. "Joan slept in my bed while I stood vigil on the chair over there," pointing to the burgundy seat with a blanket draped over an arm.

"This is true my queen!", pleaded the woman.

Margaret's eyes shifting from one to the other before the elegant woman interjected with her own query. "Please do not take my words wrongly, but why here Matthew?"

It was now time for the stoic prince to show some expression. He glanced up to the chamber's ceiling. The dilemma of exposing last night's events to his mother filled him with contradicting feelings. Maybe Joan would feel embarrassed about being a victim of an assault against her womanhood, but the young man quickly came up with an answer. "She was attacked last night."

"Oh my God!", responded his mother. "By one here in the castle?"

"Yes my lady," answered Joan.

"Were you injured?"

"No my lady. I had gone to the kitchen in an effort to prepare the proper pots and pans that would be needed for the cooking of the Yuletide's meal, and one of the cooks was already present," Joan's eyes never leaving the queen's. "He overpowered me and tried to force himself...", the woman's watery eyes dropping to the floor before she had finished. "The prince came to my rescue and then brought me here under his protection."

Margaret had already started towards Joan. Taking her hand up, she lifted the servant's chin and gazed upon the woman's face. Her eyes searching the woman's as the queen spoke in reassuring words. "I understand Joan. It sounds like it was a good thing that Matthew came along to aid you when he did."

Glancing to the prince, the queen inquired about the attempted rapist. "Where is this man now?"

"I had two guards throw him in the dungeon," he replied. "I will inform the king after we attend mass."

Suddenly a loud knock shook the room's door.

"Enter!", Matthew called out.

The chamber's wooden portal opened and King Stephen stepped into the room. He took a second to scan the three occupants standing there looking at him before he spoke. "It is not a proper time to be summoning a council. We need to leave shortly for church," advised the king.

Stephen noticed not only Joan donning his son's nightdress but also his son's unkept bed. A questioning eyebrow rose on his forehead.

"It is not as you ponder Stephen," interjected the queen at the king's silent gesture. "Let us take our leave my lord and I shall explain as we wait to depart," the elegant woman informed the prince's father as she entwined her arm with his and made for the door. Moments later she closed it behind her on their way out.

Matthew turned to Joan. "Well I shall venture to say that that went well unlike what I had imagined in the beginning." Casting her a smile, the young man headed for a wardrobe chest holding his attire for the upcoming day.

The woman sat back on the bed staring at the wall in front of her. She glanced over at the prince's back as he walked away. Turning her attention back to the stone partition, Joan smiled in relief.

Mass had ended and now the church's congregation formed three separate lines patiently waiting their turn to greet one of the members of the royal family. Three castle workers passed out rolls of bread coated in a cinnamon and sugar powder. The spices brought to England by a caravan earlier in the year.

"Well if it is not the famous Joan of Arc," greeted Matthew as Lynn approached the prince.

The fourteen year old's face spread into a grin. "You always call me by that name whenever we meet my prince," giggled the young woman.

"Because you have always reminded me of her quests since years past when you shared your story of adventure with both my mother and I," laughed Matthew.

"Do not be misled. It was far from that of a happy journey," corrected the Bradfords' oldest. "I would be willing to wager that my prince calls all the young maidens Joan of Arc," a smile never leaving her face.

"Those words know not truth," declared the young man. "I save that name for you Lynn."

A flash of flattery sparked in the Bradfords' daughter from hearing her name. Lynn was taken aback just to hear that Prince Matthew knew her name, but the young woman never displayed any kind of telltale exposing just how much the compliment meant to her. Instead, Lynn allowed his statement to pass unfazed.

"My prince, it is always pleasant to see the royal family attend mass here with us throughout the year."

Matching her agreeable words with his own, the young man shook Lynn's hand. "It is always my pleasure to see you and it be my wish that you and your family have a favorable Yuletide."

"You also my prince," she wished as the two separated until the next time the royal family attended church's mass.

Matthew watched Lynn leave for a second until another stepped right up into her vacant spot. Thoughts of the one he called Joan of Arc running through his head as he greeted another of the town's folk.

The ride through the snow from the church to the Bradfords' cottage was slow and mostly steady minus the three or four times one of the cart's wheels got stuck requiring a little help in the way of a push to free it from the snow's grip. Like on the way to mass, the Daniels followed the

Bradfords so aid was never far away if any of the wheels stopped turning. The journey took the two families a little extra time than usual but they had taken any delays into consideration when planning the day's wintery travel.

Reaching their destination, the two horse pulled carts stopped in the front of the Bradfords' small, stone barn. Both Gwenyth and Elizabeth stepped down from their seats with the aid of their husband's hands while Russell had already helped his younger sister from the back of the wagon. Her brother delivering her to her mother's side.

Leaving his sister and mother, the young man walked over to the Bradfords' cart and proceeded to offer his hand to both Lynn and Anne. The first to take his sign of assistance was the youngest daughter. Russell helped Anne out of the wagon and safely onto the snowy ground. The eleven year old smiling while heading to take up her mother's hand.

"Russell leant me aid mother," she pointed out the obvious.

Gwenyth smiled at the girl. "So I have become witness to," Anne's mother offering a smile to the Daniel's only son.

"Thank you Russell," cooed Anne.

The young man grinning and taking a bow.

Turning his attention back to the last occupant in the cart's box, the young man once again offered his hand. Lynn gazed at Russell's presented offering and then up at him with a coyish look upon her face. A moment later he was aiding her from the wooden mode of transportation, softly helping to place her on her feet in the snow.

"Thank you kind sir," came Lynn grateful for the assistance.

A smile accompanied by a nod was the young man's only reply.

The Bradfords' oldest daughter started for the small, stone cottage across the ground's blanket of powder when a tree in close proximity to both of the carts and barn had one of its thick branches crack loudly and break away from the plant's trunk. The weight of the snow the culprit leading to the loud split sending the limb along with its powdered covering crashing down onto a wooden, chicken coop underneath it.

The sudden loud outburst of smashing wood spooked the Daniel's horse causing the hitched beast to take a step back and rear up on its hind legs. When the livestock's front hooves landed back on the ground, the frightened horse took off running throwing Robert from the cart as he tried to climb back into his seat and take up the reins. He landed on the snowy ground with a thud.

Everyone heard the animal's panicked whinny before it started to dash out of control in the direction Lynn had taken on the way to her house. Her scream along with the bouncing wagon trailing it only added to the frightened horse's hysteria. It rushed on at the girl. Her hands raised in a defensive posture.

"LOOK OUT!", her father yelled trying to warn her of the imminent danger.

With the animal and cart bearing down on the paralyzed with fear young woman, Russell acted within a split second. The young man took several steps rushing in Lynn's direction and launched himself into the air tackling the would-be trampled victim. The blow knocking her out of the beast's way while both horse and cart flew by the prone two.

"Lynn!", cried Charles rushing towards the young man and woman. "Are you well?"

Laying on top of her rescuer in the snow and staring into Russell's eyes, Lynn replied in a normal voice. "I am now father. I am now." The two sharing the look for a moment longer.

Chapter 12

Hamilton, England 1440
2 years later

Russell laid on his back in the lush, green grass of summer staring up into Lynn's soft, brown eyes. The beautiful, young woman returning the look with a gaze all her own. Her long, brown hair draped around her neck and falling over her left shoulder as the young woman's body lay off to Russell's right side. The eighteen year old, young man's right arm wrapped around her thin waist.

Lynn lowered her head bringing her slightly parted, soft lips towards Russell's mouth. The descent ending when the sixteen year old's fleshy folds came into contact with the young man's. Both lovers closed their eyes losing themselves in the shared moment of intimacy while their heads moved slightly from side-to-side. The two's tongues probing the regions of each other's mouths. Lynn and Russell seemed to hunger for one another and their lips remained locked together for several minutes until finally breaking apart when the young woman pulled her mouth away to speak.

Running her hand in a gentle, circular motion over the round, mace-head ball that was his muscular shoulder, the young woman gazed down into her lover's eyes. A smile creased her lips emphasizing Lynn's dimpled face.

"Are you well?", she softly inquired.

"I am now," came the young man's answer as he felt that he was staring into the face of one of heaven's angels. His breathing slow and steady unlike that of his racing heart.

Lynn ran her hand, that she had used to caress Russell's shoulder, down over his sinewy arm following the lines caused by the veins bulging in his forearm to his hand. Placing her small hand in his and entwining their fingers together, Lynn leaned back down for another soft, sweet kiss. Russell's lips easily parting for the young woman's probing tongue. Their shared affection for one another ending sooner than later as it was interrupted by loud chirps and whistles that seemed to fill the air.

Breaking apart, both Lynn and Russell looked to the one responsible for interrupting the two lovers. Standing on the stone wall eyeballing the two was none other than Sir Robin. A small piece of Elizabeth's homemade bread sitting in front of the young man's longtime friend.

"Well there you are!", announced Russell. "Lynn and I have been waiting for your arrival."

Sir Robin offered a couple of chirps before taking a couple of pecks at the edible gift.

Beginning at the base of his throat and sliding it over his muscular chest and down to his ripped stomach, Lynn slowly ran a finger from her free hand over her lover's shirtless torso. She was enjoying watching the little bird interact with his human friend.

Guiding himself out of his lover's grasp and rising to his feet, Russell reached down extending his hand to Lynn. Taking hold of it, she also rose to her feet with the shirtless man's assistance before he broke the grip and approached the avian's temporary perch.

"How fair you on this day Sir Robin?", he inquired nearing the wall and extending his finger out towards the bird.

A lone chirp followed by a series of dance-like steps was the winged animal's only answer. The avian looked at his friend and blinked twice before half leaping and half flying onto the fleshy perch.

Russell glanced back at Lynn and they shared a smile as she gasped from the sudden surprise of the winged creature's display of trust in the human. Her brown eyes as large as saucers. "If I was never witness to it then I would never believe it!", she shockingly added.

"Sir Robin finds ease with me," he shared while gently petting the bird's crown with a finger from his other hand. "We have known one another for many years now and I am honoured to call Sir Robin my friend."

Turning his smile back to the winged animal perched on his finger, Russell formally introduced the young woman and the avian. "Sir Robin, this be Lynn. My sweet, this be the famous Sir Robin."

With impeccable timing a series of chirps shot from Russell's little friend.

Lynn giggled and offered a curtsy. "Well met Sir Robin."

The bird's head along with his body rapidly bent forward before standing back erect several times giving the two the impression that it was mirroring the young woman's move with a successions of bows all his own.

Another giggle escaped Lynn. "Always a proper gentleman with the ladies I see," she laughingly remarked.

"That or a ham," Russell smiling at his witty remark.

Sir Robin slightly turned his head gazing with an eye at his human friend before giving another series of chirps as if reprimanding the young man's retort.

"Okay! Okay!", he surrendered with a chuckle.

Sir Robin sat on the fleshy perch for only a moment longer before taking a short flight back to his spot on the wall. He offered a whistle followed by a chirp and resumed pecking at some more crumbs of bread.

Russell turned and walked back to Lynn who handed him his shirt. Pulling the article of clothing over his head and then taking a couple of minutes to tie up the sleeves laces, the young man retrieved his bow and quiver from its resting place against the field's lone tree. He strapped the arrow's case onto his back before stealing a quick kiss from Lynn. "Are you ready?", he queried.

His lover only nod her affirmation.

"Fair well Sir Robin," she wished as the young woman prepared to take her leave.

Turning back in the direction of the little bird still standing on the stone wall now eyeing him, Russell gave his concluding remark as he parted. "Until we meet on the day after the morrow take care of yourself my friend."

Sir Robin replied with a couple of chirps.

Taking his lover's hand in his grasp, Russell looked back at Lynn. "Shall we?", he asked with a slight nod.

"I will not hesitate to follow your lead anywhere," she smiled.

The two started out across the field's lush, green carpet. It was still early in the day and the sun radiated a brightness that would not perish nor be overrun by any rain clouds before nightfall. It was beginning to heat up and both Russell along with Lynn knew what to expect from this summer's day. Their destination was a small pond in the forest.

Walking hand-in-hand, the young woman glanced up towards the side of the young man's face. "Thank you for properly introducing me to your friend my love."

Meeting her gaze with his own he replied. "I just felt it be the proper time for you to meet Sir Robin. Besides my father and mother, he has taught me a lot. I am honored to call the little fellow friend," he smiled.

"I do not understand what it be that you could have learned from Sir Robin," she puzzled.

Russell once again smiled down at his love. "He has shown me that if you respect others, honour their wishes, and treat others like you wish to be treated then they will offer you the same in return. Hence, a friendship not different like that of the one in which him and I share may blossom from one another's actions."

"But not all are like Sir Robin. They only find solace in wrong doings and creating others misery," Lynn admitted.

"Your words know truth, but those kind of folk know nothing of respect nor goodwill," advised Russell. "Those people are without honour and do not deserve to be looked upon in a favorable way. They do not deserve to be treated with honour nor be allowed to thrive under God's watchful eyes. Their ill-willed actions will come back to haunt them and rear their unfavorable heads." Russell took a brief pause before finishing his thoughts. "A man who knows only ugliness shall never know the true beauty around him like that equal to the friendship of Sir Robin, nor the love given by an angel like you."

"You always have a way of speaking words that know only beauty to me," cooed Lynn while offering a squeeze to the young man's hand in hers.

Still sitting on the stone wall finishing up the last of the bread crumbs, Sir Robin watched the two disappear into the woods before taking flight.

Chapter 13

Soft moans of pleasure drifted from Joan's mouth as she arched her back thrusting her firm, round, hand-sized breast into the air. The woman's head tilting back while closing both of her eyes momentarily. Her wide open hands with fingers spread digging into her lover's back pulling him into her womanhood. The bed's dressing matching the slow almost hypnotic-like rhythm caused from the rising and falling of Matthew's hips as he planted delicate kisses on the woman's neck under her jaw. His tongue slightly touching her soft, smooth skin.

Slowly pulling away from her enough causing a slight separation of their pubic bones but still keeping a connection between the two. Matthew gazed down into his lover's face locking eyes with Joan's half-opened, lustful stare glaring back up at the eighteen year old. The thirty four year old woman's lips starting to part as he lowered himself back into her depths.

Steadily, the two lovers kept up their ballad-like dance until an oncoming, unrestrained, sexual indulgence began to arise from somewhere deep inside the both of them. Prince Matthew's slow thrusts were replaced by rapid plunges as he drove all of his manhood into Joan quicker and quicker. The woman's soft moans morphing into grunts while their bodies slapped together from the young man's excited lunges. An imminent orgasm forthcoming.

A small scream escaped Joan's lips as her sheen body, covered with sweat, began to rock and shake from her climax. The cry of ecstasy joined by his deep, relieving sigh as he shot his seed into her womb.

Rolling off of his lover and onto his back by her side, both the eighteen year old prince and the thirty four year old personal servant laid there catching their breaths staring up at the bed's canopy. A smile creasing both of their faces from the onrushing feeling of fulfillment and satisfaction.

Turning sideways and facing her lover, Joan complimented. "You never cease to satisfy my needs as a woman. You are a good lover."

"I had an accomplished teacher," smiled back Matthew.

Suddenly a loud knock on the room's door caught the two by surprise. Joan instantly wore an uneasy expression on her face as she turned from the intrusion back to the prince. His smile gone now, the young man took on a more serious look that reflected in the tone of his voice.

"Who be there?", he sternly inquired.

"It is I Matthew" replied his mother from the other side. "May I enter?", she asked.

Joan's eyes widened in horror at not only the thought of the queen being outside the chamber but the possibility of her entering the room. A deliberation going on in her head as she tried to remember if either she or the prince had locked the door last night.

"I have woken a bit late mother,..." -coolly responded Matthew- "...and I am in the process of washing up and dressing." When he was done making up the excuse, the young man offered a wink to his lover. The silent signal almost causing a burst of laughter out of the once frightened woman.

"Very well Matthew,..." -accepted Queen Margaret- "...but do not neglect the acknowledgment that your cousin should arrive for his visit on this day."

"I have not forgotten mother," he admitted. "I shall join you and father in time for his arrival," the prince confirmed.

"Very well son," agreed his mother taking a step away from the wooden portal. A last thought crossing her mind causing the queen to address her son. "Oh, and Matthew."

"Yes mother."

"Have you seen Joan yet on this morning?", she inquired.

"No mother," the prince answered giving no evidence in his voice of the contrary. "However, when I saw her last night I believe she mentioned something in the way of filling a hungering void."

Again a burst of laughter almost shot forth from the naked woman in the prince's bed but she covered her mouth with her hand just in time to at least conceal her smile. Using her other hand, she balled it up into a fist and playfully hit him in the gut. Her young lover cringing from the strike.

"My notion would be that she is either in her bed still slumbering from her nighttime snack or in the kitchen feeding her hunger," the prince composed as he offered his opinion.

"Very well. I shall go and check for her," reasoned Margaret on the other side of the door. "If you should find her first, tell her that we will require her aid in preparing the chamber your cousin will be staying in."

"Yes mother," he confirmed before the queen took her leave from outside the prince's door.

"How do you do that without any hint of feelings?", Joan smiled the query.

"I will be king one day and asked to make many decisions that at that time will require my lack of personal feelings in the matter. Being a good king, who is both fair and just along with ruling his kingdom honorably, I will be asked to do things that I may not personally agree with but must do for the betterment of my people," informed Prince Matthew. "It is not wise to allow one's feelings to lead. England wants and sometimes needs a king's rule not a king's feeling to rule."

"Thank you for looking out for my betterment then your majesty," smiled Joan before placing a kiss on the prince's cheek.

"I also find fondness when a decision benefits myself,' added the young man followed by a gentle kiss on Joan's lips.

Matthew rolled up on top of the woman mounting her, as his lover bent her knees one on each side of his body. She exhaled deeply and once again a slow rhythm was caused by the rising and falling of the young prince's hips.

<hr>

The door of Matthew's chamber slowly opened and the prince stuck his head out of the entryway scanning up and down the hallway. Waiting another moment, the young man seemed satisfied that the coast was clear. He stepped into the castle's corridor followed by his personal servant and secret lover. Once again cautiously glancing left and then right, the prince gave the woman a kiss.

"Stop by the kitchen and partake in something. When you have finished take the proper preparations and ready the chamber in the east wing for my cousin's visit," he humbly ordered the woman. "I shall go and find my mother and inform her that I have already spoken with you delivering her wishes."

Joan only nod an affirmation before starting for the castle's kitchen. An instant smile revealing her perfect, white teeth shone at her secret lover. Her expression caused from the lite slap on her heart-shaped rear by Matthew.

"I am under the notion that I will be partaking in you this night," his words marked with both anticipation and invitation.

"Of course my lord," she agreed wearing a grin before turning to leave.

The prince watched the woman's hips sway side-to-side as she strolled down the hallway and out of sight when she rounded a corner. Turning and heading in the opposite direction, the royal's destination was off to find the woman he called mother, the Queen of England.

It was just after mid-day when the royal coach carrying Prince Matthew's only cousin, Duke Paul of Scheffield, arrived at the castle. He was the only son to the king's younger brother, Duke Henry, who himself was Stephen's only sibling. Unfortunately Henry had met with an early demise two winters prior due to an ongoing battle with lung sickness. As for Duke Paul's mother, she had also left this life twenty two years ago passing at the young man's birthing.

King Stephen, along with his royal family accompanied by a couple of women servants and a male servant from the castle, watched as the young Duke of Scheffield made his way towards them across the greeting hall. An air of both confidence and arrogance appeared to radiate from the young man's every step. Paul's raptor-like facial features accompanied by his hawk-like stare locked onto his royal greeters never once straying from his line of sight.

Striding up to England's reigning family, Duke Paul took a knee in front of his uncle and bowed his head. "My king," -he addressed- "I humbly share my gratitude to both you and the queen for the invitation to stay and visit with all of you." Lifting his head and raising a hand, the duke took hold of King Stephen's hand and brought his lips to the sovereign's ring planting a kiss on the bulky piece of jewelry.

"Rise nephew," smiled his royal uncle. "Enough with the formalities. Let me have a look at you!", he added through a chuckle helping Paul gain his feet. Both wore a smile as they embraced in a hug. "It does me well to see you!"

"As it does I uncle," grinned the duke.

Everyone present shared in the royal's enjoyment.

"Aunt Margaret," came Paul. "Your beauty and elegance never seem to age," he complimented.

"That is why you are my favorite nephew!", the queen conceded with a small giggle accompanied with a smile.

"He is your only nephew mother, remember?", interjected a kidding Prince Matthew.

"A small matter of the trivial," Margaret waved off the obvious.

"I see one can no longer blind you with the pulling of wool over your eyes my prince," laughed Paul as he and his cousin shared a happy embrace.

The greeting hall's occupants all partaking in the joyous reunion for several moments.

"Is the duke's chamber prepared for his unpacking?", inquired the queen turning to Joan.

"Yes my lady," responded the woman.

Taking a second glance at the beautiful servant, Duke Paul directed his query to his aunt. "Is this the same Joan that narrated tales to the prince and I telling us of William the Brave and his heroics?"

"This be the one," confirmed Margaret.

The duke taking up the woman's hand and planting a kiss on the back of it. "One can never forget the tale of William the Brave told by a beautiful maiden such as you, Joan the Bard."

The woman's cheeks outlining her smile turned a shade red from blushing. She was slightly taken aback that he would even remember her name. "I am honoured my lord," she softly added to her curtsy.

Draping an arm over his nephew and his son's shoulder, Stephen pulled the two closer to him as they started on their way from the greeting hall.

"My dear, can you see to it that Paul's belongings are taken to his room? Us boys have a lot to discuss."

The queen gave her husband a slight nod. "Very well my husband," she affirmed while watching the three disappear into a hallway. Turning her attention to the servants, Margaret needed not use any words to get them moving.

Chapter 14

Smooth, rolling ripples flowed across the recently disturbed surface of the small pond's clear water, as the two young lovers seeking refuge from the heat of the summer's day effortlessly tread the liquid in close proximity to one another. Their voices barely audible and almost drowned out by the chirping birds housed in the branches of the surrounding forest. Trees reflected off the mirror-like surface of the small body of water joining the sun's rays sparkling off of the liquid. A small stream fed the pond, while another narrow vein led away winding through the woods.

"This place is both beautiful and peaceful," Lynn pointed out while taking in the tranquil spot. "How is it you know of its existence?"

"When I was still a boy my father began to teach me how to make my way around the forest," replied Russell. "On some nights, we would even sleep under the stars only to continue a little further the next day. After our treks he would require that I lead the way back home."

"Did you ever lose your way and wander about?", the young woman queried before slightly leaning her head backwards into the water.

"I have, but father was always with me and knew the right way," the young man responded while drifting towards the young woman. When he got close enough to Lynn, her kiss closed the gap. It only lasted a few moments then Russell slowly pulled away.

"Come on. There be something I wish to show you!", he stated while crooking his head at the pond's bank where their clothing rested in the clearing's grass. The two lovers starting to swim as one for the dry earth.

Russell was the first to leave the refreshment of the small body of water and walk towards the pile of garments. Even though he was shirtless, the young man still swam in his brown pants. A trail of running liquid fell from them onto the lush carpet of grass as he walked. Careful not to drip water on the dry apparel, he reached down and grabbed his shirt and soft, buckskin boots along with his bow and quiver.

Sitting down on a log, Russell put on his suede shoes and laced them up. Rubbing his hands over his head, the young man smoothed back his feathery, brown hair while looking skywards. "There is enough time remaining in this day," he reasoned to himself.

Dropping his gaze back to Lynn, still hidden by the pond's water, Russell addressed his lover. "I shall turn my back so you may dress and then we will go my lady," he said while spinning around on the log facing away from the young woman.

"But I thought you have something you wish for me to see?"

"I do!", he shouted over his shoulder. "I am sorry if my words gave you the wrong notion. I still wish to take you there."

Lynn emerged from the repriving dunk wearing only a one-piece undergarment. Water dripped across the grass, as she padded on the balls of her feet over to the remaining pile of her dry clothes. Underneath the apparel was a pair of soft, leather sandals that her mother had made for her last summer. The young woman's face wearing a gleaming smile as she looked over towards the back of her honour-bound lover still sitting turned on the log.

Squatting down to retrieve her white dress with matching sash, Lynn draped the two over her left forearm and swiftly slipped into her sandals. Pushing her petite feet downward against the ground, she adjusted the fit on her left foot before balancing on one leg at a time to buckle the footwear. Finally, the young woman slid her shin-length garment over her head and tied the broad band around her waist.

"Only a little longer my love," she spoke into the hot summer's air informing the young man patiently waiting for her before starting to quietly sneak up on him.

"When you are properly prepared my lady."

Like a predator stalking its prey, the fully dressed Lynn skulked over to Russell. When she was close enough to her target, the lover pounced like a playful kitten covering her man's eyes from behind.

"Guess who?", she whispered through a smile.

"Oh No! I have been cast blind by the wicked witch that resides in these woods!", cried Russell feigning his horror.

"Uhh!", shouted Lynn aghast at her lover's response. Removing her hands from his eyes, the young woman offered his shoulder a shove. "You evil boy!", she added.

Rocking forward a bit, Russell turned to take in his lover standing with her hands placed on her hips. A look of wonder written on his face as he stared at the young woman.

"I was once blinded but now I see," recited the young man. His mouth fell agape in between statements. "For in front of this wretch stands the most beautiful angel that one such as I has ever laid eyes upon. Truly a Heaven sent."

Lynn briefly shut her eyes and slowly shook her head three or four times. "You are such a poet. But know this sinner, all of your praise will get you nowhere." The young woman watched as Russell brought an accusing finger up to his own chest. An expression of shock was written across his handsome face. "Although I do find fancy in your attempts!", she added.

Laughter resonated throughout the small clearing from the two.

"I still do not see it," squinted Lynn staring into the forest's thick shrubbery.

"The place is still hidden from your view?", a slight surprise in Russell's query. Taking hold of the young woman's hand, they both started towards the area that the young man had been pointing at only moments earlier.

The two lovers walked for at least another ten yards through a heavily wooded section of the forest's trees. Their movement only slightly delayed when the two needed to walk around or step over scattered patches of small bushes. Besides spots of grass here-and-there, the forest's floor was mostly hidden from the ground cover littering the earth. The low plant life tripping Lynn up several times as she kept her eyes more focused on the place where Russell had pointed at instead of watching her steps. Her guide keeping her from taking a fall on several occasions.

A loud gasp escaped Lynn as she was now beginning to see the silhouette to a small, square structure materialize before her eyes. The young woman could barely make out the stones used to erect the house due to the numerous tendrils of vines climbing up and over the place's walls. The natural camouflage deceptively covering the undersized cottage from a quick glance of someone's vision.

"Oh my God my love!", she excitedly gasp. "I can see it now!"

A smile crossed Russell's lips at the news to Lynn's discovery. "What do you think?", he asked.

Glancing over to him before returning back to the vine covered structure, the young woman swiftly inquired, "Who lives there?"

"No one. Father and I discovered it years ago," responded the wood's guide. "The house has served us as a safe place to stay at night out here in the forest. Come on I shall acquaint you with the place."

Walking the rest of the way to the hidden cottage in the woods, both of the young lovers stood in front of a thick, oak door. Russell opened the portal with a black, iron latch. "As you can tell, father and I had to repair a few things around here," he offered as both entered the structure.

A bright ray from the day's sunlight shone through the open door allowing the two, whose eyes needed a second to adjust to the dimly lit, single room, start to make out for the most part the only chamber's furnishings. Even with the outside's radiance illuminating most of the inside, shadows still hung in the space's corners.

Lynn surveyed the place somewhat caught in awe. "Who used to live here?", she inquired.

"We know not, but neither father nor I have ever witnessed another's comings and goings."

The small, stone cottage's room was the only one in the place. With the light shining in, Lynn could make out a semi-circular fire pit in the rear of the chamber. Two chairs sat, one on either side, of the half circle and the Daniels had constructed a crude, wooden floor safely skirting the pit's stone lining. Careful in their planning for it not to be susceptible to spitting embers from a night's blaze. Two windows, one to the door's left and the other to its right, were shuttered from the inside, but sunlight spilled into the room from one Russell had just opened.

"It has an earthy smell to it," flatly stated Lynn. Her nose crinkled by the pungent odor.

"Only because it has been shut up for a time," confirmed her lover. "With the window being open, the place will air out faster now. What do you think?"

"I believe you and I have a secret place to spend our upcoming days," she replied wearing a devilish grin.

"I see I was proper in speaking the word 'wicked'," slyly interjected Russell. He reacted by quickly jumping back a step or two, as Lynn lightly swung a fist at his shoulder. The love tap missing.

"And I see you were also proper when you called yourself a 'wretch'!", she wittingly added before breaking out in laughter.

Closing the shutter, the young man unfortunately stated what was obvious to him. "We need to return. The day is growing old and its light will be waning soon."

Stepping outside the secret cottage followed by her lover closing its portal behind him, Lynn turned to Russell offering him a long, tongue probing kiss. When they finally broke apart she softly added while staring slightly up into his eyes, "Thank you for a beautiful day."

"Everyday with you my love always knows beauty," he smiled.

"There once again be the poet that I so much fancy," she affirmed before smiling and bringing her lips up to his.

Chapter 15

Gwenyth Bradford along with her thirteen year old daughter, Anne, sat at the cottage's only table watching the household's head, Charles, pace back-n-forth between the chair that he couldn't sit still in and kept constantly rising from, and the small house's only door. His feeling of unrest and anxiety emanated throughout the place's atmosphere causing an air of anxiousness and uneasiness, at least for him, in the lantern lit room. Mother and daughter calmly working on separate knitting projects for the upcoming winter.

"Charles, would you please sit down and rest," calmly pleaded Gwenyth while never looking up from her needle work and shaking her head. "You know Lynn is with Russell."

"And are you aware that it be dark?", he quickly retorted while walking towards the door throwing up an arm as if gesturing to the evening sky.

"It does that father towards the end of every day," chimed in Anne. Her mother casting the girl a slight smile and shaking her head. The woman's expression changing to one signifying to remain quiet.

Her nervous father turning on the girl with disgust in his voice. "I am aware of what takes place at the passing of the day child!" Moments later Charles returned back to his route in the direction of the empty chair.

"My dear," softly addressed Gwenyth while putting her project onto the table and giving her husband her undivided attention. "The evening's darkness just settled for the night. I am sure Russell is on his way here as we speak to deliver our daughter alive and unscathed."

Charles turned from the chair making his way back to the door. "And you have a notion of this due to?", he animatedly queried his open-ended question.

"Because that girl is safer with Russell than she would be with the whole of England's armies!", his wife sternly stated. "I do not believe that even the royal guard could protect the king and queen as well as that young man would your daughter!"

Completing the distance to the door, Charles spun back towards the chair. "You would be willing to wager that opinion of yours if you were one of those gambling souls?", he inquired.

"I would wager this whole farm on it," Gwenyth gave her matter-of-fact reply.

"I find accord with mother," agreed Anne. "Remember father that Russell has already given aid to Lynn twice in the past, and at both times saved her life."

Charles realized the truth in his youngest daughter's words and he knew that he couldn't find a way to dispute nor rearrange the facts in them. The Daniels' boy had come to his oldest daughter's rescue a couple of times already, and the patriarch had to agree that on both occasions Russell had saved Lynn's life.

Stopping at the wooden chair across the room, Charles cast a questioning look at his perfectly calm wife seated at the table. "The whole of England's armies?" he queried.

"All the way down to every last squire and stable hand," she stated in a matter-of-fact tone.

Her husband nodded his head three times and raised an eyebrow while absorbing her words. A picturing thought ran through Charles mind of a defensive scene before he plopped down into the seat. The Bradford man reflecting on Gwenyth's belief.

As if on cue, the cottage's door swung open and Lynn with Russell in tow walked into the room. The young man shutting the portal behind him.

"There you are!", excitedly blurted Charles jumping up from his chair.

The two newcomers looking in the direction of the man rising from his seat.

"Have you noticed it be dark outdoors?", Lynn's father queried the fact. "Your mother has been worried to the sickness over you!"

Gwenyth sighed as she shot Charles a glance. His wife slightly taken from her husbands blatant fabrication of the truth. The man trying not to look in her direction missing the sight of her shaking her head accompanied by a small grin on her face.

A loud gasp escaped Anne's mouth, but her father's pointed finger ordered her to further remain silent.

"My humblest apologies Mrs. Bradford," regretfully expressed Russell. "It be my error that Lynn is here after darkness has fallen. I believed we had more of the sun's light left."

"It is of no harm," she smiled.

"Well I must be returning home now myself," volunteered the young man. "I wish you all a well night," he gave a final nod before turning and opening the door.

"You also Russell," wished Gwenyth.

Charles returned the young man's nod with one of his own, and Lynn's sister waved. "Fair night Russell."

The young man nodding a second time before closing the door as he left.

Lynn took a moment to glance between her mother seated at the table and her father beginning to return to his chair. "Father," she called after him.

He turned and his daughter planted a kiss upon his bearded cheek.

"Thank you father."

"For what?", puzzled Charles.

"For worrying to the sickness for my safe return," she smiled before heading to her room.

Both Gwenyth and Anne burst out into laughter as Lynn had obviously seen right through her father's fabrication of the truth and recognized the facade for what it really was.

Watching his oldest daughter's back as she walked for her sleeping quarters, Charles glanced over in the direction of his wife and youngest daughter laughing from the amusement of his exposed ruse. Like that of a wounded thief requesting sanctuary from the church, the patriarch finished returning to his chair. He was left hoping the wooden seat would hear his petition and grant him refuge from the embarrassing moment. In time it did.

Honour

The summer, night sky was clear and a half moon, along with the dotted stars like white spots on a black canvas, shone down from the heavens illuminating the darkness covering England. Solid black shadows from lone, standing trees off to the side of the hard, dirt road littered the wide path with their dark silhouettes, as a single rider rode his leisurely walking mount. The horse needing no helpful directions from its owner in its course towards its final destination as the hoofed animal automatically began the way home.

Russell was mentally lost staring into the bright, night sky. His thoughts of the present momentarily lacking as scenes from earlier this day leapt in and out of his mind. There was no doubting his love for the oldest of the Bradfords' daughters as mental images of Lynn's twinkling, brown eyes, radiant smile ending with dimpled cheeks, and her long, straight, shiny, brown hair accenting her beauty seemed to be the only sights he saw in his mind's eye. To the young man there was only one thing that came close to his precious Lynn, and that was the time he shared with her. Whether it be with others or by himself, which he enjoyed far more, Russell was always thankful for the occasion.

The young rider had temporarily lost track of time and the distance his horse had already covered when the calls of his name brought him back to the here and now. Dropping his daydreaming eyes back to the road ahead, the sight of two figures also on horseback overtook his previous reminiscing. The young lover's thoughts of Lynn forgotten but only for the time being.

"Russell, how fairs you?", came the query from one of the two riders.

The young man quickly recognizing his friend's voice causing a smile to crease Russell's lips and reflecting the same expression he was getting from both of the others.

"Paul. Peter," he offered an acknowledging nod. "I am well thanks."

Continuing to walk his horse towards the twin brothers named after two of disciples from the bible, Russell followed his reply with a question of his own. "How fairs the two of you?", he pleasantly asked.

"We are well also," answered Paul, the twins oldest but only by a minute or two.

"What brings both of you out on this night?", inquired Russell.

"We thought the notion to bring the horses out for a stroll," again replied Paul.

"And decided this evening was a well time to do so," added Peter. "Are you attending the king's tourney? It approaches three days from now."

"Yes," he confirmed. "I shall be attending accompanied by my family."

"Not in the company of this famous Lynn that we have heard so much about?", teasingly came Paul.

His twin remaining silent but wearing a smile that matched his brothers.

Glancing from one brother and to the other, the young man's lips turned up and a smile grew upon his face. "I am under the notion that we will be traveling to the event with the Bradford family." Russell trying his hardest not to sound too embarrassed.

A burst of laughter escaped both Paul and Peter at the young man's answer feigning the playful jest. In the seconds that followed even Russell had to join the two in the laugh, considering he could not dispute the fact that he had shared his true feelings on numerous occasions with his two closest friends. Somehow, Lynn Bradford always seemed to find a way into the three's conversations.

"Damn you jesters!", scornfully chuckled Lynn's lover.

"Leave the honour-bound Russell be brother," interjected Peter trying to contain his laughter.

"He be bound alright, but honour may know only a false pretense!", excitedly chuckled Paul.

"Your words may know truth brother," Peter reasoned while looking back-n-forth between his double and Russell. The agreeing twin causing a loud roar to leave Paul's lips when he produced a cat-like meow. Their gazes meeting their friend's face.

Glancing between the two that he had grown up with since childhood, Russell wore an unimpressive expression. "Like two clucking hens," he added.

His statement drawing out louder laughter from his company of hecklers. Their enjoyment of the jest eventually led them to add tears to the nighttime roaring. Soon Russell broke into another smile and joined them in their playful fun.

Russell booted his heels into his mount's flanks signaling the animal to continue on.

Turning their horses around, the two brothers joined their friend on his journey home. "May as well join your company," admitted Peter starting to simmer from his earlier teasing fun.

Glancing at the two as they pulled up beside him, Russell threw his arms up, his hands only shoulder height, and gazed towards the night's sky. "How have I come to know such misfortune?", his jesting inquiry directed at the Almighty.

A moment later another round of laughter shot forth from the three young men on horseback strolling down the dirt road.

Duke Paul had finished unpacking his luggage for the night and had decided to take a walk though the castle in his search for his royal cousin's company. Having been in the place over a dozen times while growing up, the duke knew exactly the correct route he would need to take to get to the prince's chambers.

Strolling down one of the palace's many hallways and rounding a corner, Paul stopped instantly when he noticed the shoulder-length, brown-haired, beautiful servant, Joan, standing in the corridor outside Prince Matthew's door. He swiftly stepped back behind the wall out of sight. Cautiously, he peered down the passage where she seemed to wait.

Paul was forced to swiftly pull his head back against the wall where he now hid, as he had watched the woman give a quick glance up one side and down the other of the hallway. Patiently waiting for several moments, the duke dared another glance. He just caught sight of the servant entering Matthew's room and then heard clicking of the door closing. Another small sound followed and he knew it was the wooden portal being secured.

Taking his time, careful to not make any disturbance, Paul quietly skulked up to the spot right outside the prince's chambers. Slowly, he placed an ear to the secured oak.

The duke remained very silent in the hallway as he listened to the low, muffled laughter coming from the other side. For a second, or two, only quietness came to his probing ear. Removing the side of his head, Paul offered a fast glance up and down both sides of the corridor before placing his lobe back to its spot.

Now soft moans and groans coming from his cousin's room replaced the silence that he had known only minutes ago. The idea that his eighteen year old cousin, who was also the prince of England, was making love with an older woman, whom in herself was a servant, brought different thoughts and images to his mind's eye. A heat that had begun in the depths of his body now made its way into the lowness of his nether region.

Duke Paul scanned the empty hallway a couple more times and didn't resign from his post until he heard Joan's low moans turn into louder grunts. He had been with enough women to know her sexual explosion was near. Within a few more seconds, Paul caught the sound of her release and then only knew quietness again.

The prince's older cousin decided he had heard more than enough and the time to take his leave was upon him. Duke Paul swiftly and stealthy made his way down the corridor, around the corner, and eventually back to his room. The image of Joan's naked body with her legs spread apart while being ridden, stay burned in his mind while he undressed, closed his eyes, and found pleasure with her in bed.

Chapter 16

The bright, noonday sun shined down on the castle's royal garden, along with the two stately figures present soaking up the flaming orb's heat. Both men dressed in sheen, loose garb sat on separate, stone benches arranged in the center of the small courtyard catching up on years past as they enjoyed the beautiful afternoon weather. Their shared conversation ranging from the two's childhood all the way up to their lives present. On numerous occasions their open conversation was interrupted thanks to an outburst of laughter as both young men reminisced.

"Let's speak of seriousness for a moment cousin," interjected Prince Matthew seeking a turn in the conversation. "How have you faired since the loss of my uncle two winters ago?"

Regaining his composure from the laugh both men had shared in a moment ago, Duke Paul openly replied to his cousin's query. "I am well," -he shrugged his shoulders- "I do have some nights that are better than others, but as I have said, I am well."

"Your father was a good man and a noble man amongst nobles."

The duke nodded his head in agreement at Matthew's opinion. "No truer words have been spoken my prince." Paul raising a pewter goblet half-filled with a red wine. "A toast!"

The heir bringing his bluish-gray drinking cup up to the same height as the dukes.

"To my father, Duke Henry of Scheffield, may he have reunited with mother and the two of them share in each other's company as they peacefully walk through the heavenly fields in the Lord's Kingdom," toasted their only son.

"Hear! Hear!", called out his cousin bringing their goblets together in a slight "tinging" sound before raising them to their lips.

Taking a pull from his wine and lowering the pewter vessel to rest on the outside of one of his bent knees while obviously enjoying the taste on his palate, it was Duke Paul's time to ask a query.

"Tell me cousin. Is there any woman that your eyes have found favor with here at court?"

The question stirring up an anxiety in Matthew, who was slightly taken aback by Paul's inquiry. The young man was not ready to share the news that not only had he been attracted to and sexually active with his thirtyish year old, personal servant for the last two winters, but that he also found fanciness with a young woman closer to his age. Her only negative characteristic was that of her birth status. The girl was a farmer's daughter. A simple commoner to be exact. The fear of not knowing how his cousin would react to this information caused the young man to fabricate a ruse.

"I have not found a woman of nobility as of yet that seems to meet my fancy so I have remained abstained from another's touch," he lied while gazing into the duke's raptor-like stare. His cousin's eyes never seeming to blink causing Mathew to feel as if he was a jack being sized up for a hawk's next meal.

"But surely my prince, you must have at least sowed your oats amongst some of the castle or the town's maidens?", shockingly Paul asked feigning his disbelief.

"I have not," lied Prince Matthew. "There will be a time for that in the upcoming future, but for the present, I need this time to learn how to rule in a proper fashion," he added trying to make his facade believable.

Quickly taking the opportunity, Matthew attempted to refocus the attention from him. "How fair you in these matters cousin?"

Duke Paul sat smoothly back on the bench. A smile creasing his lips from both the knowledge of the prince's lying refusal, along with the image of the naked servant being ridden in his mind. The duke had spied the woman from two nights prior up to the last one sneaking into his cousin's chambers. From the sounds coming from the other side of the door, he had laid his ear against, the two were definitely not playing a game of cards.

Returning his attention back to Prince Matthew, Paul broke out into a small chuckle. "Since I have adorned the mantle as Duke of Scheffield both young maidens and even an older woman or two have at one time or another thrown themselves at me."

"Does that know truth!", surprisingly questioned Matthew.

"Of course cousin," replied Paul in a matter-of-fact tone. Leaning forward on his bench, the duke offered the prince a little advice. "If the obvious has gone unnoticed to you cousin, we are nobles," he sternly stated. "That means we are allowed to have anyone or anything that we wish freely. Even if we must reach out and take it," he added using his hand to close it into a snagging fist.

The prince sat there with his gaze locked on the serious stare of the duke's. The only thought that seemed to overshadow that of Matthew's awareness was the contemplating of his cousin's honour as a man; especially a nobleman of some degree of power.

Prince Matthew blinked back into the conversation moments later and decided to change the subject. "Will you be competing in the morrow's tourney?" He tried to ask his query in an uplifting manner, but the thought of Paul's lack of honour would not go away. It had burrowed into his consciousness like a mole digging into England's land.

"Are you certain you were not followed last night or any of those prior?", calmly inquired Matthew after taking a precautionary glance up and down the seemingly empty corridor the two met in on the north side of the castle.

"No Matthew!", positively declared Joan staring into her young, lover's face. "What is amiss?" Her feeling that something may be wrong beginning to grow in the pit of her stomach.

"I sat speaking with my cousin earlier in the royal gardens…," the prince softly stated as he stole another quick look to both sides of the hallway before continuing, "…and the matter of bedding woman in the same household arose.

The servant's mouth opening ajar as the troubling feeling that had started out in the depths of her body grew at an alarming rate. Her face beginning to pale in anticipation for what was to come next.

"Duke Paul offered the notion that he was aware and owned knowledge on a matter concerning the prince of England and one or two of the palace's servants," modestly reasoned Matthew. He once again checked to make sure the coast was still clear of others.

Even though her lover's tone was calm and lacking any type of worry, Joan was not as grounded as Matthew appeared. She was always self-consciously aware that not only was she almost twice the young prince's age, but the woman also knew that a royal married another royal and there was no room in the hierachy's bloodline for a servant queen. Joan also knew that king's married off their daughters to other ruler's sons causing the forming of treaties between countries.

"What are we to do Matthew?", queried his secret lover. Her panic seeming to escalate moment by moment. "Do you believe the duke to know any notion of us?", she quickly asked. Joan's second question leaving her mouth as soon as the first inquiry was fully out.

Prince Matthew slowly found and took up Joan's right hand in his own two. The young man's loose grasp causing a comforting connection between him and his nervous lover. "Calm yourself my love," he soothingly advised while holding the woman's fearful gaze with his smiling face. "I am not saying that my cousins holds any evidence of us. In truth he may be in search for any particulars that lend credence to his suspicions."

Her lover's words and his soft smile somehow seemed to subdue her surmounting trepidations causing the woman's angst to slowly fade till close to nothing remained in her body's language or utterance. Where Joan's face had been one written in turmoil, only peacefulness was found in its expression now.

Prince Matthew took one more look up and down the corridor making sure he and Joan were still alone. "Paul will only be staying here a night or two longer. After the tourney on the morrow, the duke should be parting and heading back to Scheffield," the young man advised. "We will have to remain apart this night and maybe the next to protect our secret meetings. The distance will guard and maintain our concealment."

A smile now formed on Joan's face. "Handsome and clever," she added taken with the simple plan to disguise their nighttime fun.

"Your approval makes me pleased," informed Matthew making a sweep of his hand and taken a bow.

A small giggle shot forth from behind Joan's lips, as she turned to walk away. The woman servant suddenly startled by the prince's slap on her rear.

Darkness had fallen outside and all the castle's occupants had retired for the night leaving only a small, scattered amount of royal guardsmen left stationed throughout the place. Their protective watches going undisturbed in the peaceful silence of their nighttime shifts, while the rest of the palace prepared for slumber. For some, the anticipation of witnessing the king's tourney on the morrow kept them awake. Their eyes transfixed on either stone walls or ceilings. Even sleeping quarters filled with those unlucky servants that shared them with others by the tens had at least two people in them speaking on the upcoming event. For those who would not be attending because their work here would be required thought there would always be the next one. God willing.

Joan, who was fortunate enough to have a single locking room in the servant's wing, sat at one of the counter tops on a high stool in the royal kitchen. She was eating a fresh roll that had been baked earlier in the day and washing it down with a goblet of water. The woman had her attention seized by the black, leather-bound book laying in front of her. Four of Joan's digits held the manuscript open, as she took a short pull of water and followed that sip up with a lady-like bite from her roll. When she was done chewing and swallowing, the snacking woman brought the pewter mug up to her lips for another sip. Satisfied, she returned it to the counter.

Looking up from the book, Joan let her eyes fall upon a door less cabinet containing two rows of wooden dowels and small, metal hooks. From them dangled almost two dozen mixing spoons and large, paddle-like cooking utensils used to stir the contents in some of the bigger, black cauldrons found throughout the room. Even though they only hung several feet in front of her, the woman's gaze was distant as the thought of her naked lover in bed alone ran through her mind. It wasn't even a single, full night apart yet, but already Joan missed Matthew's touch. She had kept to her blind stare for what she thought was only a minute, but after losing herself in the reel of images that ran through her mind, the longing woman returned to the here and now when she seemed to feel the presence of someone eyeing her. Quickly, the servant spun on her stool only to be caught in an observing raptor-like stare. A lump rose in her throat as soon as she realized the look belonged to a man wearing cream-colored pants and a blue tunic. The duke's high suede boots matched his shirt.

"Oh, Duke Paul!", she added after a loud gasp. "You have startled me!", placing a hand above her breast and feigning relief that it was only him.

Leaning against the frame of one of the now held open, double doors, the duke offered a pleasant smile as he started towards the seated servant. "My apologies Joan. It was not my intentions to frighten you," he expressed the slight wrong. "You appeared to be caught in thought and I did not wish to startle you," he explained. "I am under the notion now that my attempt was unsuccessful. Please forgive my wrong doing."

"No harm accomplished my lord," the woman forced a smile.

Thoughts of her conversation earlier with Prince Matthew swept throughout her mind like a blaze from a wildfire. Constantly she seemed to question herself over and over regarding the duke's knowledge of the two lovers. "Had his query of the prince earlier been a hidden warning against Matthew, or was Paul just speaking about things that young man speak on," she thought. Again, feigning her relief in the sight of the sovereign she dared conversation with him.

"Does something trouble you?", Paul inquired. His hawk-like stare piercing into the woman's soul even though he wore a smile upon his face.

"No my lord," quickly responded Joan. The woman trying harder and harder each time not to look worried. "I just located a quiet area to eat and read." Instantly memories of the night the cook had forced himself on her and attempted to rape the woman poured into her mind. She should have never mentioned that it was "quiet" here. To her, quiet could be equivalent to alone, and she didn't want to be by herself until she had a definite knowledge of whether the duke knew for sure about her and the prince.

"Can I be of some service?", she questioned the duke hoping that Paul would want something and she could make haste retrieving it and then he would be off to his chambers.

"I believe you can," he responded while pulling an empty stool over next to the one she sat on. Lowering himself onto it, Duke Paul spoke with concern in his voice.

"I am deeply concerned in regards to my cousin, our prince," he slowly started. "I was just speaking with him earlier today...," the duke stopped in mid-sentence. "Please do not think low of me for what I am about to say!"

Joan just shook her head. Her smiling face never turning from his. "Of course my lord. Please speak freely between us," she kindly encouraged Paul. The woman servant believing she might be able to pull some information out of him like a fisherman lures and catches fish.

Duke Paul once again offered a smile. "Thank you Joan. I just knew I could speak freely with you."

The woman continued to smile.

"As I was saying...," began the noble starting a conversation over. "I was speaking earlier with my cousin about women and asking if anyone has caught his fancy," he briefly paused.

"And his reply?", queried Joan intent on hearing the duke's next words.

"He said **'No'**, but I have a notion that our prince is offering false testimony.", Paul shared his opinion. "Have you seen the future King of England with another?"

The woman servant stare into the duke's raptor-like facial features for a brief moment before she responded to his query. Inside a spark of relief started to ignite and burn. It was her belief Duke Paul actually knew nothing of the two lovers. "My lord, if Prince Matthew has had his eye caught on a woman, then surely he has not permitted me to share in that knowledge. His secrets like other things are his to keep for himself, and no one else, until the prince decides to share them with others," she advised Paul. "If by chance he did permit another to know something that he deems of value then it would not be honorable for that person, whether it be you or I to spread that news across the whole of England," she added. Again a smile creased her lips, but this time it was not forced or feigned, the expression was one of satisfaction based on the duke's lacking knowledge of her and Matthew together.

"Very well Joan," Paul rose from his place on the stool. Like the servant, the noble also wore a smile and he prepared to make his exit. "The words you speak hold the truth in them but they also deceive a person not truly listening or one who does not know the real facts of the matter."

Puzzled, the woman sat still listening and gazing upon the young man in front of her. "I know not what you mean with your words," perplexedly she admitted.

A hideous chuckle escaped Duke Paul's mouth. "Dear Joan. Why would my cousin inform you that another has captured his fancy when you already know who that someone be?", his accusing question coming through gritted teeth as his stare bore down into the servant. The wildfire reigniting sparked with panic and fear. The duke's words fueling the blaze like hot oil pouring from the city's defensive walls.

"What do you notion?", she feigned her lack of understanding even though the woman knew that Paul was aware of something.

"Do my aunt and uncle retain knowledge of your tryst with their son in his bed? A woman, who is twice his age and a servant to England!", his words cutting like a knife.

Panic consumed Joan but she attempted at trying to set up a denying defense. "That is not the truth! I am only personal servant to our prince!", she tried to exclaim.

"Liar!", sharply called Paul. His intimidating stare causing the servant to cower before his anger. "I witnessed you with my own eyes calling on the prince outside his door. Then I placed my ear to his chamber's door and heard your moans and groans of pleasure carry as he lay between your legs!", the tone in his voice going from informing to condescending as he added, "Night after night."

Tears had fallen from Joan's eyes and ran down the nervous-filled woman's cheeks. She knew the ruse that she and Matthew had been playing on the whole of the castle was in danger of failing. Their shared secret exposed in the façade that the prince and the servant had built night after night would be torn down and crumble like an old ruined cottage. "What would both King Stephen and Queen Margaret think of their trust in her when told of her betrayal to the crown?", she thought as she started to cry a little harder each passing moment. Then like falling from the castle's highest tower and slamming into the oncoming ground, the servant had a thought that slammed into her head. "What kind of honorable reputation would Prince Matthew, who one day would be the King of England, have is the town or even country found out that he had been bedding a servant and not just a servant his age but one who was twice is in the years. One with possibly a barren womb?" The fact that she had visited his bed for over two years now, and although Matthew filled her with his seed every night during that time, Joan had never once conceived an heir. She knew the whole of the land would require a prince, who would one day be England's future king when Matthew had left this life.

"But I love him!", she reasoned through watery eyes. Her tears streaming down her cheeks like salty, running rivers.

"I am sure you do...", he softly agreed with an air of superiority inflected in his tone, "a given chance to move up in status. You risk England's future with the barrenness of your womb. Rightfully speaking Lady Joan, you damn our future king's bloodline with your hollowness. The prince's inability to sire a son with you will lead to the end of his name and hence his rulership," the duke put emphasis on his last statement. Matthew's honour, along with the reverence that his family has had for centuries past will be ruined!"

A burst of tears exploded from the woman servant as she dropped her head into her folded arms on the counter top. Duke Paul holding his words a moment listening to Joan's muffled sobs. Thoughts of her lover's reputation and integrity lost before he met his ending in this life due to his lack with her to sire an heir.

After a moment of silence and listening to the woman cry into her arms, Duke Paul adding a stinging shot to the wounded servant. "And to notion, my uncle and aunt raised you with open arms after the demise of your own mother. To offer another love and have that person return it by ending your blood lineage", again Paul paused letting his words hit their intended target. "I would be inclined to call it the betrayal of another's good favor! Would you be willing to agree?", he asked. The corner of his lips turning up as he started to form a smile.

Joan still hung on all of his words. With her head still buried she continued to sob. The duke's sharp words cutting to the bone.

"The king and queen need to be informed of this news immediately so they can have time to act and speak some sense into my cousin before it is too late!", informed Paul as he turned to leave the kitchen. "It is unfortunate that the future of England's kingdom falls upon my shoulders, but one must act with haste," he nobly sounded.

"No wait!", pleaded Joan jumping up from her seat on the stool and starting towards the duke. "I will end the secret relations with Matthew! I mean the prince," she corrected through watery eyes. Using the sleeve of her servant's dress to wipe her eyes she continued, "I only ask that you do not inform the king and queen. They do not need to know of our ruse."

Duke Paul halted instantly as he listened to the servant. He kept his back to her as he spoke into the air. "You would put an end to your tryst with my cousin if I was to retain my silence in regards to the matter?", he double-checked making sure he had heard her desperate bargain.

"I would!", she agreed hoping to influence his decision to drop the matter.

"But how can I own the knowledge that you will not withdraw your vow in return for my secrecy once I have left?", The duke's raptor-like stare penetrating the woman's returning gaze.

"I give you my word!"

"One's actions speak louder then one's words," he reasoned with Joan.

"What would you require of me?", she asked looking into the young man's gaze. A hopeful expression on a tear-dried face.

Taking three steps closing the distance between the two, Duke Paul wiped Joan's cheek of their salty evidence that the woman had been crying. "I swear to you that if you inform our prince on the morrow before the tourney that the tryst between him and you has come to an end, and you servant, serve me at my beckoning throughout my stay here then I will give you my word under the Almighty that I shall swear secrecy on the matter!"

The woman shaking her head in an affirmation.

"Do I have your word so an accord can be met?", he queried.

"Yes my lord!"

"Very well. When I require your assistance I will call," Paul confirmed, a smile growing on his face.

"Yes my lord," the servant added a small curtsy to match her relief. "Anytime."

"How about now," he continued to grin.

"What do you require? There are fresh rolls already baked if you hunger."

"I have a different notion," the duke revealed as his hands found the drawstrings to his pants. Pulling them loose, Paul's trousers fell to his ankles.

Joan stood with her mouth slightly ajar blankly staring into the face of the exposed man in front of her. She felt pressure on her shoulders pushing her slowly to her and knees. Once they came in contact with the stone floor, one of the duke's hands guiding her mouth to its final destination.

Paul's contorted smile watch the top of his newly, acquired, sex slave's head when he felt the wet, warmness of her engulfing mouth.

It felt like an eternity to Joan as Duke Paul used her mouth for his pleasure. His hands pulling the woman's head into the thrusts of his pelvis while her hands dug into the back of his legs holding her balance. Her sex master building up speed with each movement until finally he pushed as far as he could into her mouth. A groan accompanying his release as shots of his creamy seed flowed down her accommodating throat. Paul held himself, along with Joan, still for a minute as his climax shook his body. When it was over he pumped himself two more times and released his grip on Joan's head. Stepping back, he bent to retrieve his pants.

"I have desired to do that to you for years," he smiled tying the apparel's drawstrings. "Tomorrow night your body belongs to me," the sex master revealed his plans to be slave. "I find the agreement we made to my liking."

Joan, still in shock of the night's turn of events, stared up from her knees at Paul barely listening to the words he spoke. The woman's blank stare was disturbed when she heard one of the double-swinging doors open and close. Looking around she was alone on her knees on the kitchen floor. The servant had never been aware the duke had left her.

Using her sleeve to wipe off any of Paul from her lips and chin, she rose to her feet and rushed for her goblet still half-filled of water. Joan brought the pewter cup to her lips and swallowed the rest of the liquid in an attempt to relieve herself of the duke's taste.

Placing her empty goblet on the counter top and finding a seat back on her stool, the sex slave once again lowered her head onto her folded arms. Muffled sobs broke the kitchen's silence, as a thought came to her mind. "She had saved her lover's honour with his royal family, the folk of Hamilton, and the whole of England, but to do so Joan had made a deal with the devil himself." She continued to cry her shame.

Chapter 17

The horns blew trumpeting the arrival of the royal family. Led by King Stephen, the hierarchy of England made their way up into their private viewing box that overlooked the tourney's scheduled events. Three rich, purple thrones stood directly in the wooden, balcony-like seating area designated for the royals to not only have an unobstructed view of the mock battles, but also allowing the gathered crowd of onlookers a clear view of their king and queen. On a lower level sat eight other seats for any added royalty witnessing the day's events. A dozen of the castle's elite guards surrounded the three majestic seats, while others were posted in front of the viewing stage, behind the area, and even at the stairs leading up into the box.

Prince Matthew, who faked his happiness for the sake of his parents and the folks of Hamilton that had come out by the masses to cheer for their favorite knight, took his seat after offering a wave to the people. Dozens of young maidens blushed imagining the handsome prince was singling them out from the multitude and they would be the next queen of England.

Slowly and royal-like, he took his seat wearing a smile but inside questions ran through his mind and his heart of the new crushing blow of love lost and gone indefinitely. Prince Matthew had spent some of the morning trying to reason with his lover Joan, but the servant appeared set in her decision. Their relationship that had lasted years hidden from everyone was now over. His lover's excuse was the separation in their ages and the fact that he needed to sire an heir. She fully believed her womb was a barren wasteland.

Prince Matthew had desperately tried to reason with Joan, but in the end her decision was final and no matter how much he hated it or believed it unreasonable, Matthew could only do one thing. The prince needed to honour and respect her decision. Placing a soft kiss on her forehead, Matthew watched as Joan ran from his chambers breaking down in tears. Returning from his thoughts, he just wanted to die feeling that love had been squeezed from his heart like water rung from a tunic.

Cheers arose across the event's grounds as the elegant and beautiful queen of England gave the onlookers a wave with an accompanied smile. She was dressed all in white including her matching robe with the only other color being the gold crown she wore upon her head. Queen Margaret looked like a heavenly angel sent from God above to watch over the welfare of all the participants on the tourney's list. Even her regal walk made it appear that she glided on invisible wings.

"God save Queen Margaret!", the shout rising from a man somewhere in the crowd. The cry receiving a loud cheer from the multitude that even King Stephen joined in on a while pumping both fists in the air. All those in attendance knew who he was rooting for.

The queen smiled her gratitude and threw out another wave as she took her seat on the throne. Margaret's expression of happiness carrying over to the ground-shaking cheer her husband received from his people.

Standing in front of his throne at the center of the boxed stage, King Stephen wearing is purple robe of royalty, along with his gold crown ornate with three glittering rubies, stood waving his arms greeting the folk of Hamilton, or wherever those in attendance hailed from. A smile gleamed on his face that would rival the sun shining on this beautiful, summer day as he swept his gaze from one side of the masses to the other. In front of his majesty down on the field of mock battle, armored knights and their mounts, along with their squires, archers, and list officials kneeled displaying their respect and homage to not only the crown but also the man dawning it. Through the years he had proven to be a fair and just ruler of England. There was no doubting the honour, the admiration, and the love the people had collected in their hearts for King Stephen.

Waving his arms signaling for a quietness from the multitudes in attendance, and waiting only a moment to speak as the grounds grew silent enough to hear a pin drop, Stephen was calling a start to the daylong tourney. "My lords and ladies who make up the best country under the Lord's watchful eyes throughout this world!", his statement interrupted by the cheering from the onlooking crowd. The king giving a minute for the lively response to die down before continuing. "My family and I humbly offer for your pleasure this years first Joust à Plaisance!",he shouted while sweeping an arm over the participants filling the fielded expanse. Its perimeter lined with wooden posts connected as one by two thick oak beams.

Again a roar lasting longer than the last filled the bright day's atmosphere.

The king gestured and called for silence again. The crowd obliged him within seconds. Stephen's gaze falling on a man wearing a white tunic with black pants. A sash matching his trousers was fastened on his hip. The man also wore a pair of soft, brown, riding boots and carried a white arrow.

Looking up and meeting the king's eyes, he strolled out towards the center stage for the upcoming action.

His royalness taking his seat on the throne in between the queen and the prince. All the kneeling knights rose prepared to hear the rules of the tourney.

"My majesties, knights, participants, along with you my lords and ladies," the arrow-bearing official turning to address the royal family before returning his sweeping eyes to the folk in front of him. "I am Samuel Winchester, and I shall be the Marshall of the List for this tourney," he informed all. The man pausing a minute before continuing the rules for the event.

"Good folk of Hamilton. As our gracious of kings has already spoken, this tourney is one of peace," the marshal letting the last word to hang in the air for several moments allowing all the participants and onlookers to collect the meaning into the recognition before continuing. "Hence, all lances for the tilt will be fitted with a coronel for the protection of all the knights. The points will be scored as follows; one point will be awarded for a clean strike to an opponent's target, five points will be given for the shattering of a lance against the mark of another, and finally ten points will be earned if a man can separate a rider from his mount!"

Honour

The multitude erupting in a cheer accompanied by a thunderous applause. Even some of the knights waved a hand to the onlookers charging up the intoxicating atmosphere.

Standing by and patiently waiting for the noise to dwindle and the unrest caused by the anticipation to simmer, Samuel continued the rules. "Points for fouls, which are accidental blows to the horse or legs of a rider, will be deducted. While direct strikes to another's head will lead a knight to be disqualified."

"There be twenty riders for the tilt and each round will be a total of four lances with the winner advancing to the next round while the loser knows elimination," informed the marshal. "Till in the end only one man is left. That knight will be the winner!" he shouted.

Again cheers arose on the mock battle field but this time the horns joined the roar signaling the upcoming beginning to the day's events.

"My lords and ladies!", the tourney's marshal shouted the address. Samuels' arms waved requesting the attention of those in attendance.

A hush falling over the crowd.

"Upon determining the champion of the tilt, mock battles will be fought and the tourney will close with that of an archery contest," he laid the plans for the afternoon. "May the Joust á Plaisance begin!", Samuel shouted before turning to take his place near the miniature, wooden coat-of-arms for the knights enlisted in the first of three day long events. Their colored emblems already displaying their arrangements and opponents in the elimination bracket.

Again horns trumpeted the start, and all those who had entered any one of the three contests left the mock field of battle. Duke Paul, who was a participant in the archery event found his seat waiting for him in the royals box. Bowing to his uncle, he sat on a lower level, with his back to them wearing a grin on his face. Paul knew Prince Matthew suffered from heartbreak.

The Daniels and the Bradfords had arrived at the king's tourney earlier that morning allowing both families an advantageous spot against the perimeters fence directly across from where the royals of England sat to watch the day's activities. They joined the rest of the countryside's folk in the cheers each seeming to have picked a different knight to lend their support of encouragement to. Out of the twenty in the tilt, Sir Timothy, one of the king's best knights, had entered and found the most favor between the two families along with that of most of the crowd. The least of the overall's fancies belonged to a participant who wore black, plate mail armor. Even his warhorse was as black as a lightless night. The man seeming an enigma to all.

Nicole, Anne, and Lynn all stood on the bottom of the two wooden crossbeams allowing them a higher position to watch the contest, while Russell stood behind and off to his love's left. The family's parents took position behind the three girls shielding them from other excited onlookers caught up in the action and excitement of a dozen shattered lances and witnessing a rider or two separated from his horse. The crowd always seemed extra exhilarated and shouted their cheers louder when seeing the stimulating act of a knight forcefully dismounting his opponent. Through all the excitement no one noticed that Russell had laid his right hand on Lynn's lower back just slightly above her right hip. On several occassions throughout the tilt, the young woman was more than glad for his soft touch. The connection from her lover supporting her as she almost lost her balance caught up in the absorbing interests of the constant action.

During the late morning and into the early afternoon, the onlookers in attendance offered many cheers for both the successful and the unsuccessful knights, who had put everything they had into winning. Most were battered and bruised, along with a warrior that had suffered a broken arm when he became unseated from his charger. The eliminated men vigilantly watched the final tilt between the fan favorite Sir Timothy and his opponent wearing all black armor, Sir Rufus. The black knight hailed from no place particular in Northern England. Both men and mounts stood at the ready waiting for their lances.

Sir Timothy's stallion was white as snow and wore a royal purple skirt that started at the base of the animal's neck and completely covered it down to slightly above the mount's fetlock of its legs. The front of the cloth was split up to the band around the horse's neck allowing the steed to walk or run uninhibited. Its body's cover matching the rider's sleeveless surcoat.

The castle knight's suit of full plate mail shone as the sun's rays reflected off of it. The crown of his visored helm was decorated with a kneeling man. Strapped to his left forearm was a badge-shaped shield with the crest of a large cross with the silhouette of a figure on a knee inside it. Sir Timothy's extended right arm waited to receive his lance.

On the other end of the tilt, stood a solid, black horse with its rider waiting on his lance. The man's armor was completely black as midnight, and it matched his charger so well giving one the impression that the two were actually just one connected figure. Sir Rufus' great helm aided in making the wearer seem even larger than he already was, along with giving a more menacing appearance. On his head's protective covering was a pair of nine point stag horns. There was no doubting that the animal that had at one time worn the natural weaponry was an extremely large giant of the forest. A white symbol of the head's projecting bones from the previous owner was painted on the black knight's midnight-colored shield. The defensive piece strapped to his left arm.

"Lances ready!", one of the judges shouted.

Both of the squires handing the cornel-capped polearms to their respective waiting knights.

"Knights ready!", instructed the marshal of the list while looking from one mounted competitor to the other.

"Riders turn!", he shouted the order for the commencement.

Sir Timothy and the black knight turned their horses around the five foot tilt barrier and heeled them to charge. The animals bolting on their proper sides heading towards one another. Their riders lowering their lances both aiming and waiting for the onrushing impact. Its force enough to drive either one from their saddles.

The loud sound of the wooden polearms shattering as they found their targets split the semi-quiet atmosphere when the riders pass. A roar from the crowd followed as both knights reined their mounts to stop at the end of the barrier. The participants' hands out waiting for their next lances.

Two heralds, who had been keeping score, placed painted tiles on the wooden board near the matches bracket. Five to five was the score after the first lance.

"Lances ready!"

"Knights ready!"

"Riders turn!"

The thundering hooves pounding into the hard packed dirt carried on the air again. The two warriors preparing to meet in a collision of force lowered their lances in preparation for the imminent strike. When the point of impact came this time only Sir Timothy's polearm splintered on his opponent's shield. The black knight's lance made contact with its target but the strike only glanced off Sir Timothy's shield. His polearm slid behind the castle's knight and was still whole after the run. Throwing their blunted weapons to the earth, they both waited on the third pass.

Again the onlookers roared their approval and the fact that it now was ten to six in Sir Timothy's favor appeared to incite the crowd to offer louder cheers.

"Lances ready!"

"Knights ready!"

"Riders turn!"

For the third time in this joust, both riders pepared to meet in mock, horseback combat. Their chargers violently kicking up dust behind their running hooves. Even their warhorses seemed to feel the electricity in the air and it appeared to those watching from the stands that both animals rushed to the point where their riders would meet in hopes of dismounting the other.

The black knight took a chance of leaning towards his left and into the blow of his opponent, but the tactic paid off. The man was able to extend his lance a bit further causing the strike to connect before the other man's could. The dark warrior's polearm found its target, but the blunted weapon hit Sir Timothy's shield and roled up the badge-shaped armor connecting the man in his pauldron. The hit continued until it struck the castle's knight on the left side of his chin. The warrior's head violently turning sideways and upward with the blow causing him to remain mounted but forcing Sir Timothy onto his back. His lance, which never connected, flew from his dazed grip accompanying the broken shoulder guard.

Gasps filled the air as those in attendance witnessed Sir Timothy never leave his saddle but instead lean forward into his mount's neck as it slowed to the ready position. Some already perceived the attack was purposeful and fully expected a disqualification to swiftly follow.

The list's marshal along with the two other judges came together. After a very brief conversation, the marshal addressed the crowd. "We have ruled that the blow from Sir Rufus' strike made contact to the shield of Sir Timothy and with no ill intent glanced upward and into the rider's head. Hence, there will be no disqualification penalty addressed to Sir Rufus."

Sounds of disagreement an unhappiness with the conclusion were heard from some in attendance, but the truth that these events had taken place and were factual went uncontested by the king himself. Stephan knew accidents were the common and plentiful in the game of mock combat. His inaction spoke volumes to the people.

By now the wounded knight sat erect in his saddle, and with a confirming bob from his head relaying to Samuel, his squire, that Sir Timothy was prepared to take his last lance in the match. The victor would be the day's tourney champion. The castle's knight was still ahead on points ten to seven. He still felt light-headed and woozy, along with the fact that he had no shoulder armor, gave proof of both his honour and integrity to see the match through.

A roar rose in the air recharging the electric atmosphere. Both warhorses feeling the uplifting charge stomped a hoof into the earth preparing for one last run.

"Lances ready!"

"Knights ready!"

"Riders turn!"

Both chargers rolled around the tilt's barrier and began their rush to the finale. The two knights knew that this pass and force-filled impact that would end the one question on everyone's mind; "Who would be the champion at the end of this day?"

Sir Timothy's head was still woozy, and the dizziness that overtook him sent the entire world as he knew it spinning out of control. On instinct alone he held tightly to his horse's reins and fought to focus his aim as he was being jostled in the saddle. Without even realizing it, Sir Timothy had dropped his lance and lowered his shield as he fought to hang onto his mount.

Again loud gasps filled the crowd as they watched and waited for the black knight, who had readied his lance to deal his last blow and drive his strike into the defenseless man. By the score, he would need to unhorse

Sir Timothy or splinter his lance to win and thanks to the castle knight's condition Sir Rufus was given his chance.

Even Queen Margaret shied away from the scene of imminent carnage. The tension in the air of the onrushing disaster was thick enough for one to cut with a knife, but the black knight did something that no one in attendance foresaw. With just enough time to spare, Sir Rufus raised his polearm's tip into the air, and with the lance standing straight up on his right side, the black knight rode by the wounded and half out of it Sir Timothy. The knight giving the other mercy in lieu of a winning blow. His show of compassion cost him the match and the championship but it won him a standing ovation from the king of England. Within only mere seconds the crowd joined the lone clapper in applause. Soon cheers for Sir Rufus rang throughout the air.

"Bravo sir knight!", complimented King Stephen. "A display of honour," he impressed. "Bravo!"

Chapter 18

The king's joust a' plaisance ended late in the afternoon as early evening approached the countryside of Hamilton. Shadows cast from the slow-setting sun grew and stretched across the mock field of battle while the three winning individuals from the tourney's events stood before the royal's box seats prepared to receive the prizes for coming in the top positions of their given events. The family of the lone sovereign of England stood as the men received their spoils for first place.

"The winner of the truest shot with the bow...", informed King Stephen while projecting his voice for all those in attendance to hear, "...my own beloved nephew, Duke Paul of Scheffield."

The duke giving a bow to his royal family, as one of the judges presented him with a golden arrow. The crowd roared and clapped as Paul turned to face them and offered a sweeping hand followed by a bow.

"The winner of the Champ-clos foot combat event is awarded to Sir Lucas of Westminster," revealed Stephen.

The armored man receiving an ornamental dagger made of pewter with a small, blue sapphire decorating its pommel and an accompanying applause from the crowd.

The king casting a smiling gaze down upon the final winning participant of the day's tourney. He knew the man well and they had shared many years together walking the grounds of the castle.

"Finally, the pot of fifty gold coins to this day's winner of the tilt and champion of the joust a' plaisance, Sir Timothy."

Approaching the castle's knight and fan favorite amongst the onlookers, the marshal of the list presented him with a large, velvety, purple sack full of his winnings.

The knight took a knee and bowed his head at the royals before slowly rising and turning towards the cheering crowd. The man's arms patting the air as he tried to call for a hush quieting the multitudes. His arm's shortly receiving the folk's response of silence before turning back around to address his sovereign.

"My king. My honour will not allow me to accept the whole of these winnings. For I was wounded and at the mercy of my opponent, who could have sought the upper hand in the match. Instead, Sir Rufus stayed his hand in my unwell state and not only showed me respect but more importantly offered me clemency honorably," the castle's warrior pointed out.

"What would you find fitting for Sir Rufus?", queried the king.

"It be my will to give him these winnings my lord."

Another smile separated Stephen's moustache and beard. "An act of honour to reward another's honorable act,"

"Yes my lord," agreed the knight.

"Very well Sir Timothy. Your integrity is never lacking."

The king summonsed the black knight to come forward.

"On this day, we know the pleasure to witness a show of gamesmanship," Stephen's voice carrying over the field so all could hear. "It is the highest act of respect under our God and taught by his son, our savior, to offer another mercy," he paused so all the onlookers could collect his words before continuing. "We have born witness to a man, who found himself in that position against a weaker foe with no way to be stopped if he acted. Instead, Sir Rufus' only action taken was the honorable one of inaction."

Lowering his gaze to the black knight, the king of England spoke directly to him but loud enough for all to hear. "I find agreement with Sir Timothy's words. Hence he shall not be parting with any of his coins for I am going to match his purse with one for you of equal value. I give to you my admiration for teaching all of us here a most valued lesson.

A roar of cheers ignited from the folk and even the other participants joined into the king's revelation. Their yells and applauds lasting for several minutes until the royal gestured for their silence.

"In show of my gratitude, I humbly request your presence along with Sir Timothy's as my guests at this night's royal feast. What say you Sir Rufus will you honour my family and I?", queried King Stephen.

"I graciously accept my lord," the black knight accompanying his words with a bow.

It was obvious to all the folk who had attended the daylong event. Even though Sir Timothy was the tourney's champion and Stephen the king of England, it was Sir Rufus' words and actions that ruled over this mock field of battle.

The door to Prince Matthew's chamber slowly closed and when completely shut, the young man locked the wooden portal and leaned his back up against it. The heartbroken lover rubbing his tired face while his head cradled in the palms of both hands. The combination of the long day, attending the feast, which he had slipped away from as the festivities carried into the night, and the sudden loss of his love weighed heavy upon his brow. He had made it through the day but for some internal reason Matthew knew the lone night was about to feel both long and lonely.

Releasing a loud exhale, the prince collected himself and made his way over to the bed. A burning lantern sat on a small end table made from English Oak with a sheet of glass sitting on top of it. The light illuminated most of the room.

Finding a seat on the bed, Matthew bent down to slide off his soft boots, and when done with them stood up to disrobe. A tiny ache had started around his eyes probably caused from the stress his was under as he continuously thought about Joan. He still couldn't find the answer he had so desperately sought after offering some kind of explanation why she had been so adamant about ending their secret relationship. The two lovers were here at this point due to a hunch by his cousin over some type of facade between the two.

"I should have never questioned her or had given her any notion that Paul might know something," thought the prince as he laid back on his bed. "My unproven caprice has her fleeing in fear."

Matthew had lost all track of time as he stared into the furniture's canopy recalling the words Joan had said to him in the morning. Her dialogue played over in his mind, especially the two statements about her being twice his age and barren. She expressed how the prince needed a young, fertile womb so he may sire an heir.

Closing his eyes he felt her naked body against his and it brought back to memory the electrifying touches they shared. Unfortunately the recollection of her words could not find their way out of his mind. Matthew desperately wanted to imagine Joan was there or that she would be coming to him soon, but the reasons she had given towards ending their ruse blanketed his imagination and wrapped it in reality. The truth of the matter was whatever they had shared together was now over.

Rolling onto his side and staring at the lantern's flame, the young man tried to call to image a younger Joan roughly his age. Different scenarios ran through his mind for sometime but then that of another type of portrait invaded his thoughts. A picture of the young woman he had nicknamed "Joan of Arc", along with recognizing her earlier at the tourney standing across the field from where he sat, stuck in his mind's eye. She was the commoner that he fancied.

Laying on his side, he lost all track of time while staring into the controlled flame. The prince wasn't sure how long this young woman stayed on his conscious but in time even the only lover he had ever known lingered on the outskirt of his thoughts. Eventually he found sleep, but still the images recalled conversations that she and him had had at church. A girl his age that had grown, and even though not a birth status of royalty, carried herself like a princess. Lynn Bradford not only brought slumber, but also offered the weary-browed prince a peacefulness during his stormy time.

Duke Paul strolled across his dim lit room towards the door that only moments ago a barely audible series of knocks had come from. Keeping his naked body behind the wooden portal, he opened it to view who the caller was even though he was more than positive he already knew who it was. A smile creased Paul's mouth as the sight of his night's entertainment stepped into the duke's chambers.

Due to the festivities in the feast hall, Joan was able to get away without so much as a blink of an eye. The servant woman's heart beat a little faster at the sight of the duke's nakedness. The fact that the shuttered lantern and the accompanying small ray of light from the semi-open door only illuminated the room's bed. The rest of the place was plunged into total darkness which the frightened woman thought may work to her benefit. She knew Paul was about to use her body, but she would be able to close her eyes without his knowledge and imagine it was Matthew. This may possibly help her to endure what was about to take place. Standing at the foot of the bed, Joan watched as the man closed the door and the room knew only the dimness of the shuttered lantern.

"Remove all of your clothes and sit on the edge of the bed," ordered the duke with a condescending tone to his voice.

Paul watched as Joan got naked and sat on the edge of the bed. Her firm, round breasts with brown, tipped nipples semi-hard from the coolness of the room, along with the curves of her body, already caused a stirring in his nether region. Walking over to his newly acquired sex slave, the duke lifted his right foot onto the mattress near Joan and looked down into her surrendering eyes.

"Round one," he advised as he placed his hands on the back of her head and slowly brought her and his pelvis together. A smile creased his lips while he watched her mouth accommodate his manhood as he slowly rocked his hips. Her hands holding his left leg the whole time he sexed her orally.

Joan closed her eyes and tried to think of Matthew. The image of his naked body came to mind as she surrendered herself to the duke's guiding. Every inch of the prince's body she had explored at one time or another now popped into her head. Even the birthmark he wore on the top of his right leg near his pelvis ran through her consciousness. The servant's eyes opening when her master's pumps started to come faster signaling his oncoming release.

Again a grunt escaped the royal's lips as he pulled her head into his pelvis seeking the depths of his slave's mouth. Within moments, Duke Paul shot his warm seed down her throat. Like that of the first time in the kitchen, he gave her mouth two more pumps before backing away.

"I told you that I was going to use your body for my pleasure this night," he eagerly informed her while backing towards a chair near the small table where the room's dim light source came from. Lowering himself into the wooden seat he added, "Remember, that be round one for me."

Staring at Duke Paul wearing a questioning expression upon her face, Joan thought she caught movement from the corner of her eye. Slightly startled, the woman turned and watched a naked man, who was taller than six feet, walk out of the shadows and over to the bed in front of where she sat. The girth and size of his manhood, much larger than Paul's, was staring right at her. A fear swept over Joan's body as she looked up into the man's moustached face.

"Now it is round one for me," he deeply spoke while placing his hands on the back of Joan's head and guiding himself into her mouth. The woman's hands finding his ass and digging into it, as he stretched her mouth while finding the depths of the sex slave's throat.

"Part of my pleasure is to watch," Paul added with a devious, turned on chuckle.

It took Joan a little time but she adjusted to the man's difference. Unlike the duke, this man seemed to know nothing of finesse only power causing the sex slave to dig her nails into his rear. The gesture perceived to be more than willingly. "This wench likes it," he revealed to the duke still seated watching her pleasure his guest.

The oral assault on the woman ended when her second sex master drove his manhood into the depths of her throat. Joan's cheeks puffed all the way out from the man's girth and she could feel his hot, creamy seed running into her gullet. The sex slave swallowing as fast as she could to prevent her from drowning. Not being able to accommodate all his release some flowed out of the sides of her mouth when he backed away from her. Joan panted trying to catch her breath.

"Clean your chin," condescendingly ordered Paul throwing the woman her dress.

Joan, fighting back tears in her eyes, caught her apparel and wiped her mouth and chin. "Why is this happening to me?", she silently asked.

"Time for my round two bitch," flatly stated Duke Paul as he strode up to her. "Push up on the bed a bit and lay on your back," he ordered.

Joan did as she was commanded and even took his manhood once into her mouth trying to lubricate her master's lance, so he wouldn't cause her physical pain to match the emotional distress she suffered already. The servant only moments later feeling Paul enter her and begin slow pumps.

With tears in her eyes, Joan turned her head to the side. She could hear the grunts coming from the duke. Soon his slow pumps turned into angry thrusts, and the servant could feel his heavy, exhaling breaths on the side of her face and neck. Closing her eyes, her mind drifted and shut down. There was no way of protecting her body from her assailants, but Joan attempted to lock away her mind and feelings. When she opened her eyes they were glazed over while she blankly stared into the darkness. The duke's sex slave never noticed or felt him withdraw from her body, but snapped out of her unconscious thought and returned back to the present when she heard his demand.

"Place yourself on your hands and knees!", he sternly ordered while attempting to roll the woman over.

Joan changed positions waiting to be mounted like a mare. The woman tried to prepare for the continuing violation from both Duke Paul and the other large sex master sitting and watching from the chair, the whole time silently praying the night would come to an end soon, but knowing the realization that her strife was only beginning.

Feeling the pressure caused as Paul slowly inserted himself into her anus, Joan gripped the pillow underneath her and squeezed. Within moments his hips slapped off of her buttocks as he rode his slave from behind.

Tears ran down the violated's cheeks while her grip dug into the lone pillow. Grunts carried throughout the room and the duke's violent thrusts pushed her chest into the mattress. Joan turned her head, its side flat against the pillow as she stared into the darkness through watery eyes. The woman trying to recollect the soft touches and caresses that her long time lover had given her before this man at present began his assault on her body. What for over two years had been an embrace of heavenly love was now an attack of hellish animosity, and Joan's body was the present target.

Soon another problem came to the woman, but this time the betrayal was self-inflicted. Even though she had tried in her mind to separate herself from what was taking place and emotionally shut down to both of her attackers, Joan's body began to automatically respond to the sexual stimulus. The sounds of moans and groans began to escape from behind her lips while her body started a slow ascent to orgasm.

Upon hearing her audible response to his acts, Paul informed the still seated man. "Sounds like the bitch is starting to come into heat and fancy our play." The announcement causing his thrusts to pick up in speed. A look of determination written upon his face.

Joan's moans matched the duke's plunges rhythmically. Her body broken and subdued to the man's lust causing her reactions. With her head still laying sideways on the pillow, she suddenly felt a hand knot her hair and pull it causing her head to lift giving her only a moment to glimpse the tip of the other man's large, girth-sized manhood as it entered her mouth. The whole plunging into her throat. Joan's moans muffling around the phallus.

Joan was now pleasuring two men. Their drives finding the same speed causing all three to move as one. The woman feeling like a spitted pig as both men plunged their manhood seeking her depth as it felt to her as if they met in the middle of her body. Orgasms began rising faster in all three participants.

It was the sex slave that signaled her body's release first as her muffled grunts turned into an obstructed scream of climax. The woman squeezed the pillow underneath her as hard as she could while her body shook uncontrollably as her orgasm rocked her. Joan's physical betrayal causing the duke to release his second load of seed deep into the woman. Minutes later, the man's phallus in her mouth twitched and shot another round of his hot, creamy seed down her throat and into her stomach.

A short time later, the two men removed themselves from Joan's accomadating body and rose from the bed. Slowly, their slave slunk to the mattress.

"You have earned a reprieve...," Paul sternly informed the woman as she rolled onto her back and stared into his grinning face, "...but your rest will not last long so choose your free time well. Let your breath return or even partake in a drink, it matters not to me. The night is still young and you have much of it still to entertain."

Her tears were gone now. The woman's eye ducts all dried out. She knew that her body's act of betrayal had given the wrong signals to her masters and there was nothing she could do about her situation now. Joan knew that tonight would be a long night, but on the morrow Duke Paul would be parting back for Scheffield. Her time in hell dancing with the devil would at least come to an end until next he visited. The violated, sex slave was at least glad that he wouldn't be staying any longer and his absence from court had been about two years prior to this visit. If the time span held true again, the duke would not be able to blackmail Joan any longer for by that time Matthew should have taken a wife and the servant would only be a part of forgotten history.

Laying on her back on the bed, the woman witnessed the large, moustached man take a pull from his goblet before placing it back on the small table near the lantern. Approaching her and getting on the bed, the slave could see by his erect phallus that he required more action.

Joan drew up her legs bending them as the man climbed on.

"It appears to me that our entertainer has finally acquired the notion of the fulfillment of our requirements, Rufus my friend!", excitedly reasoned Duke Paul all the while watching the woman's total surrender in admittance to her defeat.

Smiling down into her face and watching her take a deep gasp as he slowly entered her body, Rufus started off with shallow hip thrusts. Taking time to allow Joan to get used to the size and girth of his manhood. Soon his drives became faster and deeper, and the woman swore she could feel him all the way up in her belly. The slave never experiencing something that huge ravish her insides.

Wrapping her arms under the large man's arms and digging her fingers into his back, moans rose from Joan. Inside a sexual fire started to spark again building towards a release.

Sitting in the chair and taking a pull from his goblet while his other hand rested in his lap, the devil wore a devious smile upon his face. He wished the night to move slow, however taking the pleasure in knowing that there was still a whole lot more of it left.

That night, Joan's body along with all its entrances were used over and over. She was ravished in every sexual position by either man alone or both at the same time until morning before dawn. The woman's body had betrayed her numerous times throughout the long lasting sexual encounters. She had experienced more orgasms that night than she had known all of her life. Eventually, the physical enjoyment in her body's climatic releases seemed to cast away any and all mental thoughts or emotional feelings outside of sexual pleasure. During one session, Joan straddled Rufus and rode him like she was a knight on top of a charger. The woman experiencing her release first, leaned forward and laid on her horse's hairy chest allowing Duke Paul to penetrate her anus with his manhood. The three moved in unison until reaching their releases.

The woman, who earlier believed God had forsaken her and surrendered her body completely to her two sex masters in utter defeat for the continued silence of her and Matthew's secret, gave herself willingly now. Both Duke Paul and Sir Rufus used Joan's body for not only their entertainment and pleasure but as their depository for their sexual release. In the morning when she left after a night of hot sex, along with a final drop off in her belly from both Paul and Rufus, Joan had more seed in her than a farmer's land after planting.

Chapter 19

Duke Paul stood in his doorway watching Joan heading down the hallway. Still in his nudeness wearing only a devilish grin, Paul thought to himself about the way he and Sir Rufus had used the woman's body for their fulfillment and pleasure. The idea that the two had planted a vast amount of seed into her and the possibility that soon a pregnancy might root reflected in his mind. The fact that Joan may end up being with child would cause such a devastating blow to his cousin. Prince Matthew would lose not only his lover but would also be forsaken an heir to the throne with her. Watching the sex slave disappear around the hallway's corner, the duke turned back into his room closing the portal behind him.

"If my notions hold true, than I would be inclined to say that the woman fancied in being taken in that fashion," pointed out the black knight while putting his pants on.

"Does it truly matter?", sarcastically queried Paul. His mannerism disregarding the woman's feelings. "She and I struck an agreement. Whatever I pleasure in return for my silence of her laying with my cousin," he informed his friend. "I just refrained from mentioning my interests with orgies and other perverse acts," a smile shining from his face.

"Always full of cunning," grinned Rufus sliding on his boot.

Duke Paul walked over to his bed and took a seat on it. "Besides if everything goes as planned, then Joan will be accommodating us again as we will be sowing soon." The devilish smile returning once again to his face as he thought of the seed still running down the inside of the woman's thighs as she made her way through the castle and back to her room. The idea of new sexual pleasures began to reveal themselves in his mind's eye.

Breaking his concentration on the servant, Paul looked to his friend seated in the wooden chair as he had just slipped on his other boot. "Get some rest before we depart later this day Sir Rufus. We have had a night full of feasting and negotiations."

The black knight knowing that the duke was reciting their alibi a final time.

"We have struck a bargain during last night's talks and I have decided to hire your blade for protection on my journey back to Scheffield," his words being followed by a devious grin as Duke Paul was extremely satisfied with the ruse.

Offering Sir Rufus a nod and then watching his friend close the door behind him, the cunning royal crawled backwards on his bed and lay his head down upon his pillows feeling very satisfied over the first part of his plan. His scheme to wrestle the crown of England away from his cousin Matthew caused a devilish grin to once again return. No longer would his country be ruled by a meek king concerned with mercy and fairness for an undeserving people. A ruler who believed in a God that governed his people with righteousness and justice. In Paul's eyes the Lord was a dictator, a tyrant, who made the rules to life as he sees fit and definitely to His benefit. God had not shown fairness to Paul's mother, whom he would never know due to Almighty seizing her at childbirth and leaving his heart vacant of knowing a mother's love, or the father that had worshiped faithfully the King of Kings. What mercy had he received from the Lord when the man was torn from Paul two winters ago? No. God was not a shepherd of sheep, but a lion devouring his prey. Mercy. The thought bringing a cunning expression to the man's face. Mercy was for the weak, and Duke Paul was not about to be feeble. He would choose to be a king, a lion amongst men, because he knew if you wanted something then one needed to forcibly take it. Only the strong survive.

Shutting the door and locking it behind her, Joan exhausted from the night's activities, leaned up against the portal. The tears she had battled to hold back while returning to her private, servant's chamber came now like waterfalls from her eyes. The salty liquid running over her cheeks as she uncontrollably wept. The woman's chest heaving up and down searching for air to fuel her crying.

Slowly she slid down the door to sit on the stone floor. Drawing her knees into her chest, Joan's head dropped into the small nook caused by her bent legs. The used sex slave could still feel Paul and Rufus' seed running from both her womanhood and her anus. The over-filled entrances causing the fluid to search for a release. The fullness of the woman's stomach leaving her to believe that after feasting so much on the men's bodily liquid that she would not have to eat anytime during this upcoming day. Her thoughts invaded by the replaying images causing the servant to question herself.

For over two years, Joan had only known Matthew's love and tenderness. She had given her thanks to the Lord daily for the treatment she had acquired from the prince. The woman had always found favor in his soft, caressing touches and open willingness to accept that which only she gave to him freely of her own will. Her lover had never taken what she had not offered. Matthew had treated Joan the only way she had longed to be treated, as an equal, but after last night she questioned herself when her body had betrayed that very notion.

Raising her bent head from the bony cradle of her knees, Joan reflected on her actions to the ravishing she had experienced from her two sex masters. The dilemma they caused had her questioning her own desires. Leaning her head back against the door with her watery eyes closed, the woman's mind ran over the whole night's pains and pleasures in the order she had experienced them in. From the first time in the kitchen when she was unwilling for the duke to pleasure himself with her mouth, and only accepting his sly agreement in lieu for his continued silence of her and the prince's shared love and bed. All the way to the point where she had somehow taken a fancy and became a partner in the ravishing of her body by the two men. The enjoyment of the nonstop sexual pleasuring causing her to even initiate the coupling, or in last night's case the small grouping.

The woman's confusion caused from the contrasts between the prince and his cousin, along with the duke's large friend, fueled her unrecognizable feelings. She had longed for love and tenderness but had received lust and roughness. Where Joan had found favor in her lover's soft, caressing touches, last night she had discovered her eventual likeness in her masters' rugged contact. The last part of her lack of clarity was in the beginning Joan was unwilling to give of herself to these two men. They had taken what they wanted and it mattered not to them that she had not freely offered. It was only their will that mattered not hers, but as time pass and the sex slaves's body had betrayed her, Joan's desires seemed to match those of her two masters.

There was no doubt in the servant's mind that she really did not fancy either Paul or Rufus. However the fact that she had somehow found pleasure in releasing multiple times from the two, were not only stirring questionable feelings regarding her eventual sexual willingness, but also introduced her to the burning want for Rufus' girth and largeness inside her. Even though the duke and his black knight had plundered her body against her will, Joan's only want after the first time the large man inserted himself into her and she was able to feel the greatness of his weapon was a chance at his manhood again. She wrestled with her body's longing for the knight's lance against that which her heart desired. The woman's dilemma stirring her back to once again start crying. With all of Joan's soul she yearned to be together with her true love, Matthew, but the woman's body wanted to join with Rufus' manhood. Inside the servant's mind, a battle between the two waged.

A loud knock on the door to the woman's room finally caused her to stir and slowly open her eyes. Lying on the bed, Joan groggily took in the chamber trying to remember not only when she had decided to climb onto her bed but how long after sleep had consumed her exhausted body and warring mind. Rubbing her forehead as if she was trying to polish away a headache caused from both stress and worry, the servant responded when she heard a second knock.

"Who be there?", she sleepily inquired.

"Joan," a familiar voice responded from the other side of the locked portal. "It is I, Matthew."

The woman's thoughts automatically calling back to mind her all night tryst with the duke and the knight. "I am not well today my prince," she lied while awareness that dried seed covered her inner thighs.

"What ails you?", he concerned. A worried inflection in his voice for the woman's welfare.

The fact that her mind screamed betrayal while at the same time wanting Rufus' manhood reengaged the battle of her conscious. "I have a strong ache in my head and my stomach seems to be in league with it. I just need to remain in bed," she lied. Joan's stomach feeling both content and full from her masters' night deposits and the slight pounding of her head most likely due to stress and lack of sleep.

"Very well," the prince spoke sounding dejected following a brief pause after her reply. "You are aware that Duke Paul is parting this day?", he inquired in case she wished the royal from Scheffield a farewell.

Hiding her relief from the good news, Joan asked Matthew if he would relay a message for her. "I offer my apologies for my absence, but if you could take my wishes of a safe travel home and give them to the duke then I would be much grateful."

"Are you sure your ailment may not pass before he departs?", the prince hoping that somehow she would miraculously recover and the two of them could once again share in conversation now that the threat to possibly exposing their ruse had gone.

"I am my prince," the woman trying not to let go of her tears as she answered. "I need to rest so I can return to my duties around the castle in a timely manner. I am sorry."

Desperately in her heart she wanted to be with Matthew, but her warring mind needing time apart to attempt and figure out her newly acquired personal crisis.

"Very well Joan," the dejection in his voice was recognizable again. He began to turn away from the door but added one more appeal before walking away. "I wish you well, and if you require anything please do not be troubled to call upon my assistance. I will aid you the best I can." Turning, the prince departed heading out of the servants wing of the castle.

Tears stained Joan's cheeks. She knew that if Matthew found out the real reason for her feigning her illness then Joan would be known throughout history as the servant who had betrayed a prince's love destroying the future king's honour for the desire and pleasure of another man's phallus. The woman knew some things are better left unknown and with time's assistance; forgotten.

Placing her face into her pillow, Joan's tears and accompanying cries were muffled for no passer-byes to hear.

"I offer you my gratitude on a very pleasant stay!", graciously thanked Duke Paul while delivering a kiss to his aunt's hand as he held it in his for a moment.

Standing behind him, Sir Rufus could hear the hint in his voice's inflection referring back to at least last night's conquering of the defeated sex slave in the duke's words. He knew that none of the other royals had a clue of the ravishing that took place under their roof.

"Till next we meet," Paul offering a head bow to the prince. "I hope you will have acquired a lady friend to meet at the time," his avian-like facial features casting a gaze on his cousin. His words accompanied with a smile.

Matthew feigning a return smile.

Stepping towards his uncle, Duke Paul kneeled and took up his king's hand. He placed a kiss on the ring before rising from the floor. "Thank you for the pleasure of your invitation to visit along with the tourney."

"Please allow me the pleasure my nephew," came King Stephen wrapping his arms around his younger brother's only son. "As I told you when you first arrived. It does me well to see you," he smiled.

"And Sir Rufus will be accompanying you on your return to Scheffield?", queried the king.

"Yes uncle," assured Paul. "The knight and I have come to an agreement on the price of his blade. He shall travel with me back home, but first I must stop for business in Birmingham."

"Oh. Well how long will your business keep you there?", inquired Queen Margaret.

"Two or three days," he replied knowing that the reason for the stop should only detain him for a few hours.

Looking amongst his three relatives, the duke graciously offered one more bow. "I must be on my way," Paul turned taking his leave.

Sir Rufus bowed his head to the royal family and followed his employer.

Chapter 20

An arrow cut through the air's resistance as it flew finding its mark on the newly constructed target. The shot almost striking the exact center of the bull's eye but ending up sticking half-a-hand's length away southeast of the point.

"Almost dead on!", excitedly cried Peter while turning to his twin Paul along with his friends Michael and Russell. A hint of pride beaming in the young man's face.

"True you are brother,..." replied a smug looking Paul as he stepped forward for the next shot, "...but not on enough." He pulled the bow's string back and took aim. When satisfied the twin took the shot. The arrow hitting the target closer to the center, but only by two fingers away from Peter's shot.

"Almost dead on also," sarcastically informed Peter.

Glancing over at his twin, Paul smugly replied to the other's jesting, "Closer than yours brother," he pointed out while stepping away from the spot the four had designated for taking aim.

Stepping up to take his turn, Michael, the biggest of the four, prepared to fire his missiled weapon. The young man stood a good hand or two taller than six feet and his muscular build rivaled that of anyone in all of Hamilton. Taking aim, he launched the arrow and watched as it cut through the air and hit just north of the target's center by only half-of-a-finger. A smile crossed Michael's face as he turned. His eyes doing all his talking for him.

Meeting his gaze, the two twin brothers easily showed the disbelief on their faces, and Paul who had his arms crossed in front of him shook his head in mock disgust.

Russell's laugh broke the silence in the grassy field. Followed by the deep laughter from the young man who had just shot the arrow.

"Well let us have a look at what you can do Russell!", sarcastically added Peter.

Russell offered a nod and patted Michael on the front of his muscular, boulder-like shoulder while he stepped up to take his turn. Retrieving an arrow from the quiver on his back, he nocked the string of the bow with it. Closing his right eye, the young man took aim and sighted his target. When he was satisfied, Russell let loose the arrow, firing it at the mark. Splitting the air the missile-fired weapon flew hitting the bull's eye in the dead of its center. Russell following its path of flight the whole way after it left the bow.

Michael's lone clap said enough.

"Round one goes to Russell," admitted Peter.

For the second time, the three young men stepped up when their turn arrived and took their shots. All came close to Russell's arrow, but it stood alone in the center of the bull's eye. Now Russell prepared to take his turn in the friend's mock tourney for "England's Truest Shot." Nocking his arrow and pulling back on the bow's string, the winner of the first round took aim. His sights set on splitting the shaft of his previous shot.

"So when are you going to ask for permission to take Lynn's hand in marriage?", Peter's perfectly timed inquiry catching Russell by surprise as he loosed his arrow.

Upon hearing his brother's words, Paul back-slapped Peter's shoulder. An outburst of laughter following the strike.

Michael just shook his head in disbelief at not only the directness but also the purposeful timing of the question.

Russell took a quick glance at Peter out of the side of his eye, but returned his attention to the flight path of his shot. He watched as the arrow sailed over the target landing in the ground roughly a dozen or so feet past the mark. The young man turned to his friend that had not so innocently asked his inquiry.

"That seems to have missed its mark," guiltlessly confirmed Peter while watching the arrow strike the ground. Turning to meet his friend's gaze and adding a shrug of his shoulders. "Well you cannot win them all." His words feeding Paul's laughter like oxygen fuels a fire.

"I believe we came out here to shoot and hone our skill," remarked Russell while feigning confusion.

"That be true," replied the young man whom had succeeded in helping to squander the shot.

"Or do woman now require the use of bows to be subdued into marriage agreements?", inquired Russell. Now it was his words that brought about a chuckle from the largest of the four young men.

"They do in his case," interjected the laughing Michael.

Paul erupted with laughter at the teasing jest directed at his sibling.

Turning his eyes to his brother, Peter's sarcastically retorted to Paul's amusement. "I know not why you laugh. You and I are twins, hence the same looks you court fool."

The truth stopping Paul in mid-laughter.

A laughter exploded from behind Russell's lips upon seeing the realizing expression on Paul's face. Shortly, Michael's deep roar joined in and both shared in the look of stupidity on their friends face. Finally it was Peter who brought the four's teasing to an end.

"In truth Russell," he began. "All of us here ponder the same notion. I am the only one who seems brave enough to ask what sits on everyone's mind."

Turning from his friends and staring into the field where the target stood, Russell paused for a minute and took a deep breath before speaking into the air. His words directed at no one particular. "I admit that with all my being I desire Lynn and Lynn only. I have longed for her for many years and deeply wish to make her my wife and sire children. I want for us to grow old together with our love lasting past the end of time."

Returning his gaze and sweeping his eyes from one friend to another before continuing. "I pray to our Lord that this will come to pass and hold true, but it will all be in His time not mine."

Russell lowered his eyes to the ground and held them there as he thought for a brief moment. Peter, Paul, and Michael remaining quiet waiting for the young man to continue.

"The Almighty knows that I have nothing to offer Lynn at the present," dejection sounding in his voice. "I have no farmland; nor any shelter to cover her from England's weather. How are we supposed to live? I have no way currently to support her. Never mind a family."

Russell walked over and laid a hand on Peter's shoulder. "But my friend I need not worry. The Lord tells us that we are of more value than the birds, whom even though they do not sow, nor reap are still fed. In God's time Lynn will be my wife. All I need to do is be patient and wait for Him to bestow me the right time," Russell smiled.

Hence it is you whom should worry, he added.

Wearing a puzzling expression on his face. "If the birds do not worry, then why should I?", perplexed Peter.

"Because the feathered creatures do not use bows, and thanks to that alone, never find themselves lacking in points to me after two shots," revealed Russell while witnessing his friends blank stare and slightly ajar mouth.

Taking a glance towards the target that stood with seven arrow shafts protruding from it. Only one had found the center of the bull's eye, and it belonged to Russell.

"Remaining ahead following two arrows is Russell of Hamilton!", informed Michael sounding like a tourney judge.

"It is my shot," determinedly declared Peter starting for the spot designated to shoot from.

Russell, Paul, and Michael shared in a teeth-bearing grin, with all the friends sharing in both competition and one another's comradery.

"I find fancy with this place," admitted Lynn while lying on the blanket in the sunlit cottage in the middle of the forest. "I ponder over its existence out here," the young woman confessed while staring up into the small shack's ceiling.

"What do you mean?", asked her shirtless lover propped on one elbow and watching Lynn's lips as she spoke.

Turning her head sideway and meeting his gaze, she explained her words. "Russell have you not ever pondered on how this cottage came to be built out here in the middle of the trees? Who is responsible for it, and why did that person or persons leave this place?"

The young man's thoughts searching for any kind of reasonable explanation to her queries. Even Lynn could recognize the distant look in his eyes as his brain scoured for an answer.

"Maybe it stood before the trees grew," she added.

The young woman's statement going somewhat unheard as her lover for some reason couldn't get Peter's question out of his head. His own queries forming since the four friends had joined earlier that day honing their skills with a bow.

Realizing her lover's distance between this world and wherever he was at, Lynn reached out used her finger to touch his shoulder and then trace an imaginary line over his collarbone to the indentation of his throat and finally over his chin stopping at his lips. The young woman's connection returning him from there to here.

Returning back to the present, Russell offered his prone lover a smile before placing his left hand on hers and taking hold of it. The young man planted a soft kiss on the woman's digit and then slowly removed it from his mouth. Staring into her eyes, Russell leaned down tasting his lover's lips.

Closing their eyes, both lover's shared in the softness in their touch. The two leisurely parted their mouths and their tongues began a cautious probe of their lover's oral entrances. Lynn and Russell's fleshy instruments searching and becoming caught in a dance as they rolled around between their open lips. The two's kiss of love causing their passion for each other to heat up.

Lynn softly caressed her lover's rear shoulder. Circling the round, muscular area she slowly ran her right hand over its blade eventually making her way down the side of his body stopping it right above his hip. The young woman caressing his rock, hard oblique made out the waist band of his pants. Her tongue and mouth working as one as she longed to taste his soul.

Meanwhile, Russell had interlocked his fingers with his lover's and extended their arms above Lynn's head as the two shared in the passionate kiss. The young man laggardly slid his hand down over her shirt-sleeved arm to the point where the garment's stitches connected at the shoulder.

Lynn cast a low moan into her lover's mouth. A hotness in her nether region began as she planted several kisses on his neck and chin. She returned her probing tongue back to her lover's oral cavity.

Continuing, Russell slid his hand on the border of Lynn's breast and then slowly and tenderly down her side until it reached her hip. The young man sliding his hand under her lower back while his tongue matched hers in their dance for supremacy. The two lovers' breaths ragged. His manhood harder than the wooden floor they had laid their blanket on.

Passion had filled the cottage's air and its thickness hung stationary in the atmosphere even though the window's shutters had been opened exposing the sunlight. Russell's erect phallus ached behind the cover from his pants and it desperately wanted to be set free in search of the hot, moist womanhood under Lynn's dress. The two only wanting one another.

It was the young man who slowly withdrew his tongue from his lover's mouth and delicately placed several kisses on Lynn's neck and chin. He looked down gazing into her eyes, and the look of lust that emanated from both their stares was more than recognizable. Russell had not given into the call from his body even though he knew she was about to give herself to him. The young man knew with all of his heart that now is not the time nor here like this was not the place!

There was no doubting the love that had grown and blossomed amongst the lovers. Each of their words and actions when they were together joined them in unison like the sun and day or the moon and night. Russell was the glove and Lynn the hand, and no matter how loud the call of lust from his body appeared it was always drowned out from the blaring cry of love from his heart. In the young man's world, trained always defeated untrained; humbleness prevailed where pride failed; rationality knew only the upper hand over irrationality; and most importantly true love would always conquer lust laying it to waste.

Taking a minute or two to regain their lost composure, Russell bathed in the light of his only true love. A smile worn upon his face.

Returning his smile with one of her own and staring into his eyes, Lynn quietly spoke. "My heart belongs to no one but you Russell Daniels. I give it freely bare and unscathed."

"And know without a doubt, I graciously accept your gift and will clothe it in my love. I give you my word of honour with God as my witness that I shall not allow harm or injury to come to your most precious belonging," swore Russell. "My heart is yours alone."

The young man sealing his oath with a kiss.

Chapter 21

The summer's sky was filled with dull, gray clouds. Their overcast allowing only enough illumination to be able for one to differentiate between day and night. The barely moving masses threatening rainfall upon the land at any moment. Vapors of water hung thick in the air and a sheen of wetness already covered the lush carpet of green grass and the old, stone wall separating the open field from the forest's trees. It had stormed last night, and all in Hamilton knew more bad weather was on its way.

Sheep bleated in the background while Russell, breaking up half a roll from the prior evening's supper, watched the bird swoop directly towards where he stood. The rusty-orange face and breast colored avian had darted in his direction after the young man had called for its audience. Slowing to makes its landing, the bird flapped its wings hovering over the wall before setting down with the delicateness that only a winged creature had. It's small, nimble feet finding the rocky perch.

Taking a step back with only one of his feet, Russell offered his feathered friend a bow from his head. "Good morning Sir Robin," he tranquilly greeted. "It gives me much pleasure to see you on what looks to be a fretful day upcoming."

The bird replied with a series of chirps as it turned its head to the side and gazed at its human friend with one eye.

A chuckle left Russell followed by another bow from his head. "My humblest of apologies my friend. I have lacked in visiting with you out of other obligations that required my presence."

Sir Robin took a single hop towards the young man all the while keeping a single eye on him. The avian blinking a couple of times before focusing its pupil on Russell as if waiting to see if the young man changed his explanation. After appearing satisfied with his human friend's apology, the bird took two hops and shifted its gaze to the tree behind where Russell stood. Sir Robin's neck turning from side-to-side as it searched the clearing for anyone else.

"She is not here my little friend," informed Russell. "I was with her yesterday and will not again see her until the morrow at church."

Again a short series of chirps with an added whistle in between shot forth from the winged creature.

Another chuckle escaped the young man. "I give you my word. I will bring Lynn to visit on the morrow next," he promised.

Appearing to be satisfied with its friend's answer, the bird burst into chirps and whistles with only several brief pauses in between tweets. Sir Robin bounced around atop of the stone wall at what Russell could only assume as excitement. His heart was made well to see his little friend so happy and animated.

Some time had passed before Sir Robin had calmed to a quietness and a stillness. Blinking up at the young man, the little bird finally took his first nibbles of the offered crumbs as it listened to Russell share his past days whereabouts and doings. He stopped to look over at the grazing sheep before he started telling it about the tourney two days prior. The young man speaking more on the honour of Sir Rufus' display of mercy towards the wounded Sir Timothy.

Time passed and the rains held off as Sir Robin seemed content not only to listen but with the full belly thanks to most of the roll. Eventually, his human friend began to speak on the only matter at present that sat heavy on his mind and heart. He wanted to marry Lynn.

"I find myself in a perplexing way my lifelong friend," softly admitted Russell. "I desire to ask for Lynn's hand in marriage, but I have nothing to offer her."

Sir Robin blinked and turned his neck sideways as the bird took in the sight of his human friend with his blinking eye. The avian's head jerking several times.

Russell continued, "I believe we will be together, but I fear losing her caused from that which I lack now. Every woman requires a man who has some means of providing for them. I have nothing in the way of a shelter or a definite way of supporting her. For I am still living and aiding my father on his farm." The young man gazing into the trees pass the wall as he spoke. "Even if Mr. Bradford offered a dowry, I would decline. I desire Lynn and not what her family can offer. It matters not to me if her hand in marriage comes with no coin; she is worth far more to me than all of England's riches," the firmness in his voice sounding more solid than a castle's wall.

Sir Robin still casting an eye on the young man, offered him another series of chirps. Russell's little, avian friend appeared to have listened intently to his human friend's words, as the young man shared the problem that plagued his every waking, and most of the time, sleeping thoughts. He soon felt a drop of rain which was shortly followed by a second. Another fell leaving a dark spot on the wall near the bird.

Giving his human friend a final chirp, Sir Robin took flight flying back in the direction from where he had come.

Russell took a second silently wishing his lifetime friend well in the day's endeavors before turning towards the bleating sheep to begin their short journey home. He was suddenly startled by the presence of his father who had already begun to gather and shepherd the flock. The young man had not heard Robert arrive and wondered how long he had been there during his audience.

"My apologies father," expressed Russell. "I lost track of time speaking with Sir Robin."

"No apology is necessary," his father informed while approaching his son. "Truth of the matter be, I ventured out here to ask if I can offer my aid in what seems to weigh heavy on your brow." The parent revealing again that he knows his own child.

Drops of rain began to fall at a quicker rate.

"I see Sir Robin is comfortable around you," he pointed out his assessment of the two's friendly encounter. Robert witnessed what he believed was the avian's solace with his human friend. "The bird knows you will not do him any harm."

Russell smiled as he agreed with his father. All the while wondering if the conversation he had shared with his little, feathered friend had been overheard. "I would notion that maybe you took in my words."

"Not a one Russell," Robert shaking his head. "Your words are yours alone. You have the right to decide with whom you share them with," his father stated. "An honorable man does not stand by or hide in the shadows with the intent of eavesdropping on another's conversation unless he does so to learn and reveal a plot knowing only evilness."

Russell quickly finding his words as to not make his father think that the young man accused him of sneaking a listen to the vocal expression. "I do not retain any notion that you snuck a listen. I just spoke so loudly and openly."

The two men leading the flock as they walked near each other. The clouds in the sky opening up slowly and steadily releasing their stored up waters, their rains falling earthbound.

"I was not party to your words,", explained Robert in a non- angry tone.

"They were for you and Sir Robin and that is where they shall remain until you shall desire to share them with me," his words ending in a smile.

"Come in son," Russell's father throwing an arm around the young man's shoulder. "Let's go home before this rain really starts to fall, and soaks us to the bloody bone. We shall not want your mother and Nicole notioning we are two water-logged ship rats escaped a damned vessel," his smile shortly returned by his son, as they shepherded the flock back to the stable for the rest of the day and night.

That night Russell laid in bed and stared into the darkness. His mind calling to memory the words of his father, as the young man had shared his dilemma with asking for Lynn's hand in marriage. His father's word's seeming to put some of his mind at ease, and helping Russell to concentrate and focus in on the main issue of the problem.

Robert already knew with one hundred percent certainty that Lynn wanted to be with his son. The young man's father revealing to him that he knew it for sure the second time he rescued Lynn from being trampled and run over by the Daniel's spooked horse. He had always viewed his son, and the relationship Russell shared with the oldest Bradford's daughter, as one that was like a loyal dog protecting its master. He knew as long as his son was anywhere in Lynn's vicinity that no harm would come to her. Robert fully believed that Russell would storm Hell and fight the devil himself just for a chance to hold the young woman in his arms. As for Lynn, Robert was also certain that the belief and trust she had in him rivaled only that of the belief and trust he found in the Almighty, Himself. She had made it clear on plenty of occasions that Lynn felt safer with Russell than a king did standing behind his castle's walls surrounded by an uncountable number of the royal's best knight's.

Russell recounted how the two largest problems were that of supplying the young woman with shelter and being able to provide for her daily, but the young man's father had helped to relieve some of those dilemmas.

Robert had given his son his word that he would be more than willing to aid the young man in fixing up the cottage in the woods so that the newlyweds would have a place of their own. No one owned it or even lived there. Besides in years prior, both Russell and his father had already done some work to it renovating it to at least be a warm and dry layover for when they were off venturing into the forest. Robert also believed the Bradford's family head, Charles, would be more than willing to lend a hand aiding the two.

Russell smiled to himself when he thought about how much Lynn fancied the place even though it was in a secluded spot. The distance of the cottage between here and there was at least most of the day on horseback.

The only problem that Robert could not fully relieve was the one of daily support. He agreed that the cottage in the woods was too far for his son just to leave early in the morning for work before returning late in the evening. Russell's father had no shadow of a doubt that his son could hunt and forage, but the young newlywed's place contained no area for a farm. The question of anything being planted and harvested from the ground was an enigma.

That led to another problem. Even if the soil would support the growth of wheat or potatoes, or anything of value, how would the young man cart his stuff to market? Russell owned no horse, and even if he did, the terrain was too wild and untamed for wagon travel.

Russell knew that he and Lynn couldn't stay here in his father's cottage, not because the young man's parents wouldn't allow it, but the fact there was no room for the young woman's addition in the small house. Even now the loft robbed the only main room's space and that area for Russell alone was already cramped, never mind a wife. He didn't want to even think of her being with child.

The young man finally thought of his father's last words of advice "Pray son and seek the answer to all your worries from God. Only He knows how things will turn out and it will all be revealed to you in His time",

"But what if His response to my queries takes too long?", questioned Russell. He wanted to be with Lynn now or maybe even sooner.

"Remember son, patience.", stressed Robert. "If the Lord desires it, then His will shall be, and all the obstacles you face now, He will remove."

The word's of his father running though his head over and over, as Russell continued to stare into the ceiling's darkness. The young man deciding to petition God in His own house when his family attended church on the morrow.

Closing his eyes and letting his mind drift, Russell began to replay the time he had shared with Lynn on the prior day. He imagined the two lovers entwined in each other's arms. Their passionate kiss and the feel of her body, along with the desire to take each other right then and there felt so real to him. In his mind's eyes, the young man imagined the feel of her skin, along with the smooth caress from her hands on his muscular body. The idea of her freely and willingly giving herself to him and vice versa caused a feeling of satisfaction throughout his soul. Russell's mind only knew one wish; he hoped that his time and the Lord's time matched as one, because he desperately desired to be with his heart's true love, Lynn Bradford.

Chapter 22

It had taken two full days of totally secluding herself to her chambers and remaining away from the castle's other inhabitants before Joan emerged from her room and returned to doing her day's duties within the palace. The woman only leaving the sanctity of her room to retrieve water, along with food that assisted her in the facade of being stricken ill. On one of the occasions when the woman was in the kitchen gabbing a pitcher of fresh water and some crackers another servant had asked Joan how she was feeling. The hermit quickly held up her hand flat and shook it back-n-forth several times before parting with food and drink back to her quarters.

Joan had spent a lot of time replaying the events from the other night back in her head, along with the woman calling to memory the beautiful times she had spent over the past two and a half years with Matthew. The dilemma between her royal lover and the love she quickly acquired for Sir Rufus' manhood, haunted not only her dreams, but invaded her conscious thoughts. Many times Joan either cried herself to sleep or until her eyes were dry. The servant knew that she needed somehow to right her mind because the fact of the matter was Joan would be involved in direct contact daily with Matthew. There could be no possible way that the prince could ever find out about her deal with the devil, Duke Paul, and the sexual assault on her body that eventually led her into being a more than willing participant.

Turning one of the corners in the castle's hallway and walking down the corridor that housed the door to the prince's bed chamber, Joan was relieved to know that on this Sabbath, Matthew along with his mother and father, attended the church's mass. The woman would enter his room and clean and tidy up the place before he returned later in the afternoon, allowing her a little more time to dodge his company. The woman fully realizing that he and she would once again be spending most of their time together, but the sexual relationship they once shared would only be a platonic one.

Standing in front of his door, Joan inhaled deeply holding her breath for a moment, and then audibly exhaled. The servant knocking even though she knew his room was vacant and Matthew was at the week's service. Waiting another minute verifying the chamber was empty, she slipped a chain with a key hanging from it over her head and used it to unlock and open the wooden portal. She then slipped inside closing and locking the door behind her.

Taking a quick survey of her one time lover's room, the servant involuntarily gave a little smile. For the most part it was in order with only a small pile of the prior two day's clothes lying across an ottoman, and the water in the pitcher and the wash basin was dirty, and required a fresh refill. Without time to waste, Joan got to work taking care of the two obvious duties that needed performing. She only found a couple more out of place items, or small messes that demanded her attention. The woman wished to have it all completed before Prince Matthew's return.

"Peace be with you."

"And also with you.", responded the church's congregation as one voice when the day's mass came to an end. The town's folk prepared to meet and greet the royals of England.

King Stephen and his family lined up waiting for the first of Hamilton's people to begin the humble opportunity to speak with their ruler for a brief moment. Many folks commented on issues anywhere from the tourney that had taken place earlier this week to the day's overcast that loomed outside, and threatened rainfall for the second day. Whatever the topic may be to their conversation in passing the royal family gave the congregation, and any who had entered the line, their undivided attention. Prince Matthew was raised by his parents to respect his loyal subjects, and was taught in the days of his childhood that everyone has a voice and sometimes something of value to share. He had learned from both the king and the queen that all deserve to be heard, and his father would make it a point to see all those that day, who stood in line awaiting their chance to exchange words with him. The prince smiling as he watched the next in line start towards him after greeting Queen Margaret.

"If it be not Hamilton's own Joan of Arc," jokingly came Matthew

"My Prince," curtseyed Lynn with a returning smile.

"It does my eyes well to witness you," he offered before continuing with a further inquiry. "Have you been away on adventure as of late?"

The young woman offering a small giggle before replying, "No my Prince. I have discovered a fondness in letting those better suited to journeys or quests adventure here, or there.," she added a dainty-like nod and smile to her words.

The prince chuckling at her response. "Then maybe you have a new found fancy with jousting or even archery," he reasoned. "I had witness of you at the tourney two days prior."

"Oh no Prince Matthew!", Lynn taking a surprising gasp to his inquiry. "Could you even notion me in a suit of armour? I would not be able to walk never mind ride on horseback. As for archery, I would be fortunate enough to draw the bow's string back enough for a small bend to take shape.", the young woman briefly laughing at the thought. "I am more than happy performing the tasks of women than the toils of men."

Pausing a moment, as he looked the Bradford's daughter up and down,

Prince Matthew was impressed with the words Lynn spoke. He shook his head in the affirmative. "Very well said Lynn Bradford," he complimented.

"Thank you my Prince," she softly accepted his compliment. Consciously knowing the line behind her had come to a standstill, Lynn decided in everyone's best interest to end her conversation with Matthew. " It has done my eyes and heart well to have spoken with you again my Prince, but I request my leave so others may find joy in your company," again she accompanied her words with a smile and a curtsy.

Matthew offering a nod in both agreement and farewell. He watched as the commoner that he had found fancy in walked away. The prince's mind never thinking about his ex-lover who had broken his heart.

Joan laid the last article of wet clothing down on the wooden, drying rack in the corner of Matthew's room before turning and starting for the bed. The servant earlier had left the prince's chambers after tidying up a few things that were out of place and washed all of Matthew's dirty clothes. She had dumped the used water out of the basin and the pitcher before cleaning and refilling them with fresh liquid. The woman was done for now, and was relieved she had finished her duties before he had returned. Joan desperately wished not to experience an uncomfortable encounter with him.

Making her way to his bed, and taking a seat on the edge to the side where she had slept for more than two years unknowingly to everyone else, Joan took hold of one of the bed's pillows, and brought it up to her face. The woman taking a deep breath as she buried her nose into the soft headrest inhaling Matthew's smell. Her lover's scent soothing her as images reeled through her mind's eye. The feel of his comforting touch appearing real to her while the memories of the times, both days and nights, the two had shared slowly flashed through her head.

Joan lowered the pillow to her lap and felt a tear forming in her eye. She wanted Matthew more than flowers needed the sun's light to grow and blossom, but she knew that he wouldn't desire her if he discovered that she had given her body to his cousin and the knight. The woman painfully acknowledged that even though she required his love in her life, Matthew's future kingship demanded an heir for him and with her womb a baron wasteland, no future prince of his would grow there anytime soon.

Joan placed the pillow back into its place at the head of the bed and rose from the mattress using her sleeve, she wiped the tears from her eyes and her cheeks. The servant used her hand's to brush out the bed's wrinkles, and when satisfied made her way to the door. Before leaving the prince's chambers, Joan looked back to the canopied piece of furniture. Two thoughts of gratitude crossed her mind. The first thing she was grateful for was the opportunity to have at least known love, true love, instead of never experiencing it in her lifetime. Joan was also thankful that Duke Paul and Sir Rufus were gone and wouldn't be coming back anytime soon. She figured since the duke was not one for visiting, and the last time he was here at the castle was at least two years ago, the elapsed time would help create a void between Sir Rufus's phallus and her slight feeling of wanting it. By the time Matthew ever found out, if he did, about that night it wouldn't matter a bit. The prince might be king and have taken another as a wife. She would only be known as a servant conquest.

The thought brought a depressed smile of irony to Joan's face, as she left the room. Locking the door behind her she made her way down the hallway and around the corner. With tears in her eyes, she knew that the fairy tale of a servant sharing a love with a prince was just a child's dream.

After what seemed like an extra hour at church, England's number one family had finally just finished speaking with the last person in line. Even though their stay had been extended none of them, especially King Stephen offered forth any complaints. He knew how important it was not only to his people to meet and speak to their crownless ruler on their ground, but the experience always seemed to joyfully humble him. It also gave him the chance to speak freely with the folk of Hamilton and help to make him fully aware of any problems that the crown might be able to mend and repair. Anyone who knew King Stephen could tell that the ruler lived for his people, and that is why they loved him and his family so much. With the Lord, no prayer went unanswered and with King Stephen, no voice went unheard.

Following their ruler's lead, both Queen Margaret and Prince Matthew took a knee in front of the church's spokesman for the Almighty.

"May God go with all of you and be ever vigilant over your lives," proclaimed the priest. "England has never known a finer family or a greater king in all its existence," he smiled watching the three rise.

Wearing a smile, Stephen embraced the priest and planted a kiss on his cheek. Margaret and Matthew followed by giving the man a hug and a peck on the cheek as well before the four started for the church's large double doors. A crowd had formed outside waiting for the royals.

"When can I expect to be honored by the royal family again?", inquired the church's spokesman

"The usual," informed King Stephen. "Within the next month."

The priest nodding his head in affirmation, as they strolled closer to the door. Already all of them could see the royal carriage and some personal guards waiting for the three on the city's cobblestone street.

Stopping outside the church's door, King Stephen turned back to the holy man. "Thank you again for the opportunity to use this place not only to worship the Almighty, but to speak with the folks here."

"Everyone is welcome in the Lord's house your majesty," the priest smiled while laying a hand on his ruler's shoulder. "What you folks do here and the way you lift everyone's spirits is surely a blessing to not only me but these people. To have knowledge that you and your words mean something in this kingdom is a notion that creates most men and women to have the belief of one's existence here on earth," praised the holy man.

King Stephen gave a slight bow with his head, "We are all God's children."

Turning and motioning for one of his royal guards to approach him and the priest, Stephen returned his gaze back to the man. "Here is a tithe that should aid you in assisting the homeless," he handed the man a leather pouch full of coins that the guard had just given the royal. The king's smile shone from between his salt and peppered beard.

"Too kind your majesty," humbly remarked the priest. Two other guards had carried both Stephen and Margaret their crowns. Both ornamental headpieces sat on small purple pillows. They bowed as they presented them to their wearers. The king and queen downed their respective symbols of their rulership, and began their descent downstairs to their awaiting royal carriage. The crowd roared.

A member of the royal guard opened the carriage door waiting for King Stephen to step in. Suddenly, without any warning at all an arrow flew over the onlookers heads finding its mark. The missile fired weapon biting into the front of King Stephen's throat and not coming to a halt until its point stuck out the other side of the ruler's neck.

Screams of horror and chaos broke out in the street. "Stephen!!!", screamed Queen Margaret, as she along with some of the guardsman rushed to the king's aid.

The royal woman watched the arrow's force drive her husband four steps back before he began to topple to the ground. Blood sprayed skyward.

Matching the unblinking stare of her dying husband, the queens rational thought subconsciously took hold of her actions. Quickly turning, she hastily grabbed hold of Matthew as he started to rush to his father's aid. The woman's body releasing adrenaline as her motherly instincts to protect her child from harm consumed her somehow finding the strength to force him towards the safety of the carriage.

Time seemed to stand still, as Prince Matthew tried to comprehend what was happening in front of him. All sounds from the screaming crowd, along with the shouts as the guards rushed to the aid, were tuned right out. The young man began to rush to his father's side, but suddenly felt someone grab him and pull him from his original course. At first he thought it was a guardsman but when he turned his head to look at the one impeding his progress, the young man's glance met the tear-fulled eyes of his mother. Somehow she had gained the strength needed to physically force him toward the royal carriage.

A searing hot pain bit into Queen Margaret's back causing her to issue a small grunt of pain, but her focus was on that of getting her son to relative safety inside the wagon. With the help of the armored door man both he and she got the prince, who had been calling for his father, inside. Margaret followed the young man laying over him to shield her son with her own body.

Three guardsmen rushed to the aid of the fallen king while a couple others, whom had bows, scanned the building tops for any sign of the assassin. The crowd was still scattering; their hopes in not being the next target at the forefront of their panicking mind.

Grabbing the king, and his fallen crown, the three guardsmen cautiously carried his slump body over to the carriage. One of the men broke the point of the arrow off and slid the shaft out of Stephen's neck. With help from the other door guard, the four got the king into the carriage.

"To the castle!", screamed one of the men to the driver. Reins slashed the two horses and the royal carriage began its hastened trip back to the palace.

"Out of the way!", cried another guard trying to clear the getaway route. "Out of the way!"

Townsfolk ran everywhere, their chaotic panic causing the carriage to move slower than the driver liked. All knew the royal family would not want harm to fall on Hamilton's people. The man knew that if just one person was purposely run over it could be his life at the hangman's noose.

The driver was able to locate another less crowded street. As he turned the corner, a guard seated on the bench beside him witnessed a figure fall from a rooftop of a building in the direction the arrow had come from. Soon wind rushed by as the two horses ran at full gallop.

Sir Timothy had joined the royal family in the carriage, who were now being jostled and bounced from side-to-side. The prince still shielded by his mother's body could see his murdered father laying on the floor between the two seats. Tears filled the young man's eyes as the thought of the lifeless man, who was so full of energy minutes before the attack, was stolen from him and his mother.

Looking down into the eyes belonging to his fleshy body shield staring back at him, he faintly heard her words.

"You are safe now Matthew," she softly spoke. Margaret's long, wavy, brown hair was wet and matted to her head. The queen's face pale and robbed of any color.

With a puzzled expression on his face, he looked to Sir Timothy, who had his eyes down on his friend.

Prince Matthew removed his hand from the side of his mother's ribs, and was about to use it to wipe the hair from her face to get a better look at her, when he noticed blood on their tips. It never occurred to him that she had been hit, with his only thought being that his mother's full body weight rested on him from her grief over her long time companion's death.

Frantically, he tried craning his neck looking for any signs of a wound. The prince finally found an arrow's broken shaft roughly protruding from around her rib area. His scream filled the carriage and seized the attention of not just Sir Timothy but the driver and other guards as well.

"Mother!!!"

Chapter 23

A dark, gloomy mood hung in the atmosphere throughout the castle and sullen feelings spread across the countryside of Hamilton. The people's spirits mourning from the sudden assassination of their beloved king earlier this day. A dismal cloud suspended over everyone that even the storm clouds alone could not come close to rivaling. Today all the folk of Hamilton suffered a devastating and heart-wrenching blow.

Tears of sadness filled the eyes of all the castle's occupants, from the servants to the honorable knights, as King Stephen's dead body had been carried to one of the palace's sitting rooms. Four men at arms had been posted there to watch over the deceased. King Stephen deserved proper burial, but for now his lifeless form laid on a settee covered by a linen. Everyone's attention was focused on the number one priority at hand; Queen Margaret's welfare.

When the coach had first arrived at the castle's main entrance, Sir Timothy with the aid of another guardsman had hastily taken Queen Margaret into the royal, dining room. A twelve candle candelabra hung over a long, wooden table that was used to dine on, whether it be just the royal family or dinner guests, but now it had become a makeshift cot for the wounded woman. Ten chairs, that had been pushed under the piece of furniture, were strewn about the chamber. Water had filled the wounded woman's eyes and her face lacked any coloring at all. Margaret's wheezes and gasping breathes was a possible sign that the arrow, which now had most of its shaft broken off, had struck the woman between her ribs and punctured a lung. A large blood stained red circle covered part of her right side and her lower back. Holding Matthew's hand she had passed out before the castle's surgeon had rushed through the room's door. Eventually a makeshift litter was made, and the queen had been carried upstairs to the royal's chamber and placed in her bed. The prince never leaving her side throughout the remaining day and into the night.

Slowly, Margaret opened her eyes a bit and looked laggardly around the chamber. A throbbing pain from the newly received wound ached on her side and lower back. The queen's lips turning into a grimace from the uncomfortable feeling that her body tore more from any small movement.

The light cast from a blaze burning in the room's fireplace, lit mostly to keep the dampness and the chill from the storm outside at bay, allowed her gaze to fall on the only other occupant in the chamber. Across from her royal bed in a plush seat, sat Matthew staring into the fire's flickering flames. The young man's mother knowing his thought's lost to another time.

"Matthew," she softly wheezed.

Hearing his mother's call, the prince quickly looked to the bed realizing her eyes were open. Swiftly he went to her side concerned, "Mother!" "How do you fair?"

"I have been witness to better days,.." Margaret's words labored, "but it does me well to see you and to take knowledge in your safe being," his mother offered a smile and one of her hands.

"Try not to speak mother. You need to rest," came Matthew while taking up her hand. The prince returning the smile with his own anxious-filled grin. The young man's heart pounding in his chest.

Releasing his grip and rising from his seat on the edge of the bed, Matthew started for a full pitcher and a goblet that sat near it. "I will retrieve you a drink of water," he informed her. "Your mouth and throat must suffer from dryness."

Again Margaret offered a smile with an approving nod.

Pouring some of the pitcher's contents into the bluish-grey cup, the prince returned to his seat on the bed's edge and slowly brought the goblet to his mother's parched lips. Margaret took two small pulls from it as she attempted to catch her breath in between the drinks. When the woman was content with the sips, her son placed the goblet on the wooden stand near the bed.

Returning his watery gaze back to his mother and taking her hand up in his, Matthew softly spoke confirming the day's obvious, "Father is dead."

"I am aware my son," she sadly admitted. "I am sorry for your loss Matthew." The queen added mustering her strength over the loss of her lifelong companion for the sake of the young man.

Matthew leaned forward and rested his head in the crook of his mother's shoulder, as his grief finally left his body through his tears.

His mother, ignoring the pain of her wound for her son's sake a second time, embraced him with both of her consoling arms. A tear that had fought free of her controlling grasp rolled down her cheek going unseen by the young man's crying eyes.

<hr />

Sir Timothy sat alone in the sitting room where the body of not only the dead king but his best friend laid. Tears from the knight's eyes had flowed freely over his cheeks leaving salty rivers in his grieving for the loss of his friend and what he believed was England's, if not the worlds, best of men. They had known each other since the two were lads growing up together in the castle. Timothy's father was a guard to Stephen's father, and the boys had grown close to one another. "I am sorry my friend, but everything happened so quick and unexpected," apologized Timothy, "My lack of awareness cost you your life, and England the best king it has ever known,"

The knight pausing as if he awaited a response from Stephen. Again silence filled the dimly lit chamber for almost a minute before Sir Timothy's words began. "Even now I believe that you sit at the right side of the Lord gazing down amongst your loyal subjects," firmly stated the knight slowly rising from his seat to take a knee beside Stephen's lifeless body.

"I ask that you do not anger at me for my folly and cast away any worries that even now trouble your brow," he humbly requested. "As I have served you all these years, I will give my blade in defense of your son." Sir Timothy drew his sword from its scabbard and held it pommel up by its blade. The upside down weapon forming a cross. "This I swear to you as the Almighty be my witness. My death in exchange for the life of King Matthew!"

Taking the hand of the deceased and planting a kiss to the royal's ring, the knight placed the cold, limp hand on Stephen's chest before he rose to his feet.

"I give you my word. I will not fail you again," the honorable man swore.

Turning from Stephen's limp body, Sir Timothy started for the door. Stopping in front the portal, the knight turned and addressed his fallen king one more time. "Fairwell my friend," he offered a bow with his head, "Until we meet in the next life." Sir Timothy took his leave.

Outside the door to the room, the four guards turned their gaze upon their commander as he closed the door behind him.

"I want three of you men too stay here and keep this room off limits to everybody except family or the castle's undertaker," sternly ordered Sir Timothy. "He should arrive to take the body to the palace's mortuary where you men will accompany him and remain guard there."

"Yes Sir!", responded the guards to their commands.

Casting his gaze on the fourth man of the group, the knight gave him his directives, "I want men out on this night retrieving as much information as they can on the day's events leading up to the assassination. I care not that the rains fall. Somebody knows or saw something."

"Yes Sir!", the one guard responded.

"I believe not that only one man is responsible for both the attack on the king and queen, and since the folk of Hamilton bludgeoned to death the man that fell from the rooftop leaving any secrets to die with him, then we need to locate anything that leads us to another assassin," informed Timothy. The commander was about to walk away but added one more order glancing amongst the other four soldiers, "And take heed in knowing that Prince Matthew is now the King of England, so look alive. No other king will perish from an assassin on my watch!" The guards saluted him while the one took his leave to follow his commander's orders.

The knight leaving the men posted outside the door to the temporary resting place of the fallen king. Sir Timothy had places to go and people to see, but most importantly he needed to discover the information behind the assassination. He needed to find out if his friend Stephen's end was actually just the beginning to a plot that would leave England in turmoil.

"Who be there?", Matthew answered to the light knock on the door.

"It is Joan," the servant hesitantly giving her identity. She dreaded to see Matthew and these present conditions didn't aid her cause.

"Enter," the prince's sadness evident in his tone.

Joan entered Queen Margaret's bed chamber cautiously in case the woman was asleep. Slowly and quietly she closed the wooden portal behind her.

The woman's eyes taking in the sight of Matthew sitting on his mother's bed while Margaret wore a grin on her lips. The deceptive expression covering up and hiding the queen's pain. Joan returned a slight smile of her own. The servant's red eyes caused from crying.

"Can I retrieve anything for you my lord or my lady?"

"I am fine," responded the young man.

"No thank you," wheezed Margaret. Her gaze watching the woman she had known all her life uneasily standing at the door. "Come sit with me for a time Joan," labored Margaret's breaths.

The servant happy for the invitation, started for the queen's side.

Queen Margaret, who along with King Stephen had somewhat adopted the woman when her mother passed leaving Joan as a only child, knew when the servant felt uncomfortable or needed some type of reassurance. The child was kept on as part of the castle's staff, and her time growing up was also overseen by the king and queen. Stephen and Margaret made sure that even though the girl was not of their conception, the child would not be cast away to hunger or die in Hamilton's streets.

"Son, let me speak with Joan," his mother requested.

"Yes mother," he nodded and rose from the bed. Placing a soft kiss on the back of mother's hand, the prince found the chair he had sat in earlier.

A smile crossed Queen Margaret's face as she softly patted to the spot on the bed's edge indicating Joan to come to her. Her loving eyes never leaving the woman.

Softly taking a seat on the mattress, the servant's hand took up the queen's while her eyes fought desperately to hold back tears. "I am deeply sorry my queen," quietly came Joan's words. The woman who had always seen the two as a mother and father figure began to cry at the loss of the king.

"Shhhh," reassured Margaret as she weakly pulled the woman toward her. The queen arms open to accept the grieving girl.

"The king was like a father to me," her sobs briefly breaking the sentence apart as she melted into the woman that was always the mother that Joan had lost.

"And you the version of the daughter that we never had," informed the queen with a soft kiss to the woman's head. "Stephen was proud of you."

Prince Matthew witnessing the servant and his mother from the chair. Their conversation audible to his ears causing the boy's eyes to water up.

Tears flowing heavy from Joan's eyes.

Queen Margaret never withholding any of her motherly love for the crying woman. Her hand smoothing Joan's hair, as she rubbed her head.

After sometime, the crying woman straightened up and used her dress' sleeve to wipe her wet eyes and cheeks. "My apologies my lady. It is I who should be consoling you; not you I."

"Nonsense my adopted daughter," she wheezed. Her words bringing a smile to the sniffling girl's lips and a feeling of appreciation for the woman's love filling her.

"God found reason to bless me with your family in my life," she praised Margaret.

"No my dear, it was Stephen and I who are extremely blessed."

Joan wearing an expression that showed Margaret's words had touched her heart and soul.

"I must find some rest now...," admitted the wounded queen through ragged breaths, "...but on the morrow I will be awaiting your company," she smiled at the woman.

"On the morrow," confirmed Joan rising from her seat on the bed. "My lord. My lady," the servant addressed the two occupants before leaving the room.

Both the prince and the queen watched as Joan left the room closing the door behind her.

"Rest now mother. I will be here when you wake on the morrow."

Margaret's wound throbbed more than it had earlier. Smiling at her son, she eventually found peace in her sleep.

The Daniel's household was overtaken with an atmosphere of somber quietness as the storm continued both outside their cottage and inside their hearts. The sound of thunder seemed to split apart the heavens and bolts of lightning flashed bright through the sky. Their sudden bursts of bright light illuminating the inside of the small structure for an instant on numerous occasions around the cracks left by the closed shutters. A blaze flickered in the fireplace to help chase away any dampness from the down-pouring rains.

Sitting at the table with his family, Russell was drawn back from the thoughts by his statement to the young man's mother.

"Even the Lord is maddened by the murder of King Stephen," Robert expressing his opinion on the day's earlier assassination. "His tears of sadness are in the company of the Almighty's display of anger towards the murderous act."

"But who would want to see the king dead?", inquired Russell. "King Stephen was a good man."

"Truth to that!", interjected Elizabeth. "The fairest of rulers," she added.

Robert shook his head in agreement. "And now Prince Matthew has the murderer's sight on him."

"I saw a second arrow strike the queen as she shielded the prince," Nicole stated. "Do you think she lives?", the sixteen year old girl queried.

"I am not of the knowledge to the answer of that query," responded Elizabeth shaking her head.

"Can we do anything father?", determinedly questioned Russell after the chaotic scene he had witnessed earlier flashed in his mind like the bolts of lightning did outside.

"Our hands are somewhat bound," Robert admitted. "If we do however become witness to any questionable act of another, we must with haste report it to one of the city's guards. Our future king's life could depend on it," his words spoken in a serious tone.

"Let us pray for Queen Margaret's health and Prince Matthew's well being," reasoned Russell's mother while extending her arms over the table for the closest sitting person to grasp. Once the four had completed a circle from holding each other's hands, the woman of the house bowed her head and offered the Lord a prayer. Elizabeth asking for His protection and safety for the wounded queen along with her son, who soon would be England's king.

"Amen," the four Daniel's added when the woman's request had come to an end.

Looking at his son with a gaze that could not be mistaken as anything else but seriousness, Robert admitted, "I have no definite notion of what to expect, and for all I know Hamilton could become unsettled in upcoming days." Glancing to Elizabeth and then back to his son, Robert firmly advised the young man, "I feel it best for you to start carrying your sword with you at all times."

"And also your bow," added his mother.

"Your mother is correct," agreed Russell's father. "We may need both of us to watch over this place for some time."

The young man nodded his acknowledgment.

Lynn sat quietly in a wooden chair by a lit fireplace listening to the storm outside, along with her mother and father speaking on the king's murder. Her thoughts lost briefly as she remembered the way Russell had taken a hold of her and his younger sister pulling them to cover behind the steps leading up to the Lord's house as soon the first arrow had struck King Stephen. Lynn's lover had used his body like a shield to protect her and Nicole from any missile-fired weapon that may come their way. Russell's display of love for the Bradford's oldest daughter was never once questioned by Lynn. The young woman knew he would stand against an army to protect her, and the odds of their victory would not be in their favor. Russell's spirit became one of a dragon if forced to defend the young woman.

"There is no question now that the future king will have to take a bride quickly!", Lynn's father excited words stealing her thoughts from her. "The young man's first act as England's king is going to be to sire a heir!",

Charles continued while traveling his favorite route between his chair and the cottage's door as he paced his anxiety.

Sitting at the table Gwenyth, along with her daughter Anne, watched the head of the household go back-n-forth. If not for the sad events from earlier and the actual truth in the man's words, the two would be jesting the usual worry wort.

"I have no knowledge of the young man's love life, but if I was in his place there would be a line of servants outside the door to my room awaiting their turn," he revealed on his way to the door

"Charles!", aghast Gwenyth while listening to the giggles coming from both her daughters. "Have you lost your wits about yourself or have you been stricken weak of mind?"

Stopping in midstride, he cast a glance at his wife. Name it as you wish woman, but my words only hold truth. Without an heir to the throne, the reign over England ends with the last beat of his heart," Charles pointed out.

"What about love father?", questioned Lynn from her seat by the fireplace.

Tuning his gaze to his oldest daughter, "Love has no place in the matter! It is about duty! A king's obligation to his country and a woman's loyalty to lie with him in order to produce an heir, who will one day inherit the thrown from his father."

"I agree with father," came Anne

Her mother quickly turning on the girl pointing a finger. "Do not bolster your father's words!"

"It is the truth!", he appealed. "With no heir to the throne, England will fall in on itself giving birth to those who seek the throne for their own wickedness. Their rise to rulership will only bring strife and chaos to Hamilton, and then this love that you speak so fondly of will be nonexistent."

Trying to regain the air of composure in the small cottage, Gwenyth spoke softly to her pacing husband, "My dear, we have not yet ventured to the crossroads of which you speak. Already you put dread in the future, but the truth is none of us notions what is about to come. "Only God retains the knowledge of what will transpire in the young man's future up on the throne. You need to sit, and remove the extra worry from your brow. It may prove to be premature." Reaching his chair and dropping into it, the man added, "I am just saying Gwenyth, if I were the queen I would be lining them up outside the young man's door and handing out towels and goblets of water for the next several days until he at least sires one heir."

"Charles!", she yelled. The finality of the matter no doubt at an end by the tone of her voice. Casting a glance at her daughter Anne, as the thirteen year old girl began to smile and a small giggle escaped from behind her lips, Gwenyth's gaze put an end to that instantly. In seconds Anne's face knew not a smile.

Chapter 24

Flashes of lightning outlined the two, hooded cloak men as they secretly met in the rain-soaked alleyways behind one of Hamilton's lower class sections of the city. The foul smell from the filth-covered cobblestone seemed to rise thanks in part from the saturating that the ground had been receiving since shortly before late afternoon. Unpleasantries dumped from the buildings lining the narrow passageway floated on by as the running water carried them in its constant search for lower elevations. The two were careful to make sure their footsteps never came in contact with the grotesque obstacles bobbing in the miniature rushing river.

"Have you acquired any information in regards to today's assassination?", inquired the slightly larger man.

"Nothing yet," confessed the smaller of the two. "Maybe that one that fell from the rooftop after the two attacks worked alone," he reasoned.

"I believe it not," quietly revealed the larger man. "So you notion there is another?"

"I would believe,", the larger man confirming his hunch with a nod to accompany his words. "Those shots, especially the one that murdered the king, were made by one with a balanced aim and a true shot. Not a bumbling fool, whom is unsure footing causes him a one way trip off a rooftop."

The smaller of the two hooded men casting an unseen grin at the other's sleuth-like skills. "Well what of the second arrow that struck the queen in the rear of her side," the man questioned. "Why not in her throat like the one that struck Stephen?"

Taking a moment to pause, as a loud crack of thunder tore into the night, the larger hooded man responded, "I believe that arrow was intended for the prince not the queen. Ponder this for a moment. Our queen turned to shield her son and push the prince into the safety of the carriage. The arrow hitting her in her back toward her side," he displayed the hit on his own body.

The other man following the larger man's lead, "I see."

"Well if the queen had not placed her body in harm's way then the arrow would have struck here," the hooded man pointing to the round about spot on his body. "Below his heart."

"I am impressed Timothy," the smaller of the two admitting while taking a quick look around the rainy alley. "You were always the one between us two that would not rest until discovering what appeared to be the truth."

"Do you still hold doubt that another was not present on the roof at the time?", queried Timothy

"Not even a notion anymore," truthfully answered the other. "In truth, now I have begun to ponder the notion that the dead assassin is truly not the one who made those shots, hence the distraction to a cover up."

"My beliefs exactly," agreed the knight who had removed all his plate armor and dressed in pants and hard boots. The men's hooded cloaks covering a chain mail shirt and hidden dagger.

"Look alive you vagabonds!", yelled a woman from a second story open window. A wooden bucket in her hands ready to heave its contents. "If you stand there with a lack of taking heed there will be more on your heads than merely rain!", she warned as she gave them little time to dodge the pail's dumped contents.

Making sure to get clear of the plummeting filth, the smaller hooded man shouted, "Many thanks to you my lady for casting fair warning to an undeserving soul such as myself and another poor wretch, who has come to know misfortune," the man sweeping his hand to the undercover Sir Timothy. "I further ponder, if you can find it in your heart to part with a coin and cast one or two our way? If so we can be removed from this ungodly weather. Your gift could purchase a chance for us to depart from the bludgeoning of this night's rain for the warmth of a roof overhead," he begged.

The woman's face formed a questioning look as if she recognized the man's voice. "David, will that be you?", she perplexed.

"Why yes it be my lady," his smile hidden by his cloak's hood along with the dreary night.

Upon hearing David's recognition to her inquiry, the woman holding the bucket began to scold the beggar. "You need to be at the end with seeking charity from others you pauper, and acquire your person an upstanding way to come into the presence of coin!", she yelled before slamming the window. Its bang rivaling that of the boom's caused from the storm's thunder.

"Is there at least mercy in your heart for a donation towards a cup of spirits to warm ones bones on this night?", David shouted at the now closed window.

Returning his attention back to Timothy, David began to softly speak, "That Mary sure is a feisty woman. A character like that of an adder."

Timothy gave a quiet chuckle and then proceeded to comment on David's pauperish act. "You have always been one for the dramatics and the stage. I wager that there will not be another in the whole of England who can keep to an act like one's self."

The smaller man taking a bow at the knight's words.

Casting a glance around the alley to make sure the two were still alone, Sir Timothy returned to the topic of the two's secret meeting, "Find out as much as you can, and we will meet again on two nights from this."

"Very well," David agreed. "But until then I would also accommodate this notion. There may be a voice coming out of the castle itself."

Taking a second to ponder the man's words, the undercover knight inquired. "Do you believe this to be truth?"

"I know not the fact in the matter and it be only a notion," he advised.

Sir Timothy slid his hand into his cloak and withdrew a hefty, leather pouch. Handing the clinking bag to David, "I won this at the tourney. There be twenty five gold coins," he informed the beggar while releasing his grip on the pouch. "This should buy you a roof for the night and spirits to accompany the lodging. What you do with the rest is your business."

David took the gift and quickly secured it to his belt hiding the bag on the inside of his pants near his crotch area.

"Why not return to the castle? It was once your home," the knight queried.

David closed the small gap between Sir Timothy and placed a hand on his shoulder, "You know why my brother. I have never found a fondness in the daily running of castle life nor the stuffiness of its hallways."

"But you would make a fine knight."

"Oh, but I be one now...," informed David, "...but instead of a castle's solider, I am a knight of the road. Free from the ways of the stifling corridors."

Removing his hand from his older brother's shoulder, David the beggar turned and began to walk down the alley away from Sir Timothy. A crash of thunder followed by a flash of lightning outlining his silhouette.

"And you find fondness with the suffocating stench of back passageways or living life like this?", came Timothy's question to the man's back.

David turned, "It is all a guise. Props to life's stage brother." Taking a bow, the town's beggar disappeared into the rain-filled night. The thought of lodging and spirits locked in his mind. David's determination to find out any information that his sponge-like hearing could soak up leading him to an assassin of royal's before Matthew found himself in the murder's sight was his only interest.

Chapter 25

Lying in her bed, Queen Margaret's eyes were fixed on the sight of her son sleeping in the plush chair he had sat in last night. Ever since the assassination of his father and the injury his mother had received at the hands of the attacker's second arrow, the prince had refused to leave her side. She knew he feared losing the only person he had left to guide him in his rule as King of England, and even though confident in Stephen's teachings, Margaret knew Matthew second guessed himself right now. The people couldn't afford an indecisive ruler. When Matthew was king, the young man's decisions would be final, and he wouldn't want his rulings to be open to interpretation. This would definitely invite problems.

Margaret grimaced as she slightly moved and pain shot all around the wound. The saturated feeling from the bandages, didn't add to the woman's comfort, and by her wheezes and lack of breathes she figured its tip had at least punctured a lung. The queen not only feared the extent of the injury, but the possibility of the wound becoming infected. She knew that if it did, and her body couldn't fight off the germs that took up residents at the spot, then the rest of her life would be short lived. Margaret realized that England needed its queen to act.

Two thoughts flooded through Margaret's mind in the stillness of the room. The first thing that needed to be done was Matthew needed to be declared king. The young man's coronation was imminent now that her husband had passed. The fact that the country needed to stay united under one sovereign before factions rose up throwing England into civil war fighting for an attempt to seize the crown made the ceremony that much more important. The time was now for Matthew to ascend to his rightful place.

The second issue pertained to her son's heir. The soon to be crowned king needed to sire a child. Margaret already knew that Matthew wanted to marry and father children out of love for the woman he would call his queen, but now he would have to accomplish the partnership and siring out of duty. Her son's obligation to England took precedence over his own wants. Matthew would have to choose a bride and grow to love her later. His mother knew no envy on the matter that now plagued her son.

Turning her head so the side of her face now lay on the pillow, the queen stared in the direction of the bed chamber's door. Tears began to fill her eyes as she imagined Stephen walking through the portal alive and well. Margaret thought about past times she and her lifelong companion had shared. Whether good or bad, the two had always seemed to make it together. The woman's memories passed before her mind's eye. From the moment Stephen asked permission to court her, up to their royal wedding, onto the birth of their son, and finally ending abruptly with Stephen's untimely death. The woman taking full knowledge in her belief that because of this man, her life was made whole. The grieving wife never taking notice of her labored breaths as she wheezed in her crying.

The prince abruptly woke when he heard his mother's strained gasps for air. Rushing to her side, the grief-stricken woman never felt the mattress sag as he sat on the bed. His mother's eyes filled with tears as she took in her son's appearance. He looked so much like his father she thought. No words were spoken between the two, but Matthew instantly recognized that his mother's painful expression was not caused from the arrow's piercing wound to her body, but instead by the one that robbed her of her love's wholeness and shattered her heart.

Battling back tears, Matthew took up his mother's hand and planted his lips softly on her forehead. Leaning back, Matthew met her watery gaze. "I am sorry mother," he offered his condolences before resting his head lightly against the crook of her arm.

Embracing her son, Margaret held the young man for a long time.

The queen watched from her own majestic bed as the royal's chamber housed more occupants now than it had at any time in the past. The room had been transformed into a makeshift chapel. Its furniture had been moved to the perimeter of the room allowing more open space for the commencing of the private ceremony to crown England's new monarch. Earlier today a dozen of the castle's servants had hastened in their duties of preparing the chamber and relocating the dias and a cross from the palace's divine temple.

After taking her chance to grieve some from the loss of her husband, the queen emerged herself into deep conversation with the prince. Margaret had informed Matthew that he needed to ascend to his place on the throne. Even though the young man suffered the tragic loss of his father, the prince still had a duty to perform for all of the people of England. With all the majestic elegance of the country's queen, Margaret gazed into Matthew's brown eyes and gave him the advice he would need to be a great leader, not only for the rest of his life but for the sake of his people.

"I know your heart mourns my son, but take heed in knowing that not only do the folk of Hamilton share your sorrows, but all the land partakes in your grief. What you must do now to keep the union of England strong and unwavering is separate your heart and its feelings from you mind and its reasons!", the woman touching her son's chest then the young man's forehead. "Use your heart to show reverence and compassion and your mind to be fair and just."

"I will mother," admitted the prince.

"I take heed in knowing that your father has taught you well," the woman smiled at her son. "In the name of your father, and for the sake of all of England, you cannot publicly display the open wound of a prince who has just lost his father. Rather, let the people gaze upon the sight of a king whose ways know not vulnerability from the actions of another's evil and treacheries," firmly stated the queen.

"I will mother," swore Matthew as he leaned forward and gently embraced her. "Let the Almighty be witness to my words!"

Now Margaret took witness, as did Sir Timothy, Joan, several other household workers and most importantly God himself, as the city's priest finished his coronation and placed the royal crown upon the young man's head. Matthew slid the same ring his father had worn on his finger before turning to the kneeling gatherers. His gaze falling upon his bed ridden mother whose title as queen had now changed to queen mother.

"All hail King Matthew!", shouted Sir Timothy being the first to seal his allegiance to the crown with a kiss on the ruler's ring. Every witness in the room pledged their allegiance with the symbolic gesture before the newly crowned king made his way back over to the bed. The young man took his mother's hand in his while his smile met hers. Margaret raised the ring to her lips and gave it a delicate kiss.

"I am your loyal subject my king," the woman pledged.

"And I am your most loving son," the crowned man offered.

"I promise to rule England as my father did and embrace all of my people. No voice shall go unheard!", firmly stated Matthew.

"Long live the king!", shouted Sir Timothy, but this time he was joined by the room's other occupants.

Queen Mother Margaret raised her eyes to the heavens and gave a silent petition from behind closed lips, "Please Stephen watch over, protect, and guide our little boy." A moment later she returned her attentions to her son bringing a goblet of water to her lips.

"Take a sip mother," he offered.

The private coronation ceremony that had taken place here in her chamber had been over for at least an hour. Sir Timothy had been both happy and more importantly relieved that it had taken place here in her secure room rather than in front of a crowd of Hamilton's folk. The knight believed a second assassin still lurked in the shadows waiting to strike. The queen mother and the newly crowned king watched as Joan, along with another one of the castle's servants, slid the last piece of furniture back into its original place. Both mother and son sat perfectly quiet as they waited for the two servants to finish tidying loose ends up and leave them in private. A grimace finding Margaret's face more often than not from the pain of the festering wound. In time Joan and her helper took their leave.

"Mother you appear to be in more pain this day than that of the prior," Matthew worried. "Should I have the healer fetched?"

"That not be needed. The pain comes and goes like the rain," Margaret feigned. The truth being she was in constant pain. The woman's breaths still strained when she spoke.

Before the king could put any more worry into her predicament, the queen mother quickly changed the topic. "I see the storm has broken and the sun has reclaimed its place in the sky," she pointed to one of the half opened double balcony doors. Sunlight beamed into the room.

Matthew only nodded.

The chamber took on a moment or two of silence while the queen mother reasoned with the beginning words to her next topic of discussion. Her smile falling on Matthew's quiet gaze.

"What do you ponder over mother?", inquired the king.

Letting a silence hold between his query and her response, Margaret forewarned Matthew of her soon to be exposed thoughts. "I know of no other way to put this with the lack of directness," she warned.

"What be it mother?", suspiciously he asked.

"Matthew you need to choose a bride and sire a heir," she revealed.

"But mother what of love?", the king's question shot out automatically from his mouth. "You and father fell in love before you two were wed," he pointed out.

"That be true Matthew, but your father was only the prince and his seat on the throne was still removed when we wed," her words reasoning the situation.

"There is still time for me to find the right one to call my queen," images of Joan quickly flashed through his mind's eye. Matthew wanting to know another's love before learning to love another.

"I am deeply sorry son and I envy your position not. You must marry not out of love now, but instead to continue on your father's bloodline," sadly informed the queen mother.

"But mother I desire love!"

"I have always known that love is your wish, but as the king it is not a decision made with your feelings at the forefront," softly consoled Margaret. "It is a duty-bound choice for what is best for England."

The king's spirit seeming to slowly deflate upon hearing the raw truth in the matter. His mother's words spoken more out of care and concern instead of out of unconcern and disregard for his own feelings. The fact that no matter how much the queen mother tried to dull her hurtful revelation of what needed to happen, the words were like sharp daggers slashing his hopes and desires to minute pieces.

"And what if I were to try to sire a heir and the woman's womb proves barren?", Matthew thinking his word's catching his mother off guard.

Pausing while she caught her breath, and knowing the lack of comfort in her next words, Margaret internally winced. "You must find a bride that is fertile and can produce a heir. If the woman's womb be barren and no life will take root in her belly then you must find another until an heir is sired."

Matthew's mouth fell ajar at his mother's statement. Her word's sounding less and less of love, but rather more of lust and plunder. Collecting his composure the king queried one final question. The desire to be with Joan written all over his conscience even though his love swore barrenness. "You make it sound more like conquering victories instead of love for another. What if I choose a woman and it turns out she cannot sire children, but I make the choice to live happily in love with her? England will survive many years after I leave this life," Matthew pointed out.

"Then your father's bloodline will meet its end with you," the queen mother's reply cast the two into silence and her bed chamber remained quiet for a long duration of time.

Matthew's heart knew only Joan, but the king's mind realized he needed an heir. The son's decision to love a barren woman could be more deadly to his father than any assassin's arrow.

Chapter 26

When the private coronation ceremony had come to a close, the castle's royal pages had already been sent out into both the cities along with the countryside to declare the public announcement of newly crowned King Matthew. Word of England's new sovereign seemed to spread like wildfire thanks in part to all the mounted, dispatched messengers traveling to all corners of the land. The throne which sat vacant upon the death of King Stephen was now filled by the ruler's only son. Most of the scattered people, who knew about the murder, found a bit of relief in the knowledge that the crown once again harbored direction for England. The fact that the new king was the heir of the much loved King Stephan and daily life would remain relatively the same aided in relieving the built up tension caused by another possible hierarchy and new decrees and doctrines throwing the land into possible chaos.

"I am telling you Gwenyth, it be only half of fine news," firmly stated the Bradford man. "Now if the announcement added to it the news that King Matthew sired an heir or two then it would truly be pleasant on the ear."

"Do not begin on that again Charles," his wife's staring eyes expressing the woman's serious warning to quit while her husband was ahead.

The Bradford man knowing to end any talk on the matter abruptly. "I will be in the chicken coop," stated Charles walking out of the cottage and closing the door behind him.

Turning to glance at Anne seated at the table and dicing potatoes for the evening's meal, Gwenyth picked up a knife joining her daughter. "If he keeps up with that, the birds are likely to throw him out of their enclosure too," she thought. Not a word was shared as the cottage's shutters were open absorbing the summer sunlight.

Charles mumbled to himself as he walked across the semi-dry ground towards the wooden enclosure that housed the sixteen chickens he owned. The brown with grey highlighted, hairy-faced man prepared to let the flightless birds out of their coop to stroll around and peck the ground in search for some food while he would check for any eggs and clean their roosts. The man's worrisome disposition caused by both witnessing the fatal attack the day prior, and the memories caused by a damn fox that had raided the bird's enclosure for the past four nights. Each time the orange-furred thief made off with one of the defenseless chickens. Charles was determined to outwit the crafty rogue.

"Alright ladies, come on out," he ordered after unbarring the coop's only door and opening it wide.

The hens exiting the enclosure with a bobbing stroll. Their eyes blinking as they took in both Charles and the bright sunlight. Soon all sixteen birds promenaded around with their heads and rears jerking up and down repeatedly.

The Bradford man waited till the place was all cleared before he entered heading to the spot of the night's costly break-ins. Squatting down, Charles inspected the hole dug in the soil going under one of the coop's walls. "So this be your new way in and out you four-legged trickster," his hand brushing some hay used as floor covering, along with more than a dozen white feathers from the crime scene.

"I have something in wait for you that you are not about to find fancy with," Charles firmly stated while rising and placing his hands on his hips.

For the next hour, the household's head collected a total of eight eggs; refilled in the thieves entry hole; and laid a new bed of hay on the dirt floor. When he had finished, Charles retrieved a wooden wheel-barrow and headed for a small pile of stones that he had been collecting from his tilled field for the last two planting seasons. Making several trips back and forth between the coop and the pile, the Bradford man began straightening and arranging the poultry's protective, rock defense.

"We will see how fond you are of this."

"What are you doing father?", inquired Lynn watching the kneeling man toil.

"I am keeping that damn fox out of our hen house," he replied without even turning to look at his daughter. "I will not have any chickens left if I defend not the bird's against that four-legged rogue."

"Can I aid you father in your toils?", the young woman asked.

"If you wish," was the only three words he spoke, but Lynn knew her father really would like her assistance. Stepping up to his side, she dropped to her knees and started picking and rearranging the stones. Taking a glance from the side of her eyes, the man's determined face while he worked appeared to have grown a small smile upon it. Charles' daughter knowing her father always appreciated her help even though he would never ask Lynn nor Anne for it while they were growing up. The man's motto: "Men toil, where women care take!" In Lynn's mind, her father was a worry wart of a man, but a good man none-the-less.

⊰≡⋄→

Standing near her father and gazing down at the stone moat surrounding three of the walls to the chicken coop connected to the rear of the small barn, Lynn queried, "Do you think it will work?"

"I do not notion why not," Charles reasoned. "It not be the castle walls but the barricade should turn away the bandit," the man's opinion sounding confident in the hens future security.

"Now I have to come to some kind of agreement with the Smiths for a second time," her father revealed. "I was hoping to wait past the winter before purchasing my own cock to sire more hens, but now I need to use theirs for mating," a touch of anger in the tone of his voice.

"Why the notion of now and not later in time?" slightly puzzled Lynn.

"It may be too late at that time," revealed her father. "The cock could die by then, or more importantly the chicks will be hatched an almost grown by winter's time. The weather will not be too bad on the little ones so they should live, as long as we keep that damn fox out of the hen house! Creature be as bad as that assassin that murdered King Stephen," the Bradford man starting for the enclosures's open door. "But unlike that new king of ours, I am going to make sure there is new ones sired before it be too late. It falls on me to make sure you two girls and your mother are fed and not begging for charity on Hamilton's streets. You may not notion it a big deal, but it is my obligation as a father and husband."

Lynn knew the truth in his words, but also realized her father was speaking on the worries he carried now. She retained the full understanding that the house's head really loved the royal family. Her father was also concerned for not only King Stephen's bloodline ending with his son's death, but that a war over the throne would cast Hamilton into a chaotic mess and Charles would not want to witness his family caught in the middle of such troubling times. For the whole of England to draw swords against itself was a sign that nothing good would come out of its unruliness.

"Father," the young woman called after the man before he got too far from her

Turning, Charles watched as his oldest daughter walked up to him and planted a peck-like kiss on his bearded cheek.

"Thank you father," smiled Lynn. Turning she started for the house.

"Matthew is going to need you now more than ever," revealed Margaret speaking privately to Joan. The servant sitting on the edge of the bed puzzled at the other woman's words. Joan had originally entered the room in order to retrieve the dirty dishes from the evening's meal and found herself alone with the queen mother. The newly crowned king had sat all day with his mother, and had just recently left to partake in a bath.

"I believe an infection has begun to take root and grow," confessed Margaret. "Earlier the healer had dressed the injury and said the wound festers. I can feel my body grow with heat," she admitted.

Joan's face becoming pale white at the distressing news. "But, but queen mother, you cannot leave this life now, " her tone invaded with fear. "If you die think about what that would do to the king!", tears beginning to well up in Joan's eyes.

"It is not of my doing, nor my wish to depart at this time Joan rather the Lord's will," pointed out a wheezing Margaret. "Besides, I say not that I die so do not fill yourself with worry at this time," the bed ridden woman doing her best to sound sure of a pleasant ending while experiencing a nonstop pain and her body's heat rise.

"I fear you have wrongly heard me and have caused yourself unnecessary distress. I ask that you not ponder over a matter that is yet to happen," assuredly smiled Margaret.

The servant returning a watery smile while nodding her head in agreement. "You are right my lady. I was already pondering over the worst," Joan acknowledged.

"We all leave this earth someday," Margaret admitted while taking up Joan's hand in hers. "The question is what did we do with our time allotted to us and how did we live our lives?" Her eyes gazed up beyond the servants shoulder as she offered words one would hear from a priest at a funeral. "I would like to believe that I used all the time I was allotted by the Lord to live my life to the fullest everyday he graced me with breath. I treated others the way I wished to be treated and my belief is one of richness," Margaret dropped her eyes to Joan and gave her a smile. "Not because I was queen, or knew riches, but because my spirit is wealthy due to having known folk like you."

Gazing into the red, tear-filled eyes of the woman, who the queen mother had known for all of the servant's life and had treated her like she was born from the royal, "I query two requests from you Joan."

"Please my lady," anxiously waited the servant.

"I ask that you watch over Matthew when I am gone. He will need you, and I hold the knowledge that his trust is held high in you. You have always loved him and he you. He will need you now more than any other time in his life."

"I will," softly sniffled Joan. "I give you my word."

Smiling, the queen mother continued, "I ask that you, who has always been the daughter that Stephen and I longed for but never had; the child who came to us as a blessing from God; embrace me like that of a daughter and mother and speak on the good memories you have given to me and your father.

Joan's tears came as the woman slid on the bed next to Margaret and melted into her adoptive mother's embrace. She knew in her heart that she was about to lose the woman soon from the same attack that had robbed her of her adoptive father. At the same time Joan's soul felt the wealth of the royal's love. The adoptive daughter was England's richest servant.

When Matthew had returned to his mother's chamber after his refreshing bath, Joan sat beside Margaret on the queen mother's royal bed. They both shared in stories and laughter. Even though the wounded woman's injury plagued her with pain and her breaths came in the company of wheezes, Margaret really enjoyed the time she was spending with Joan. King Matthew couldn't tell if the servant's red eyes were the cause of sadness or laughter, but just the appearance of the servant and queen mother together on level ground seated next to one another on the bed intrigued his suspicions.

"What is this about?", the king queried to neither of the two particular.

"We share in stories about old times," the queen mother responded. Patting a spot near her on the open side of the bed she invited, "Remove the weight of your crown son and join us in our talks of less complicated times."

Matthew glanced between the two before reaching up to remove the crown from his head. Placing it on a small, wooden table, the young man made his way onto the bed and sat in the spot where his mother had patted minutes ago.

Turning toward her son, Margaret placed a soft kiss on his cheek. "You hold the knowledge that I love you with all my heart and soul," she spoke quietly wearing a smile.

"I am aware mother," he confirmed her words with a peck on her cheek.

"As I you."

"Well as for now we will pretend that these troubles in our household lack and royals we not be," spoke Margaret while looking from her son to her adopted daughter. "Tonight we relish in times and memories of yesteryear totgether," she declared.

"Do you remember when you were but a boy, Matthew, and found fondness in Joan's story telling?"

"I do," he replied.

"It was the tale of William the Brave that you favored. Is there truth to my memory?", queried his smiling mother.

"It holds true."

"I would find fancy if Joan would be kind to share with us the hero's tale. What say you?", smiled Margaret.

Taking a second to glance between his mother and his childhood storyteller, Matthew gave the two a smile, "I believe I would also take fancy in hearing the tale if Joan is up to narrating the story."

"I would be honoured," grinned the woman at her audience of two. In no time at all Joan retold the story she narrated to Matthew as the boy grew up. The woman's words, along with her facial expressions and body language captivating the two listeners.

When Joan had finished, the three found joy continuing to retell events they had shared with each other throughout the years. Not one of the three were left out, and even Stephen was included in their stories, which brought laughs to the atmosphere that only knew somberness for the last few days.

Margaret had done her best to block out not only the pain from the injury but the lack of comfort from the infection's slowly rising fever. Matthew and Joan's joyful laughs lent aid as the bed's three occupants burned the midnight oil.

Chapter 27

Joan, along with the two royals, had spent most of the night remembering past events from their memories together before finally finding slumber in the wee hours of the morning. In fact, it had been so late the woman upon request from her adopted mother took up her night's sleep in the company of Margaret and Matthew. Her body's muscles were still slightly tight even after her cat-like stretch from her stay in the room's only settee. The thought of knowing and hiding from Matthew, the truth that his mother was possibly dying haunted her mind now, but the servant was at peace last night by the happiness the three shared. The joy seemed to cast the worries from her resting mind. Presently, she was collecting the tray with last night's supper dishes on it and preparing to bring them to the kitchen.

Queen Mother Margaret still lay at peace in her sleep, but Joan could see she wore sheen, pale skin and tell her hair was wet and slightly matted from fever. The servant being able to tell that the germ causing infection in her injury was now at battle with her body. The woman issuing a silent prayer that Margaret would defeat the infection and her fever would break. The woman hoping that the queen mother would be back to health soon.

Looking over to her true love still finding slumber in one of the plush chairs in the chamber, Joan's heart sunk into her belly. A look of lost hope and sadness covered her face like a mask. She knew he loved her, but she was unable to give him back what he so desperately needed, an heir. The two had shared numerous nights together finding pleasure in each other's arms, but no matter how many times he needed her Joan's womb denied his offer. Her chance at a family with him nonexistent.

Grabbing the tray, she quietly opened the door. Closing it behind her as she left the room, Joan offered the two posted guardsman a smile and a slight nod. Obviously, Sir Timothy was not taking any chances, and after his secret meeting with David the beggar the other night, he had doubled up on security. If there was a danger in the castle, Timothy didn't want the king or the queen mother to be jeopardized from his lack in caution.

Starting down the hall carrying the tray with every thought on the dreariness of Margaret's degenerating condition heavy on her mind, Joan turned the corner. In her lack of paying any attention to her surroundings, the servant jumped in startlement as she almost collided with a person coming down the corridor from the other direction. Locking her grip onto the tray so she wouldn't drop any of the dishes on it, the woman looked up from the flat receptacle.

"My apologies I was lost in my thoughts," Joan's justification trailing off as she looked upon the raptor-like gaze staring down at her. A grasp of fear slightly taking hold of the servant. "Duke Paul, but I thought you were in Sheffield." The startled woman feeling like a mouse under the watchful eyes of a hawk. Memories from a night past instantly running through her mind.

"Good morning to you Joan," the Duke sarcastically stated.

"Ah yes, my apologies my lord," stammered the servant. "Good morning to you also."

"I believe it is apparent that I am not in Sheffield, but if you must know, I was in Birmingham conducting business when I learned of the tragic news," sternly informed Paul. "I rode all day and the two nights prior to get here. It is my wish to see my wounded aunt and cousin!"

"Yes, of course," agreed Joan. "The king and queen mother are in her chambers now as we presently speak."

"Very well. If you will pardon my leave."

"Of course Duke Paul," bowed Joan.

The servant began to continue her walk down the castle's corridor with the royal kitchen as her destination. She had made it roughly ten feet away when Paul's call to her stopped her dead in her tracks.

"Oh and Joan if I might inquire?", the duke asked while starting towards her.

The woman turned, "Yes my lord."

"Have you mentioned to the new king regarding your willingness to be taken over and over again all night by Sir Rufus and I?", a devilish grin that the servant knew so well dressing his face. "Or even the truth behind you finding fancy and your fondness for the hugeness in Sir Rufus', shall we say lance?"

Fear returned taken hold of Joan, but she put forth the best battle she could muster. "Matthew will not believe your lack of the truth and will not hear your lies. When the king finds out you took what was not freely given to you, then you might find yourself to be the first to hang at the new king's hands!", the

woman's anger obvious in her voice. "Besides you can say nothing that will begin Matthew's new rule in ruins now that he is England's king!"

"And that be your belief?", Paul calmly queried. His tone sounding smooth like ice pumped through his veins.

"That is my belief in as much as that be the truth!", she huffed.

"My cousin believes in honour," Paul flatly stated. "The kind showed by a knight to another, who be weakened and unable to defend oneself. Just the kind of honorable mercy that Sir Rufus showed Sir Timothy," the duke pointed out. "Matthew saw it for himself and he along with my uncle were taken with the action."

Duke Paul paused a second pretending to think to himself. The young

man's word's hung for Joan to ponder, and she knew he was right. Both Matthew, along with his father spoke on the issue for days after the tourney.

"No, I ponder my king will believe his noble cousin and an honorable knight over a phallus-loving, barren servant. Whom, I might remind you, called off their coupling relation on the same day we stayed as guest in the castle," Paul's devilish smile and raptor-like stare had an intimidating effect on Joan.

"Sir Rufus, as a matter of happening, is here with me now," the duke informed the woman as he started back towards his aunt's chamber. "I will need to summons him. I take heed in knowing that both the king and the queen mother will desire to hear the words of truth second by someone they have seen has honour!"

"No! Please stop my lord!", cried Joan to Paul's back.

The duke took two more steps causing her to cry out to him a second time. "Please my lord. That will not be necessary."

The woman knew that Matthew was already facing two extremely hard situations; the loss of his father and the reality of his dying mother. He could not stand to have his heart ripped from his chest and shattered into anymore pieces with the news of being taken at her will by two other men. Joan had given Margaret her word that she would do whatever it takes to be there for her son, not be the one to hurt him more. No matter what the danger, Joan would protect Matthew even if it meant damning herself for his benefit. The woman's head and shoulders appeared to slump as all the fight seemed to leave her body.

Duke Paul spun on his heels content in knowing that Joan still belonged to him. He knew she wanted desperately out from under his boot hold, but a deal was a deal he laughed to himself.

"What be my cousin and aunt doing at this time?" the duke inquired.

"They sleep," the defeated woman replied. All hostility gone in her voice.

"Then they cannot miss what they do not know is present," Paul admitted grabbing Joan by the arm.

"Let us be away from here," he remarked as they followed the hallway back from where he had just come from. The servant still carrying the tray.

It was not long, especially since Duke Paul had some general acquaintance of the castle layout, that he led Joan to one of the many nooks. Standing in the hidden place from others roaming the halls, he watched the woman place the tray she carried on the floor and turn back to him while he untied his pant's drawstrings.

"You are aware what be required by you," he remarked as his pants fell to his ankles.

Without any coaxing, a defeated Joan slowly dropped to her knees taking his manhood into her mouth.

In time he placed his hands behind her head and pulled her engulfing mouth into his thrusting hips. She felt him twitch as his hot seed shot down her throat.

Joan wished it was her dying instead of Margaret. She had made a deal with the devil and thought the bargain had been fulfilled days ago when the duke had left. The woman not expecting to see Paul for at least two more years when he showed up to visit following his regular routine. Joan believed she would never see Sir Rufus, or his huge phallus again, but now he was in the castle too. The defeated woman also thought that her body would never be ravaged by the likes of the of those two again. The feel of the knights manhood inside her using her and pleasuring her like no other before could be forgotten and put in her past. Joan realized one thing as Paul mounted her from behind; the sex slave thought wrong.

Chapter 28

Leaning with her back against the tree across from the stone wall that her lover and his friend had taken audience at, Lynn's tongue probed the young man's mouth as she and Russell were locked in a passionate kiss. The young woman's hands roaming all over his back, along with moving up and down his sides. They had been apart and not seen each other since the assassination of King Stephen. What was only two and a half days ago, felt like an eternity to the two lovers.

"I never desire to be apart from you and only wish to feel your touch every moment of my wakefulness," Lynn informed her lover in between their hungry kisses.

"Nor I you my love," Russell confirmed her words while his actions cemented his desires. The young man's hands resting on the woman's hips. "I have longed for your scent; the beauty in your eyes; along with the feel of your touch; and I truly know now that God cannot create another to rival you here on earth nor in the heavens." Her lover smoothing her hair back over her ear. "The looks of an angel," Russell softly added.

Lynn gazed into Russell's eyes the whole time he spoke searching and knowing without a doubt his words were not coming forth from his mind, nor his groin, but they were a declaration from her lover's heart that held no underlyings.

She knew without a shadow of a doubt the truth in his words. Instantaneously she brought her lips to his, the young woman's mouth trying to devour Russell's in a passionate kiss searching to touch his inner life force. Their bodies and spirits melting from two separate individuals into one entity.

Slowly, Lynn's right hand slid across his chest making its way over his stomach. The young woman feeling every definition of his separated abdomen through his shirt. Continuing its journey, the lover's hand glided over the outline of his stomach toward the waist of his pants. Their pelvises slowly beginning to grind each other, and she could feel his hardness against the lower part of her belly. Russell wanted his lover as much as she wanted him.

Without hesitation in his movement, Russell's hand quickly grasped hold of Lynn's as she reached the drawstring to his pants and began to pull on them. Before she accomplished releasing the knot, the young man broke their kiss and backed away her hand still in his.

"What's wrong my love?", surprisingly inquired his lover. "I desire you and wish to feel your nakedness against my skin."

"I you, but not in this manner," Russell softly responded.

"My heart is yours and I freely give my body," Lynn informed her lover.

Russell brought his empty hand up to the young woman's cheek tenderly laying it there. He gazed into his lover's eyes a second before he spoke. "And I give all of myself to you, but I vowed an oath to you when I gave you my word that I shall always protect and defend you against any rival. That is what I do now." The young man pushing strands of hair behind Lynn's ear with a finger. "My restraint is not from a lack of desire to receive the gift you offer, but I safeguard your virtues which even now are under siege from our obscured judgments. I wish you not at a time later know regret in the decision made today. For if ever you ponder the choice you make now, then my words know not truth and I have failed you." Lynn's lover placing a delicate kiss on the young woman's forehead.

His word's lacked reproach toward Lynn's action's caused by the heat of the moment, and Lord knows he, himself, desperately desired his lover's naked touch. The young man's truthfulness in his statement was one weighed down by Russell's undying love for Lynn.

The young woman not only heard but felt the lovingness and truth in her lover's honor-bound and oath-filled reluctance towards her tempting advances and the heat of the moment.

"Do not feel ill towards me," she humbly requested.

"Never I will", he confirmed with another kiss on her forehead.

A smile took form on Lynn's face upon hearing her lover's reply. "Always my hero. Even when I need rescuing from myself," The young woman embraced her own personal protector and defender of her virtues.

The hug they shared only lasted a brief time as the advancing sounds of angry chirps carried on the air. Instantly Russell recognized the irate tweets.

"I have angered my friend with the lack of bringing you here after church," he admitted to Lynn whispering in her ear.

"Just explain to Sir Robin, King Stephen's assassination."

"But my love, birds have no care in the troubles of men," remarked Russell. "They face their own hardships."

Releasing the embrace they shared, Russell spun and took in the sight of Sir Robin spouting anger-filled tweets from his perch on the stone wall. "My humblest apologies my little friend...," he tried to begin, but it was obvious to him he was in for an earful first. Behind the young man Lynn's giggles added to Sir Robin's irate chirps. Russell who carried his sword and bow with him stood defenseless to the verbal attacks from the bird's maddening chirps, along with his lover's joyous outbursts of laughter.

The mood in the castle took on a somber atmosphere contradicting the bright, sunny, summer day outside its walls. The queen mother's fever had risen. Margaret's skin was pale and clammy, and perspiration constantly leaked from her still body soaking into the bed's sheets and its mattress. King Matthew had stayed by her side all day constantly giving her water in an attempt to shake her thirst. Even Duke Paul got his chance to see the woman, but any conversation was kept to a bare minimum. Everyone knew the queen mother needed her rest because her body battled a foreign invader.

Joan knocked softly on the chamber's door she now found herself in front of. The woman knowing that this night she belonged to Paul and Rufus. Her thoughts confrontational as they ran amuck in her head. On one hand she hated being used for the Dukes pleasures, but on the other, the woman's mind anticipating the feel of Sir Rufus' manhood inside of her. Upon hearing the invitation to enter, Joan slowly opened the door and started into the room.

Like the last time she found herself in the Duke's chamber, the room was dimly lit mostly illuminating the bed while the edge of the room was shrouded in darkness. Instantly she recognized Paul lying on the bed in the nude. Wanting to desperately run, she shut the door behind her. Without being too obvious she searched the darkness for Rufus while Joan removed all her clothing. He sat in the chair he had the last time she was here although his presence was more noticeable this time.

When Joan had removed her last article of clothing, she made her way over to the bed. The woman could tell by Paul's manhood he was ready to go. Climbing onto the mattress by the foot of the bed, she crawled her way up positioning herself between his spread open legs.

"Good evening Joan," he sarcastically smiled fixing his hawk-like eyes on her.

Lying flat on her belly, she took his phallus into her hand slowly lowering her lips to it. Paul watched as his manhood disappeared into her mouth.

"That is it you bitch," remarked a satisfied duke. "You seem to have acquired some skill."

The woman's thought's not on what she was doing to Paul, but what she hoped Rufus would be doing to her. She could feel the wetness between her legs as the woman rubbed herself against the bed. The pleasurable feeling causing a few muffled moans around Paul's manhood.

A smile returning to his face.

Several minutes had passed, and Joan still working on the duke felt the mattress sag when the knight climbed onto the bed. Knowing what was about to happen and secretly desiring it, the woman pulled her knees up from her position lying on the mattress causing her ass to rise into the air. Joan presented herself inviting Rufus' hugeness. Moments later she felt the tip of his lance slide into her. A muffled groan escaped from her mouth, as Rufus fed his large, girth sized phallus into her. The knight slowly beginning to rock his hips, but soon his tempo began to speed up. Both Joan's mouth and vagina were being filled with man flesh, and the woman not only liked it but loved the pleasure she was feeling. She had secretly longed for the feeling of Rufus in her lower belly.

Listening to the muffled groans and moans issuing from Joan, Paul while laying his hands behind his head was caught by surprise when the woman gripped both thighs and used them to not only brace herself against the knights thrusts, but actually used them in an aid to push back into Rufus. The woman's groans turning into grunts. Joan wanted everything the huge man gave. Reaching down Duke Paul pulled her head up until she released her hungry grip on him with her mouth. Her grunts filling the air of the room.

"Sounds to me like she likes your phallus my friend," revealed the smiling duke. "Do my words know truth?"

The woman only nodding her head.

"My apologies," offered the smiling man. "I seem to have not heard you."

"Yes my lord!", she replied between grunts.

Her words causing Rufus to slow in his thrusts. Paul just smiled at him. The two had done this act before and were on the same page. Joan softly whining from the man's change in speed. Her body wanting his manhood bad and no matter how hard she attempted to back into Rufus, the knight held her at bay. He teased her with his weapon.

"What do you fancy of him." again queried Paul.

"Please," she openly begged.

"Just say what you desire," the devil grinned.

A soft cry came from Joan as Rufus slowly fed her wanting body all of himself. When he withdrew only the tip sat inside of her. She waited in anticipation for the next thrust, but he held steady. The rider breaking his mount.

"His huge phallus taking me!"

Both men laughed.

"Truly a vixen," offered Rufus beginning his thrusts again.

"I believe you are correct in your words," agreed Paul. "She is a bitch in heat."

"What would you do for more of the knight's phallus, Joan?"

Being ridden again by the knight and feeling the pleasure he was giving her, the woman never wanted the two to tease her again. Joan could feel an orgasm building up inside of her and now was not the time to stop. With no thought to her words she answered, "Anything, my lord! I will do anything you require of me!", she grunted.

The devil grinned forcing her down onto his manhood. In a short time the three shared in their releases.

After taking a moment to catch their breaths, the duke rose from the bed and began to dress. "I will return in a bit," he informed the two.

"Where are you off to?" inquired the huge man.

"I need some air," Duke Paul pulled his shirt over his head. "Until I return I am quite sure Joan will take care of your needs," he smiled.

Minutes later he was closing the room's door behind him.

Joan smiled at Rufus and took hold of his limp weapon. Even in his state now the man's phallus seemed to dwarf her hands. "Time to prepare for round two my lord." It wasn't long after that she felt the sleeping giant begin to awaken.

Joan laid on her back with her knees bent and her feet flat on the mattress. She watched as Rufus lowered himself on and into the woman's body. Joan accepting all of him. Her mouth gasping for air. Unlike before, the huge man took Joan slow for a time. The woman enjoying the pleasure he was giving to her. Eventually his slow steady thrusts began to quicken, and Joan loved the coupling she was receiving now that the duke had left the room. Little did she realize through her moans, and the fact that her attention was on the feeling of the man's hugeness touching her belly deep inside, that Paul had actually returned. The night's entertainer hearing his voice before actually seeing him.

"Bring Joan down this way," the duke advised the knight. "I would like to witness her face."

Responding to the request, Rufus removed himself from the woman only to hear a soft whine signaling her want for his unsheathed weapon. Joan never taking her eyes from the man repositioning both of them and now facing the chair that Paul sat in. The woman's eyes watching her hands feed Rufus' phallus back into her hungry vagina. His thrusts picking up where they had left off causing the atmosphere to once again come alive with groans of pleasure.

Joan wrapped her legs around the knight and placed the heels of her feet in the bends of his knees. She wanted to keep him inside her so she pulled herself off the mattress trying to melt into the hovering man over her. The young woman could feel an orgasm building for a second time this night. Joan's attention lacking in the duke sitting in the room, as her eyes tried to make a connection between her and the man riding her. Feeling one of his muscular arms forcing her back so she laid fully on the mattress, Joan felt the bed's support end at her shoulders causing her head to droop over its border. Looking through lust filled eyes towards the duke, Joan watched as a naked man she had never recognized before approached her prone body being pleasured. The night's entertainer witnessed his rock, hard manhood as it came closer to her face. The woman able to tell that even though the man's body was smaller than Rufus, his erect phallus rivaled the one taken her now. Unconsciously she opened her mouth and took the man into her. For the second time this evening she was being spit like a wild boar.

Joan's muffled cries of pleasure fought their way out of her working mouth. The newcomer's size and girth causing her cheeks to expand, as he sought the depths of her throat. The woman gave into her wanton lust at the hugeness of the two phalluses ravaging her body, along with the hands belonging to the man she orally pleasured as he fondled her breasts. His gropes adding to the feel of a building climax.

The ravished entertainer wrapped her arms around the man feeding her taken hold of his ass. Using her arms to guide his thrusts, the three quickly found a matching rhythm. Their moves in unison. Joan's muffled screams coming faster now as the two men's plunges picked up in speed. The woman's body helpless as they drove deep into her.

Joan was the first to release. Her orgasm shattering her body as she tried to scream out her pleasure. The woman's climax followed by Rufus' hot seed shooting into her womb and the newcomer's seed flowing down her throat. The entertainers cheeks puffing out as she swallowed fast in an attempt not to lose any of the deposit. The sex slave's hungry vagina and mouth milking the two men of all their offerings.

The whole time Duke Paul sat naked in his chair watching the woman finally give in to her wanton lust. A devilish smile crossing his face as he thought about how the woman's riders had broken their mount. The duke knowing that he wasn't finished yet and still needed to fuel the fire a little bit more.

For the rest of the night and into the morning the three men satisfied not only themselves but what now appeared to be Joan's insatiable appetite.

At roughly the same time that Joan had entered her chamber of desire, two hooded cloak men met somewhere in one of Hamilton's alleyways away from any watchful eyes or any foul unpleasantries. The two were glad the English rain had been reprieved and tonight the sky was clear holding nothing but stars. The minds of both men knowing not of pleasure at this hour, rather only conducting business of the highest form. An assassination plot needed to be solved and foiled before any further attempt was made on the newly, crowned king. An appointment to the gallows for anyone involved also required a quick investigation, arrest, and conviction. The murderer's neck or necks would certainly be stretched at the hands of the hangman's noose.

"Anything yet?", inquired an armorless Sir Timothy.

"I hear not a word so far," -dejectedly revealed David the beggar- "but I am under the impression that you have installed safeguards in the castle."

"You speak the truth," pointed out the undercover knight. "Although on the morrow, the king will be putting his father's body to rest in the vault below the church. Like that of an adder, danger lays still waiting for it's time to rear up and strike I fear!"

"I will be there hidden, but in plain sight to aid in Matthew's protection," revealed David.

"Keep in mind brother not one person holds knowledge of who you really be, nor that of which you protect," he pointed out to the beggar. "If anything were to go wrong, then you could find one's self mistaken and a date with the hangman."

"My humblest of thanks for your worries, but I have sworn my allegiance to the defense of the crown," the beggar responded. "If my life be forfeit in exchange to safeguard the one who wears it, then it was worth the trade."

The two brothers from two different worlds clasped forearms.

"Keep an eye on your back on the morrow," warned Sir Timothy.

"Do not trouble your brow with worries regarding my loss. It be you not I that another is shooting at," revealed David.

The undercover knight watched as the hidden protector of the crown walked away from him. David's word's holding truth, as Sir Timothy knew he would be more in the line of fire than his brother. Raising his eyes to the heavens, the knight spoke softly to his longtime king and friend, "I need your aid on the morrow Stephen. Matthew may require more than mortal eyes to watch over him."

Chapter 29

The last of the city's people, including all of the folk of Hamilton that lived in the countryside, had been making their way in line past the laid out corpse of their heart's most loved king. Stephen's body laid on one of the church's wooden tables located on the dias that had been decorated with bluebell flowers for the occasion. It had taken three and a half days since his assassination, but with everything else going on both the queen mother, along with England's new king knew this would have been what Stephen had desired. The man always wishing to be one with his people instead of a royal that looked down on his subjects from his throne.

Behind Stephen's lifeless body sat the church's priest. To his right, the chair that doubled as a seat for the realm's sovereign when attending the house of worship sat empty. To that seat's right was seated Duke Paul. The Queen Mother would have sat in that chair if she was in attendance, but she had taken a turn for the worse and now slept from a high fever. She had gone unconscious the prior night and had not yet awakened from her battle with her wound's infection. Margaret's life was under siege from the bacteria.

On the floor besides the dias, a crownless King Matthew stood awaiting the next town folk, who kneeled before the deceased's body offering a prayer. Sir Timothy stood behind the young man ever watchful for an attack that had not shown itself yet while other members of the royal guard remained ever vigilant both inside and outside the church. Their eyes darting to-and-from. The royal's wake had begun late this morning and with the mid afternoon hour passing the last of Hamilton's people gave Matthew their condolences. When done, they found themselves a spot to stand in, as the young man took his seat upon the dias. The priest making his way over to the podium to begin the fallen king's eulogy.

Not a dry eye was present in the Lord's house when the holy man ended his reverence-filled words. Sounds caused from the muffled crying from those in attendance could be faintly heard, as Matthew made his way to the lectern. He paused only briefly to place a kiss on the back of the priest's hand.

Taking his place at the podium, the crownless king surveyed the people, his people, throughout the chapel. The somber atmosphere matching that of the room's saddened hearts. Glancing about the congregation, a hush fell over Hamilton's folk, as he began to speak.

"We have lost one of England's most honorable kings to one who only knows treason and wishes our beloved country know chaos and turmoil. Most of you folk have known me since my days of childhood. When my father and mother brought me here as a boy and it appeared that mother spent more time preventing her son from playful runs throughout these corridors than praying herself," King Matthew's words seeming to bring forth several sad smiles from mothers throughout the congregation.

"My knowledge does not lack in how my father had time for every one of you," he said slowly gliding a pointing finger from right to left. "Take heed in knowing no voice should go unheard to my ear neither. I solemnly swear and take an oath before God…," the young man dropped to a knee while keeping his gaze on his people, "… that I will not cower like a mutt in fear before this unholy murderer, nor any other who come to rival the crown. Like my father before me, I will rule with kindness and justice. Take heed good people of Hamilton for I am not just your king and leader, but I am your brother under the Almighty, who stands beside you in the largest battle one can fight," Matthew paused while his gaze searched the crowd. "The battle for life's freedom and the right to live as free men and women. I swear to rule in the likes of my father, who knew not tyranny, but love. With your helpful guidance we will remain as one, as we have under King Stephen!" The dark and somber cloud that hung over the people of Hamilton was pierced and broken apart by the inspiring words of King Matthew's address. His oath like that of the winter's grip on the land broken by the dawning of spring.

"Long live the King!" someone yelled from the place's seats in the balcony. Soon after others joined into the chant caused by the young man's enlightened words of inspiration.

"Long live the King!" the chant continuing to rise as one voice.

King Matthew remained kneeling and slighly shook his head no towards Sir Timothy when a little girl, a child no more than eight or nine years old, ran for the young man her arms open wide.

A gasp filled the air only to be subdued when Matthew opened his arms swallowing the child. Rising to his feet, the king's smile fell upon her, and it wasn't long before his expression pulled a single tooth-missing smile from the girl. Giving a slight nod of his head, the congregation cheered as the royal along with the commoner raised an arm as one would in triumphant.

"Long live King Matthew!", a collective voice chanted over and over.

Tears steamed from people's faces at the sight symbolizing unity, but for Joan sitting in the first row of pews, her watery eyes gazed on the sight of what she wished could have been for her and the woman's true love. A family of their own.

"You would have been so proud of the king," advised Joan with a smile on her face while she held Margaret's hand. The queen mother's unconscious form covered in a sheen of sweat from her internal battle. The woman being rendered unable to do anything but slumber, as her fever rose in an attempt to fight her wound's infection. Unfortunately, the adopted daughter realizing she was on the brink of losing a second mother in this life although this one she had come to know and love.

"I am telling you my lady he spoke like King Stephen. Matthew turned what was a church full of people that knowing only dread and despair into folk that had been refilled with hope anew. He dispelled all of Hamilton's fears with their questioning of the future." The woman pausing before she continued as her gut wrenched from the image of her and him with children. "His words were full of inspiration that even a child ran to seek solace in Matthew's arms, and like you my lady he never questioned twice when he embraced her. I wish you could have witnessed the little girl's face when he lifted her up and held her with a smile," Joan's words causing tears to form in her eyes.

"I hold a secret, and I can no longer bear the burden of keeping it from you. After seeing Matthew with that child today, I cannot keep in my grasps any longer," the woman servant quietly admitted. "I lay before you my confession in my love for your son. I desire him and I know his wish for me, but I believe my womb barren. We have coupled for years past, and I have not yet had a child begin to grow inside of me," Joan's eyes became watery accompanying her sniffles. "I wish God would have blessed me with a much needed heir, but even now I believe the Lord has forsaken me."

"Duke Paul knows of our coupling and has threatened to ruin Matthew as king by breaking the news of our trysts due to my barrenness," Joan began to cry. "When the people of Hamilton along with the whole of England takes knowledge of his love to a woman, who cannot give him an heir, then they will rise up and threaten his seat on the throne. To save Matthew I struck a deal with the duke, but never was I aware of the deception amongst his words. I believe Paul wanted me to serve on him hand and foot while at the castle, but he required another type of service. Even now he uses my body for his and any of those he wishes to be entertained. Duke Paul, and his acquaintances take me for their own sexual pleasures. To protect Matthew's reign in exchange Duke Paul rapes me," the woman confessed through crying eyes. Joan's head slumping to the mattress. Her tears running onto her hand and Margaret's.

Minutes went by before the confessing woman's head rose from the bed and her composure started to return to her. "The duke also requires me to end my coupling with Matthew, along with any type of relations we had or no bargain can be met. I have for his sake."

Releasing her grip on Margaret's motionless hand, Joan dried her face, "I have one request my lady that I beg from you. When you reach Heaven in the life after and see God, please ask him what I have done to be forsaken from his graces and cast into the grip of the devil himself?"

Joan turned the corner heading down one of the castle's many corridors. Upon Matthew's arrival he had suggested her to retire for the night and get some sleep, but the woman couldn't return to her chambers yet. There was still a full night of activities ahead for her at the duke's beckoning. Throughout the day, she had unfortunately come in contact with him on several occasions, and Paul's words were always the same even though his gropes were on different parts of her body, "Don't be late on this night!," he would firmly state. On one occasion, he boldly pulled her off to a secluded spot in the church and sat her on a flat, stone table-like stand. When he was more than satisfied they were alone, Duke Paul's head disappeared under her dress. His mouth hungrily devouring her until her release became imminent before he would back away leaving her wanting closure. Paul enjoyed hearing her lust-filled begs until finally on the third time with her legs bent over his shoulders his mouth brought her to release.

For the second night in a row, Joan stood in front of the door to his chamber and softly knocked on the portal. When Paul opened it he stood completely in the nude and already his manhood was hard as a rock. He wore just a grin on his face, and Joan could already recognize the sounds of a woman's moans coming from inside. Seizing a hold of her, Paul swiftly ushered her into the room.

The duke's chamber was dimly lit, but instantly Joan recognized Rufus on the mattress riding another, who by the sounds of pleasure and the words lustfully spoken was obviously a woman.

The huge knight took her from behind while the duke helped relieve Joan of her clothes. Once she was completely naked, Paul ushered the newcomer to the chair on the side of the bed sitting the mesmerized Joan into it. She watched as Rufus took the other woman, who she recognized as the young, twenty two year old blonde haired servant named Ruth. The young woman sounding like a whore at a brothel, as she moaned and confessed her love of being taken by a phallus so big. Joan wondering what Paul hung over her head.

Caught in a trance-like grip, Joan watched as the knight rocked his hips back-n-forth purposely showing the voyeur his large manhood stretch Ruth's vagina. The blonde haired Ruth begging for more when he withdrew his lance only leaving the tip in her clutches. Joan knowing the pleasure the young woman must be feeling deep inside her belly every time Rufus thrusts into her. Ruth's moans, accompanied by her dirty words carrying through the room along with the sight of the knight's hugeness as he ravished another, instantly brought Joan excitement. Her own womanhood glistened its wetness in the room's dim light. The voyeur never taken notice to Paul using his hand to check her nether regions.

"You find fancy in watching your Rufus take another woman?" the duke questioned.

Joan never even realizing she nodded her answer, nor recognizing the smile on the man's hawk-like face.

"Do you long for Rufus' phallus?", he asked barely audible in comparison to Ruth's declaration from the pleasure she received.

"I do," replied the voyeur.

Joan sat and watched as Rufus unsheathed his sword before motioning to the voyeur. She rose from her seat and climbed onto the bed. The smiling duke delivering a slap to one of her ass cheeks on the way.

Laying on her back with her feet flat on the mattress and her knees bent, Joan watched, felt, and gasped as Rufus leveled his manhood and slowly fed it into her. The knight's weapon stretching out her fleshy sheath as he began to rock back-n-forth. Her moans of pleasure filling the air where moments ago Ruth's had. The blonde woman now the voyeur as she hungrily watched the two coupling.

"I fancy Ruth over there due to her declarations from my pleasurings," informed Rufus.

Joan feeling the knight slowly withdrawing his phallus from her looked at the man puzzling his statement. His expression quickly changing when he slammed himself back into her. His drive creating the reaction he sought.

"Oh yes!," moaned the woman.

He repeated the move and again heard the response he desired.

"Oh yes!," her moan having the edge of a cry of pleasure.

Rufus knew his manhood was breaking Joan and he kept up the process until the woman was crying out in ecstasy. With only several more drives accompanied by some speed, along with a little coaxing from the two voyeurs, Joan herself sounded like a whore at a brothel. Now she was completely lost to her sexual pleasure. Both Paul and Rufus knew the mount had been completely broken.

Slowing down the speed while backing off a bit of his driving force, the man took Joan leisurely. She had reached ecstasy and watched with lust-filled eyes, as Ruth straddled her head lowering her womanhood down onto her face while Rufus rocked inside of her. Joan had never tasted or pleasured another woman before, but automatically in her coveting state Joan's arms wrapped around Ruth's ass cheeks pulling the young woman down onto her tongue.

Soon Rufus' thrusts turned into deep drives that seemed to push not only against her body, but the air out of her lungs. Hungrily, her vagina fed on the man's phallus, as she heard Ruth's cries from the devouring of the young woman's vagina by Joan's mouth.

In moments, the knight pumped hot, creamy seed into her causing the woman's release to rock her body. The feeling causing Joan to pull Ruth further to her mouth until the young woman finally yelled her release. Joan's tongue frantically probing the girl's cavity, as she milked Rufus for all of his deposit.

Throughout the night Joan enjoyed being taken and pleasured over and over. The woman also found it a great joy to watch Ruth in action as she was numerously mounted and ridden by both the duke and the knight. Both women were spitted and Joan joined Ruth in her brothel like dialogue. She had finally become very verbal during her episodes of being used as a sheath for especially Rufus' flesh weapon. Her wanton search for her ecstasy brought a devilish grin to Paul's face. Whether it was two participants, or all four at once, the sexing never found a lull. Even the two women took each other greedily devouring each other's womanhood at the same time.

At one point Rufus sat and watched the duke aid Ruth in strapping on a leather harness around her waist with a bronze replica of a phallus covered with sheep skin.

Their round, firm, breasts touching as the blonde-haired woman climbed on top of Joan and plunged in and out of her. The older woman's hands reaching around to grab Ruth's ass pulling the young woman and the imitation manhood deep into her. Their tongues probing each other's mouths. Soon it was Joan's turn to dawn the harness and take Ruth.

Both Joan and Ruth left the duke's chambers right before the first of the castle's bakers woke for the morning's breakfast preparations. They both knew that they needed to get some sleep before the start to their day, but with Duke Paul's gift Ruth joined Joan in her private, servant chambers. They both desired each other and wished to play some more. Soon moans filled Joan's room.

Chapter 30

The two women had awoken in each other's arms a short time ago, and Joan had watched Ruth get dressed before leaving her room. Both servants not only wished to clean up before their work duties began this day, but they had made the decision to keep the harness, along with its replica phallus hidden in Joan's room.

Laying back and resting her head on the pillow, Joan stared up at the ceiling. The images of last night with both Rufus and Ruth ran through her mind's eye. She enjoyed the feeling the knight had given her especially when he sought her lewd remarks from his tactics on taken her and giving her pleasure. How he had made her beg for what she desired. The unexpected fact that somehow unknown to her, she had found a fondness in Ruth made her both astonished, but also left her questioning her own feelings. It was undeniable that Ruth seemed loving with her soft, delicate touches, and more like that of her true love, Matthew. The young woman knew how to please her in a tender and sensitive way, where Rufus used his manhood and the roughness that was in his nature to deliver pleasure to Joan. She was taken aback on how she had found fancy in the feel of a man's phallus and the pleasingness of a woman's vagina.

Closing her eyes, Joan called back to memory the times she had shared with Matthew coupling all night long. Her hand finding its way to her breasts as she imagined him touching her. While fondling her hard nipple, she slowly slid the other hand down her belly. Bending her legs and spreading them, Joan's finger found her hot nether region. She inserted a digit followed by a second and a third as she imagined Matthew pumping into her.

Small groans of pleasure came from the woman's mouth, and in time her hand found both a rhythm and speed. Her moans matching the pace of her digits as Joan's ass flexed and thrust into her plunging fingers. The image of Matthew above her faded out only to be replaced by Ruth working to seek Joan's release. Almost instantly the woman grunted and her body shook as she opened her eyes.

Staring at the room's ceiling while catching her breath, a smile crossed Joan's face as suddenly an idea crossed her mind. The woman already taking full knowledge in knowing that her desire to be with Matthew was plagued by his need to sire a heir, or risk not only having a city rise up against his rule but actually the whole of England. Joan's womb had proven its barrenness, and no matter how hard Matthew tried to plant his seed in her, it just would not take root denying a child to grow in her belly.

The woman would choose her love any day over his forked-tongued cousin and the knight's huge phallus. She discovered the prior night that she had found fancy pleasuring and being pleasured by another woman. Already her fondness for the blonde-haired servant, Ruth, was growing inside her body, and for some reason she couldn't wait to couple with the young woman again. Joan had come up with an answer to her and Matthew's problem.

The young king wished to be with Joan and she yearned for him. The servant had also discovered in a short time that she coveted for the touch of the other woman. With Joan being twelve years the senior to Ruth and realizing that due to the young woman's youth it most likely meant a fertile womb, along with being witness to the blonde-haired servant's love for both men and women, Joan would need to speak to Matthew and Ruth alone at first and then together for her plan to work. Her idea still allowing her to be with the king even though he sired an heir with another woman. Joan would seek sexual pleasure every night in the royal's bed with King Matthew and Queen Ruth. In her mind, the only way she could still be with the young man was to share him with the young woman. Besides, the way she was feeling towards Ruth, Joan had made up her mind that it wouldn't be a bad thing neither.

Quickly bouncing out of bed, the naked woman found and hid the harness she and Ruth had used on one another. Joan wished to be cleaned up before she faced the day's duties ahead of her. The idea of being taken by the two caused a moistness in between her legs, but Joan brushed aside the urge at self satisfaction knowing that she had to get things started at least with Matthew.

Strolling down the hall to the Queen Mother's royal chamber, Joan seemed to glow as her plan came together more and more in her mind. The fact that she had not come upon Duke Paul for most of the day definitely brightened her disposition, but she took heed in the knowledge that her body would be used in his presence this night again. At least Rufus' manhood would be there, which was something she had gotten used to and had actually learned to like. Her fancy was not for the man himself, but she knew only fondness over his huge weapon. Joan had also run into Ruth four times already, and along with the young woman verifying her attendance in tonight's activities, the two had actually stolen some kisses fueled by their newly acquired passion for each other. The older woman never mentioning her plan until she spoke with King Matthew and he agreed on the love triangle.

Stopping in front of Margaret's door to her room, the woman knocked only walking in when invited. She was hoping to speak with Matthew about her idea while at the same time wishing she and Ruth would join him in his bed maybe as early as this night.

Closing the door softly behind her, she turned only to have the enlightenment she felt stolen from her when the sight of the teary-eyed king sitting in the plush chair met her gaze. Fear grasped her for a moment as the woman quickly looked to Margaret's unconscious form on the bed.

"What be wrong?", she anxiously asked walking up and standing in front of the seated king.

Gazing into her eyes, Matthew's tears began to flow down his cheeks. "Mother is dying." Wrapping his arms around the woman's waist, her former lover buried his head into Joan's lower stomach. The emotion to cry taking over him, as the servant could not only hear his anguish but could feel his pain as well.

The display of vulnerability causing the woman to wrap her arms around his sobbing head and lower hers while her eyes knew only tears. Now was not the time to speak on her idea.

Some time pass between the two's embrace before Joan in a mother-like fashion delicately released her consoling clutch on the king and lowered herself to her knees. She gazed into his watery eyes with tear-filled ones herself.

"Margaret suffers right now my love," she softly spoke to the young man. "She longs for reprieve from her fight, and one not to our liking might be in her leaving us." Her words stinging as much as they held the truth. "Do not forget, even though Margaret may lose the battle against the infection now laying siege on her body, the Queen Mother has won a war versus an assassin's strike," she tried to point out.

"Why do you mean?", Matthew asked between sniffles. "My mother dies from that same attack's arrow."

Joan laid her hand on the side of Matthew's face, "Your mother conquered a murderer the moment she sacrificed her welfare to protect her son, and by doing so foiled some type of plot to rob England of its king. The Queen Mother knew the country would fall into turmoil. She not only took the arrow in her attempt to rescue you, but Margaret has saved all of England." Joan's words causing Matthew to ponder their truth. His eyes glancing over the woman's shoulder letting his gaze fall on his unconscious mother on the bed. He knew she was right.

Looking back to Joan still kneeling in front of him, he confirmed his feeling of loneliness. "I miss her and my father already." The young man pausing before he continued, "I also know the absence of your touch." Matthew slowly leaned towards his true love and tenderly kissed the woman. With no hesitation, the servant returned the display of his true feelings with a show of her own.

"I have longed for you Joan and desire your touch," the king admitted.

"And I you my love."

The two melting into one another, as Matthew sought solace from his imminent troubles at hand, and Joan attempted to find sanctuary from the castles evil.

Joan had remained with Matthew for a long time that day in the Queen Mother's chamber leaving only to retrieve a meal for the two of them. They had sat making small talk as they ate, and he had eventually kindly asked her to take her leave for the night only to return to his side in the morning. Before Joan left, the lovers embraced in a hug giving each other a passionate kiss. When the woman carried the tray with the dirty dishes on it out the door and passed the two guardsmen, the glow that she originally had earlier relit in her disposition. Joan believed her idea may work out for everyone involved. The woman making her way to the kitchen to drop off the dirty, supper dishes.

King Matthew took up his mother's hand in his before softly speaking to the unconscious woman. The young man somewhat coming to grips after spending a good amount of time speaking with the one who was his personal servant, his trusted companion, but more importantly his lover. Joan had come back to him when he needed her most and he never wanted to lose her love again. Matthew was willing to be the woman's life partner even if it meant ending his ancestor's blood reign as King of England. He knew his mother would be extremely upset. Staring at her for a moment, he spoke to her knowing that she had sacrificed herself for him, and the young man knew that his mother tried to hang to life more for Matthew's benefit than her own. It was time for her boy to become a man. Where once he clung to her leg seeking comfort, Matthew knew his mother needed to find peace that only the Lord could give. It was time for the young man to release his panic-stricken grip on her and stop being afraid to be alone. Matthew knew he had to let go.

"I love you mother,..." the young man began. Already his eyes fought to hold back the tears. "...and I know you and father have always been proud of me. I humbly give you many thanks for the life you have given to me along with the knowledge you have taught me over the years. How you always lifted me when I fell and never stopped protecting me from a world that knows cruelness and hardships. You have instilled in my heart compassion and love. I am a better man because of you and your ways mother, and thanks to that I have grown blooming like a flower in your sunlight," her son smiled behind the tears that fell from his eyes. The young man's vision obscured through watery orbs. "I take heed in knowing that you have always worried over me and I owe you my life. I beg for you to end your troubles for me for I am no longer a child, but a man who can handle these times ahead, so it is time you remove the bothers from your brow. You must seek father and with him the peace you so much deserve. I will be well," tears ran like rivers from Matthew's eyes, as he pecked the back of her hand and softly placed a kiss on his mother's clammy forehead. "I love you mother. Leave your torment behind and find father. For he shall be waiting for you with the Lord. The Almighty surely needs an angel in the Heavens the likes of you." The sobbing son placing another kiss on his unconscious mother's forehead.

Matthew sat holding his mother's lethargic hand for the next hour until Duke Paul had entered the room. The cousin's hawk-like gaze meeting Matthew's watery eyes, as the king relayed the somber news. "The Queen Mother has passed from this world," her son's heavy heart knowing only grief.

Shortly after Joan dropped off her tray of dirty dishes in the royal kitchen, the woman made her way to the duke's chamber only stopping to grab the harness for her and Ruth's pleasure. She hid it in a piece of wrapped cloth and had placed it in one of her clean dress pockets. The thought of her and Matthew being together ran through her mind. She only wished Paul would just disappear.

When she finally arrived at his room, and was invited in by a half-naked Rufus, Joan saw Ruth present but the duke was missing. The lantern on the table was unshuttered bathing the chambers in light. She made her way over to the other servant embracing her and passionately kissing a fully nude Ruth.

All three entertained themselves with a little foreplay, as the young woman and the knight helped remove all articles of clothing from Joan. Standing in the middle of the floor, the newcomer draped her left leg over Ruth's right shoulder, as the young woman kneeled in front of her starting to feast on Joan's womanhood. She could feel Rufus' hugeness rub up and down the crack of her ass while he kissed her neck. Joan was more than happy Duke Paul was not present and the question of where he was soon slipped from her mind.

Rufus, Ruth, and Joan had spent some time with each other, and the fully illuminated room seemed to up the sexual desire amongst the three.

The fact that each one was clearly able to see the others appeared to make the moment hotter for all involved.

The man finally directed Ruth to lay on the bed with her legs hanging off the edge of the mattress. He had Joan place herself on her hands and knees facing the young woman's legs disappearing over the foot of the bed, while he positioned himself behind the woman closer to the head of the furniture. Joan's body starting a little when Ruth gave her clitoris a lick from below. The blonde-haired woman on her back taken all the man's phallus in her mouth before using her hands to guide it into Joan's awaiting vagina. Ruth hearing the woman's moan while watching her fleshy sheath stretch swallowing all of Rufus' weapon.

Slowly he rocked his hips into her, and Joan could feel him deep inside. Her moans coming at every thrust, but when she felt Ruth's tongue make contact and massage her puffed clitoris, the sex slave's moans turned to groans. The young blonde-haired woman watching and feeling with her tongue every time the knight thrust his hugeness into Joan.

Rufus began to pick up speed increasing force to his plunges, driving himself into Joan's vagina. The slave not only trying to meet his thrusts with ones of her own, but also trying to push her womanhood down onto Ruth's hungry mouth. The young woman wrapping her arms around Joan's ass adding to her movements. Joan's pleasure became so intense, she had stopped feasting on Ruth's nether region and raised her head up grunting her declarations at the ceiling.

"Oh yes!," she grunted. "Take me you two! Feed me your mighty lance knight!", her cries filling the room seeming to cause an added excitement to both Rufus and Ruth.

Joan lowered her head to feast on Ruth but her loud grunts kept impeding her hungry tongue. The woman repositioned one of her hands before sliding three digits into Ruth's wetness. The pleasured feeling caused the young woman on her back to attack Joan's clitoris with a renewed vigor. Her arms working to not only pull the woman above downwards, but helping to impale her with the knight's manhood. If it wasn't for his hands on her hips pulling Joan into his thrusts, along with the assistance offered by Ruth's embracing grip, the mounted woman would have been driven from the bed. Joan swearing she had never felt Rufus' phallus bigger, wider, and deeper inside her.

"Yes my lord!", she cried in ecstasy.

Sliding a fourth finger into Ruth, the woman's digits began rocking the young woman's body as they searched to feel her womb.

The crescendo between the three had almost reached the point of release, and Joan had never even with all the times her body had been mounted, ridden, nor, ravished come to know pleasure like this. She was lost in her lust, and the feeling of both Rufus deep inside her and Ruth's tongue brought her a climax that she had never experienced in the past.

Rufus drove into Joan so hard, with the aid caused by the woman on top pushing back while being pulled by both the knight and Ruth, that he buried his long, thick phallus the deepest it had ever touched Joan. His weapon's tip seemed with the help of the young woman's tongue action to hit a target causing the slave a release like no other. Her yells like that of an animal's guttural screams.

"I feel you deep inside me! Please plant your seed my lord! My body belongs to your mighty weapon!", Joan's body shook as she felt Sir Rufus pump load after load of his hot seed into her. Her vagina hungrily milking the man for every bit of his deposit. The woman's buried fingers bringing a loud groan from Ruth underneath her. Joan was both still being worked over and ridden by the knight, as she noticed the two men standing in the doorway to the duke's chamber. Her gaze falling on the betrayed stare of her watery-eyed lover. Behind him unnoticed to her, was a smile from ear-to-ear on the raptor-like face of Matthew's cousin.

Joan's first thought was to jump up, but with the other two still holding her as they pleasured her body, a tear began to form in the corner of her eye.

She had let the Devil tempt her introducing her to an uncontrollable lust, and Joan knew when her true love needed her the most, the woman had deeply hurt him.

Like Judas, Joan had used the dagger known as betrayal to strike a fatal blow to another king.

Chapter 31

"What be this?", shouted the duke feigning both his degree of acsending anger and surprise at the three on his bed. His inquiry snapping Matthew from his stillness. "My apologies cousin. I only expected Rufus, not any festivities in my chamber none the less!" Paul knew that the presence, along with the sight and hearing of Joan's damning words while being willingly taken by another, was the final ounce of weight needed to completely crush the king's heart. The duke silently congratulating himself for not only breaking the woman that Sir Rufus now mount, but using the broken woman to destroy any belief Matthew had in his lover. His soul only knowing betrayal and loneliness for sure now.

Blinking his eyes from the sight of his lover finding obvious pleasure at the hands of another man and a woman, Matthew changed his betrayed look not only in his eyes but also on his face, to a stoic, kingly expression. The young man successful as he removed any telltale of pain from his voice.

"Forgive me Sir Rufus," he humbly apologized with a bow. Backing from the room feeling both hurt and anger build up inside his body, Matthew turned to Paul. "I tire my cousin finding myself in need of rest," the young man offering the duke a slight nod of his head. "On the morrow the Queen Mother will be prepared for sepulchering."

Glancing from his cousin's hawk-like features to the three on the bed before returning his gaze back to Paul, the king added, "Hence it appears that your presence is required, and by the looks and sounds of one so spirited, Sir Rufus may be able to use your assistance." Matthew remarked as he turned and took his leave. His words cutting Joan to the bone.

Joan's tears ran down her face as her gaze met the betrayed stare of her true love. The woman had heard his hurtful words before he turned his back on her and walked from the doorway. She knew that her lust-filled declaration directed at the knight had pierced the young man's heart. The sight of her being ridden only added to the damning evidence against her. The woman catching the news of Margaret's passing only seemed to douse her fiery promise of never leaving him alone. Joan had sworn to protect him and keep alive the young man's spirit, but ended up killing his soul.

Joan desperately wanted to jump up and chase after him, but she was unable to if she had tried. Rufus held her in place with his limp manhood still in her, along with Ruth's embrace, who even now placed delicate kisses and blew small breaths on her excited clitoris. The knight knowing that the show of her restraint would be seen as a lack of caring for her lover's feelings.

Closing the door behind him and securing the lock, Duke Paul shared a devilish grin with Sir Rufus followed by a short series of claps.

"Very well done my friend," Paul smiled as he disrobed. "Not only has Joan confessed her body to you, but her king has given us the gift of her company," he smiled kicking off his boots.

Joan feeling Rufus' phallus start to rise again in her body while Ruth offered several slow licks. The woman, who even though she had tears falling from her eyes automatically felt her body start to respond to the knight's soft thrusts with rocks of her own .

Joan watched as Paul completely stiff now strolled over to the bed looking straight at her. A devilish smile emanating from his approving face.

"Why thank you Joan!", he sarcastically responded to her unspoken words. "I know Ruth probably needs not the aid, but it fails not to help."

Grabbing the woman by the head, the duke forced her mouth onto his manhood bobbing her head on him several times. Removing her lips from him and releasing his grip on her rocking body, Paul placed Ruth's legs on his shoulders.

"You do the honors," Paul said to Joan, who now had soft moans coming from her as she once again started to be taken from Rufus and Ruth.

Taking the duke's stiff manhood in her right hand, the watery-eyed woman, who once again had been betrayed by her body, fed Paul to Ruth's vagina. When it was engulfed by the young woman, Joan grabbed hold of her ankles as they rested against the duke's shoulders. Soon the sounds of pleasure filled the atmosphere, as the devil and his knight from hell impaled the fallen, castle's servants. The men's erect phalluses piercing the women like Satan's trident. Joan's body desired the fleshy pleasure while her heart and soul longed for death.

King Matthew's tear-filled eyes were believed by all he encountered in the castle's corridors to be the cause of the loss of the Queen Mother. From all the palace's servants to the highest knight in the place, everyone who had the opportunity to know the deceased woman was filled with a heavy heart along with a somber mood to match. Queen Mother Margaret not only gave her life to her son, but her presence and maternal love over-filled all in the royal household.

The king offered a slight nod to the two guards posted outside his chamber as he unlocked the door and entered the room. Closing the portal, the young man's eyes gave way to his oncoming tears, as he tried to make his way across the dark room to his bed. His obscured sight blurring out the mattress' edge.

Standing in front of the largest piece of furniture in the lightless chamber, Matthew collapsed onto it. The king crying into a pillow from his heart only knowing aloneness and pain. The loss of his father, his mother, and the young man's only love in less than a week was more than he cared to bear at this time. He had caught Joan being pleasured by another man and liking it. She had openly declared her body his for the taking.

The image of her breaking their coupling the first night Sir Rufus had stayed as an invited guest of his father came back to memory now. The young man not fully understanding at the time why she had rarely been seen the day after that night, but by the way she acted when he had seen her being ridden like a charger and what she professed solved that mystery.

Through his pain and muffled sobs, King Matthew realized now what needed to be done not just to continue his father's bloodline, or for the benefit of his country, but for his own self. The young man coming to grips with not only ruling England as its king, but picking up the shattered pieces of his broken heart and putting it back together again. He needed to make it whole replacing the loneliness he felt now with a completeness that only a family of his own could provide. The time to wed and sire an heir of his own was now. The king would have to arrange his own marriage, but tonight wasn't the time for vows and promises between a man and a woman. No, this night was about grieving and letting go.

Into the wee hours of the morning, Matthew's pillow became a sponge. The young man crying his eyes dry.

Chapter 32

Joan had lost track of the numerous times she had been taken by Duke Paul, Sir Rufus, and Ruth before the king's cousin had thrown her naked into the hallway.

"You have served your purpose," he condescendingly stated while looming over the woman seated on the corridor floor. A distant look filling her eyes, as she stared at his hawk-like face. "Ruth will relieve you of your duties now," Paul grinning his confirmation while tossing her, her clothes. The sounds coming from Ruth being used faded out, as the duke closed the door.

Joan's thoughts were locked on Matthew's betrayed expression as she remained seated on the floor for a minute blankly staring at the closed portal. Gathering her clothes and quickly slipping her dress over her head, the woman made her way to her own private chambers to clean up. Joan wanted to go see Matthew, but seed belonging to both men ran down her inner thighs. She was lost in her thoughts on her walk to her room, and Joan's eyes never left their distant connection with the rug covered floor. The heart broken and used sex slave retired to her chambers.

After washing up, Joan laid on her bed curled up staring at one of the walls. Her thoughts on her betrayal to her true love and death itself. The woman knowing the hurt she caused, along with the troubles she had experienced would exist no more upon taking her own life. Joan had dealt the final blow to Matthew's wounded heart murdering any desire he would ever have for her. She pondered over taking her own life. Joan knowing that dead people no longer needed or wanted anything. A lone teardrop ran down the side of her face and into her pillow.

Honour

On the following day the town folk of Hamilton once again gathered at the church to pay their respects for their beloved queen mother. Unlike Stephen's royal wake there were no inspiring speeches made, but only a king who looked troubled and defeated. Matthew had accepted his people's condolences and blessing as he stood in the same spot he had only two days prior. Today the king's mournful people only heard the words of the deceased woman's eulogy given by the priest. Only one person came to know a small bit of relief that day, and that wasn't until Sir Timothy had gotten King Matthew safely back inside the castle walls.

Joan had made sure she was by purpose absent when Matthew had seen Duke Paul off. The man would return to Scheffield, along with the accompanying blade of Sir Rufus, and the woman was glad that she wouldn't have to lay eyes on neither of them for at least awhile. Then again she thought the same thing the last time they had left. The image of the first night in the castle's kitchen where she and the duke had struck the deal to protect the servant and the king's secret tryst had come back to memory. Shortly after that is when she surprisingly realized she had sold her soul to Satan, eventually damning herself in front of the one she truly loved.

Knowing that at this moment, Matthew could be alone in his chambers, Joan started for his room and in no time at all was knocking on the quarter's door. Two posted guards stood on either side of the servant. Upon hearing the young man's invitation to enter, the woman walked into the chamber closing the wooden portal behind her. Joan's eyes falling upon Matthew seated in the plush chair with his back to her as he faced the open double doors to the room's balcony. The woman pausing a moment to swallow hard before she made an attempt at any words.

"My love, may we speak for a time?", her voice barely audible.

The young man's head slowly shaking. His voice carrying both an inflection of anger and disgust at this time. "You may address me as king or King Matthew, but nothing less," he paused before continuing. "Do you lack any understanding of that royal order, Joan the servant?"

Matthew's words cutting Joan to the bone while the woman felt as if all hope she had of trying to explain what had actually happened, and how she truly felt towards the young man rush from her body with an exhaled breath. The woman's lips quivered in pain from the staggering her body felt from the king's verbal punch in her gut.

Taking a moment to gather herself, Joan attempted to press forward.

"No my lord," she humbled herself before continuing. "King Matthew, may we speak for a time?", the woman beginning again.

"On what matter Joan?"

"On the issue of last night, and what you saw."

"I take heed in what I saw, and know there is not a word you can say in objection to that which my eyes took in," angrily answered the king.

"But it is not what you think," she pleaded.

Like a bullfrog leaping from a pad of lily, Matthew jumped from his seat and spun on the woman standing on the other side of the chair. "And what do you know I ponder?", angrily shouted the young man. His face's expression matching the rage his body felt.

Joan started and cowered from his anger. She had never been witness to this side of Matthew wrath, and tried to explain herself the best the woman could.

"I never gave of myself freely! They took me and plundered my body!"

"In accord with my eyes and ears woman, you helped the knight as he impaled your nether region while in your own words declaring your body to him!", Matthew yelled walking around the chair towards the woman. "Not the actions nor words of one who does not seek coupling! No. A woman not knowing only the pillaging of her womb or her virtues, but the ways of whores and harlets!" His fiery words cutting off and strangling Joan's pleading ones. "No, you found fondness in the way you were being mounted and ridden."

"But! But! You are wrong, Matthew!", tears flowing from the woman. Joan knowing that she had wounded him, and now faced a wall he had erected to guard his betrayed heart.

"What I thought was a dove was in real sight a bitch in heat!", the king's face only inches from the servants as he stared into her tear-filled eyes.

"For how long Joan?", he asked through gritted teeth. "Ever since you called off our coupling?"

Tears fell like rain from the woman's face as she nod the affirmation while she attempted to speak. "Duke Paul forced me, for he knew of us!"

"My cousin's knowledge lacked!", Matthew remembering the shock Paul displayed in the doorway to the room last night. "I saw his face for myself!"

"Please my love you must believe me!", she begged. "My words hold only truth!"

"Just as they did when Sir Rufus took you from behind?", Matthew stressing home the point. The young man knew he had struck the target in her and hit the mark dead in its center.

"No. You must hear me my love!", Joan sobbed uncontrollably as she reached for Matthew.

Her former lover quickly grabbed her hands and threw them down away from him.

"I have told you once," he growled his anger while his stare met her watery gaze. "Lovers we are no longer! I be your king and that title is how one such as you will address me!" Glancing from the servant to the door and back to Joan, King Matthew added, "Now that Sir Rufus is gone, one such as your kind should not lack the difficulty in finding a new knight to mount and ride you."

The hurt and pain caused by Matthew's stinging words brought forth a reaction that the woman never saw or felt coming. Joan's hand swiftly left her side slapping the king across the face before joining the other one in front of her mouth. The servant frozen in place wearing an expression of shock.

The king turned his head slowly, and his angered stare bore into the surprised woman. "Thank my father and mother that I choose to overlook your offense this night. Take heed in my words Joan, if you ever in the future commit even the slightest of touches against me then punished you will find yourself," the king spoke through clenched teeth. "I will not look kindly upon you and you will share your dinner with the dungeon's rats. You are no longer my lover, but a servant that lives here. I suggest you decide what kind of chamber you want to lay in at night."

Joan knew their audience was over. Her former lover had made up his mind. No matter what, she realized he would not be changing it anytime soon.

Lowering her defeated head while crying, the woman offered a curtsey. "Am I dismissed my king?", she quietly queried.

"You may go,..." affirmed the steady voiced king, "...but Joan, I suggest you ponder over my words."

"Yes my lord," she sadly choked out the words. "Thank you, my lord."

Matthew watched as Joan approached the door before burying his final dagger. "Oh, and by the way Joan."

His defeated former lover turned, "Yes my lord."

"I am relieving you from all your duties as my personal servant. I will no longer require your daily obligations," his eyes never leaving the woman. "However I do consign you to become the personal servant to the queen upon my marriage in the weeks forthcoming." Matthew's piercing revelation driving the point home and robbing Joan of any final thought of the two sharing each other in the future. The king's word's making the woman dizzy as she knew there was to be no reconciliation between the two.

Opening and closing the door behind her, the woman passed in between the two posted guards and started down the hallway. When she turned the corner Joan's legs seemed to give out and she plummeted onto the corridor's floor. Leaning against one of its walls, the servant buried her face into her hands. Her chest bouncing as she wept uncontrollably. The woman thought to herself how she had lost her adopted father and mother to an assassin's arrows, and now her lover to another's piercing weapon.

Matthew witnessed how his spoken words to the woman were equal to that of a knight's killing blow. Their bluntness like that of a spiked mace crushing an enemy's skull. Returning to his seat, tears fell from the young man as he recognized that within the short time he had been king, and what he had just done to Joan, this night would be the hardest choice of his whole rule.

Chapter 33

Lynn's body bounced several times as the young woman's eyes took in the sight of the carriage's interior while it carried her from her house to the castle. Not only was she surprised beyond belief when the majestic coach had reined to a stop on the road in front of her cottage, but the idea of being formally invited to the palace by King Matthew himself was still unbelievable. The two had spoken with one another throughout the years during church services, and the Bradford's had recently attended the two wakes for the king's deceased parents. The notion that Matthew sought audience with Lynn, and she was on her way to the palace, was a vision that the young woman would have never dreamt about in the next half-a-dozen lifetimes.

"This is pleasing to one," the young woman openly speaking her declaration while glancing around the carriage's plush interior. "Would you not agree father?"

"The question you should be seeking is; For what reason would the King of England have to summons me?", he anxiously remarked.

Lynn raising her eyebrows as she pointed out an obvious distinction to Charles, "King Matthew did not summons me father, he invited me. One summons a dog demanding its presence now; whereas one who invites another encourages their presence at some future time." The man's daughter smiling at the clarity she had given him.

"Invite is just a pleasant way that royals use the word summons," the bearded man stated leaning slightly in the direction of his daughter. "Are you of surety that you and Russell have never found yourselves in the limits that know only those from the castle?", Charles inquired behind squinted eyes that searched for a telling sign.

"Of course not father!", huffed Lynn. "Do you think Russell and I weak of mind that we would lack heed to century old prescripts and decrees?"

Sitting back fully against his seat, the young woman's father tried to quell her angry astonishment. "I only query to your summons," he explained.

"Invitation!", she corrected.

"Whatever it be you call it!", the frustrated man's gaze falling on his daughter witnessing Lynn calmly sit back in her plush seat.

"Thank you father," she smiled knowing that the battle of words was won by her.

"You are your mother's daughter!"

The young woman knowing the man's two biggest characteristics were the shared traits of a worry-wart and at times a blow hard.

Still wearing a grin of victory on her face, Lynn accepted the words as if they were a compliment. "Thank you father, but I am also of no doubt your blood," Charles' daughter pointed out before blowing him a kiss.

Her father appearing as if he would jump from the moving carriage just to seek a reprieve from the victor's smile, but knowing with his fortune the door would probably be jammed and unopenable.

Both Lynn and her father stepped from the royal coach and made their way up the castle's stairs escorted by one of the many servants. The two's faces both wearing an awe-filled expression at the size and grandness of the king's house. The palace's splendor becoming more magnificent when they were led though the wooden double doors and into the main greeting foyer. The young woman believed that just this one room appeared to equal in size to their whole cottage. Both Lynn and her father eyed the murals on the walls along with the stately, purple rug with the gold fringy border that they walked on now. Nobility seemed to emanate from everything in the chamber.

"I see my guests have arrived," came King Matthew crossing the foyer to meet and greet the young woman and her father. "I find gladness in your acceptance of my invitation."

Lynn's lips turned up in a smile as she and Charles shared a quick glance at one another. Her father's face less than enthused with the victory grin.

The three dropped to a knee.

"Your majesty," the servant's head bowed.

Matthew offered the man a returning nod which was an unspoken sign granting the servant dismissal.

The greeter taking his leave.

"Please rise," he humbly requested. "You folks are my guest."

Taking up the young woman's hand in his, Matthew gave it a soft kiss above her knuckles. "Thank you for coming Lynn and Sir Bradford," he added releasing her hand and smiling towards the man.

"Please allow me to show you around the palace."

"I would fancy that sire," Lynn's face radiantly glowing finding fondness with the idea. "My father and I would be honoured."

"Sir Bradford," the king respectfully addressed the young woman's father.

"After you my lord," humbly smiled Charles.

"Very well," agreed Matthew as he and Lynn started side by side across the room followed by the man.

The Bradfords eyed their noble surrounding all the while they briefly strolled about the castle with Matthew. For more than a couple of hours the three just leisurely walked sharing conversation, along with outbursts of laughter. Even worry-wart, Charles enjoyed the royal trip and like both King Matthew and Lynn, had missed spotting the teary-eyed servant watching from behind one of the majestic hall's stone pillars as the three left the great room. Joan's watery orbs taking in the sight of the one who would possibly be her love's queen.

"It be a beautiful, summer's day outside and I would be honored by your company if you would join me in partaking the mid-day meal in the royal garden?", King Matthew humbly inquired.

"That sounds very nice," smiled Lynn. "We would be honoured by your graciousness sire."

King Matthew offered the two a pleasing look accompanied with a slight nod. "Very well. This way," the royal extended an arm ushering the Bradfords in the direction of the kingly picnic.

King Matthew, Lynn, and her father had shared a delicious mid-day meal consisting of roast venison, vegetable soup, warm, freshly, baked rolls and red wine. For dessert the three enjoyed a jam-filled pastry just made this morning by the castle's royal baker.

"I believe you have a sister some years younger?", queried Matthew
"Yes my lord," replied Lynn. "By three winters."

"Then before we part ways at the conclusion to the our shared time this day. I will have a small basket filled and wrapped with some desserts for her to enjoy," sweetly offered the king.

"Why thank you your majesty," gratefully nodded the young woman accompanied with a bow of her head.

Taking a pause momentarily, King Matthew decided it was time to unveil the reason behind his invitation. "You must be pondering why I have asked for your presence here on this day."

The young woman held her inquisitive eyes on the royal. The king's words sounding more like the meaning of "summons" then "invitation." "As you are aware of, my father and mother have passed from this place somewhat before their time," the young man started.

"And again, please accept our humblest of sympathies," the young woman interjected, as she reached and found the top of his hand with hers for a moment. Lynn's show of compassion automatic.

"My many thanks to both of you," he added glancing between her and Charles. A feeling of warmness shot alive inside by the young woman's physical display of humanity.

Matthew continued, "I have swiftly found myself in the position that I am in now as we speak. The king of a country with neither an heir, nor a queen. I believe these attacks on my parents were attempts to acquire turmoil and chaos in our country that knows peace at these times."

"I, myself am in accordance with you your majesty," chimed in Charles.

"Thank you," responded Matthew to the Bradfords' head of household.

"Take ease in knowing that not only would I be humbly gracious, but in lieu of a dowry that I would be recipient to, I am more than aware of the situation. I am willing to compensate your family with land, coins, and a tax reprieve," the young king looking between the two seated at the table.

Lynn wore a puzzled expression on her face as she attempted to sort out Matthew's statement looking for what it was that he was trying to say.

The young woman's father seeming to have an idea where this discussion was heading.

"Please forgive me my king, but I know not what you are saying," perplexed the young woman.

Taking a minute to locate the words he required to sum up this audience with Lynn and her father, King Matthew finally found the epitome he needed. "I have always spoken of you as one who seeks adventure like Joan of Arc. Do you find truth in the words I speak?", he inquired.

"Yes Sire," she remained confused.

"Well I query Lynn Bradford, that now you seek to accompany me on an adventure as my queen. Not only do I yearn for someone such as you but your country needs a compassionate, giving soul like the one you can offer them. Will you offer me your hand in marriage and not just make me a joyous man, but a king along with a country, who longs no more for a queen?"

The inquiry seeming to not only hit Charles, but Lynn also, like that of a blow from a knight's charging lance strike. An atmosphere filled with both silence and tension fell upon the three at the table. A king asking for a commoner's hand in marriage was unheard of, and the young woman felt as if the air was hard to breathe. The weight of the man asking, along with England, seemed to be compressing down on her shoulders.

"But what about love?", she queried while her mind still desperately tried to comprehend what it is that her king was asking from her. "Do you not believe in love for another?"

"I have known love and have come to lose it more times this week than I would prefer to remember." Slowly taking her hand in his, the young man added, "Henceforth, we can learn to love one another on our journey from now to then."

Time seemed to stop from the anguish Lynn saw in King Matthew's eyes. In front of her was a young man who had just been beaten and battered with losses that could only be justly worded as devastating. The young woman had no notion that the young king, who only two nights prior was witness to his only love being pleased by another. In her own damning words finding fondness and proclaiming her body a field to be seeded by the man who took her.

Lynn's own thoughts on her one and only true love Russell, and how no matter what he did or how hard he tried, her lover would be unable to rescue her from the one-sided decision she needed to make.

"Your mother and I have only wished for the best for both you and Anne," Charles had told her when they had first entered the coach back at the castle. "This is a decision that really is no choice at all. I am truly sorry," her father placing a kiss on her forehead before sitting fully back on the carriage's seat. The ride home was quiet.

Gazing out the coach's window, a tear rolled down the young woman's cheek. She knew in her heart and soul that Russell was the only one she wanted to be with forever. Lynn thought about how King Matthew was a fine, young man but she never desired anyone but her true love. Lynn's heart, mind and body had been given to Russell, but now her king had requested both in honour and duty, the young woman's hand in marriage, along with her fertile womb to plant his heir in.

Her choice wasn't who not to honour, but unfortunately who to dishonour. On one side was Russell and on the other side king and country with her caught in the middle. Lynn's heart was experiencing a turmoil that England would never know even if strife fell upon the land. Tonight, the young woman had a decision to make, and even though she wasn't entwined in her lover's arms, Lynn wished this night would never come to an end.

Chapter 34

Russell leaned back on his horse and closed his eyes in an attempt to soak up as much as the sun's rays as he could. Today was a beautiful, summer's day, and the young man knew that soon this season would move onto the next. Fall would be here and with it the harvest, bringing an end to his free time. Russell would be working long hours with his father, and his shared time with his true love would be coming to a halt for a short duration until the farm's reaping and gathering had come to an end. For now, the young man was thankful that he had gotten to spend the sunny day with the one that could make it more beautiful than it already was. The time that he had shared with Lynn more precious than life itself.

The horse clopped down the dirt road, that even now shadows from the tree tops dotted the throughway on both sides. Sitting straight in the saddle, Russell witnessed a castle's messenger on horseback come from the direction of the Bradford's cottage. Clouds of dust kicked up from the carrier's mount, as it appeared obvious to the young man that there was information that needed to be relayed to the castle. Maybe even the city guard regarding the recent assassinations. The last thought causing a small hint of nervousness to dawn in his stomach. He heeled his mount's flanks pushing the horse into a canter towards the Bradford's home. Russell was not that far away from the place so it did not take long before he was reining the animal to a stop in front of the place. With his bow and quiver slung across his back and sword strapped to his hip, Russell dismounted and headed for the stone house's door.

The young man's knocks on the wooden portal come both loud and swiftly. One could almost hear the determination in his raps. Their summons ceasing to exist when the man of the house answered their call.

"Is all well Sire Bradford?," inquired Russell without making it to obvious to Lynn's father that he was trying to see past the man.

"Where be the barn's fire?" queried Charles as he opened the door to allow the young man in. His expression stoic.

Lynn's love never taking notice of how Charles avoided his question by not answering Russell as he made his way into the shack, and the man closed the door behind him. Sunlight shone through the open, shutter windows bathing the cottage, and a thin cloud of dust slowly danced through the air in its rays. The young man glancing around the small house, but finding no sight of his love or her mother.

"Who be it Charles?", queried Gwenyth yelling from her bedroom.

"It be Russell."

"Lynn will be with him in a minute."

"Sit down son," requested Charles while pointing to chair at the table.

The young man removing his bow and quiver, along with pushing the sword's scabbard to the side before taking a seat.

"Lynn will be with you in a minute." her father reiterated what the young man had already heard from Mrs. Bradford.

"Hello Russell," waved Anne

"My lady Anne," he winked while feeling a sense of relief for overthinking that something may be amiss.

The young man only waiting a short, quiet-filled time before Lynn made her way out of her parent's bedroom followed by her mother. The look of dried red eyes caused by tears upon the young woman's face. Automatically the feeling of angst reignited in Russell and quickly he rose from his chair.

"We need to speak my love," she informed him.

Lynn's confession was the first time her parents had ever heard her heart's declaration for the Daniel's boy openly. Even though Gwenyth and Charles knew of her desire for him, the two also realized this address between the young man and their daughter may be their last. The three Bradford's watched as Lynn's pain-filled smile, accompanied with a single tear rolled down her cheek, escorted the worry-faced young man out the cottage's door. Her family knew what was about to happen and a sullen atmosphere engulfed them. Even a teardrop escaped from her mother's eye.

Lynn rode seated in front of Russell, as the mount entered the forest. The two had previously planned on spending the day at the small cottage in the woods. The young man along with his father's aid were intending on beginning the renovations needed to transform it into a house for the newlywed couple after their marriage. Both Russell and Robert notioned that it would only require a couple of minute alterations, with the two more difficult ones being a free-flowing chimney and an outhouse. A vertical structure to a fireplace already existed, but it would definitely take some care giving as not to allow smoke to back flow into the cottage. The outhouse needed to be built anew.

Lynn had promised Russell that she would speak on the important matter between him and her, but she wanted to do it at the hidden cottage. The young woman had asked her love if they could wait until they reached their destination. The young man secretly yearned to discover the reason for the somber attitude, but again he was willing to trust her now like he had for years. No matter how bad he desired to know, her love would never push her or force Lynn in to uncomfortableness. Russell believed love is patient, so the two shared the silent ride. All the while inside each of them was the chaotic noise of knowing and not knowing what was about to happen.

The horse had weaved through some oak trees eventually making its way to a river bed. Following the water the mount came to a pond, the same one where Lynn and Russell had shared many hot, summer days swimming and cooling off in. Memories of those times seemed to slam into the young woman's mind as she knew that after today there would be no more of these memories to create.

"My love," softly spoke Lynn looking back over her shoulder into Russell's face. "I wish to stop here and speak on that which has plagued me all the night."

Signaling the mount to halt with the pull of its reins accompanied with two clicks from his tongue, Russell dismounted and assisted the young woman down off the horse. Wrapping her arms around the young man, the two embraced while they kissed each other tenderly. After several minutes, Lynn pulled back from her love and tears began to fall like rain from bursting storm clouds. The young woman sobbing uncontrollably. Russell still had no clue what was causing her sadness. The young man pulling her into his embrace offering his love comfort.

"Shhh," he consoled. "What troubles you my dear?"

His love weeping into his chest met his gaze. Her obscured vision was watery, as she made the hardest confession of her life so far. Lynn felt that in all the years Russell had always been there for her, she was about to repay his loyalty and love by breaking the young man's heart. The idea of wounding the one who had protected her since she was eight years old and had never let her down killed her inside. The young woman feeling that her words were equal to that of the arrows used to murder King Stephen and Queen Margaret.

"I cannot marry you my love," she cried.

Her words shocking Russell before stinging him to the bone. Russell's mind working hard to understand the world-shattering news.

"What?", he blankly stared desperately trying to comprehend the young woman.

Sobbing harder than she was only seconds ago, his love repeated her startling news, "I cannot marry you Russell and be your wife."

The young man felt that his heart had been ripped from his chest and was being smashed under a boot heel. The surrounding trees seeming to become instantly silent, as he tried to make any sense of what was happening. Russell stumbled back a step, or two, as if struck from a blunted weapon. His eyes glued to the devastated expression worn upon his the young woman's face.

"What do you speak?", he asked again in hopes of misunderstanding what she was saying.

Lynn realized she had torn this young man asunder. "King Matthew has requested my hand in marriage," she cried. "I feel for me to honour my king and my country, it has caused me to dishonour the one I truly love."

She suddenly felt her knees go weak and start to buckle. Within seconds darkness consumed her and her body went limp.

Russell witnessed his love's eyes roll up in her head seconds before her body gave way as she fainted. With the speed of a darting robin, the young man caught the young woman's dead weight. Both softly and slowly, he lowered her into the lush green grass.

"Lynn! Lynn!", he called to her while trying to use a hand to fan her face.

The young woman laid unresponsive to him.

Ripping a piece of cloth from his shirt sleeve, he swiftly ran to the pond and dunked it. Ringing out the excessive water, Russell ran back to Lynn and dabbed her face before placing the damp material on her forehead. The young man fanning his hand in the air as he attempted to help her regain her consciousness. "Lynn," he tenderly called her name.

Finally after a couple of minutes, Lynn's eyes slowly opened. The young woman was disoriented at first as she looked up into the smiling face of her rescuer. The memory of her world-ending confession slowly entering her mind even though the expression on Russell's face did not match her thoughts. Moments ago he wore an expression of devastation, but now it had been replaced with a warm smile.

"I am sorry I have hurt you my love. My heart knows only sadness," Lynn tried to explain while attempting to rise, but Russell's strong hands held her down.

"Rest for a moment," he advised her. "Your attempt to rise too soon may call forth more light-headedness."

The young woman instantly thinking that no matter how much pain and hurt the young man was in, it was her welfare and well being he always put first.

"No matter how good a person King Matthew was, he would never be the kind-hearted and honorable man Russell is," she thought to herself. She knew her heart belonged to Russell, and any attempt to grow to love Matthew would be like catching all the sky's rain in a cup.

"I desire not to be the Queen of England, but take heed in knowing you will always be the king of my heart," sniffled the young woman looking up into the young man's eyes. "Know that I made this choice not out of love, but rather out of duty. I own a responsibility to my king, and an obligation to my country," a tear rolling down the side of her face. "My father also grows older and has no sons to aid his toil around the farm. He will slow leaving him and mother to search for ways to live when all the years have sapped him of all of his energy. I cannot sit by and watch the man, who has provided for us all his life wish death to come in the stead of bearing witness to failing his family. King Matthew has offered father and mother a small country estate and a little amount of coin. After this harvest he will never have to toil again for the rest of his life in this world," Lynn sat up.

"This choice was not a notion that I made with ease," the sobbing young woman informed him. "I never intended to hurt you, and I beg you take heed in knowing that you will always own my heart and soul. I forever in this lifetime and the next love only you Russell Daniels. I pray that you will find forgiveness for me and not think ill of me." Inside, her heart was being bound by royal shackles.

Russell's heart was wounded and broken. The only one he had ever desired in his life was Lynn, but the young man knew she was unattainable to him now. That reality took hold of him like winter's grip on England. The thought of them together ran away from him like water over a fall. The completeness he felt in her company was draining from his soul and its void had already begun to fill with loneliness. After today and this last time, it would only understand the emptiness caused by the loss of true love.

The young man was devastated by her announcement, but he pondered on the helplessness and hopelessness his love must have felt. He knew deep down inside, Lynn never would have given up on their love for one another, and the truth that the young woman never could've made a choice to deny her king helped him to realize that her marrying Matthew was not about disrespecting or dishonoring him, but more about herself sacrificing her own wants and desires in lieu of the needs of a ruler, a country, and a father. Russell believed that Lynn had not forsaken his love dishonorably, but had honored the other three with her unyielding dedication to do what is right. Putting his own feelings aside, Russell did what he had done since he was ten years old and found Lynn alone and frightened with a twisted ankle in the forest. The young man would lend his love, and soon to be queen, support and protect her from the feeling of helplessness and fear.

Smoothing back Lynn's long, brown hair, as he kneeled next to her still sitting up on the ground, Russell gazed into her eyes while he softly spoke to the young woman.

"Do not fear my love, for today you have not betrayed me nor dishonored me," the young man offered a smile. "I will never think ill of you, and I ask that you accept my thanks not only for myself but for the whole of the country. You have sacrificed all in exchange to save many from chaos and strife, and to know that I shared love with one of England's greatest of queens, and she with I, knows only honour." Russell paused briefly and looked to the sky. "Take heed in my words Lynn Bradford. You have aided me in the man I am today, and no matter where our paths may lead us on our journey through life my heart, my loyalty, and the truth that I will never love another in your stead is for you to keep." Russell wiped away a tear drop under Lynn's eye and placed a tender kiss on her forehead before adding, "If the time we have left together is to be our last, then I wish to share it in the laughter and joy that you have always brought to me and not in a mood that knows only somberness." The young man stood up and offered a helping hand to the young woman. "My love will you honour me with your joyous presence, in that we may know a memorable finality to an adventure we partook in as one?"

Taking a hold of her love's hand, Lynn was helped to her feet. "Russell I want you to know...", her words drowned out, as the only love she ever knew slowly brought his lips to hers. The two wrapping their arms around each other as they began to passionately kiss. They both realized that the rest of the day would go by as quickly as it takes to exhale a breath. The two's tongues hoping to intercept the other's expired air.

Russell and Lynn had spent the rest of the day at the small hidden cottage in the woods leaving the place right before nightfall. Once again the young woman had offered her body to her lover, and like before he had refrained from taking her. The king would most likely be able to tell if she was a young virgin of virtues or an experienced woman in the bed, and Russell would not want Matthew to look upon her unfavorably or already spoiled.

The young man had dropped her off at the cottage, and the two shared a goodbye kiss. They both knew that the intimate show of affection signified the end of a love life for one another. Soon she would be the young man's untouchable and unattainable queen, and their time together would be forgotten to the ages.

The ride home for Russell was one of the loneliest and pain-filled treks that he would ever make. The young man was deeply lost to sadness and his thoughts causing him to lose track of time. Fortunately for him, the Daniel's horse had traveled this route day after day; year after year; and automatically knew its way back to the stone barn. The horse's footfalls were the only things breaking the silence.

Arriving at the cottage, Russell was zombie-like removing the mounts saddle and blanket, along with its bit and bridle. He was only going through the motions. He put the animal in its pen and barred the small stable's door for the night. The memory of his love's announcement running though his mind, as Russell now fought to hold back his tears. He had done earlier what Lynn so desperately needed, but now in his solitude her words assaulted him again and again over and over. The weight in her revelation finally being too much of a burden that he could shoulder and driving the young man to his knees, as soon as he closed the wooden portal to the cottage behind him. His head slumped toward the floor.

"Russell!", screamed his mother witnessing her son fall to his knees. Already Elizabeth was up from her seat at the table, and running for the young man. Her yell causing both Robert and Nicole to take notice, as she read to her father by the light of a lantern.

"Are you hurt son?", frantically queried his mother squatting down in front of him looking for any physical signs of what could possibly trouble her son.

Looking up through watery-blurred eyes as tears ran down his cheeks, Russell cried out his pain. "I have lost my love to the crown," he sobbed.

"What be it you mean Russell?", perplexed Elizabeth.

"Lynn is to marry King Matthew two days from now," informed the defeated young man.

A loud gasp of shock shot forth from both his mother and his sister. His father remained silent seated in his chair. Of all the women in England, Matthew could have picked to wed, it had to be his son's only true love.

No matter how good the young man could fire a bow or fight with a blade, he would have to yield the battle to the crown. Russell had no defense for a blow wielded by a king, especially one who was so revered by the people. A young man that his son would defend with his dying breath.

Robert rose from his seat and headed to console his son. The young man suffering a defeat that would eclipse every victory that Russell would ever experience. His son suffering a wound that time itself may never be able to heal.

Chapter 35

Sir Robin's head jerked from one side to the other while he made two bounces on the stone wall. The bird's eye taking in the sight of the young man standing in front of him breaking the roll he brought with him into small, easy to swallow portions for his little friend. Even the winged creature could somehow tell something was amiss with his human confidant by the strange vibe Russell's body language, along with his deflated stature put off. Sir Robin stole a look behind the young man at the tree where Lynn usually stood nearby.

"She be not there my little friend," sadly informed Russell. His head never turning to see where the avian had looked to, but instinctively knowing.

Sir Robin glanced to him as if waiting for an explanation to his words.

"Lynn will not be coming anymore. Our roads have parted and on the morrow she will be wed to King Matthew."

Russell's little friend giving a couple of chirps to the heart broken man, as he bounced towards his hands splitting the bread. When Sir Robin was directly in his line of sight, the bird took in the human confidant with its eye.

"She has made a choice based on honour and self-sacrifice," heavy-heartedly admitted Russell tearing the last piece of roll in two and placing both hands on the wall. "I take heed in knowing that the conclusion was one of hardship that had kept her awake on the prior night. I understand in, but my heart only knows pain and distress. Already I long for her," the young man mourned his loss.

Bouncing up and making slight contact with his human friend's finger, as his hand laid open on the bird's stone perch, Sir Robin offered the dispirited young man a short series of tweets. The small bird bringing a sad grin to Russell's face.

"Thank you my friend."

The two confidants standing in silence, as Russell used a finger to tenderly rub Sir Robin's small head. The young man not noticing at that time the bird's small display of empathy was actually a big show of support from the little winged creature. Right now Russell could use all the assistance he could receive bracing him against the onslaught of pain attacking him. Even though the two lifelong friends stood in silence, already Sir Robin's quiet exhibition of encouragement spoke aloud.

Lying in her bed in her own private servant's room, Joan blankly stared at the wall. The woman knowing that on the morrow she would lose her true love to another, as Matthew prepared to marry the young woman she had seen on the day prior strolling the castle's hills with the king. The servant knowing that her actions with Rufus and Ruth, along with the damning words she had cried out in her lust-filled frenzy of pleasure destroyed any chance of her in not only Matthew's bed, but his future as well. Duke Paul had pillaged Joan's body in order to ruin the love she shared with the king, and unfortunately for her, he had succeeded. The woman trapped so deeply in her own subconsciousness that she never heard the door to her quarters open and shut. It took half a minute for her to realize, who had walked over and stopped in front of her. Leisurely, as if Joan had not a care, she shifted her eyes upward and met the gaze of the young blonde-haired servant, Ruth, looking down upon her.

"I worry about you Joan," concerned Ruth. "I am so sorry that I aided in causing you distress," she apologized.

With her sight locked onto the young woman's apologetic gaze, Joan sat up on her bed. "Why did you aid the duke and the knight that night when King Matthew stood in the entrance way?", the woman accusingly queried.

"I had no knowledge that you and the king were lovers. Only later that night did I ever find out the truth. I honestly never knew!", Ruth pleaded.

"Besides you never ceased rocking back into Rufus' phallus the whole time so I believed you present by your own will."

Joan unfortunately knew the truth in the other's words. Even though her lover had witnessed her being ridden, the woman's body had never stopped attempting to milk the man for his full deposit.

"No my choice to be there was no doing of my own," Joan's head lowered staring into her lap. "Duke Paul discovered my secret with Matthew, and threatened to expose it to everyone unless I came to a bargain with him. He used a slight of tongue to disguise his intentions." Raising her head, so that once again her now tear-filled eyes met Ruth's, whose orb's had also filled with water, Joan's tone knew only vulnerability. "They raped me until I grew to know fondness of Sir Rufus' manhood. They broke my spirit and trained me to confess my fancy in his weapon. The same weapon the two used to not only slash apart our connection, but to bring forth those damning words that would run through and kill Matthew's loving heart."

Ruth squatted down in front of her.

Joan could not hold back her sobs, as the reality of the king's wedding and coupling with another was coming on the morrow. "Matthew is forever lost to me!", she cried while wrapping her arms around the blonde-haired woman coming forward and embracing Joan.

"Please forgive me my trespasses," weeped Ruth. "I never took heed in the notion that the duke blackmailed another."

The two servants locked in a vice-like embrace as they cried.

"What does Paul have to keep you bound to his wishes?", inquired Joan.

"He has threatened to have my younger sister, Antoinette, hung due to our mother breaking a family heirloom of his accidentally while she cleaned his chamber. Duke Paul said his father passed it onto him when his father died," sniffled Ruth. "The duke was on his way to reveal the unfortunate mishap to King Stephen, but he was going to reiterate the tale as one that excluded mother's accident and include an act of malice by Antoinette."

"But the king would have known his story lacked the truth," interjected Joan using her sleeve to dry her eyes.

Ruth shook her head. "Duke Paul said his uncle would believe nobility over one who served the crown."

Joan realizing he had spoken almost the same words to her before she made the deal with the devil. There was no doubting that Paul did not lack of incriminating threats to others, but who and how?

"I am truly sorry I hurt you," sniffed Ruth.

Joan gazed upon her not in an accusing fashion any longer, but only knew forgiveness for the young woman.

"I pardon you. I know now that your choices in the matter lacked as mine did."

The two women again embraced in a hug. Joan pondering how to expose Duke Paul for what he really was; a scoundrel possessing no honour; not a person of nobility.

Not only had the sun risen shining its radiance upon England, a wedding gift from the Lord above, but all the townsfolk of Hamilton came to the House of Worship to bear witness on the country's new queen. People filled both the church along with the streets, but on this day unlike the two earlier this past week, was one of happiness and joy instead of sadness and fear. It was a day that was dedicated to those of history when a king of royalty would take a commoner to be his queen. All of the royal guard were in attendance, and all had been informed by Sir Timothy to look alive. This was the kind of day that assassins found fondness with. It was their chance to be known forever throughout time.

The service was both particular to its distinctive cause of unity under God, along with the unstated obligation of the new queen to both her king and country. It was also lengthy as both King Matthew and Queen Lynn met and received the folk of Hamilton.

Queen Lynn enjoyed her time with her people just as Queen Margaret had done before her, and on numerous occasions folk both inside the chapel and outside in the streets cheered "Long live Queen Lynn!" The young woman breaking out in a smile when one group seemed to set off into chants after hearing the other half of the crowd. Even King Matthew offered his new wife a grin when he could tell the uplifting show of spirit by the folk appeared to initially embarrass the new royal. The only time throughout the reception line that a dark cloud hung over the young woman was when her true love came to stand in front of her.

Lynn stood staring into the eyes of Russell, as the young man gazed upon her majestic appearance. The young woman's long hair was braided into a roll on each side of her head, with its length still flowing down her back. She wore make up, along with a beautiful dress of white that seemed to trail behind her when she glided across the floor. Even King Matthew noticed the lack of a smile that was on her face when the young man stood in front of her. An unspoken tension filled the air from their locked gazes.

"You truly are the fairest of all royals that I have had the pleasure to lay my eyes on," Russell smiled at the only young woman his heart had ever known. His expression contagious enough to bring a grin to her face.

Lynn had more butterflies in her stomach now, than she had had when she married King Matthew. Somehow this young man chased them away with his words, but then again he always had a way of soothing her angst and fear. "Why have you the chance to gaze on many queens before I?", she grinned.

"No, but now I fear I cannot thanks to you," Russell bowed his head before adding, "My eyes will never know one as beautiful as you my queen."

Taking a knee in front of her, causing many alert glances from guardsmen, townsfolk, and even puzzling King Matthew, Russell looked into Lynn's eyes. "With God as a witness to my words, I swear my dying loyalty to you my queen. Take heed in knowing that at any time my life is yours to forfeit in the protection of your life and your good name. My sword and bow are yours to command as you see fit," the young man's words bringing the chapel to silence. "Your love may be unattainable to me now, but my defense in your honour will never lack. All you need do is call on me." Russell rose to his feet and bowing at the waist to his queen and former love took his leave.

Watching her true love walk away from the chapel, Lynn knew firsthand the truth in his words.

"Thank you Joan. That will be all," a night robed King Matthew confirmed while entering his chambers.

"Yes my lord," she responded with a torn heart The fact that she knew her former lover was about to consummate his marriage was unbearable.

Lynn, dressed only in a robe, stood near their bed. She knew what was to come next, and the fact that she had never coupled made her nervous inside.

Joan closed the door behind her, and Matthew secured it for the night before turning towards his new wife.

"Were you and the man in church close?", he serenely queried.

"Yes my lord."

"You can call me husband or Matthew my dear," he informed her while he approached.

Lynn only nod the affirmative.

"Please accept my apologies. For it was never my intentions to break up love," Matthew humbly offered. "I hope you can learn to love me and replace the void this all has caused with me."

As if an unspoken word directed the two newlywed royals, they both removed their robes and Lynn climbed onto the bed followed by Matthew.

"You are my first," she nervously informed him.

"And I promise to be gentle," swore Matthew. Already his manhood had grown hard, and the young husband placed delicate kisses on the young woman's neck and breasts.

Lynn soon felt pressure in her nether regions, as Matthew slowly penetrated her virgin body. Taking his time, the young man worked himself into her allowing her body to adjust while taking several pauses. The young woman's face grimaced, as for a short time her body only knew pain and discomfort. His phallus splitting her hymen for the new wife's first time.

Soon the pain and discomfort that Lynn experienced surpassed, and Matthew rocked his hips into her. In time slowly meeting his thrusts with rocks of her own. Her breathing built up to gasps until for the first time she heard her own moans. Lynn's mind more on Russell, the one she wished was on top of her. She shut her eyes and imagined it was him.

Feeling Matthew start to quicken his movement, Lynn experienced another first when she felt the young man's seed shoot into her cavity. The young woman knew no release on her first time, but eventually received that pleasure later when it was their third time coupling. Matthew sowed his seed all that night. England needed a heir.

By the time Joan had returned to her room, the woman knew that Matthew laid with another. Tears had already fallen from her eyes no matter how much she had tried to prepare herself for the inevitable, but at last she knew a little relief with the absence of Duke Paul's appearance from the castle. The young man not coming to his cousin's marriage to the new queen. The reason why, Joan had no clue and she didn't care.

Soon there was a knock on her door, and she got up to see who would be calling on her at this time of the night. Opening the portal, the woman's gaze took in the young blond-haired woman.

"I cannot slumber," quietly informed Ruth. "Would you find fancy with a guest?"

Stepping to the side Joan watched Ruth walk in before shutting the wooden portal.

"What ponders have you this night ?", queried Joan.

Pulling the leather harness with the replica phallus from her dress pocket, Ruth offered the woman a little smile. "Would you fancy in play with me?"

Soon Joan lay naked on her bed as she watched the young woman fasten the harness on and double check the buckles. A wetness had formed between her legs, and she watched Ruth climbing onto the pallet. The prone woman pulling her legs up bending at the knees with her feet flat on the bed accepted Ruth as she slowly fed the woman's vagina the imitation manhood. If Joan couldn't have Matthew then she would have the next best thing. Closing her eyes the woman imagined him and her in bed coupling. In no time Joan's moan's filled the air.

Chapter 36

It was a sunny and crisp, autumn day throughout Hamilton. Already the swaying leaves on the trees had begun to change their coloration from green to a rusty-red and orange mixture. Eventually the new fiery shades found themselves dancing on the ground when the wind blew. The trees shedding the dead foliage in preparation for the upcoming winter.

Along with the giants of the forest, most of the plant life had started to bunker down for the grip of the cold weather across the land. Only sporadic patches of bluebells and dandelions scattered the countryside in spots. Even the farm crops were being harvested leaving the soils barren of life. The town, along with its countryside, made ready for the inevitable; signaled by the diminished daylight.

Already two months had passed and England's new queen spent most of her days familiarizing herself with the castle's staff, but more importantly the place itself. Everyone from the palace servants to the royal guard had been taken with the kind-hearted young woman, and if someone amongst them hadn't they dare not say. If it wasn't for the fact that she was Matthew's wife, all amidst them would have sworn that Queen Lynn was a younger version of the young king's mother, Margaret. The young woman always treating them as if they were all equal family members, especially her personal servant. Joan had begun to develop a baby bump roughly a month ago, and even now in the privacy of the two month old queen, the woman seemed to always be graciously instructed to act at ease.

"But my queen," concerned the woman sitting in a plush chair watching Lynn tidying up the royal's room. "What if King Matthew should enter?"

"Was he not the one who allotted you to me?", the young queen answered the servant's question with one of her own.

"Yes my lady, but...", Joan's words trailing off due to the look Lynn was giving her. The young woman finishing tucking in the bed's sheets.

"Did the king speak on how you are to do as I wish?", the queen inquired taking a seat in the other plush chair.

"Yes my lady."

"Well I fancy you as you are now speaking with me," the young queen smiled. "Should King Matthew enter this room and find trouble with what he sees then I shall be the one he needs to deal with rather then the one fulfilling my wishes!" Lynn's words, along with her accompanying matter-of-fact body language, caused a giggle to burst from Joan. Soon the queen joined her in her laughter.

A brief moment past while Lynn glanced at the woman's puffed out stomach and became lost. She thought to herself about how she and Matthew had coupled just about every night since their wedding night; and how the young queen not only expected it but found fancy with the late night activity. Russell's love still remained in her heart, but she was attempting to learn how to love Matthew. The young woman imagining how a child of her own might aid her in reaching total fulfillment with her husband. Lynn could give herself fully as the queen to a country or her womb to an heir, but still her heart belonged to another from a life prior. The young woman not realizing that she had been blankly staring over Joan's shoulder until she heard the woman speak.

"My lady, do you not feel well?", her personal servant inquired.

The woman's voice returning Lynn back from her thoughts.

"Is all well my queen?", concerned Joan again.

Blinking at the pregnant woman, Lynn's lips turned up in a grin. "Yes. Yes. I am sorry. I just was lost in my own day visions is all," confirmed the queen.

"May we speak freely?", the royal questioning her servant.

"Of course my lady," came Joan.

"Do you find happiness with the one who sired the child now growing in your womb?"

The young woman's question taking the other woman by surprise. Joan was not happy that she had coupled with Matthew all that time and never once had his seed taken root in her womb, but after being mounted and ridden by Paul and Rufus one of them had planted the growing child in her belly. Glancing at the bump she now wore, the servant softly replied. "I know not happiness with the father of my child."

"He be one who lives and works here at the castle?", inquired Lynn.

Joan lacked the knowledge of even knowing which one, the duke or the knight, was the father of the child growing inside her. What she did know was that she was not about to tell the queen that she had been raped by the king's cousin and Rufus. "He is one from town that won fancy in my eyes," Joan lied. "I only wish that I had attained knowledge of him before instead of after," the woman depressingly smiled.

Leaning forward from her chair, Queen Lynn placed a hand on Joan's knee as she looked the woman in her eyes. "I am truly sorry if I caused you memories knowing only pain," she humbly apologized. "I give you my word that the king and I will aid you with your child."

Joan met her expression with a hopeful one of her own, but hidden down-deep inside of her, the woman servant did not want the bastard child sired by the devil nor his minion from hell. She would never be able to look at the innocent one without remembering the atrocities done to her by its vile transgressor of a father.

King Matthew had visited this room many times throughout his years growing up in the castle, and it still brought back to memory times both he and his father had shared in audience with one another. Even now the young man could still hear his father's voice giving him advice and teaching him about everything from wisdom to women. If it wasn't for the armored man that stood before him, King Matthew may have broken down in tears. The young royal still grieved the murder of his parents only months prior.

"Your majesty," addressed Sir Timothy with a slight bow from his hip. "Again another threat of death to your life has arrived at the castle's gates. This makes the sixth parchment in two months," the knight informed the royal.

"Are you of the belief that the French may be involved?", inquired the king. "A war has always lingered between our countries."

"I possess no definitive knowledge, but your words my lord speak the truth. The unfortunate in the matter of this is I cannot find the one, nor a group if one should exist, that is responsible," Sir Timothy shook his head. "I toil day and night, trudging in my efforts, to turn over rocks that would lead us to the discovery of the adder, but the serpent still eludes our efforts!"

The young man knowing the knight all his life and realizing the man had burdened himself with the pressure to catch those responsible for killing his parents. The load taxing the honorable captain to know only a weary brow overrun by constant worry.

"I do not trouble myself taking heed in the efficiency of your efforts my trustworthy friend," Matthew placing his left hand on the knights shoulder. "My father believed in you and trusted his life to your sword, and like him also will I."

"But my lord. I let King Stephen down and he paid for it with his life," Timothy's eyes starting to fill with water.

"Nonsense," peacefully spoke Matthew. "My father would contest your words, and even I find they lack the truth. Stephen has shared with me on many occasions on how you have come to his aid numerous times throughout the years whether it be with sword or council. He had told me growing up that there is no better man in England than you. Let us sit as equals this day and speak on times you and he shared in your younger years. It would do me well to not only take a moments reprieve from my grief, but to also hear happy tales from one who was the closest of friends with my father. Please sit with me Sir Timothy."

"You are your mother's son my lord."

Soon the chamber was filled with laughter from the two, as the older friend reminisced over times he had shared with the younger man's father. The knight's present burden relieved for a time by the narration of pleasant memories. King Stephen's life living on past his death.

Matthew rolled off of Lynn as the two had begun to catch their breaths after both of them found pleasure in their mutual releases. It was their first time this night that the king and queen had joined in coupling in attempt to produce an heir. Both of them knew it would not be the last. The young couple laid on their backs staring up at the bed's canopy gasping for air.

Lynn's thoughts caught in both the present and the past as she remembered a period in her life that now appeared lost and forgotten by time. An era not so long ago when she only fathomed herself with one man and not as an elaborate princess or queen, but of one who was a simple commoner or farmer's wife.

Lynn could see Russell's face in her mind's eye. The image causing her to wonder how he was doing and if he had found someone to replace the emptiness she had left in his heart. The young woman had seen him at church when the royal's had attended, and on each occasion even though she longed to speak with him when receiving and greeting the folks of Hamilton, her former love never took part in the opportunity. Instead Russell would always take his leave, and Lynn would be stuck hoping in his mother's advice. Elizabeth would always say, "He will come and speak with you eventually, but in his time. You know he has always loved you, and even though Russell understands and honours your decision, his heart still knows pain. Do not lose hope my queen. The day will come."

For Lynn it wasn't coming fast enough! The young woman desperately wanting to feel his hand in hers as the two shook their greeting.

Lost in her thoughts, the young queen almost missed when her husband addressed her.

"Are you aware I speak with you my dear?", placidly queried Matthew.

"I am sorry Matthew," she apologized. "I was lost in my thoughts considering the morrow is all."

"Is something troubling you?"

"No. No. It be nothing," explained Lynn. Turning to her side so she could gaze at her husband, the young woman placed a hand on his chest. "What be it my dear?"

"I find myself pondering the thought of taking a trip to see my cousin in Scheffield," revealed the young king. "The ride will have to be before winter is upon us and the snow begins to fall. I wish for you to accompany me to see the duke."

"I would find fancy with that notion," happily agreed the young woman.

It will allot me the opportunity to meet him personally especially since business required his attention and kept him away from our wedding day."

"Very well then. I will send a messenger to him on the morrow."

Matthew leaned over and gave his wife a kiss before positioning her on her stomach. He lie on top of the young woman and slowly planted kisses on her back as he mounted her from behind. The queen pulling for air when she felt her husband enter her body.

Slowly and tenderly, he rocked into her until his hip movements picked up speed. Moans of pleasure escaped Lynn until eventually seizing the mattress' sheet in a vice-like grip. The young woman could feel the sowing of Matthew's seed being shot into her. His release causing Lynn's body to react with one of her own. Even now in the heat of the moment with the pleasure the king was giving her, the queen's heart still wished the man inside her was her true love. Lynn wished nothing more than to be made love to by Russell. The young woman's body and mind had been swayed and purchased by obligation to a king, a country, and an aging man and woman, whom had provided for her all her life. No amount of coinage or land would ever buy Queen Lynn's heart. She had already sworn its love not to a royal man rather a common one.

Chapter 37

Both Russell and his father had spent many of the beginning days of harvest time toiling in the fields as they reaped the wheat and gathered potatoes. The daylight had started to shorten caused by the sun setting earlier and earlier. Even Russell's mother and sister aided in some of the daily chores, so the two men of the household could keep collecting the crops. It was now up to the women to shepherd the sheep every day, along with their daily upkeep of the cottage. After roughly a week of keeping the work up with very little breaks in the activity and most times toiling to after sundown, the Daniel's rode over to the Bradford's so Robert and Russell could lend aid to their lifelong friend, Charles.

"I am glad you two have come!", relieved Charles while leaning on his scythe wiping the sweat from his brow. "Now we will witness who gets the better of who," he added gazing out over the wheat fields.

"We would not miss this even if the king were to throw another tourney," remarked Robert with a smile and carrying his own curved bladed tool.

"Besides Sir Bradford, our ears took heed in hearing this be the place to be," added Russell with a wink.

Looking over the young man's shoulder, Charles eyed the sight of three other young men and two older ones walking towards them all carrying scythes. He knew the largest of the young men, Michael, along with his father owned the farm four away from his. The other two young men were the twins Peter and Paul accompanied by their father, Thomas Smith. He provided most of Hamilton with both milk and cheeses, and had been one of Charles' friends for many years.

"We have come to aid thee," smilingly declared Thomas.

The Bradford man realizing the extra hands were all in part due to the young Daniel's man. A wide grin grew on Charles' face. "My many thanks to all of you. Today I am truly humbled."

No one noticed Gwenyth and Anne, who had been lured outside by the small gathering.

"What be this?" perplexed Charles' wife looking amidst the group.

"It seems to be the works of Russell," her husband replied. Approaching the young man and embracing him in a hug, Gwenyth leaned up to his ear. "Thank you Russell. Your heart knows more richness than any king throughout the world." The woman holding back a tear as she realized it would be her husband's last harvest at this farm.

For over the thousandth of times throughout the years, Anne once again witnessed first-hand why her older sister had given her heart to the young man. She herself had grown to hold her sister's previous love in a fond way, and even now wished there was a way both her sibling and Russell could reunite.

"The crops know not how to harvest themselves," someone interjected.

"Those words know only truth," remarked a happy Charles. "What say all?"

"Onward!", excitedly came Paul.

For the rest of the day, and most of the next, the small group of laborers collected all that the soil had produced this season. Most importantly Charles and his family learned how much they meant to some in the small, farming community. The Bradford family knew they would deeply miss the Daniels when they moved to the country estate bestowed on them by King Matthew. Charles could only begin to fathom the absence that Lynn's heart knew for her true love by her self-sacrifice not only to the crown or her country, but for them and their future. The idea keeping her father awake long into the night, as he had already begun to miss not just his friend Robert, but also the young, honorable, Russell.

Lying on her side facing away from her husband Gwenyth stared into the darkness. Russell had once again come to the aid of someone in her family, and she pondered over somehow repaying his show of kindness with one of her own. Closing her eyes, she offered a silent prayer to God. Lynn's mother knew only He would have an answer. Soon the corner of her lips turned up as an idea entered her mind. The king and queen would be at church in three days. "My humblest thanks my Lord," she silently praised. "I ask that you guide my words and my ways."

On the following day the four members of the Daniels traveled to the Bradford's cottage, so both Robert and Russell could aid Charles in preparation of flailing the wheat grain and separating it from its stalks. The three would then bag up the grain into burlap sacks and it would be sold or traded at market. Usually the Bradford man would keep several sacks for himself, but where he and his family were moving to they wouldn't need it. Secretly he had other plans for it.

Elizabeth, along with Nicole, were also busy helping Gwenyth and Anne pack some of their belongings the family had decided to take with them on the move.

"I was not of any knowledge that Charles owned a sword," surprisingly came Elizabeth while holding up the weapon.

"Oh yes, but I ponder he would rather use the sharpness of his tongue in the stead of the blade," his wife laughed. "Even Charles could lay waste to the king's army with his irritableness."

Her words bringing laughter from the other three. The four women caught up in their moment of mirth that none of them paid any attention when Charles stepped through the door. Just the look of unknowing he was the object of the four's fun, as he glanced from one to the other brought forth more giggles from the foursome.

Forgetting what he had come in for the man rolled his eyes and stepped back out. Shutting the door behind him he thought, "That is the dilemma of women gathering. The lot eventually become that rivaling cackling hens." Charles stole a glance to the chicken coop. "And everyone ponders why I call the birds ladies," he added rolling his eyes. Sire Bradford made his way back to his toiling with still no memory as to why he went into the cottage to begin with.

It was late in the day when the three finally had finished their work and had decided to join the four women in the cottage. Charles had made plans to travel to Robert's place on the morrow to finish assisting him with his final stages of labor. The two men had decided that on the day after church they would go to market together and peddle off what they had decided to part with. The Daniels were just in the middle of their goodbyes to The Bradfords for the day when Charles decided to speak.

"Please. Everyone I have words to speak," informed the head of The Bradfords household. "If I may?"

Once all were silent and their gazes on him, Charles began. "My family and I not only found pleasure in knowing you folk, but also knowing a fondness in our heart for your friendship and kindness all have displayed to us throughout the years. Robert, not a man alive could have ever asked for a friend that I have known in you. Through all these past years at harvest you have always chosen to lend me your aid."

Letting his gaze fall upon Elizabeth, Charles continued. "My lady, I offer my humble gratitude for all the aid and love you have given to this family."

"Nicole you have always been like that of a third daughter. My home will remain a place that you may find shelter whenever you find the need to and are forever welcome in."

"Thank you Sir Bradford," Robert's sixteen year old daughter replied.

"And finally there be you Russell," pointed out Charles as he walked over to place a hand on the young man's shoulder. "You have always been like a son to me, and have treated both my wife and I with the highest respect allotted to a king. I cannot begin to count the times that you have been there for my family, especially when it came to Lynn."

Just the mention of his lost love's name caused a slamming blow to his heart, but Russell never showed outwardly the inner strike he reeled from.

"The kindness you gave to me on the yesterday was above and beyond a man's normal reverence for another," a tear starting to form in the corner of Charles' eye. Taking a brief pause to gather himself, he continued, "I am not one of words, but because our Lord has blessed me with two daughters and a friend with a son whom has always treated me as his second father, I give him this cottage and all that accompanies it."

Elizabeth couldn't contain her gasp at the Bradford man's revelation.

"But Sire Bradford! What about...", Russell's words cut off by the man's facial expression.

"I have no use for it any further. King Matthew agreed to a country estate for my family as you are aware of. Lynn did that due in part to the years creeping faster and faster by on these old bones. Anne will eventually marry and move with the one she is wed to leaving this place to only ruin over time. Pure idiocy and nonsense to leave it here to loss when someone deserving as you can use it son."

"I cannot find words," stunningly revealed the young man after almost a minute of silence as his brain tried to work out the comprehension of what just happened.

"Lynn would want it, and I desire it," Charles placed both hands on either side of Russell's face. "My daughter loves you son and always will. You must know that I rode with her in the royal carriage to the king's request, and when we sat in his garden partaking food and drink, she defended her love for you. The ride home was one of silence, and I take heed in knowing that her heart only knew pain as it wept for you and the decision she had to make."

Charles spoke the truth and everyone that was there knew he did. All had wetness in their eyes.

The Bradford man made a final appeal. "I know your heart aches from the loss but I beg you son, please speak with Lynn at church on Sunday. She desperately desires to hear your voice along with gazing upon your face in the stead of your back."

Teardrops fell from Russell's eyes at the man's request.

"You have always put her first, but at the chapel do it for both of you," Charles pleaded. Slowly he lowered his hands and walked away from the young man. Wiping his eyes with the sleeve from his shirt, the Bradford man added one more thing. "And accept the gift I offer to you Russell. It is what Lynn wishes."

Taking a moment to wipe his own face dry, Russell accepted.

Glancing up, Gwenyth silently offered a prayer of gratitude to the Lord. It would appear He had his own plan, and it was one that only required her silence. Her husband was the right tool God needed for the job.

The sun hung low in the sky, and it was already releasing the grip it had on the day to the full moon and the stars. Already one could tell the temperatures would be dipping into the lows tonight, and an accompanying wind had already started to pick up causing all of the Daniels during their ride home to lift their coat collars. It wouldn't be long now that they'd be in the shelter of their own cottage near a warm fire out of the nippy air. On the morrow the land may be introduced to the first frost of the season.

During the cart ride home, Russell seemed to be lost in his thoughts. In one night, the young man had come to own not only a cottage, but also a horse and a cart along with sixteen hens and a rooster. He understood that Lynn was behind the gift, but he still felt odd. The other reason for his silence was the issue that Charles wished him to speak with Lynn. There was no doubt that he loved the woman with all his heart, but it was still broken and he just wasn't ready to speak with her. Church was still two days away, and maybe Russell would have a change of heart. For now the young man's number one priority was to spend time on a trip through the part of the forest folks called "The Vale" with his three friends Michael, Peter, and Paul. Russell knew he needed to heal until eventually he and Lynn were a thing of the past, so he figured some time camping and spending it with his best friends could benefit him. Besides, at least the comic relief provided by Peter and Paul would always make for a good diversion from his ongoing heartache.

Pulling his coat's collar close to guard his neck from the wind, Russell had one more thought. He was glad that he and his father had fixed up the hidden cottage in the woods during the last couple of months. The four would be able to use it since the place was almost a midpoint allowing only a little more than half-a-day travel to "The Vale". He would be able to hunt for deer, and it wouldn't be impossible to return home with some butchered venison or maybe even a hide if the four stayed at the cottage in the forest. The image of a nine point stag rack mounted above the fireplace to his soon to be gift brought a smile to his lips. It also seemed to make him forget about the chilliness in the air.

Lowering his head in an attempt to hide most of his face behind the protection of the jacket and its collars, Russell was sure glad that he was almost home.

Chapter 38

Hamilton, England 1438
6 years later

Russell drew the bow's string back fully behind his ear and shut his right eye using his open left one to take aim for his upcoming shot. The weapon's strain from its pull no longer affecting him like it had first done when the boy began to learn how to use the missile-firing instrument. His years of practice and strengthening up had made Russell a very good shot with the bow.

Standing in the tree line, Russell used his one aiming eye to sight and lock on the wild boar making its way across the grassy bank of the slow, flowing stream. The pig's nose to the ground in search of a scent that led to food. Grunts and heavy, exhaling snorts following deep sniffs of the land escaped from the animal. The beast raising its large head displaying six inch tusks to the sky every now and then sniffing the air. The sixteen year old, a smart enough hunter to know now how to stay downwind from the boar.

Slowly and cautiously, Russell waited for the right time to let loose his nocked arrow. Only when he believed the swine was in the right spot, the shooter fired the bow. Its arrow flying from the trees and finding its mark in the pig's hairy body behind the animal's front leg. A high-pitched squeal erupted from the swine more from the surprising hit then from the actual piercing of its heart. The kill shot dropping the wild boar to the ground dead. Russell waited a brief time before running out of the tree's cover and exposing his position to the animal. The hunter wanted to make sure the pig was dead before he ended up having a wounded and angry animal regain its feet and charge him. The young man knew things could go bad quickly if he was careless.

"Father!", yelled Russell satisfied with the encounters outcome. "I have fallen one by the stream!"

Looking around the young man left the forest heading into the small clearing that ran the perimeter of the water. He jogged up to the dead beast to get a closer view.

"Father, I have got one!", he shouted a second time.

"I am coming Russell!", came a voice carrying on the air out of the surrounding forest.

Russell couldn't believe the size of the deceased as he got closer to it. The pig would definitely be enough to feed his family of four for at least a couple of days. "Got some pretty big tusks on it," he softly said as he examined one of the enlarged, protruding teeth.

Bushes and shrubs rustled in the background off in the distance and the young man knew his father had finally arrived to help him gut the pig and then bind it to a pole made from a thick tree branch. The three had brought it along on their hunt to carry a deer or a boar out of the woods and back home.

"Did you retrieve the pole and the rope?", he inquired while looking back in the direction of the noise. Russell's eyes grew to the size of gold coins when only twenty feet away stood another large, hairy, wild boar. Its own eyes set on the young man. Issuing a high-pitched squeal of anger, the ornery beast charged at the hunter kneeling next to the pig he had moments ago killed.

With the oncoming swine closing the distance between it and its prey, Russell had very little time to act. Still gripping the bow in his left hand, the young man moved with lightning speed as he reached for an arrow housed in the quiver on his back while propelling himself forward rolling over the dead boar. The hairy pig armed with at least five inch tusks of its own slashed at the hunter as it ran by. Russell's quick acrobatics allowing him to dodge out of the way of the animal's attack. The boar's momentum causing it to run right by the spot where Russell had been kneeling only seconds ago. Fortunately for the swine, one of its protruding bone weapons caught the young man's lower leg ripping his pants and causing Russell to suffer a superficial slice. Blood began to trickle from the shallow cut and the hunter now turned prey grimaced from the pain of the wound.

Russell had no time now to worry about the injury to his leg as he swiftly nocked the arrow he had retrieved and drew the bow's string back preparing a shot. Hitting the ground and landing on his lower back almost in a laid back position, the young man held the weapon across his body with the arrow's feathers drawn to his hip.

The ferocious animal spun quickly after its direct miss and came again at the elusive hunter. Rage in its eyes as it once again set its sight on Russell and charged. An angry squeal came forth from the boar.

Fighting through the burning pain in his leg, Russell took aim and concentrated waiting as long as he could making sure that his one shot would give him the best chance he so desperately needed to escape a mauling. The young man whispered a small prayer before letting loose the arrow. He watched as it flew towards the charging pig biting into the animal's head right above its eyes while at the same time a second arrow sunk into the middle of the beast's skull. The onrushing boar instantly dropped to the ground. Its momentum carried it forward plowing up the grassy terrain. Clumps of dirt shot skyward before it came to a rest only inches away from the original swine. The rage in its eyes now replaced with the unblinking stare of death.

Russell turned his head looking behind him to see his father rushing in his direction carrying his own bow and Lynn's father following carrying his bow along with the pole and ropes needed to carry the first dead boar home.

"Are you well son?", anxiously cried Robert.

The young hunter laid back on the grass and exhaled a breath of relief before he responded. "I am fine father." Gazing towards the sky, Russell softly added, "Thank you."

"I would be inclined to say we both got one," pointed out his savior looking down at his son.

The prone hunter cast a smile up at the two grinning faces looking down upon him before sharing in a brief laughter at the now relieved close call.

It had taken the three hunters twice as much time to carry the two kills out of the forest after finding another pole-like limb to lash the second boar to and dividing the rope out evenly securing both carcasses to them. Russell also required several minutes to clean and wrap a cloth around the bloody cut on his leg. The wound leaving him with a slight limp in his gait. There was no denying that all three men struggled with the loads of dead weight.

Once the hunters had returned to the Daniels' small farmstead, both Robert and Charles decided to hang the boars up in a stone slaughterhouse that would allow for the pigs' blood to drain from their bodies. The two had made the decision that at some point on the morrow they would skin the animals and start butchering the meat from the kills.

Meanwhile, Russell had limped into the cottage where he was welcomed by the sounds of a loud inhalation from not only his mother and sister but also the three women of the Bradfords' household. Elizabeth ran to his aid when she noticed his torn and bloody pants accompanying his limp.

"Oh my!", gasped his mother as she jumped up from her seat at the table. "What happened Russell?"

"It's nothing mother. Just a nick," her son brushing off the seriousness of the close call. "It appears worse than it really is."

"Come take a seat," she offered helping him to the chair she had just been sitting in. "Let me have a look at that."

Russell laid his bow on the table and removed the quiver from his back placing it near the weapon before dropping into the chair.

Lifting his leg and cradling his boot on her lap as she kneeled in front of him, Elizabeth rolled up the torn pant's leg revealing the wound caused from the animal's tusk. A makeshift bandage from a piece of the pant's material covered the cut. Slipping the field dressing down, a small trickle of blood ran from the shallow injury.

"See mother, I told you it's not bad," confirmed her son.

She looked up at Russell smiling and pat him on his foot's instep. "Okay son but I shall clean it and put a fresh bandage on it," she informed him. "How did this happen anyways?", she inquired rising up from her knees.

"A boar almost got me."

"From what I have witnessed already I would say he did."

"It is not that bad mother."

"Where was your father?", Elizabeth queried while filling a wash basin up with water from a pitcher.

"He saved me," Russell answered.

Returning to her seated son, his mother stared up into his face. "Tell me the whole of it Russell."

The young man spent the next ten minutes or so narrating the events that led up to his injury. Russell finished his story just before his father and Charles walked through the door.

Elizabeth was just rising from the floor finished with cleaning and bandaging the wound, but before she could say anything Russell addressed Robert. "Father, did you get them both up and hanging?"

"Yes son, but the query is how are you feeling?"

"What do you mean both?", Elizabeth puzzled. Her eyes glancing between her husband and son.

"The boy shot two of them today," advised Robert.

Turning her attention back to Russell, a small scowl began to make its way onto her face. "I thought you said there was only one boar!"

"Well I did not want you to worry mother so I left out a few details in my tale," came her son.

Before anyone else could say anything, Charles walked over and placed a hand on Russell's shoulder. "You should be proud of the lad Elizabeth for the boy's actions earlier this day are the only reason why he is still here. Most men I know, never mind a growing boy, would have been badly mauled or even dead right now." Charles glanced back-n-forth between the two Daniels' parents before returning his gaze back to Elizabeth. "Robert has taught this young man well," he proclaimed.

Russell's mother looked over at her husband. "But he said you killed one."

"No my dear. Russell killed both of the beasts," corrected her husband. "My shot was only to make sure that the animal would not be rising up anytime soon."

Walking over to Russell, his father patted him on his shoulder. "You did a fine job son," he praised. "You have come a long way with the bow."

"Thank you father," smiled the appreciative young man.

The next day the Bradfords made the trip back to the Daniels' farm so Charles could help Robert skin and butcher the two boars. With all the meat that they would both be getting from the wild pigs, the two had decided to give some of the pork to the neighbor who lived roughly a mile on the other side of Robert's small farm. Both Paul and Juliet were in their early fifties and would definitely appreciate the edible gift.

"I shall be right out father to help you and Mr. Bradford," informed Russell seated at the table while starting to slip on one of his boots.

"No son," corrected his father. "I think you should stay here and take care of your leg. You do not want anything to cause an infection and plague you."

"But father, I will be fine," he tried to plead.

"Your father is right," softly interjected Russell's mother who had also been sitting at the table along with Charles' wife, Gwenyth. "Stay and do your mother the honour of partaking in a hot cup of tea and shared conversation with both Mrs. Bradford and I."

Russell badly wished to go to the stone slaughterhouse but he had been raised to honour thy mother and father, so the young man accepted their wishes, placing them above his own desire. "Yes mother," he softly agreed.

Elizabeth gave her son a small grin while patting his knee twice. She then cast a smile at her husband along with Charles before finally glancing across the table to Gwenyth sitting down. "Very well. Let me heat some water for tea," she proclaimed rising from her seat and starting for a pot she used specifically to heat water.

"I know you would rather be out with us son but I want to make sure that your leg is well so we can continue with your sword lessons in a couple of days," remarked Robert before following Charles out of the cottage's door.

"How are your sword lessons coming along anyhow?", inquired Gwenyth looking over to Russell. Her face wearing a pleasant expression and her eyes shifting to Elizabeth, who met the glance with a smile of her own.

Even Gwenyth's oldest daughter Lynn, who was now fourteen years of age and only two winters younger than Russell, seemed to have her interest peaked by her mother's query. The girl was not into the same boyish stuff Russell liked, but after overhearing her father retell the events from the hunt to her mother in the cart on their way home yesterday and recalling the time from six years earlier when the boy rescued her from the forest, Lynn was slightly taken aback by Russell's bravery. She was still a girl by age's standard but mentally she was like that of a young adult. Even already Lynn knew that if her mother and father were to find a proper suitor for her that she would soon be of marriageable age in two more years.

The Bradford girl liked everything about Russell's character. He was both brave and honorable, and those two traits seemed to cause the girl to gravitate towards his personality. The fact that Russell never looked down on her and always treated others with respect was definitely a plus, but the one thing that had always stuck with her in Lynn's heart and mind was the fact that Russell had saved her. He, a ten year old boy, had come looking for her years ago and had promised to reunite her and her mother back together again. That boy had done what he had said he was going to do and upheld a promise to a scared, little girl. She never forgot that. Somehow Russell had taken root in Lynn's heart and a flower had begun to grow there.

Chapter 39

Bouncing up and down in the royal carriage, Lynn accompanied by the other three members of the Bradford family caught a glimpse in the distance of the stone, country manor as it peeked in and out from behind the trees. The place only being somewhat revealed to the private, dirt road they traveled thanks in part to most of the leaves that had already fallen to the ground leaving the hardwood beeches almost naked of their cover. The red, orange and yellow foliage, along with the perennial plant's smooth, gray bark helped to add to the breath-taking scenery.

"This here be beautiful!", Gwenyth confirmed what the other three were thinking as she was taken with the observations she had made before she finally arrived at the estate's stone structure.

"The king said that there be a small pond behind the manor, and one can witness deer come to drink," excitedly added Lynn.

The Bradford's were given assistance, as they stepped down from the carriage and headed for the place's front door. Charles offered his arm to his oldest daughter and ushered England's young queen into her family's new villa.

"Thank you father," the young woman smiled while entwining her arm with his.

Anne, Gwenyth and Charles froze instantly as they were all filled with the awe-inspiring sight of the structures immaculate, first floor. Candelabras hung from the ceiling suspended over rug-covered surfaces. Most of the furniture, especially the ten chair dining table set were made from the hardwood of English Oak, and the manor's sitting chairs were soft and plush. There was even a beautiful staircase that led upstairs to the second level.

"Mother look!", excitedly pointed out Anne before grabbing her mother's hand and dashing for the flight of stairs. Both disappearing up the stairs.

Both Charles and Lynn offered a chuckle and giggle when they heard the youngest Bradford shout.

"Ease yourself child!", happily demanded her mother. "In all your haste you will drag me like a sack of grain."

Glancing to her father, Lynn looked into the man's eyes now filling with water. "Oh father," she compassionately spoke. "What troubles you?"

"I am sorry this has happened to you," he expressed softly.

"I am well father," his daughter sounding as if she attempted to convince herself of the matter more than Charles. Tears already beginning to form in her eyes.

"My beliefs differ in opinion," her father pointed out tenderly placing a hand on both sides of her face. "It is my notion that my words pushed you into the decision you made and away from that of which you desired."

A teardrop rolled down the young woman's cheek.

"I can never thank you enough in one hundred lifetimes for this place that your mother, sister, and I share now, but for your happiness I know my way around our farm. I will always choose a life of toil in exchange for my daughter's well being."

"You, nor mother, ever need to thank me for this place," admitted Lynn as another tear fell from her eyes. "You have given of yourself for all of us father for all my life. It was time to do for you."

"Nonsense child," he calmly disagreed. "I am your father graced by the Almighty with two blessings; you and Anne. It was your mother and I who desired you and sent forth query time and time again until the Lord filled our wishes. My daughter it was not you, who asked to be born, but in the stead I who petitioned for you!", Charles clarified. "Therefore the duties of a father to protect, provide for, and nurture were of my own will. It was I who partook in that oath to God himself with the promise to always do so."

"But father I have grown to lack fondness in watching you toil year after year," confessed his daughter. "I made the choice not based on the words you spoke, but I too know England needs an heir. I swore a duty to the crown, and what kind of person would I be if I turned away from my obligation?"

Charles looked over his daughter's shoulder because he knew the answer before she said it.

"One who knows happiness but knows not integrity nor honour," the young woman pointed out. "If I must forfeit my own complete happiness and the love that I have for one who knows me better than I do myself, than I will not surrender the whole of me for a lacking value. I shall barter a price that I deem equal and use it to give to the one who has given of himself all my life, and not once known complaint over the matter. A man who has left me unwanting and given me the best life one could," tears flowed from his daughter's eyes as she lovingly embraced her father.

Hugging Lynn, Charles watched as Gwenyth and Anne walked down the stairs taking notice of his watery eyes.

"Is all not well?", queried his youngest daughter. "It would appear that I swallowed a bug seeking sanctuary from the cold outside," lied Charles. "Even now I can feel the creature's wings in my throat."

"What troubles Lynn?", suspiciously questioned Anne.

"Oh, your sister here will be well once she has finished laughing herself to tears," her father informed her. "Lynn's words were something on the line of; Father, at times even the bugs will do what they must to silence your words of worry."

"Your daughter's words know both wisdom and truth Charles," laughed Gwenyth.

Not one of them ever laying eyes on Lynn's wet smile as she and her father still embraced. The young woman pondering on the fact that Charles had once again fulfilled his duty as a father and protected her private feelings even if it caused some laughter at his own expense.

"There she be," pointed out King Matthew while both he and Duke Paul watched Queen Lynn enter the sitting room they were both in. Behind her, and definitely not of her own design, followed the young woman's personal servant. The two strolling up to the young men, who had now risen to their feet. Joan's baby bump surely a tell tale sign to all.

"My husband," addressed the smiling queen offering the king a hug and a kiss on the young man's cheek.

The two royals paying no heed to the raptor-like stare accompanied with the sly grin Paul had given to the discomforting servant after a quick glance at her slowly growing stomach. The uneasy woman could almost read his thoughts by his facial expression.

"This be my wife and the new Queen of England cousin," introduced Matthew.

Dropping to a knee and taking Lynn's hand, the duke placed a kiss on it. "My lady, the pleasure is all mine. I believe you have been witness to me at church, but I offer my greetings and allegiance to the crown formally. I am the king's only relative, Duke Paul of Scheffield, and your wish is my command," he informed his new queen before rising to his feet.

"Please let us sit and speak on our trip to your land," invited Lynn wearing a smile. Turning to Matthew she added, "If you were not speaking on things more important my king."

"Not at all," revealed the young man. "The duke and I awaited your return. How are your parents fancying their move?"

"I believe they were taken with the place," she informed him with a grin.

Standing back and witnessing the conversation going on between husband and wife, along with Paul's several glances between the uncomfortable servant in his presence and the queen's breasts, Joan wished desperately that she would be dismissed.

"Take your leave Joan," sternly came Matthew. "That will be all. The queen will summons you if she requires your assistance."

"Yes your majesty," bowed the woman before making her exit.

Closing the door behind her, Joan couldn't get away from Paul's presence fast enough. Swiftly making her way across the castle's main hall towards the servant quarters, she desperately needed to find and warn Ruth that the duke had come back to Hamilton. Joan had a strong feeling that neither of them would be safe this night from evil.

Watching Joan close the door behind her, Lynn quickly glanced at her husband. She had never remembered him being so hard in his words to any of those who worked in the castle. The young woman's thoughts disrupted when she heard Duke Paul question her for a second time.

"How be that?", queried Paul.

Letting the subject go thinking maybe her husband tired, Lynn apologized to the man. "I am sorry. My mind was a wonder. You were speaking on?"

Offering the new queen a smile, the duke retold the story leading up to his inquiry. The three continued their conversation through supper.

Lying on her side with her head resting in her hand propped up on an elbow, Lynn gazed down at her husband who laid on his back staring up at the bed's canopy. The thoughts of the conversation she and he had in the carriage on their way home from church running through his mind.

"Are you well my husband?", concerned his young wife placing her hand on his bare chest.

"Yes," he answered while turning his head to gaze into her eyes. "I know I am not the one that you have grown to love throughout these years, but I give you my word that I will protect and provide for you. I also believe if you give us a chance, a love will grow and blossom in your heart," he softly added.

"I have given you my word that I be willing to make an attempt my husband," she placidly responded.

Lynn felt Matthew's hand closest to her touch her body and slide down to her nether regions. While remaining on her side, she pulled her foot flat and bent her outside knee. The young woman momentarily closing her eyes while taking a gasp of air, as she accepted a finger and then another. Slowly, she slid her hand on her husband's chest down in search of her husband's manhood.

Soon the queen's moans filled the air. Slowly she rocked back and forth while mounted on top of the king. He made sure the two with their gazes locked on each other held constant eye contact. Never once did Matthew lose a visual connection with Lynn, and the one time she had begun to close her eyes and lean her head up, the young man gently held her face in place and adjusted his upward thrusts. The hip move caused the young woman no pain, but it had accomplished in opening her eyes wider as she felt him deeper inside. This night's love making would be strictly between Lynn and Matthew. There would be no room for Russell nor Joan in their bed henceforth.

Making his way skulking through the castle's semi-lit corridors, Duke Paul slowly peeked around the corner to the empty hallway in front of him. Continuing to his cousin's chamber door, the young man took a knee and placed his ear to the keyhole. Paul's manhood began to instantly stir when he heard the moans of pleasure coming from the new queen. Remaining long enough to hear her groan her release, the duke rose and began back to his room.

On the way to his chambers for the night, he thought about how many times he had found joy in listening to the pleasures of another. Paul added Lynn to his list of auditory voyeurism with both Joan and his Aunt Margaret, along with the women he had heard his father pleasure before his death.

Stopping at a door before his room, Paul quickly opened it to the muffled sounds of women being taken. He watched for a short time as seven of his men took Ruth, along with her thirty eight year old mother every-and-any which way, and in every possible combination. At one point before Paul left. He witnessed both mother and daughter pleasure three men at the same time while one waited his turn.

Finally making it to his chamber, the duke opened his door to the groans of another. Laying on his bed with Rufus mounted on top of her gripping the large man's ass was Joan.

"Turn her this way," instructed Paul while removing his clothing.

In one motion, Rufus changed both their positions causing the woman's shoulders to lay on the edge of the mattress.

Joan watched, as Paul strolled over to her. Squatting down a bit near her head, the duke supported it with his hand.

"Well it looks like the barren womb be with child," Duke Paul grinned his devilish grin. "One that looks to be sired by a father of Scheffield I might add." The duke looked to Rufus still rocking into the woman before he continued, "All I would need to do is take claim, and Matthew would surely send you to live with me. There you would give birth to the child, whomever it may belong too, and shortly find yourself pleasuring most of Northern England."

"No!", Joan answered between moans. "Please I beg of you Duke Paul release me from your grasp!"

Again the duke laughed at her and gave his head a nod signaling Rufus to plunge hard into the woman.

Joan groaned.

"You desire that over this Joan?", inquired Paul.

"Please my lord release me," she pleaded.

Again the duke nodded, and the knight responded with a series of plunges and quick hip thrusts.

Joan began to groan even loader with the movements. Her hands finding the knight's rear, as she felt the sparks beginning in her body.

"I will inquire again Joan. You desire that over this?", questioned Paul. This time he received no answer. The woman's body starting to build towards her release.

"I thought not," he sinisterly stated.

Directing Joan's head back to hang over the edge of the mattress, Paul slowly fed her his manhood. Leaning slightly forward his hands found her breasts, as hers found his ass. The duke closed his eyes. All images, along with the muffled sounds of pleasure from Joan disappeared. A thought caused that devilish grin to return. On this night he imagined both he and Rufus ravished the new Queen of England.

Chapter 40

King Matthew, along with his family's most trusted knight, Sir Timothy; his cousin Duke Paul, and the duke's most trusted Sir Rufus; all met in the king's private study finalizing the route the royal carriage would be traveling on their way to visit Scheffield.

"My Lord," addressed the captain of the guard while pointing to the map and tracing the planned route they would be taking. "We will travel on the King's Road through The Vale stopping once we reach Birmingham upon dusk this day," informed Sir Timothy looking up from the open drawing on the table.

Matthew remained quiet, but his nod silently instructed the knight to continue.

"There be a handful of scattered villages we could stop at to water the horses and partake in a hot meal between Birmingham and Scheffield," Sir Timothy's attention on his king as he straightened up. "Unless your majesty wishes to travel straight through to the latter?" The guard gazed upon Matthew's indecisive face.

"How many days from here to there making at the least two stops one at Birmingham, along with another?", inquired the king.

"At least five or six," calmly injected Duke Paul looking towards his cousin.

"And if we stop in Birmingham before traveling to Scheffield both day and night?"

"By my assessment, at the least three days and a half," replied Sir Timothy while mentally double-checking his estimation of arrival. "What say you?", he directed his query to both the duke and Rufus.

"I would agree," the two admitted almost as one.

Turning his attention back to King Matthew, Sir Timothy gave the young man a moment to think over this decision to stop or continue to ride straight on through. "To which do you fancy sire?", the armoured man inquired.

"We go to Birmingham this day, but plan to hold over for the night before we ride without a further stop to Sheffield," announced Matthew. We will take some provisions with us and pick up more if we require it," the young man smilingly added.

"Yes your majesty," came Sir Timothy. "As you wish," he added before bowing to take his leave. The knight needed to prepare the royal carriage, along with the eleven man royal guard accompanying the king and queen on their trip.

Accepting a nod from Duke Paul, Sir Rufus followed the captain of the guard out of the room. He himself had a coach and seven men to prepare.

Imagining Lynn's breasts and naked body moving as one in unison with him and Rufus, a smile decorated the raptor-like facial feature of Duke Paul, as he placed a hand on King Matthew's shoulder. "Days from now, you and the queen will be my honoured guest."

The young king reflecting his cousin's smile with one of his own. "I am sure the queen will find the trip to her liking," innocently admitted Matthew as his thoughts of Lynn the adventurer was about to witness some of Northern England.

Sitting on the soft, plush seat of the royal carriage next to her queen, Joan was at least more than relieved that she would not have to accompany Duke Paul, who rode by himself in his own private coach, along for the trip. Just the thought of what he would be doing to her body caused the woman to shiver momentarily from the idea.

"Do you suffer from a chill?", concerned Lynn. She had been traveling with the window shutters open allowing her to take in the beautiful, fall scenery of the multi-colored foliage and half bare beech trees.

"Oh no my lady," the servant replied. "The fresh air actually is to my liking. I believe my shakes were caused by the thought of the coldness we are about to partake upon in Scheffield," she smiled her lie. Joan was not about to tell her queen with the king seated across from her the vile truths of the young man's cousin or what he had done to her. Joan was smart enough to know Matthew would never believe her based upon what he had both seen and heard. Quickly she changed the topic.

"Look my queen!", she pointed out the window. "There still be patches of Blue Bells."

Lynn swiftly turning her head in time to catch a glimpse of the passing flowers, while Matthew engrossed himself in reading one of the books he chose from his private study.

For at least the morning and into the earlier part of the day, the royal carriage surrounded by Sir Timothy and his eleven guardsmen, along with the duke's coach and his eight guards following, made their way through The Vale on the King's Road. The solid, dirt road ran in between the continuously rolling hills on each side. Their beginning to die grass covered by both patches of soon to be dead bluebells and piles of fallen leaves from the many beech trees that rose from the land. In the summer their canopies casting shade on the throughway.

Making their way around a slight bend in the road, the royal caravan slowed to a stop when one of the two escorting guardsmen yelled for the movement to cease. "Halt!"

King Matthew's eyes rose from above his book, as both the queen and her servant looked to him wearing puzzling expressions. They both turned their gazes to the open windows. The young man leaning forward and peering out to watch Sir Timothy approaching the coach on horseback.

"It appears a tree has fallen across the road my lord. The men are making preparations to hook it to some horses and reposition it so we may continue," the knight stoically added. "We should be on our way briefly."

"Very well," came Matthew with an accompanying head nod. The king glanced up towards the hills ridge before sitting back down and leaving his book closed on the seat near him. A thought-filled gaze following on the two women.

The captain of the guard had just turned his horse to head back towards the two men preparing to move the beech tree blocking the road.

"The tree is not fell!", one of the men anxiously shouted his discovery. "It has been cut!"

No sooner had the investigating guard cried out his find, two arrows struck the man in his upper chest piercing his plate mail and driving him backwards over a fallen branch. The man dead before hitting the ground.

"Ambush!!!", Sir Timothy cried out as he drew his sword. "Protect the king and queen!", he shouted while racing back to the carriage window.

In the short time it took him to get there both the driver and his helper on the royal's coach fell dead from their perch, along with one of the lead horses to the four animal team. Three crossbow bolts stuck from its neck. The blood stain they caused were a good indicator the horse drew no more breath.

"Close the shutters before one meets the sting of the arrow's tip!", anxiously warned the knight.

Already over a dozen men wearing cloaks covering chain mail shirts underneath, rose from piles of leaves or poured over the ridge on just one of the hillsides. Their shouts breaking the serenity of the forest, as they rushed down the slope brandishing swords.

Reining his horse to turn around, Sir Timothy was launched in the air from his saddle. The force and power from the blow driving him into the front side of the carriage causing the royal's coach to lurch. The knight fell to the ground and laid still with a piece of a pointed tip lance embedded in his left shoulder.

The carriage's three occupants watched in both horror and shock as Sir Rufus' surprise attack not only dismounted the captain of the guards, but also sent his sword skyward and his armour's guard brace into the coach where it landed between the queen and her servant. The two's screams being held by the surprising astonishment they had just taken in.

"Timothy!", yelled King Matthew.

Duke Paul was more than aware of what was about to happen when the caravan came to a stop. He had waited to see the appearance of the black knight by his carriage, so he could hand him a pointed lance. The duke had chosen to ride by himself so no one would see the three polearms allowing his trap to be sprung with no hitches. Paul could have requested Joan to accompany him, and several times he thought how the bumpy road would assist her movements up and down as she rode him, but what was taking place now was better than any sex he could ever imagine. "Today the height of my plan has arrived," he thought when he saw the charging men rushing down the hill. "The crown will finally dress my brow."

Duke Paul knew no fear of being on the wrong side of the arrow strike, because simply put, none were shooting at him. He leaned out the window to take in the chaos and evilness of his perfectly, designed plan. He witnessed Sir Rufus' charge on the undefended Sir Timothy, and hideously laughed when he took in the sight of the lance shatter causing the knight's body to fly though the air, bounce off the royal carriage, and flop to the road like a child's rag doll.

"If the young queen does not want a date with the gallows then she will be the one tonight feeling Rufus' impaling lance." The thought of conquering both the king and queen gave birth to an appeasing smile on Paul's raptor-like face.

"I have to check on Paul!", reasoned the young man. "You may be wrong about him."

"Please Matthew trust me!", pleaded his true lover. "I am not!"

Looking at the two women as the carriage rocked from the battle outside, King Matthew leaned across Joan and quickly opened the other window shutter. Taking a moment to scan the other side of the coach, along with the slope on that side, the young man was satisfied the coast was clear.

"My dear," he calmly addressed his scared wife. "Take Joan and run up the slope over to the other side. Get to the tree line, and do not show yourself until I come seeking you." The young man continued, "If others should look for you make your way into the woods and hide until later. Follow the road to Birmingham, and under guise send word to the church's priest. He will instruct you from there."

"Come with us Matthew!", pleaded Joan.

"Yes Matthew, please!", joined Lynn. "England has enough martyrs to worship already."

Desiring to go get his cousin from this attack and realizing deep in his heart that the only way his queen and the servant could flee out the back undetected was to draw everyone's attention to himself, the king glanced out the window he had just recently unshuttered. Making sure the coast was clear, he turned to his wife. "Now go my queen before it is too late,..." Matthew quickly spoke as he kissed her on the cheek, "... and take Joan with you. That is a royal order from your king."

"The words causing Lynn to blink away the fear as she looked at the man she knew was saving her life. Opening the carriage's door carefully, she stepped down and turned to give the young man a nod. "Yes my husband."

"Till next we meet," he softly stated to both women.

Knowing that those words were symbolizing a departing farewell, Joan replied with a tear in her eye and feigning a weak smile. "Till next we meet. I love you Matthew," she added.

Gazing at the two as they ran up the hill seemingly undetected, the king shut the door and in seconds stepped from the other side into the fray.

Duke Paul quietly watched the carnage taking place in front of his coach. Even though his ambushers outnumbered the royal guard two to one, the king's men were not easily over run by their attackers. Testament to the training they had all received from Sir Timothy. Although Paul knew that it wouldn't be long now for his men to taste victory. Already half of the royal guard had been killed.

The duke silently chuckled to himself as he witnessed the door to the king's carriage open up and Matthew deliver a boot strike to one of the ambushers preparing to run through the still prone Sir Timothy with a sword. The would be attacker's head snapping back from a kick in the mouth driving him back several steps before falling to the ground.

Surveying the area quickly, King Matthew with his gold crown donning his brow, picked up the knight's fallen blade. Paul's cousin stood over his fallen friend in a defensive stance. Weapon on guard.

Standing at the ready, Matthew quickly scanned the melee taking place around him. The young man taking in the sight of two of the ambushers seizing the upper hand when a third delivered a strike to one of his guards from behind. The man screaming out his pain, as the three pounced on their wounded prey.

Looking to the fallen man he had just kicked in the head, Matthew could tell his strike had left the unexpected attacker dazed. The ambusher only semiconscious lie on his back gazing skyward.

Squatting and placing the sword by his side, King Matthew placed his hands under Sir Timothy, and somehow seemed to summons enough strength to roll the knight under the carriage offering a limited protection for his friend. The young man digging the balls of his feet into the dirt road while using his legs to push Sir Timothy a little bit further. Satisfied with the knight's place, the young man grabbed the sword's pummel and returned to his feet. Matthew started for his cousin's coach, but a kick from behind by Sir Rufus still on horseback as he rode by drove him into the right, rear wheel of his carriage. The force from the blow causing the royal to hit face first and turn towards the hill, as he bounced off the solid, circular object.

Before Matthew could recover not only his breath but also his bearings, along with the king's crown that had been dislodged from his brow and rolled several times on the ground, an arrow followed by a second, and then a third bit into his unarmoured torso. The combining forces driving the young man back into the wheel. His arm wavered back and forth, as he loosely gripped the sword's pummel, and within a moment or two, Matthew dropped it as he slowly lowered to his knees. Instinctively, the young king reached for his crown and with a snail-like motion placed it back on his head. Everything and everyone around him seemed to move in slow motion.

Queen Lynn and Joan ran up and over the ridge of the hill before quickly laying down and peering over the edge watching the battle below wage on. As luck would have it, the two were concealed by a small, patch of bluebells leaving them feeling secure that they would not easily be noticed. Both women anxiously waiting for Matthew to flee up the slope.

Horror met their eyes causing both of the secluded women to start a bit and gasp as one as they witnessed the young king take two sloth-like steps at the rear of the royal coach before falling to his knees. The sight of three feathered arrow shafts protruding from his body. The king's gold crown falling from his brow.

Collecting his crown and placing it back on his head, King Matthew slowly rose to his feet. He took a couple more sloth-like steps and fell back to the ground. Blood flowed from the three arrow wounds staining his robes around the shafts. The young man watched through a watery gaze, as his cousin walked towards him.

"Well, well, well my cousin," smiled Paul. "It looks like your reign as King of England has finally met its end."

"Why cousin?", quietly inquired the wounded king between ragged breaths. "Why have you betrayed me?"

"I have not betrayed you cousin. What I have done is save England from the ones who would rather show weakness and mercy to our enemies. A leader that displays softness in the stead of strength and dominance."

"You are wrong Paul. Meekness be not rivaled by that of weakness," the young man corrected. "To show an enemy mercy and respect is not a task of ease for any man, but the display of honour be one that quells wars and knows patience and peace. My father knew of that truth," the young king stopped to pull air.

"My uncle was a fool!", sharply stated Paul. "He was weak! Stephen sheltered and protected those who would drive England to ruins with their frailness. They know not strength, and only the strong survive! We are of noble blood and therefore by birthright we take what we want. Stephen held these weaklings to his bosom with protection and reverence that clouded his judgements to do what is right," angrily spoke the duke.

"You be correct cousin. My father did hold everyone to his bosom, but his sight was not clouded or obscured as you say from it. He did it under the clarity of love and the knowledge that as nobility we burden the right to provide a life for our people. Not the other way around where we know the right of birth and the riches it brings using them to drain life from our people," firmly stated the prone king. "The people of England serve the crown, and to hold connection with our people the crown serves them with respect, honour, love, and integrity in our words of peace and protection not in the displays of tyranny and abuse of power."

Stopping to take several pulls of air, Matthew watched as his cousin walked over to him and took the crown from his head and placed the headpiece upon his own brow. A wicked smile crossed Paul's face.

"You will truly never know how to be a king," pointed out Matthew.

Paul laughed. "I know this cousin, and take heed of my words for you might be able to use them in the afterlife. I know strength over weakness. Look around you," he stopped to take a glance at the scene of carnage. "I know to save my country from weaklings, whom have no courage, I had to have you mother and father murdered. Although know this, the second arrow was meant for you not her. I had plans to pierce her body with a different kind of shot," the duke's hand resting on his crotch.

A tear rolled from Matthew's eye.

"And as for your secret coupling with Joan, once again like your crown, I took her from you or should I say we took her from you," he laughed as he motioned to Sir Rufus. "She allowed me to blackmail her to protect you from not only the king and the queen, but the people of England. How do you think they would have acted when I told them not only is the woman a castle's servant, but she was also barren?", Paul offered a brief chuckle. "To gaze upon her now with undeniable proof she be with child. The bastard sired by one of us who forcefully took her and raped her," the duke devilishly grinned. "Know this, she was not so easy to break. The declaration you witnessed her scream out was more in part to let's call it, a moments gratification than a feeling of the heart. Joan was forced to know pleasure by three men and a woman throughout my stays at the castle, and she always remained loyal to you."

Finally realizing the truth to his lover's words when she tried to speak on his lack of understanding in that which had taken place, the truly defeated Matthew's tear-filled eyes were accompanied by the groan of failure. The failure to his true love. If the assassination of his father, along with the death of his mother, and the loss he experienced when he believed Joan's heart had betrayed his didn't fully break his spirit, his cousin's words sacked it like a ruined city.

From their hiding spot, Lynn and Joan watched as a self-crowned Duke Paul stood for several minutes over his royal cousin and obviously spoke to him. Redirecting his attention, the duke looked to the hills. "I am the new king of England now!", he shouted into the air. "If I may deliver a notion to the queen and her servant. I will offer you asylum on the grounds that you both accompany me back to Hamilton with the story that our late king died at the hands of the French." Paul briefly paused and scanned the hillside before continuing, "All here fought hard to protect my cousin, but in the ambush the brigands murdered him. The rest of us barely survived with our lives. Due to my blood line, Lynn has decided to name me king, where you will remain as my queen to sire me an heir to the throne," this time his lips drew back in a devilish smile as he waited a response.

Upon hearing no words and witnessing no movement, Duke Paul added to the quiet surroundings, "Then you will receive no sanctuary anywhere you go in this land. All of England will learn that the king's assassination will have been a conspiracy between you and the French. From henceforth, I decree as King of England that you and your servant be hunted down and put to death not only for your treason to this country, but known as a traitor to the crown!", he shouted.

The young, crownless king lie on the ground dying while lost in his own thoughts on all that his cousin had just revealed to him. Matthew had heard Paul's shouts and speeches to both his wife and his true love, but he had not attempted to listen to the self-proclaimed king's exact words. He could only hope the two had fled and not bear witness to his imminent plight.

Catching movement from the corner of his eye, Matthew watched as Paul strolled up to a man, whom he did not recognize. His cousin spoke to the stranger for a moment before addressing the remaining men under his command.

"I am your king now. "Who of you swears allegiance to me and my crown?", the self-proclaimed king calmly inquired.

The duke's remaining men bent to a knee. "I do your majesty," they all swore as one.

"Then rise," he commanded before delivering his first orders as king. "Sir Rufus, you and two others will accompany me back to Hamilton where I will relate the terrible murder of King Matthew to the townsfolk and send messengers to all of England. Nathaniel, you and another will remain here after we leave to finish the job with my dear cousin," Paul's sarcasm causing both men to laugh. "The rest of you will ride to Hamilton, but separate before we enter the city. You will take up residence at different inns and remain there awaiting the arrival of the next Sabbath. I will send for you."

The men nodded their heads.

"Oh and Nathaniel," Paul addressed the man he assigned with finishing off Matthew. "You and whomever remains with you, I desire you hunt down the other two traitors."

"Should I kill them my lord?"

The self-proclaimed king offered a laugh. "You assassins are all the same. You only ponder on death."

"It be my nature your majesty," he grinned.

"No bring the queen to me alive. The people of England will always find favor with a king who deals a traitor a fair trial at the end of a shortened rope."

"What of the other woman my lord?", questioned the assassin.

Paul glanced over at Rufus with a look that silently asked in case the child in her belly his. The black knight only shaking his head no. An expression of disdain on his face.

"She is of no need. The one time lover of my cousin has served her purpose," the new king informed the man. "Take her for your pleasure if you wish before you dispatch of her. Joan did seem to fancy you that night you and Rufus took her."

Paul's men had already turned his coach around facing back towards Hamilton.

Opening the door, the self-proclaimed king was approached by the black knight.

"How was it you knew that the queen and the servant had fled into the woods my lord?", inquired Rufus.

Because only a fool-hearty king, who believes himself honorable would ponder a diversion knowing he has no chance of victory," replied Paul, as he handed the two pointed lances to him. "Dispose of these here. We wish no signs of betrayal," he added.

Soon the king's coach and all the remaining men except Nathaniel and one other disappeared around the slight bend in the road.

Both Queen Lynn and Joan watched without revealing their hiding spot on the hill's ridge camouflaged by a patch of bluebells, as two men stood over Matthew's body looking down at the young man. One of the two men saying something causing the other to briefly look to the trees. The man's face instantly recognized by Joan, as the third man she had pleasured while he raped her one night in Paul's chambers.

The two women desperately wanted to go to their king's side.

Joan began to start as she watched the other man who had not used her body raise his sword over his head prepared to plunge it into her prone lover. The second man leaning against the cart's wheel closest to the hill they hid on gazing upon the king.

Suddenly without warning a blade erupted from the chest of the man with his sword raised over his head. His body fell sideways, as it was pushed aside by a battered Sir Timothy. Lynn and Joan could tell by the knight's limp shoulder with the lance tip still embedded in it that Sir Timothy only had use of one arm. His eyes locked on the other man as he started from the sight of the captain of the guard.

The queen and her servant watched as the battle between the knight and the assassin started and continued for several minutes. Both women could tell that the man allied with the duke, or now self-proclaimed king, had the upper hand against the wounded knight.

Sir Timothy held his own for a short time even though he could only use one arm and his movements were hindered from the surprise attack earlier, but in the end the assassin got the best of him.

Lynn and Joan looked on as Sir Timothy's sword flew in the air three feet from him, as Nathaniel disarmed the knight. Moving with the speed of a striking adder, the assassin drove his sword into and through his adversary's stomach. The queen covering her gasping mouth and the servant looking to the ground, as the sound of tearing metal accompanied the blow. Paul's ally withdrew his sword while the two women watched with tears in their eyes, as Sir Timothy dropped to his knees and fell sideways.

Hovering over the fallen knight and convinced he was now dead, the assassin walked back over to Matthew. By his movements the two could tell he was still alive. The man said something inaudible to the women's ears before bringing the sword above his head ready to run the young man through.

Lynn was caught in the grasp of a haze-like awe, while Joan began to rise to a knee panic stricken for her lover. "No!!", yelled Joan.

The pleading filling the wooded area causing the killer to look up towards her.

The two women watched as an arrow bit into the assassin's throat sinking through till the point found day light on the other side of his neck. Their bodies flinched when a second one embedded into the man's chest, followed by a third and a fourth. The sounds of thumping bow strings lost in the moment to the queen and the servant's ears.

Taking one, then another step backwards, the assassin dropped his sword. The man wavered for a second and followed the weapon as his carcass plummeted to the dirt road.

Trying to comprehend what exactly had just happened, Lynn and Joan quickly turned around. Their surprised gazes falling on four young men holding bows. The shaking servant had never remembered seeing the men before now. Her eyes taking in the large, muscular young man and the two, who were obviously brothers, on guard with arrows ready. The three scanning the road.

Meeting the young man's soft brown eyes with her own, the queen took a moment to comprehend what had just happened and who she gazed upon. She knew his face and recognized everything even down to the sword's pommel. His concerning voice she knew from all the years back when the young man had first rescued her in the woods.

"Lynn are you well?"

The young woman caught by the sight of her rescuer kneeling down in front of her while she sat in the dying grass.

Using a finger to push a strand of her long, straight, brown hair back and tucking it behind her ear. "Lynn are you well?", he softly asked.

Tears began to fill up in her eyes while a drop rolled down her cheek as she leaned forward and wrapped her arms around the young man's neck. "I am now Russell! I am now!", revealed the frightened woman.

Chapter 41

"We are going to get you out of here your majesty," calmly reassured the young man kneeling at his side inspecting the king for any other wounds beside the obvious three caused by the arrow strikes.

Gazing through watery eyes, King Matthew took in his rescuers short, wavy, brown hair and soft, brown eyes. The young king believing in the truth to the other's words, along with his look of peaceful determination. It is said that the eyes are the windows to a man's soul, and Matthew knew that to be correct. He recognized that this man's soul was one bathed in truth and honour.

Matthew's face took on a look of concern when he inquired about the two women. "The queen and her servant were with me. They both fled into the hills. Have you seen them?"

"Yes my lord," confirmed Russell. "My friends and I had to make sure the coast was clear before calling them from hiding. They come to you now," he added while watching the two jogging down the hill.

Taking in the sight of the young man at his side glancing over his shoulder and speaking to another, King Matthew's softly admitted, "I know your face."

"My lord?", surprisingly queried Russell.

"I know who you be," repeated Matthew. "You are the one I witnessed in church. Lynn's Russell."

The acknowledgment causing the young rescuer to feel somewhat awkward, but the arrival of Lynn and Joan drove away Russell's discomfort.

Honour

"Matthew!", cried the teary-eyed Joan falling to her knees on the young king's other side. "What has he done?", she asked into her hands covering her mouth.

Rising to his feet, Russell handed Lynn his waterskin, "I am going to aid Michael and Paul checking for any more survivors. If an arrow falls from the sky, you and the woman run for the trees," he pointed up the hill. "Peter has gone to the road's bend watching for anyone who has decided to come back. The young woman acknowledging his words with a nod before kneeling next to her husband.

The young man taking his leave to assist his friends.

"Take a sip my dear," the queen offered the waterskin to his lips, as she supported his head and neck.

"You two are safe," meekly smiled Matthew.

"No doubt to your bravery my husband," reasoned his wife with a smile.

"Paul," called Russell.

Peter's twin looked up from another body littering the ground. "What say you?", the young man queried.

"Round up these horses," the young rescuer advised. "We will find the mounts needed now."

Offering a nod, his friend rose and went to collect the wandering animals that had belonged to either the king's royal guard or those who perished at their defending hands.

"Over here Russell!", called Michael kneeling down over the popular known knight of Hamilton, Sir Timothy.

The young man hastily walked over to his friend and the fallen guard.

Kneeling next to Sir Timothy's bloodied and beaten body, the knight weakly spoke. Both Russell and Michael could tell the man was close to death.

"Your friend has told me that you saved both the king and queen," quietly confessed the man. "Now the protection of the crown and England falls in your hands. If Duke Paul wins victory over Matthew and his wife then all will fall into darkness and know only war and tyranny. You must aid in retaking the throne and the crown from him," he coughed up blood. "My sword, bring it to me," Sir Timothy requested.

Russell left to retrieve the weapon, and returned with it moments later.

Retaking a knee, he held the weapon out to the knight. "Here Sir Timothy."

"No young man," the guard denied. "You will need it to aid you in the defense of the real king and queen of England. There are those amongst Hamilton and the castle that will aid you in this," informed the knight before once again coughing up blood.

"Take the blade, and find David the Beggar. He will know I am dead, and what to do."

"How will a beggar know what need be done to regain the crown?", queried Russell.

"David the Beggar is my brother," revealed Sir Timothy. The words escaping his mouth, along with his last breath.

Russell closed the knight's eyelids shut, and along with Michael lowered their heads in a silent prayer to the Lord. Both young men believing that Sir Timothy would once again be reunited with his long time friends King Stephen and Queen Margaret in the after-life. The Heavens would be one champion of righteousness and honour heavier.

Michael had just finished, as carefully as he possibly could removing the last arrow from the unconscious king, before dressing the wound with rags for the moment. Matthew had been so overwhelmed by the pain that it had caused him to pass out cold after the second arrow had been removed. Holding his hand throughout the ordeal Joan glanced around a worried expression dressing her face. "That should do it for now," informed Michael as he sat back away from Matthew's limp form.

"Get the king and queen on these horses and prepare to leave," announced Russell to the small group. "You and your lady may want to grab some clothing to bring with you. Make haste though," the young man added.

"What do you wish to do with the bodies Russell?", inquired Paul.

"Let's place the castle guard in the royal carriage," he sympathetically replied. "We will turn the coach around and hook up the last charger you found in the stead of the dead horse, and send them back to the castle," Russell advised.

"We are going back there?", anxiously queried Joan.

"No," he confirmed. "We will hide you folk out until we have devised a plan and know what needs to be done," compassionately advised the young man. He knew they all needed to get away from here before someone came along and caused more trouble than the four young men could handle.

"Paul up on your horse," Russell instructed. "Michael and I will hand you the king. He rides with you."

In a short time Paul; mounted with the king, Michael; leading a horse carrying Joan with a small bag of clothes, and Russell; also leading a horse with Lynn and a roll of clothes wrapped around Sir Timothy's sword-filled scabbard watched as Peter approached. His bow in hand.

"Take this charger, and ride alongside Paul and the king," instructed Russell while handing the young man the reigns to a fourth horse. "We head to the cottage," he informed his friends.

"What of the coach holding the dead men from the castle? Do you ponder it will even get to Hamilton?", queried Joan from atop a horse.

"Oh there is no doubt in my mind it will arrive there tonight," stoically replied Russell. "All horses instinctively retain the knowledge on how to get back to their stables. However, when they arrive with the carriage full of dead heroes, the duke will have no choice but to give each man a proper burial," the young man humanely pointed out to the woman with child. "Take heed my lady, even the townsfolk of Hamilton fear the Lord and disease before they dread a king. Even a self-proclaimed one at that."

"What of them?", questioned Peter while pointing to the scattered bodies of the dead ambushers on the King's Road.

"Like the horses leave them for the foxes and crows to scavenge," responded the young man. "Traitors and men, who know no honour do not deserve proper burials especially not ones who would attempt to assassinate an honorable king."

Lynn remained silent the whole time Russell had formulated and relayed the plan to the others back at the site of the battle. Even though the young woman was the Queen of England and her words commanded the whole of a country, she knew Russell would be looking out and protecting her, along with the entire group's best interest.

It was far beyond nightfall when the small group of rescuers and refugees made it to the quiet, secluded cottage. They had left the beech trees of "The Vale" hours ago following Russell walking the mount that carried a wrapped up Queen Lynn. All were more than glad to be there because on this night the air only knew coldness and an autumn wind bit their skin.

"We will move the king indoors under shelter first," reasoned Russell. The stars illuminating the darkness just enough to make out each other's faces. "Michael get a fire going and warm up some stew. Peter, you and Paul secure the horses."

His friends only giving a nod of affirmation.

Aiding Lynn down off the charger, Russell led her to the door opening it. The young man's hand locating the lantern on his right and taking a few moments to light a small flame. The portable light brightening the interior enough for the occupants to see. Lynn hesitated when her eyes took in the renovation work Russell and his father had put in over the last couple of months. A one person pallet, along with a wooden table and four chairs made up cottage's the furniture.

"Lay the king on the bed," advised the young man, as the brothers carried Matthew inside.

Both Joan and Michael followed them. The young, muscular man went straight to the fireplace and quickly got to work igniting a flame.

Peter and Paul gently placed the semi-conscious King Matthew on the cot before returning outside to tie up the chargers and bringing all the stuff they had brought with them indoors for the night.

"You repaired the fireplace and chimney?"

"Yes my lady," replied Russell while checking the young king's bandages. "These dressings may require changing already," he pointed out. "We are safe here this night. Partake in some food and drink. Get some rest, for the morrow may be a whole other matter."

That night Matthew slumbered on the pallet routinely being checked upon by his lover, his wife, and his rescuer. Michael, along with the two brothers found rest either laying on the floor or leaning against a wall. Joan slept on the floor near the head of her lover, while Russell leaned in a corner. He gazed upon Lynn as she approached him and knelt in front of him.

"Thank you for what you did Russell," gratefully spoke the young woman. "If the four of you had not shown up when you had, we would all be dead right now," reasoned the queen. "How did you come to be there today?"

"We were hunting a stag, and I had it within my target when the fight broke out and spooked it. "Hence the four of us went to get a look and stumbled on you and the woman lying in the grass. The four of us saw the wounded king preparing to be murdered."

"No matter what brought you there, I thank God you showed up."

Taking a finger and tucking a strand of hair behind the queen's ear, Russell added, "You are safe now Lynn."

His words reflected by the young woman's smile as she leaned towards him.

Joan lie on her side watching the queen lean into the young man losing herself in his engulfing embrace as if seeking to hide from the world. "It would appear I am not the only one with a secret," she thought to herself glancing towards the bed.

Melting into Russell's body, Lynn succumbed to sleep quickly. Tonight the queen knew the surety of safety with a vigilant commoner. The royal finding protection in her ever loving and caring guardian.

Chapter 42

It was late in the afternoon, and the sun had already begun its slow decline over the horizon. Soon the light of day would give way to the darkness of night, and only the stars would dot the heavens casting some illumination down on England. The temperature had also begun to drop, and a wind had slowly started to form. Its blowing, picking up over time until it bit into any exposed flesh. The city's night watch would surely be in for a long, cold shift.

Taking up their posts on the wall above the main entrance to Hamilton, a couple of soldiers peered out into the fading daylight at the four horse carriage being accompanied by three riders. Both men had seen this coach throughout the years that they had spent in the king's royal army recognizing it instantly as belonging to the duke.

"Did not Duke Paul set out with the king and queen to Scheffield earlier this day?", queried one guard to the other.

"Your words know truth," perplexed the second sentry.

"Lieutenant!", shouted the first guard. "There appears to be something amiss on the horizon!", he warned.

"What is it Adams?", curiously inquired the senior officer in charge walking out of the doorway to tower and towards the two watchmen.

"There sir," pointed Adams. "It appears to be the duke's coach, but where be the king's royal carriage?"

The lieutenant gazing out to watch the approaching coach with the three riders rapidly making their way up the road to the city's main entrance.

"Christ Almighty!", he loudly swore before taking off running for the stairs leading off of the wall's battlement. "Look alive you two!", he shouted. Adams quickly headed to the tower that shortly earlier the lieutenant had come from. "Relay the order to stand at the ready and look alive for anything amiss to the other wall's sentries!", he anxiously advised the four other guardsmen preparing to begin their relief duty. "There may be trouble this night!"

With their steps hastened, the four took off running to inform the others of the possibility.

No sooner had Lieutenant Cobb cleared the stone stairs and arrived at the wall's entrance did the duke's carriage pull to a stop. Its door opened revealing a lip-quivering, teary-eyed, dirty, bleeding from several superficial cuts, trembling Paul. The young man stricken with grief.

"What be amiss Du...?", the lieutenant's inquiry being cut off as Cobb's eyes took in the sight of King Matthew's golden crown dawning the young man's brow.

Feigning not to notice the lieutenant's unfinished question or his body hesitate from the reeling view he had just taken in, the hurt young noble through agonizing words explained what had taken place earlier.

"We were riding on King's Road when we came under attack by a clever set ambush," revealed Paul. "The men fought as hard as they could, but the numbers were far too much for us to handle. The king was killed," the young man began to sob. The weight of the painful news driving him to his knees as he stepped from the coach. Tears running down his cheeks smudging his dirty face.

"My cousin be a hero," sobbed Paul. "King Matthew picked up a sword and dispatched two men before he himself was hit by three arrows. Our king handing me the crown, and in his dying breath ordered me to flee with these four men into the trees until the battle had ended," the young man sweeping a hand pointing out Sir Rufus, the two riders, and the coach's driver. "It was my cousin's last words that due to our bloodline I bear the burden of the crown and lead England to not only avenge his death, but protect his people." The self-made king looking up towards the sky, "Why my uncle and aunt? Why my cousin?" Lowering himself, he wailed into the dirt.

Staring at a prostrate Paul, the befuddled lieutenant, along with other members of the city's guard posted at the gate, stood in shock to the young man's words. It was the senior officer who comprehended first that the duke was now the king of England. Quickly he dropped to a knee.

"Your majesty," Cobb addressed. "Who be the ones responsible for the attack?"

Casting a watery gaze on his kneeling city guardsman, King Paul's anguish turned to a growl. "The French."

"What of Queen Lynn?", sadly inquired Lieutenant Cobb.

The young man looked upon every man present listening to his tall tale of tragedy before he spoke the largest of lies.

"The queen is with the French now, but not as a prisoner. From my hiding spot amongst the trees she seems to have fallen into some type of arrangement or partnership with them," he relayed in a disbelieving act. "If I had not been witness to it with my own eyes, I would have never believed she be capable of the treacherous act. I fear the attack that we encountered on this day she conspired with them and planned it precisely in order to alleviate England of its king."

His words seemed to rob the guards of their air, as his verbal blow of her treason was unsuspected by all of them. The men slowly realizing that her acts of kindness could possibly have just been a guise for her true intentions.

"We will avenge my cousin's death and make plans to war with the French. Their land and women will come only to know English seed. We will deliver swift justice on them after winter's snow," the new king pledged. "As for our treasonous queen, I, King Paul royally decree that from this day henceforth the woman formerly known as Queen Lynn to all of England be hunted and put to death! The succubus shall be known for whom she truly is; a traitor to not only my cousin but to the crown!", swore the self-made king.

King Paul had made it to the castle before sunset, and of his own free will spent time throughout the evening relaying the exact same detailed events that he had told the men he had first spoken to at the gates of Hamilton. The young man ordered the portcullises to the city's three entrances be lowered and closed for at least the night. "Who had the knowledge on how many French the former queen commanded?", he had reasoned before ordering them shut and the town off limits to all for now. On the morrow, Paul would send messengers out to spread the news of the assassination and post wanted posters for the traitor, Lynn Bradford. Already he had discovered her last name with the assistance of the castle's scribes from the royal wedding contract, and put them to work producing the scrolls. King Paul knew he needed to tie up loose ends.

Wall guard Adams strained his eyes in the darkness as he caught some type of movement on the road off in the distance. The man wasn't exactly sure what it was at first, but with the illumination of the star-filled sky it wasn't long before he knew exactly what he saw.

"Look there!", he pointed out to the other men who had been patrolling this section of wall with him.

Staring in the direction Adams pointed, the other guards also caught sight of the movement.

"Be that not the…?"

"Royal Carriage," ended Adams.

"Lieutenant! I have something!", pointed out the wall's sentry.

Stepping from the protection of the tower and into the stinging wind, Cobb gave the man a questioning look. "What do you see Adams?"

"It be the king's royal coach sir! By the look of it, there be no driver."

For the second time in so many hours, Lieutenant Cobb made his way down the stone stairs off the battlement and to the portcullis sealed entrance. He watched with a half-a-dozen other guardsmen through the gated closure, as the coach came to a stop. The senior officer glancing from face to face of the other men standing beside him.

After several long minutes of listening to snorts and whinnies from the horses, whom appeared to be requesting entrance into Hamilton, Cobb along with three other men rolled out of a narrow opening under the slightly raised portcullis. The lieutenant was not about to take any chances that this may be a French trap, so he had the gate lowered. Slowly and cautiously, the four soldiers with swords in hand approached the dark, silent coach.

Positioning themselves at the ready, the lieutenant cast a glance up to the battlements taking in the sight of six men, whom had bows ready to let loose their arrows. Grabbing a lit torch from one of the guards, Cobb quickly flung open the door to the carriage, while swiftly jumping to the side so he wouldn't be in the direct line of fire for a crossbow bolt. Nothing came from the darkness.

Waiting for brief, but tense filled moment, the senior officer extended the torch forward peering into the coach's interior.

"Christ almighty!", he start jumping back. Drawing a cross from head to heart and then across his shoulders, Cobb blessed himself grievously adding, "May you find peace in the Lord's House my friends,", as he gazed upon the dead corpses of the royal guardsmen packed in the carriage.

King Paul sat on the throne pondering over the arrival of the royal carriage carrying the bodies of all of Matthew's personal guardsmen. The only corpse that was missing, if it was an informing sign from Nathaniel, was the body of his cousin. He had already accounted for the queen and her servant, but he couldn't fathom the fact that a highly accomplished assassin, along with another man, could be overrun by the likes of two women. Could they have somehow killed his two men and rescued Matthew only to flee into the woods. Paul rose from the throne and started out for his new royal chambers.

"It be highly unlikely that Matthew still lived only to return and expose his cousin as the true traitor to the crown," thought Paul as he climbed the elegant staircase. Just the idea of the two women trying to care for the wounded king out in the wilderness during the weather this time of year seemed to quell his suspicions, but an indication of doubt had been planted in his head. Subconsciously, the thought still remained. Turning down the corridor, a smile crossed Paul's raptor-like face. Ruth was waiting at the door to his chambers.

Paul had not been coronated under God as England's new king, but already the crown burdened his brow. The young man just wouldn't admit to himself that the weight of the gold-decorated head piece, and all that he had planned and committed to get it, already pressed down on his head. The self-made king planning to escape his duties already this night as he opened the door and ushered the sex slave into his room. Hail to the king," he thought as he smiled.

Chapter 43

Russell's eyes flashed open when he heard King Matthew beginning to stir. The young man slightly sleeping in one of the room's corners with the queen engulfed by his protective embrace, scanned the place making sure there was no unwanted visitors in their midst. A fire still burning in the chimney's hearth lit up the room enough for Russell to make out his three friends still partaking in slumber, and the woman he now knew as Joan sleeping on the floor near the head of the king. From the dancing shadows on the walls caused by the flickering flames, and the lack of any type of sunlight coming through the cracks around the window shutters, the young man knew it was still the wee hours of the morning.

Slowly and carefully, so not to awaken the young woman, Russell repositioned Lynn so she now leaned into the corner he had been sleeping in while sliding his way out. Taking only a couple of minutes to accomplish his task at hand, the young man successful in his tricky escape made his way over to the wounded royal. His gaze meeting that of the weak, upward stare of King Matthew.

"My lord how can I aid thee?", his rescuer quietly inquired.

The corners of Matthew's lips turning up as he offered the young man a weakened grin. "You already have Russell. You and your friends came to the aid of the crown when we needed you most. Because of the actions you took both the queen and Joan live, and I am allotted valuable time to not only give my farewells to those whom mean the most to me, but to right any wrongs doings that I have made against the one I truly love."

Upon hearing his words, Russell investigated the dressings that Michael had bandaged Matthew's wounds up with earlier. He discovered that they were already soaked with the royal's blood. The attempt to stop the bleeding had been unsuccessful.

"I need to change your bandages my lord," calmly reasoned the young rescuer, but the young king lightly grabbed Russell's wrist.

"Do not find worry with the dressings Russell for I will pass from this life to the next soon," confessed the dying Matthew. "I would fancy with a pull of water though. My mouth knows only dryness."

Reaching and unstopping a waterskin that hung from a chair, the young man slid a hand under the king's head offering Matthew support, as the royal took two sips. Wiping his mouth, Russell gently laid him back on the pallet, and stoppered the skin. A shadow fell on both the young men drawing attention away from each other, as they sought out the reason for the covering darkness. Standing above them was the young woman, Russell had left alone in the corner where she slept.

"My queen," nodded Russell beginning to back away from the pallet.

"Do not leave Russell," came the weak voice of the king, as he smiled up at both of them. "What I say now I desire the both of you to hear."

"I found fondness with you my queen, and the tales of adventures from your youthful years, but believe me when I say I never meant to hurt you," softly spoke Matthew. "Nor you Russell," he added. "To ruin a true love between two people by stealing one from the other be an act rivaling that only equal to theft and murder," regretted the dying king. "I have committed a grievous act to you both, and only hope that the two of you can forgive my actions."

"Do not blame yourself my lord," sadly responded Lynn. Already a tear rolled down her cheek as she took up one of his hands in hers. "You did not know and only wished to do that which you felt right. It is I who am honored by your choice my king. I came to you not on terms set by your royal decree, but on those governed by my free will," pointed out Lynn as she placed a delicate kiss on the back of Matthew's hand and offered her husband a smile even though her eyes only knew tears.

"I only wish now my feelings and the decisions that I made were based in that of love and understanding in the stead of anger and blindness," disappointedly reasoned Matthew.

His wife, nor her true love, not knowing what he meant by those words.

"Lynn never stopped loving you," the king quietly revealed to the young man. "Do not harbor ill feelings towards her Russell. Her choice was not made with ease, and the queen never once let go of her heart that already belonged to you."

"I wish we could have known each other and perhaps we will in another life, but now I charge you with the largest task that I have ever given as a king," slowly he brought his hand with hers in it towards his young rescuer passing it off to him. "Take the queens hand. You have sworn an oath to her and God that you will protect her. I, as not only your king, but as a dying husband ask that you fulfill your sworn obligation." Matthew's own hand covered the joined hands of both Lynn and Russell.

"I swear with every ounce of strength and breath in my body that I will!", sternly the young man pledged. The look in his eyes solidifying his words, as Matthew knew in his heart that Russell would battle the devil himself and all of his minions of hell if he had to in order to defend Lynn from damnation.

"Lynn is your true love and you hers. Never let each other go," pleaded the king. "Her heart is yours and she will never love another. As you take her hand now in defense of her life, you must take her hand in marriage and keep her knowing safety as your wife," softly advised Matthew.

Both queen and commoner looking at each other momentarily and then back to their dying king.

"Never surrender true love," Matthew added. "Now I need to speak with Joan before it be too late."

"I am here Matthew," gently spoke the woman as she moved into his line of sight. Both Russell and Lynn moved to allow her and the king to share in a private moment.

"I lay in front of you a humble and broken fool who can only wish and pray that you forgive my trespasses against you," meekly confessed Matthew. "You tried to tell me the truth, but through foolishness my ears were deaf to your pleas. Instead of love I knew only pain. My cousin labeled me a jester with his acts of deception," angrily spoke the dying young man. "Can you forgive me my love?"

"I forgave you that night your verbal lashes my love," Joan weepingly admitted while sitting in the chair holding her lover's hand. "Paul forced me or he would have tried to see your ruin. You must believe my words that my heart only knows you, and will always know only you!"

Hiding his pain, the young king leaned up and wiped a tear from Joan's cheek. "I love you Joan, and know I chose you over a family until my cousin covered my sight with his mask of lies. I let his guise work and it rendered me blind." Slowly he pulled her to him and the two embraced in a kiss. After a moment his head found the pallet.

"Russell I burden you with one more request," softly stated Matthew.

"Yes your majesty."

"I beg of you, like the protection you offer the queen please give the same to my true love!"

"I swear my lord I will," sternly he pledged while dropping to a knee. "I shall see no harm come to the queen nor her!"

"Neither will I. Nor I. Nor I," swore Michael, Peter and Paul, whom all had been awoken by the attempt at Joan's quiet weeps.

The king put on a smile. "Already the two of you have four elite guardsmen."

"I love you Joan," peacefully pledged Matthew.

"I love you Matthew," responded Joan as she witnessed her lover exhale his final breath. "Do not leave me Matthew I need you!", she pleaded. Her words futile. For in the wee hours of the morning, England lost another king.

Weeping from the passing of Matthew, Lynn stepped forward to console Joan, who was now sobbing heavily. Her head resting near her lover's face.

Turning and looking to his three friends, Russell started for the cottage's door. The young man stepped outside with both brothers and Michael behind him. The queen and Joan needed to mourn their losses of a young man that they knew more about than being just their king.

Minutes passed and quietly Lynn stood over Joan rubbing the woman's back while Matthew's lover cried her loss. Eventually she straightened up in her seat.

"I love you Matthew," she said, as she softly placed a kiss on the dead man's forehead and using two fingers closed his open lids. "Till next we meet my love." Standing up, Joan embraced her queen and her friend.

"At first light, Peter and I will go back to the farm and grab more provisions," reasoned a chilly Russell while the four friends had left the two women to mourn the death of the king. "Michael, you and Paul wrap up King Matthew in cloth and find an elevation that the rains drain from. Bury the royal there, but do not make the grave too deep. When the cousin is relinquished of the crown, we will have to dig up the king so he may join his family sepulcher at the church."

His three friends just nodded their affirmation in the slowly lightening sky.

The four young men checked on the horses before making their way back inside. Lynn met them at the door,

"We need to bury Matthew," she matter-of-factly stated.

"Michael and Paul will carry out the task this day," confirmed the young man.

"Thank you," she humbly expressed before leading the four back inside.

Joan was still seated near her deceased lover, but her sobs were gone now. She knew the queen and her future was slowly caving in around them and the two were about to be hunted to extinction. Her only hope of survival lay in the four rescuers.

The sun had just broken the horizon and began its slow ascent into the sky. The wind was gone now, but still the crisp cold air of autumn kept its hold causing smoke to billow forth from anyone who had something to say. Russell and Peter packed their mounts preparing to make the trip back to the old Bradfords' cottage, along with the Daniels' farm, to select the necessary provisions. Russell knew they needed to buy some time while he found David the Beggar. The young man having a solid hunch that the man of the streets would be at the city's entrance a few days from now on the Sabbath. Breaking his thoughts, he turned his head when he heard the call softly behind him. Alone in the brisk air was Lynn's personal servant.

"Yes my lady," he responded while he packed one more item in a saddle bag and slowly begun to turn all the way around.

Peter overheard the encounter, but never lifted his eyes from his charger.

"I just wanted to offer you my humblest gratitude for what you and the others did for us on the yester day," the woman thanked. "It gave both Matthew and me a chance to know reconcile in the end rather than falsehoods." Taking a step to close the distance between the two, Joan placed a kiss on Russell's cheek before turning to go back inside.

"My lady," his words stopping her spin. "Matthew was a good king and a man who knew greatness. Do not fear I gave him my word I will protect you."

"I do not doubt that Russell," optimistically stated Joan. "The queen tells me that I am safer with you than if I was a half a world away." She smiled before starting for the cottage.

"Looks like someone may have an admirer," Peter broke the silence.

"Do not begin your jests with me on this day," retorted Russell.

"I am just making a possible observation," the other young man offering his explanation while mounting his charger.

Sticking his foot in the stir up and swinging the other leg over the horses back, Russell's head looked at the door when he heard the woman add before entering the cottage.

"God speed."

Without even looking to his traveling friend, Russell warned the young man. "Save your looks for another, Peter."

The brother only breaking into a small chuckle, as his friend's mount started the journey.

Russell only shook his head.

"Rise King Paul," placidly instructed Hamilton's priest after slipping the crown of England onto his brow. The clergyman had been summoned to the castle in order to ordain the young man. "May God, along with all those present, recognize their new ruler."

Slowly rising to his feet, Paul offered the holy man a smile before turning to face the castle's audience. The small congregation of servants and guardsmen dropped to a knee as one and pledged their allegiance to their new king. For those, whom happened to be most, who had a hard time believing the story of Matthew's demise and their queen's treason added a silent prayer for their fallen king.

"My most trusted of Hamilton," addressed Paul. His eyes roaming over the limited audience. "Today we need mourn my cousin. He was a good king in his short lived reign, but his time has come to an end. Today I will change some of our appearances from those that know weakness to those of strength forged like that of steel. We shall hunt down the traitorous queen, along with her French accomplices, and show them swift English justice! This I swear before God." King Paul's words not receiving the exact reaction he was looking for from the dispirited gatherers. The young man quickly coming up with an explanation for the lack of enthusiasm they displayed.

"I know you are saddened by the loss of Matthew, but I ask that you return to your duties and perform your tasks well," he feigned his sadness.

King Paul, Sir Rufus, and the priest watched the people slowly file out of the castle's chapel.

"When can Hamilton expect to be gifted by your presence at mass your majesty?", optimistically inquired the Lord's servant.

"On this upcoming Sabbath," replied the new king.

"Very well your highness," smilingly nodded the priest before taking his leave.

Both Paul and Rufus stood alone on the dais, as the last of the occupants filed out the doorway.

"They will come around my lord."

"Of course they will Rufus," agreed Paul. "And the ones who do not will have their necks stretched!", evilly smiled the king. "Take a couple of our men with you and bring me the queen's family."

"Yes my lord," nodded Sir Rufus before stepping from the dais heading for the room's doorway.

Chapter 44

Russell and Peter, both on horseback, emerged from the trees and made their way around the end of the stone wall. Both had been by this way throughout their lives, and knew all they would have to do is follow the barricade between the forest and the rolling grassland. The two would end up near the Daniels' cottage before going to the Bradford's old farm and resupplying their provisions.

"We make haste," informed Russell instructing his charger into a gallop.

Peter flipped the reigns belonging to his mount and heeled his horse to follow.

Already it was almost early afternoon, and Russell had one quick stop to make before the two young men would arrive at his father's farm. He and Peter were glad that even though the weather was cold, it had been sunny and clear with no wind nipping at the two as they rode.

After making a stop and leaving crumbs of bread on the stone wall across from a lone, leafless tree, Russell and Peter finally gazed down a hill at his father's cottage. Smoke billowed from its chimney, as the young Daniel's man scanned the grounds for any signs of his father about.

"It would appear that the cold has driven my father inside to seek shelter. "Tie the horses over there,..." -Russell pointed behind the small stone barn,- "...and give them some hay and water."

Peter only nod his affirmative before the two heeled the chargers toward the structures.

"What are you boys doing back here already?", excitedly queried his mother, as Russell and Peter walked through the doorway. "Where be Paul and Michael?", Elizabeth added looking past the two for the rest of the four.

"There be trouble mother," her son revealed trying to blow the coldness from his hands. "King Matthew has been murdered by Duke Paul."

Elizabeth dropping the clay bowl that she had been holding and was about to ladle some stew from a pot she simmered near the chimney's hearth.

"What of Lynn?", gasped Nicole.

"She be safe," admitted her older brother. "We came upon the scene of the slaughter in time to rescue her, another woman, and the king. Unfortunately he succumbed to his wounds and passed this morning."

Both young men sat down while Elizabeth retrieved a couple of bowls and gave them some hot potato stew and a roll to aid in warming themselves.

"Right now Lynn, along with the other woman, are with the four of us at the cottage," confirmed Russell after a swallow. "The new king has already declared Lynn,..." his words trailing off as Robert stormed through the doorway waving a parchment.

"Matthew be dead, and now the new king, Paul, has decreed the queen a wanted traitor! She is to be charged with treason against the crown and to be hung once she is found!", excitedly revealed Russell's father shutting the door behind him.

"What are you doing back son?", perplexedly questioned Robert while gazing at the young man.

"Lynn be innocent father."

"Of course she be!", he answered in a matter-of-fact tone. "The cousin's accusation only knows falsehood. Truth lacks in his words. We need to find her if she still lives before this self-proclaimed king does!"

"She be safe father," admitted Russell.

"Lynn be with you son?"

"We have hid her and her servant at the cottage. Peter and I came for provisions."

Pulling out a chair, Robert sat at the table as both of the young men told him of the ambush on the day prior. Russell's father would aid the four rescuers with a plan to not only protect England's queen, but save the young woman's life and neck length.

"Is the traitor here!", shouted the large black knight that the Bradfords had seen and remembered from the tourney.

"Traitor!", perplexed Charles jumping up when the manor's front door had been kicked open. The wooden portal had swung open so violently that it had slammed against the inside wall and quickly bounced back towards the entering intruders. "What traitor?!", he shouted.

"You know who it be that I speak of," growled Sir Rufus almost ripping the rebounding door from its hinges.

"What be the meaning of this?", madly inquired Gwyneth rushing down the staircase. Her daughter Anne in tow.

Three other men followed the black knight through the entrance way and into the country estate. Fanning out, they began their search from room to room. The three men taking great pleasure overturning furniture while ripping and tearing the place asunder. Miscellaneous debris flew throughout the air.

"Do not...", Charles tried shout the order, but his words were cut short when one of the men pushed him down to the floor.

Both his wife and his daughter screamed as they rushed the rest of the way down the stairs and to the head of the Bradford family.

"There be no traitor here!", Gwyneth shouted afraid. "When the king and queen hear of this...", the woman's words cut off by a back hand. Gwenyth tumbling backwards from the strike.

"Leave her!", frighteningly screamed Anne who had been squatting near her father.

"King Matthew has been assassinated," growled Sir Rufus staring down at the three Bradfords.

The news shocking them to a loud gasp.

"What of my daughter?", demandingly inquired Charles bouncing to his feet like he was a spring buck.

"The queen conspired with the French. She be the traitor."

"Liar !", shouted Lynn's father. He attempted a swing at the larger Sir Rufus but the knight just took a step back watching the attempted blow go by.

"You dare to attempt to strike a king's royal guardsman?", he laughed as he used the man's momentum against him carrying Charles into the wall. Hitting his head on the wooden partition, the queen's father went limp and dropped to the floor unconscious.

"Father!", screamed Anne.

"Charles!", cried out Gwenyth, as she rushed to his side squatting near the unconscious man.

The four king's men laughed.

"You two take a look outside," commanded Rufus. "The queen and her servant may be in hiding somewhere out there just waiting for our departure."

"Yes sir."

The knight giving a mischievous smile to the remaining guard before starting for Gwenyth. Lynn's mother trying desperately to get an answer from her unconscious husband.

"Let us see if we can jar your memories," Sir Rufus growled while pulling the woman up by her hair. "Come with me Jonas," instructed the knight.

"If you do not wish to see your mother hurt, I would suggest you be here when we return," intimidated the man named Jonas before he followed the large man with Anne's mother into another room.

"No! No!", Gwenyth screamed over and over.

Her daughter could hear her struggling. Without a seconds delay, the thirteen year old ran into another room. She reappeared minutes later with her father's sheathed sword, and quietly ran to his side. Anne could hear the creaking of a piece of furniture and grunts from the guard Jonas and her mother as he was taking her.

"Father! Father wake up! Mother needs you!", she quietly cried trying to stir the man from unconsciousness. Her eyes watery as tears rolled down her face. "Father wake up!"

Slowly Charles began to come to attempting to blink the darkness from his eyes.

"Father get up! Mother needs you!"

The grunts and furniture creaks in the other room came a little faster now.

"Anne?", perplexedly asked her father while he began to stir trying to call back to memory what had just happened.

"They are hurting mother!", agonized his crying daughter.

Charles began to rise to his feet while blinking away the pain. He could hear the grunts and the creaks come at a much faster pace now, and automatically he knew what type of violation to his wife was going on. Taking a second to peek into the room, he grabbed his sheathed sword and one of the chairs by its back support.

"Do you know your way to the Daniels?", he inquired.

"Yes father," sniffled Anne.

"Go tell Robert what be going on."

His daughter only nodded her head.

"Be careful Anne and do not stop for anything. Do not let anyone see you," he warned her. "I love you. Now go."

Jonas had just shot his seed into Gwenyth when he began to pull himself away from the crying woman. The sound of the wood splintering caused him to turn and take in the sight of Sir Rufus reel before falling from the chair strike. The guard not having time to pull his pants up from his ankles witnessed Charles draw the sword across his neck. Blood splayed on the wall as Jonas' head fell to the floor followed moments later by his limp body.

"Can you run Gwenyth?", he queried while on guard, as the knight began to rise.

Tears fell from her eyes and she quickly smoothed down her dress. "Yes," she nodded.

"Run!", instructed her husband. "I will allot you as much time as I can."

"I love you Charles," she cried running from the room. The last two things his wife heard is her husband response followed by the clash of swords, as she fled from the manor.

Gwenyth did not have to worry about going back for her daughter when Anne intercepted her coming out of the stone structure. Hand in hand, they ran for the cover of the half naked trees going unseen by the two guards, who had run into the back door. Like all of their lives, Charles had given all he had to provide for his family and this day was no different. The Bradford man provided for them the time the two needed to flee at the cost of giving it his all.

It was already past sundown when the four occupants in the small cottage heard the whistle of the robin. Silently they all took heed to the call.

"What be that?", frighteningly asked Joan.

"Do not worry yourself my lady," calmly advised Michael. "It be only Russell and Peter returning."

"I will check it out," Paul slipped out the door with his bow.

A short time later both Russell and Peter opened the door to the heated place and walked in. Michael, along with Lynn and Joan, could tell the two were cold and tired. The young queen rising from her seat at the table.

"You be cold," she pointed out the obvious. "Come warm yourselves by the fire."

"There be wanted posters of you already around Hamilton," her love confirmed while taking one from his pocket and placing it down on the table.

Both women glanced on it and within moments Lynn gasped. Bringing her eyes up from the parchment, tears had already begun to well up in them. "My parents and Anne be in grave danger!", she aghast. "We need rescue them!"

"I am sorry Lynn, but we cannot do anything this night," the young man apologized. "Peter, Paul and I will ride on the morrow to get them."

"You be right my love," sadly admitted Lynn. "Already my crown and my life gives burden to you and your friends."

"Your words lack truth," corrected Russell while gazing into her eyes. "We need a plan and cannot ride into a possible trap blindly. Tonight we devise a plan for if we fail then you will fall and I lack the acceptance in that outcome."

Taking a moment to ponder her love's words, she agreed. "Once again you know what is best for me," she smiled through watery eyes.

On this night Joan witnessed her queen be the servant, as Lynn prepared both Russell and Peter a bowl of rabbit stew from the two hares that Paul had snared earlier in the day.

Picking up the wanted poster, Russell threw it into the chimney's fire. The blaze consuming the parchment quick. On this night the rescuers planned on returning on the morrow with the rest of the Bradford's.

Eventually sleep consumed everyone, but Lynn. Even though she found comfort in her love's arms, her thoughts could not rest. Uncomfortably her mind knew that her family was now in close striking distance of England's most deadliest creature. The young woman hoping the morrow would not be too late, nor would Russell and his brave friends find themselves snared like the two hares Paul had caught earlier. Their ending did not come out favorable for them.

Chapter 45

The sun had risen over Hamilton this morning, but frost covered the ground and there was a cold breeze blowing in the air. Warm vapors being exhaled by both the horses feeding on buckets filled with oats, as well as the three young men who were finishing preparing the chargers to leave so they could retrieve the queen's family, drifted from their mouths and nostrils into the frigid atmosphere. Soon winter would fully fall on the land bringing the snowfall in its descent. The small group knew that that time wasn't far off now. They would have to hide here for the winter with at least one person returning back to Russell's farmhouse to replenish their provisions and create the illusion that the place was being inhabited.

"Please be safe," cautiously advised Lynn as she approached Russell.

"We will be back as soon as we can," came the young man finishing securing some rations in his saddlebag. "For now you two will stay with Michael while Peter, Paul, and I retrieve your parents and Anne."

"I am sorry I got you into this," she sadly apologized.

"Nonsense," he waved off her words. "I will always protect you Lynn because you mean so much to me and you be my queen."

The young woman leaning into him to give her true love a hug and a kiss, but Russell turned his head to the side. Lynn's lips meeting his left cheek.

"Why do you turn away my love?", she surprisingly queried. "Because you be my queen, and wife to the late King."

"But Matthew knew the truth in his heart and gave us his blessings," Lynn tried to reason.

"My heart desires you more than the trees do the sun, but under God's ever watchful and knowing eyes you are still the king's queen," pointed out Russell. "We cannot know love like we did before your marriage. At least not now."

Lynn felt her heart drop into her stomach. "Why Russell?", her question only bringing her to know more pain.

Reaching up, he lovingly took hold of the young woman's hand. "Because God has commanded thou shall not commit adultery my love," he tenderly affirmed before continuing. "Even now you cause my soul to sin because of the desire and need I have for a married woman. If I be damned for breaking one of our Lord's commandments then so be it, but I will not allow you to lose your soul to the devil, nor your virtues."

"But the king is lost to us!", she tried pleading with him. It was to no avail. Russell had already made up his mind.

"When this is over, you and I will set things right in the Lord's Eye, but for now you are off limits to me and I you in that form of mannerism."

Her true love raising her hand to his lips and placing a delicate kiss on it. "My queen we need to ride and bring your family to safety before King Paul strikes."

Releasing her hand, the young man swung up on his mount. Looking to the brothers, who were mounted and waiting to leave, Russell made a "clicking" noise from the side of his mouth and the three mounted men began their journey. Lynn's true love only hoping they would get to the country estate and return with the Bradfords in time. The young man knowing that King Paul's lie circulated and stretched quicker than he could ride. The rescuer heeling his horse into a jog-like gallop. Peter and Paul's mounts keeping pace.

The day warmed a little bit removing the frost from the ground, but still a cold breeze blew lightly through the air. More leaves had fallen coming to join the others as they rested on the forest's floor. The light wind carried them dancing and skittering amongst the tree's trunks throughout the woods. Already the multi-colored foliage dotted the rock covering to King Matthew's resting place.

"I miss you my love," quietly admitted Joan standing over the grave site while bunching the hooded cloak that she wore at her throat. The woman not given any attention to the leaves crunching under Lynn's footfalls as she came up behind her.

"I am sorry for your loss," the young queen softly consoled her servant. "I know you miss Matthew as do I. He was a good king and a great person," she added behind a saddened smile.

The other woman turned to meet her gaze with tears in her eyes. "I miss him more than the heavens hold clouds. My heart has died with him."

Joan felt her friend's arm wrap around her shoulders. The action causing the personal servant to melt into the young queen's body and the comforting support she gave. Joan's tears came faster now blurring her vision. "It is not my business, but overhearing your words to Matthew, and he you, what happened between the both of you?", inquired the young woman.

The air only knew the sounds of Joan weeping and the rustle caused by the leaves skipping in the breeze.

"It be alright if you wish not to share," compassionately admitted the queen. "You need not say a word. Your dealings are yours."

"I was present the day Matthew was born into this world," Joan began a minute or two later between sniffles and wiping her eyes. "From that moment, Queen Margaret assigned me to the duties of Matthew's caretaker and personal servant. Through the years I watched the boy grow into a young man, and as he grew so did my love for him," a small smile creased Joan's lips while waves of memories throughout the years rolled through her mind's eye. "Until one night when he had just started to begin life as a young man, we sat in his room speaking. To this day I cannot bring to memory what it was that we even spoke about. Before I knew what was happening, Matthew and I were partaking in a kiss."

Staring at the almost bare tree branches, Lynn brought back to her the memory the first time she and Russell confessed their love for one another. Even now the young woman could feel the softness of her true love's lips on hers.

"That night we coupled for the first time," admitted Joan. "We had loved each other ever since."

"I do not understand why Matthew wed I not the one he truly loved?", perplexed Lynn. "What occurred that changed that?"

"His cousin occurred," disappointedly informed Joan. "Paul took witness to me sneaking into Matthew's chambers one night during a stay at the castle and threatened to tell King Stephen and Queen Margaret, along with the whole of England that the prince coupled with a barren servant. The duke also planned on adding the fact that Matthew had decided to honour our love which would not produce an heir to succeed him on the throne. He exposed his plan to ruin Matthew to me one night in the palace's kitchen. I begged him not to and we struck an accord. In exchange for his secrecy, I would be at his beckoning call for the remainder of his stay. The duke's words were nothing but a trick. I thought he wanted me to wait on him, but the devil used me as his sex slave. He made me call off my visits to Matthew and summonsed me to his chambers every night where Paul raped me alone or with Rufus, and who I now know as his assassin on the King's Road," revealed Joan behind watery eyes.

The horrific explanation shocked Lynn beyond any words known to her and for seemed like several minutes. The two standing in silence before the queen pointed out the obvious. "But you are not of a barren womb and a child grows in there now!", she pointed at her servant's stomach.

Slowly and instinctively, the woman began to rub her belly in a circular motion. "Yes, but I know not whom sired the child," cried Joan. "I only wish now that I truly be barren in the stead of birthing a child whose father be either the devil himself or one of his minions from hell!"

The revelation causing a shiver to run through Lynn as she thought back to how many times she had desired to meet the king's cousin.

"Matthew did not believe you when you told him what occurred?"

"I never told him believing that he would not believe my words," corrected the woman. "On one night Paul had devised in his plan that he would bring his cousin to his chambers. Once the duke opened the door, Matthew witnessed me caught in the throes of pleasure being taken by Rufus and another. My body had surrendered and responded to their actions," she sniffled.

Lynn embraced her friend and held her tight in both support and understanding for the woman's plight. "I am sorry this happened to you Joan," softly she spoke into the woman's ear behind tears of her own.

The queen realizing at that moment that no one needed a crown to be burdened, especially not one whom had been unwillingly taken and left to bear her rapist's child as a single mother.

"I promise to aid you and your baby as much as I can," compassionately stated the young woman. Already through her listening and unjudging kindness, Joan felt the burden weighing down on her from the tragic secret she had kept to herself begin to lighten and ease in Lynn's supporting words and embrace.

It was close to midday and Michael had left a short time ago to check the cottage's grounds and make sure the area was clear of the new king's men looking for the outlaw queen. He had left important words before taking his leave. "No matter the cause, do not open this door unless you hear the hoot of an owl or the call of a robin," he had instructed before closing the portal.

Both Lynn and Joan busied themselves with preparing this evening's meal. The two women had returned back inside shortly after the servant's horrific revelation and the shared hug between them. Now, both shared in a much lighter conversation bringing smiles and laughter to them like young maidens who knew of no worries.

"What of you and this Russell?", inquired Joan out of the blue while cutting up another potato for the cooking pot.

"What it be you mean?"

Her servant looking up from the cutting board on the table. "I believe you know what I speak of," she mischievously grinned.

"Well we were born commoners and our families have always been good friends since my father and his father were small boys. Russell and I grew up together and he always protected me, along with my younger sister and his. Eventually a love blossomed between him and I, and he is my true love," she replied while glancing up from the lamb fillets she was tenderizing with a block-shaped cooking utensil. "One time when I was a small child, I got lost in the woods. Russell looked for me and found me hiding and afraid with a hurt ankle. He was holding a stick for protection." Lynn smiled and let out a little laugh at the memory. "He gave it to me so I would not know fear and remained with me until our fathers came and got us. From that day on, I have loved Russell with all my heart." The young queen about to go on when she heard the call of the robin in the distance followed by a hoot.

"Speak of Russell!", she excitedly said while jumping up and placing the utensil down. Hastily, Lynn started for the barred door.

"Are you sure it is them?", cautiously queried Joan.

"Michael said an owl or a robin," affirmed Lynn unbarring the wooden portal.

The young woman slowly opened the door, peeked out, and checked to make certain the coast was clear. That was when it hit her and a bad feeling crept into her body. Quickly she closed and barred the door.

"What be wrong my queen?", perplexedly queried Joan jumping up from her seat at the table. The spud she had been cutting fell to the floor.

"It cannot be Russell," she quietly responded. "He should not be returning soon."

"What do you mean?", panicked Joan while hoping to see through the cracks of a shutter. Without even realizing it, the knife she had been using was still in her grasp.

"It took Russell all of the yesterday to go for provisions," Lynn stated while she was looking for something to use to defend herself. "It be only midday, and it would have taken him longer for he must travel further to get my family.

The queen's truth causing her servant's worry to rise by the moment. Joan swore she could hear he own heart pounding off the walls of the cottage.

Both women started and gasped when they heard the knock on the door. The frightened women feeling like mice caught in a trap. Their panic-stricken bodies relieved when they heard Michael's voice.

"Lynn. Joan. Open the door," he requested. "It be I, Michael. Russell be close."

The young women ran to the portal and like before removed the solid piece of lumber barring it. Opening it and taking in the sight of the muscular young man, Lynn walked out from the cottage.

"Where be Russell?"

"He, along with Peter and Paul, will be coming from there," pointed Michael.

Searching the half dead undergrowth and the semi-bare trees, the queen and her servant watched as Russell came into sight leading his mount. On the horses's back sat Lynn's mother followed by Peter leading his charger. Anne took up residence in its saddle, but the third animal was ridden by Peter's brother Paul. Lynn's smile disappeared when her father never came into view. The anticipation to see her family was beginning to give way to panic fueled by the worrisome look on Anne's face, along with the sad, distant gaze of her mother.

The young woman's question barely audible at first. It grew louder the closer she and the procession came together.

"Where be father? Where be father?", fear reflecting in the queen's voice

Russell's expression of anguish told Lynn all she needed to know. Tears flowed from her eyes. The young man holding her pained gaze, as the two came together.

"Russell. Where be my father?"

"I know not Lynn," he answered. "My father met me on the way and said they had both made it to his cottage last night."

"Mother. Where be father?", the young queen tried to inquire between tears, but Gwynth was distant and lost inside herself.

"They said you had King Matthew murdered and you be a traitor," interjected her younger sister.

"Where be father Anne?"

"They were hurting mother so father told me to run to the Daniels' farm. I hid at first, but within minutes mother came running from the manor. We made our way there together. Father saved us," her younger sister's words causing both of Lynn's legs to buckle. The queen dropped to her knees on the leaf-covered ground. The image of those horrific events sending her into uncontrollable sobs.

"Michael," called Russell. "Take the Bradfords into the cottage," the young man handing his horse's lead to the other.

Dropping to his knees, her love tried to console the devastated daughter. The young man embracing the crying young woman as he watched the rest of the refugees head to the cottage. Russell only knew one thought. "I should have ridden last night to get them."

Chapter 46

The Sabbath; November 1st, 1440
All Saints' Day

The weather was both cold and damp with the pewter-colored storm clouds overhead threatening to dump rain on Hamilton at any moment. A biting wind ripped at any exposed flesh, and the three Daniels whom had ridden into the city to attend church on this Sabbath wore reddened cheeks and noses. The days rawness helping things to move quicker due to the townsfolk not desiring to be out and about for extended periods of time. Hamilton's streets were somewhat clear now rather than being jam-packed like they had been only a month ago. Still one man braved the gloominess the outdoors had to offer.

"Alms for the poor!", cried out the street urchin bundled up in rags and wearing a hooded cloak. "Alms for the poor please!"

"Keep it moving folks!", shouted the gate's guardsman while waving pass incoming carts from Hamilton's countryside on their way to church.

"Pleasant morning Daniels family," the beggar greeted while walking toward their horse drawn wagon. The man noticing the missing presence of Robert's only son. "My eyes take in the sight of only three of your family rather than four," he pointed out.

"You are correct David," responded Robert as he pulled his cart off to the side of the road so others could keep moving past. "We find ourselves short Russell today in thanks to a cold that keeps him bedridden," he explained. "He does however send his greetings."

David the Beggar offered a slight bow from his hip. "Please return my wishes for a speedy recovery. He is a fine young man no doubt in thanks to his mother and father," the street urchin smiled as he glanced to Nicole.

"Greetings David," he sixteen year old smiled.

"Well hello to my favorite lass," grinned the beggar. "There be no arguing that you be your mother's daughter. Your beauty rivals that of hers day to day."

Both Elizabeth and her daughter turned and smiled at one another. A giggle escaped from Nicole.

"Terrible news regarding King Matthew," disappointedly brought up David. "King Paul says the demise is due to a plan between the outlaw queen and the French.

"Keep it moving folks!", shouted the guardsmen gazing over in their direction.

"Please my lord," pleaded David turning towards the soldier. "I know not sharing words with another in conversation. People spend the greater part of their time yelling down at me to move away from under their window or take the risk of being flogged by their unpleasantries." The visual image of the street urchin's words causing the guard to grimace. Even Elizabeth and Nicole shared a look of disgust.

Turning back to the Daniels' cart, David the Beggar smiled. "Till the next Sabbath when we be able to speak again."

"We do not part ways until you take this first," Elizabeth's statement leaving no room for compromise as she held out a large, roll of bread wrapped in cloth. Nicole also held out a rectangular-shaped object wrapped up. "You know this be bread while that there be three lamb fillets already seen the cooking fire," Robert's wife happily pointed out.

David accepted the food wearing a gracious smile accompanied with a bow of his head. "You folks have always been good to me. May God forever bestow his blessings on your family."

"And also you," quickly added Nicole, as already their cart began for the city's entrance.

For this day had been designated a Christian day to honour all of the saints. With both hands full, David the Beggar smiled to himself knowing that not only could he give reverence to any saint he desired, but he was fortunate enough to speak with and be fed by a family of God's finest ones.

"Good day to you sir," he wished the gate's guard as he strolled past him on his way to his favorite alley.

"Peace be with you," humbly wished the church's priest, as mass came to a close.

"And also with you," returned the full congregation there to not only worship but meet their new ruler.

Turning, the holy man bowed his head to the young man seated on the dais relinquishing the podium to the royal.

Returning the priest's nod with one of his own, the king rose from his throne-like seat and made his way to the lectern.

"My loyal subjects," he addressed the church's crowd. "This day be All Saints' Day. It be a day to feast and honour all those whom have lent aid to others throughout their lives. A time to call to memory the deeds performed by another in an attempt to lighten the burden of the crosses that we all bear," movingly convey Paul. Taking a moment to pause, the tone in his voice changed more to reflect a somber mood. "On this day, as we feast and pay reverence, please find it in your hearts to remember not only my cousin King Matthew, but importantly both King Stephen and Queen Margaret. None of them be named saints, but all of you know their actions and mannerisms were those that rival that of sainthood."

His words brought the congregation to a low sound of agreement.

Waiting for the murmur to die down, King Paul gazed out amongst the congregation before continuing. "The burden of the crown now falls to me to aid you all in the protection against those who work evil against our land. The same heathens who even now desire war with our country."

Suddenly, two doors, one on each side of the throne-like chairs where the royals always sat when joining the church in worship opened up, and a large group of men poured out of them to join the priest and Sir Rufus on the dais behind the new king at the podium.

Another low murmur arose from the surprised crowd, and even the holy man appeared in shock by the men dawning chain mail.

"People of Hamilton!", Paul raised his voice suppressing the low tone throughout the chapel. "We plan for a war against the French, but to do that we need to gather our forces and amass coin to pay for the war support. Thenceforth, taxes shall be paid at a cost of two and a half gold every month, along with you good folk of Hamilton being expected to open up your homes to at least one guardsman. Those that refuse will have three choices; join the battle on the front line; be thrown in the castle's dungeon; or have your necks stretched as traitors to the crown."

Gasps filled the air as the townsfolk, along with those from the countryside sat in complete shock over King Paul's proclamation.

"This be only a small number of men," the young man turned to sweep his hand and pointed out the guards. "In time more will arrive with some men from here joining the gathering army. It be my wish to protect not only England from invasion, but every home in Hamilton!", the king confidently reasoned.

"Now go in peace good folk, and when a soldier comes knocking at your door welcome him in with open arms. Take heed in knowing that like those saints that this day honours, you too will be aiding a man who is giving more to England than a mere shelter over a stranger's head and food to eat."

Turning his head around, Paul nodded at Sir Rufus and the two took their leave from the church. The new king, his knight, and the royal carriage were already down the next street and on their way to the castle before the whole of the congregation attempted to recover from their shock. There would be no sanctuary offered at church today, nor refuge from the increase in taxes, or the armored men who would eventually come knocking.

A light shower had begun to fall on the land shortly before darkness, and David the Beggar was glad to be out of the wet weather. The wind from this morning had picked up slightly causing the rain to come down a little on a slant. The street urchin was glad that he had found shelter in a wide alleyway underneath a two-wheeled cart out of the elements. David carefully repositioned the small wagon to butt up against a building's wall. Its roof's overhang helping to block the exterior partition from the falling rain, allowing the man to climb under the cart and remain dry while leaning back against the building.

Placing the cloth covered roll on his lap, David slowly folded back the materials edge exposing a piece of the baked item Elizabeth Daniels had given him this morning. Just the mere sight and smell of the fresh bread caused the beggar's mouth to water as the memories of her always soft and tasty rolls came to mind. He knew this time would be no different. The recollection quickly and momentarily causing him to lose his train of thought over the new king's dreary decree.

"My trust lacks in King Paul's choices and decisions," he thought. "I wish Timothy was around so I could learn more about the hastily rise of this new royal and the sudden fall of the old one." Just the mere mention of his brother caused David to draw a cross with his fingertips upon his body. "I knew castle life would be the death of you before your time," added David while looking up at the bottom of the cart and sending a silent prayer towards the heavens.

Ripping a piece of the roll and inhaling a waft of it, the man took a bite. Chewing, David's thoughts returned to the news days ago of the ambush on the royal carriage and how Queen Lynn was responsible with aid being lent by the French. The fact that the English and French stood on a blade's edge ready to fall into war with one another held true, but the story that the queen had conspired and planned the attack that would rob England of its beloved king or take the lives of good men like his brother was not adding up in his head. Timothy had told him on several occasions when they had met, that Queen Lynn reminded him of a younger version of Queen Margaret. The descriptions; ruthless, unkind, and plotting were words that were never used to describe the prior royal, so if the new one had been compared to the previous one by his brother than how did his brother's comparison know truth.

"Something be not right," he thought to himself while tearing off another piece of the roll. His eyes glancing down to the contents in his lap when he heard a piece of parchment rustle.

"What be this?", he perplexed.

Moving the piece of roll aside, the street urchin could make out a small piece of parchment under the bread's base. Removing it from the cloth packaging, David held it up, but it was too dark to read it here. He puzzled over a note from the Daniels.

Folding up the cloth, David tucked the remainder of the uneaten portion along with the parchment back inside a pocket located on the interior of his hooded cloak and crawled out from under his shelter for the night. The beggar figured it had to be of some importance, for never had he received a note from the family throughout the years of receiving food.

Making his way to the center of the alley, David pulled the note out of his cloaks inside pocket and opened it to read.

David,

> *King Paul be not who he pretends to be. For he is the one responsible for Sir Timothy and King Matthew's deaths. Our queen be innocent, and I can prove this. Meet me on the morrow night outside the city. Just keep walking on the main road far enough out of the wall guard's sight and I shall be there.*

Russell

David looked around to make sure no one watched before tearing the note into little pieces. When he was satisfied with their small parts he brought half the stack to his lips, threw it into his mouth, and began chewing. A minute later, the beggar swallowed the other half with ease. David reached in his pocket and felt for a small pouch of coin he still had left from the day's work outside the city's walls. The street urchin headed for the local tavern as he thought to himself, "An ale would wash down any evidence of the note." For even though he knew the young man's words were soaked with honour, the swallowed correspondence was one that only knew dryness.

Paul sat on his throne wearing his majestic, royal-purple robe, his gold crown, and a look of disgust on his hawk-like face as he waited for the two guests to be ushered into the throne room. His plans to leave the church right after his shocking announcement and exchange meeting and greeting his people for a bath followed by some rest and relaxation had been carried out until now. King Paul was hoping the two visitors, who had arrived hours ago at the castle, would get sick of waiting and take their leave, but that was not the case. Even now holding audience with them was postponing his supper plans.

Paul looked up and feigned a smile as he watched one of the palace's servants lead a young man and woman into the throne room. Automatically, he could tell the two were commoners by the way they were dressed. The king knowing that the clothes these people were wearing were their Sunday's best.

"Welcome," Paul greeted, as the three dropped to a knee in front of the steps leading to the platform where the two thrones sat upon. "My humblest of apologies for the wait," he offered. "This turmoil with the French robbed me of my time."

"There be no trouble your majesty," the young man responded. "We be grateful that you took the time to see us and listen to our troubles."

"You are dismissed."

"Thank you my lord," the servant rose to his feet and gave a nod. "Please rise," instructed Paul sitting back in his throne. "You folks seem to be farmers. Do those words know truth?"

"Yes your majesty," they both replied with a smile. "I am Ronald and this be my wife Martha."

"What be your trouble?", King Paul inquired feigning his pleasantness. He had witnessed his Uncle Stephen go through the same routine several times here at the castle, along with numerous times in Scheffield when the king and queen came North to visit. The only difference is his uncle never faked his courtesy or concern.

"It be the extra taxes my lord," cautiously admitted Ronald while glancing between his wife and the king several times. "I wished to see you this day and speak with your majesty before there be a misunderstanding."

"I am not quite sure what you mean," Paul feigned his ignorance. "You be not required to pay extra taxes only the two and a half gold every month to support in the protection of our country from the French."

"That be what I address with you now my lord," nervously revealed Ronald. "We did not pull enough coin to carry us to the next season if you raise our taxes." Stealing a glance to his wife he continued, "Even now my lord, Martha and I go hungry more times than not just to pay our current fair. More coin would bring about our dying of starvation. Please your highness, be there any way you could offer us a reprieve at least for this upcoming winter?", pleaded the young commoner.

King Paul sat in silence for a minute contemplating the young couple's dilemma.

"You say you hunger?"

"Yes my lord," humbly replied Ronald and his wife.

The seated royal turned his attention to the young woman and calmly addressed her. "Martha, would you please step forward and allow me to gaze upon you?"

Taking a step forward, Ronald's wife gazed upon the king and smiled.

"You hunger?", he puzzled.

"Yes your majesty."

"I am sorry Martha," apologized Paul. "Remove your clothes, so I can know a better look."

"But your majesty," shocked Ronald when he not only heard the request, but also met the questioning eyes from his wife.

"You folks come to me for help correct?", the king's firm tone rising a couple of decibels as Paul's hawk-like stare displayed only intimidation.

"My apologies my lord." he humbled. Turning to his wife, the young husband watched, as the young woman began to remove her dress.

Paul glared at the nude woman taking notice that she still wore her soft shoes. "Remove your shoes as well."

Responding to her king's request, Martha removed her footwear. The thin, young woman standing fully exposed to Paul.

"I will help you," he broke the moment of silence in the room. "Martha come hither," the young king instructed while pointing on the platform right in front of where he sat.

The young wife began to pick up her dress, but was stopped before she could grab the garment.

"You shall not need your clothes. Now come hither!", he snapped.

Ronald stood in awe watching his sweet wife climb the two steps and stand in front of the king's throne.

"On your knees!", ordered Paul.

Honour

Ronald's wife wore a look of fear as she dropped to her knees and the king spread his robe only to reveal that he was nude underneath. Already his manhood hardened. Reaching forward, he guided the young woman's head into his lap. "Since Ronald cannot feed you I will," Paul devilishly stated.

Martha's eyes pleaded but to no avail. The king entered her mouth.

"Your majesty!", begged Ronald in shock. "That be my wife!"

"I will not let a woman hunger in my kingdom," he smugly assured her husband as King Paul placed her palms on his chest.

Ronald watched in horror, as Martha's head continued to bob in the royal's lap.

"I will continue to feed and take care of Martha while now you will have only one mouth to feed. You shall still be required to pay your fair share of taxes as ordered by your king. This aid that I offer to you and your wife should help assist you in making it though the winter," he arrogantly informed the young husband.

"But my king, I beg you mercy!"

"Mercy be for the weak!", the king shouted. "Or do you wish I show you mercy at the gallows?", his hawk-like stare causing Ronald to back down.

"No your majesty! That will not be necessary."

King Paul could feel both the back of Martha's throat and a release began to build in him.

"Stand here," he ordered Ronald pointing to a place where the young husband could see a side profile of his wife's working mouth. "Let it not be said that King Paul does not take care of his people. Your wife's first royal dinner."

Soon the young commoner witnessed Martha's hands ball up and clench at the king's chest, as Paul shot a load of seed into her mouth. The young woman's swallowing as fast as she could in an attempt not to choke.

After a couple of moments, the king stopped twitching in her mouth, and the young woman lifted her water-filled eyes to the young man she just pleasured.

"Do not trouble yourself with any more worry," Paul softly spoke in a deliberate tone. "For I swear to you and your husband that I will never let you hunger again." With those words, he smiled a devilish grin and guided the young woman's head back to his semi-erect manhood. "Round two," he added.

Ronald was ordered by King Paul to stay and watch eventually being witness to the royal feed his wife a second time before he was ushered out of the castle by two guards. Martha was now seized property.

After watching the defeated young husband leave the throne room, Paul laughed to himself and led the naked woman through the castle's hallways.

"Do you still hunger?", he sarcastically inquired, but her reply really didn't matter. For on this night, she joined him and Rufus in the knight's bed. Martha would be filled in more ways than one.

Chapter 47

The small group of refugees at the cottage awoke on this morning to an atmosphere that matched the gloom of the sky above. Yesterday's news of the death of Charles Bradford, along with the violation of his wife by the king's men, left a feeling of both sadness and hopelessness in the air. Even Michael and the two brothers seemed to share Russell's anguish over the decision to wait the remainder of the prior day before going to retrieve the queen's family safely.

The forest floor was matted by wet leaves, and water from the prior day's rains had soaked into everything especially the trees that would be needed to supply a warming and cooking fire. For now the heavens held off dumping their showers on the land, but everyone knew there would be more rainfall on the way. Like yesterday, the weather was raw but at least there was no wind.

Both Peter and Paul went hunting hoping to catch more than just hares for stew. Their sights were already set on a wild boar or small deer. Michael had found himself outside the cottage taking care of and grooming the group's four horses. The young man knowing that if the chargers were not thoroughly maintained or attended to with the proper welfare, then when they might be desperately needed for a life or death situation, the mounts may falter and fail leaving possibly all of them with an unfortunate outcome. Russell had left his bow and quiver behind wearing only his sword for protection while he grabbed the cottage's axe and headed to cut some lumber to dry. Everyone knew he blamed himself with Lynn's father's demise, and desperately needed the alone time. Inside the stone structure, the four women set to tidying up the place, their sadness was apparent. Even Joan grieved for the Bradford's loss.

"Russell needs you my dear," sympathetically pointed out Lynn's mother to her from across the room. Her words causing both Joan and Anne to look up from their knees as they washed the floor.

"What is it you mean mother?", sadly inquired the young woman.

"I see it in his eyes. He holds himself responsible for your pain," Gwenyth softly informed her daughter.

"But that knows no truth!", responded the queen. "Russell and the others rescued Joan and I. He saved the king from a murderer's sword, and even now he burdens himself with risk by giving aid to one who is labeled an outlaw. He be a hero! To rival that than one would be said a liar!", the young woman's anger apparent at the thought of those holding false accusations against her love.

Gwenyth crossed the room to Lynn, who now had tears of frustration rolling down her cheeks. Tenderly the young woman's mother laid a hand on her daughter's face and gazed into her eyes. "Your words are filled with the truth my dear. It not be any of us that needs convincing, but rather Russell who needs to hear that he be holding onto a false guilt. Go to him Lynn. For only your words can remove the feeling he harbors of being the one responsible for your pain." Gwenyth offered a smile followed by an embrace.

"It be I mother who have brought burden and pain to his brow," Lynn cried on her mother's shoulder. The woman pulling her daughter away from her to gaze upon the regretful queen.

"Do you truly believe that? Everything happens for a reason, and even though we may lack an answer to it or an explanation may escape our knowledge, it be God who only knows the truth behind the happening. Why has the Lord always kept your life and Russell's entwined as one?", Gwenyth pondered wearing a questioning look in her eyes. "Only He holds the answer. I believe God has a purpose for you and Russell. Like He uses him, our Lord uses you at least for a cause to guide the young man to His will. How was it that the only one you know protection with more than any other happens to show at the ambush?", she queried. "You ponder God put him there?", a watery-eyed Lynn answered her mother's question with one of her own.

"Go to him Lynn."

The king's raptor-like stare watched the defeated man leave the throne room, as the commoner's wife fed on Paul's manhood. A smile creasing his lips as he appreciated the fact that this was the second married woman he had taken from her husband requesting an audience over the raising taxes in less than a full day's time.

Glancing down at the woman's hands balling up and clenching his robe's lapels as she swallowed his seedy offering, King Paul turned his attention to Sir Rufus standing beside the throne watching.

"I believe if this slows down to a halt than I shall raise the taxes twice fold," he sarcastically laughed nodding at the knight. The unspoken word between the two causing Rufus to walk up behind the naked woman and loosen his drawstrings.

"Round two," Paul smugly informed the new sex slave while wearing a smile. Knowing what was about to come, the king removed her hands from his lapels and placed them on the throne.

The royal watched the woman's eyes open wide and her mouth gasp pulling in air. The seized wife's face contorted while Rufus entered her from behind beginning to rock into her. Moments later she began groaning, and King Paul guided her head to his lap.

"We would not want her to be heard by another unsuspecting wife on her way into the throne room," he laughed while Rufus began to plunge into his new mount.

"There will be too many mouths to feed at the castle if you keep seizing more wives," pointed out the large man.

Taking a moment to ponder, as muffled moans of pleasure filled the chamber and Susan responded to the mounting she was receiving, an idea crossed Paul's mind. "Your words hold truth my friend. Round up all of the male servants and have them hung," demanded the king.

"Women whose bellies be filled with seed eat less," he reasoned before looking down at the woman's head bobbing in his lap. "Be that true Susan?"

A moment later Paul answered, "She be in agreement." He devilishly grinned.

Sir Rufus amused by the king's sarcastic quirk began to laugh and quicken his plunges.

Russell's pain at the hurt that his love felt and displayed with every fiber of her body when he returned without her father drove his axe swing as it bit into the small tree. Splinters of wood leaped from the trunk at the spot of his anguish-fueled assault, and once he had dislodged the tool's blade, the young man would no sooner sink another direct score into the wedge that he was hacking at. Just the thought of failing Lynn by resting for the night continued to cut away at his soul. To Russell, who loved Lynn more than life itself, failure was not acceptable.

Driving his axe swing one more time into the trees trunk, Russell heard the large crack that signified that the hardened plant only needed to be pushed to cause it to fall to the ground. Leaning his weight into it, the young man watched as the small tree fell.

Russell had decided he would chop the tree into reasonable sizes and have the horses pull several back to the cottage where him and his friends could take turns splitting the timber. Hovering above the fallen oak he swung his bladed tool down. More splinters flew into the air. Even though the weather was wet and raw, a sheen of sweat began to cover his body. Russell took out his regret-filled pain on the defenseless, felled tree.

Soon the young man stopped to remove his hooded cloak. Unhooking the barrel shaped button from the small loop of material fashioned to secure it at the front of his lower neck, Russell hung the clothing on a damp, leafless branch and reached for his axe that had been leaning up against the oak he had been chopping. Suddenly he heard the soft call of his name. He turned taking in the sight of Lynn standing roughly ten feet away.

"May I have a word with you?", she gently queried.

"You should remain hidden. I wish not for your discovery."

"I care not Russell," she plainly admitted. "I need to speak with you, for you be the only one that matters to me!", Lynn stressed walking towards her lover. Already a tear formed in her eye.

Taking in the sight of her pain, the young man lowered his eyes to the ground. He just couldn't deal with the hurt he caused his love. "I am truly sorry Lynn."

"You need not be. You own nothing to be sorry for."

"I should have ridden that night," his anguish radiating on his face like a lantern in the dark.

"My dear you be only one man, and what you have done for me thus far knows more love than Paul's letter to the Corinthians," she offered a wet smile. "You be the one that speaks on how you have known fortune because of me, but it be I who be truly blessed by a man like you. Throughout our years I have loved you since the first time you rescued me in the woods," Lynn revealed. "It be you Russell Daniels, who through all of these years has given me your strength, your protection, and your undying love. Because of that my heart remains one."

"It be your love that allows me to know only wholeness," the young man revealed, as he placed a strand of hair behind her ear. "I love you, and I swear..." Russell's words being cut off, as the young woman with the speed of a striking bolt of lightning engulfed her love's mouth with her own.

Lynn's passion and desire for her true love seemed to set off an uncontrolled chain reaction throughout Russell's body. He answered her hungry mouth with his own, and the two's tongues probed reaching for each other's souls. Even though the day was cold and damp, the two only knew heat. The heat of passion that blazed out of control like a wildfire. Time seemed to stand still, as their passions for one another had finally reached an apex. A yearning filled the air, and with every fiber of Lynn and Russell's hearts and souls they surrendered to the other. The young woman not only let go her feelings, but her body began a release of its own. A wetness formed between her legs, and she noticed her love's hard excitement against her lower belly.

Dropping her hand down, Lynn began to rub his cloth-covered firmness. Her touch causing Russell to start and offer a deep groan. She massaged his manhood before her fingers nimbly loosened the drawstrings of his pants. Without any resistance, they fell to his ankles. Returning to his rigidness, the young woman deeply moaned for the first time when she felt the skin-to-skin contact of his bare erection.

"We cannot," her love warned in between the passionate kiss they shared. Although Russell could not deny how good her tender touch felt.

"I do not care my love," she sexually crooned. "I love you and I need you now." Lynn reached for his cloak hanging from a branch and tossed it on the ground behind her. Slowly she pulled him down on top of her.

"My love we should not do this now," protested Russell, but it was Lynn who had the upper hand.

"I care not," she whispered. "To know love completely with you, be to know that our love existed in this life. That in and of itself cannot be labeled a sin nor a wrong doing. I beg of you my love, give to me freely what I freely offer to you," the young woman softly pleaded.

Suddenly Lynn gasped for air when for the first time she felt Russell enter her body. Her lover's hip thrusts were slow and rhythmic knowing only tenderness in their rises and falls.

"I love you Russell Daniels."

"And I love you Lynn Bradford."

Their tongues joined their bodies in an entwining embrace that seemed more like a slow dance. On this day the love that had grown over the years finally blossomed, and knew not protected and protector nor queen or commoner, but it only recognized one complete heart.

None questioned the queen's disheveled hair or robe when she finally returned to the cottage. Even though the young woman mentioned not a word about her coupling with her love and smoothed her clothes, both Gwyneth and Joan knew. Lynn had a glow to her and a bounce to her steps. To her mother and her personal servant, the slightly disarrayed queen not only looked regal again but appeared to have forgotten about all her recent troubles.

For most of the day, she and Russell seemed to stay away from one another busying themselves with tasks. The young man wished to have most of the lumber split and in the cottage drying out before he left to meet David the Beggar that night.

"I will make certain that whatever it may be that Paul and Peter catch today will be warm for you when you return," Lynn informed Russell when the time came to prepare his horse for the journey.

"I fathom not when I will return my love," he unsurely revealed as he secured the wrapped up sword in its scabbard and then tied it behind the saddle.

Everyone, except the two brothers who had not returned yet, held witness to Russell and Lynn embracing in a passionate kiss.

"Be safe my love," wished the young woman watching the young man step in the stir up and swing his leg over his mount.

"I shall return."

Heeling the horse, Lynn watched as he rode into the nearly bare trees and out of sight. Already she missed him. "Please God I beg that you protect him like he does I," she silently prayed before making her way back indoors.

David the Beggar knew he wouldn't be entering the city tonight, at least not in plain sight, with the gate already closed. Following his way down the dirt road as the note had stated, it took the man a little time to get to where the almost naked trees began. With the cover of darkness, along with the overcast night sky, his secret meeting would not be seen by any of the wall's watching guardsmen. It wasn't long before he heard someone call his name from the shadows.

"David. Have you been followed?"

"No. I took no witness to anyone behind me," David replied into the darkness.

The man watched as a silhouette materialized out of the shadows.

"Russell be that you?", the beggar inquired.

"Yes. The king was killed in an ambush attack planned and executed by Paul and his henchman. For now as we speak the queen is safe with me," informed Russell in a low tone and glancing from left to right checking to make sure the coast was clear. "I am sorry for the loss of your brother. He asked me to give you this," the young man held out the knight's sword to David.

Sir Timothy's brother accepting the scabbard housing the blade. The air only knowing silence for a moment. "Did my brother die well?"

"He died defending and saving King Matthew. The king passing later from wounds caused by arrows he had received earlier in the fight."

"Be you with plan," quietly inquired the beggar.

"None at this time, but I believe we need be rid of Paul and return the queen to the throne," Russell matter-of-factly stated.

"I agree," acknowledged David. "For now I will try to find out as much as I can until we can plot how to rid England of the scoundrel. As for you, keep the queen alive and well," the beggar advised. "Paul's men have already begun to arrive and take up residence one man to every cottage. The traitor has also had all of the male servants at the castle hung this day," he informed the young man.

"Be any others who will fight?"

"Yes, and Paul knows it," confirmed David. "That is why the change in the castle's staff and some more of his soldiers will arrive."

"Then we must plan to take Hamilton back by force."

"Let me find those who will join us first. How shall I contact you?"

"For now I will find you." The young man fading into the shadows.

David turned and hid the wrapped up scabbard under his cloak the best he could. Already he knew that Russell possessed the one weapon that would lead to the fall of the self-made king. It was not a blade nor bow, but in the stead it be Russell's determination to see dishonour and evil thwarted.

Chapter 48

Already one month's time had passed, and the small group of fugitives were already experiencing both major and minor changes. One of the biggest changes came in part due to the weather. The cold, crisp days of autumn had released its grip on the land giving way to the clutches of the winter season and Hamilton's first snow. A blanket of white powder covered the ground hiding any proof of the strewn leaf litter from fall and the trees, which at one time wore a canopy of foliage, were now adorned with icicles.

Another change was the erection of the rough-lumbered structure for the horses that had been built by the four young men. They all knew that caring for the chargers was one of the top priorities toward success of their plan to hide out in the forest through winter. If there was no way to ride horseback and reprovision themselves then everyone in the cottage knew without a doubt that they would have to return back to civilization and risk the danger of being caught and hung by King Paul's men.

"It struck you!", happily pointed out Joan after hitting Michael with a ball of snow. The servant's stomach had grown a bit more as the days passed.

The young, muscular man only laughed and showed his empty palms to the woman. "I yield."

"That makes three against three," pointed out a joyful Gwenyth, who had been first to be hit by a sphere of powder.

Peter, who attempted to hide behind one of the stone walls of the cottage chanced a peak around its corner. The skulking move being caught by Joan as she was already cupping her hands to form another globe.

"I be seeing you Peter," the woman warned the young man.

Quickly turning to abandon his post, Peter unsuspectingly spun into the line of fire of both Lynn and her younger sister. Both not only striking him in the chest causing the air to become full of powdery spray, but aiding the surprised twin in an errant throw that went wide.

"You be out!", excitedly informed Anne followed by a giggle.

"For my brother!", shouted Paul from behind the queen and her sibling, as he let loose his sphere of white. The shot catching Lynn on the rear of her shoulder.

"Save yourself Anne!", cried out Joan launching her snowy attack.

The girl running towards the women offering cover-fire.

Paul slipped as he tried to dodge the throw, and before he could regain his balance, got hit on the right side of his head.

"Argh!", he yelled acting like he was just hit by a catapult launching a giant stone.

Both Joan and Anne missed his performance while running around the corner to the cottage, but Lynn giggled at the theatrics.

"Keep to farming Paul," sarcastically advised his brother.

"You need to keep to farming. At least I hit someone," the young man adding a grin to the end of his words.

The banter caused the queen's giggles to turn to straight laughter, as the three eliminated players strolled out from around the corner heading towards Gwenyth and Michael standing in front of the cottage's door.

"Watch for Russell!", warned Lynn speaking to her sister and Joan.

"Two against one," informed Anne's mother.

Everyone scanned for the only young man left in their snowball battle. Cautiously the girl and the woman armed with their powdery weapons slowly began to move toward the shelter that held the four horses. Their heads on a swivel as they searched for their last target.

Without any warning, Russell burst out from around the corner to their rear and charged at his two assailants. His only weapon; one ball of snow.

"There he be!", Lynn yelled. Her waning drawing the attention of the two whose backs were turned.

Both the women and the girl spun. Joan threw her globe towards the charging young man, but Anne waited.

Letting loose his sphere, Russell launched himself into a roll in hopes of dodging the airborne projectile. His nimble evasion worked, as Joan's snowball flew over his head missing him altogether. The woman with child wasn't as lucky. Her assailant's throw struck her in the left thigh exploding into a cloud of white.

Russell grabbed some powder as he began to roll and quickly tried to pack another sphere for his last attack. Unfortunately when he came out of the acrobatic move, he was at the mercy of the youngest Bradford daughter. Anne had waited to launch her ball of snow. With Russell down and at point blank range, she fired at him striking him in the chest.

"I won!", excitedly she yelled. "I be the winner!"

The crowd clapped and cheered.

"Bravo young Anne," congratulated Russell lying on the white ground clapping and smiling. "Bravo."

Losing the field of battle was something that Russell always found hard to accept, but at this moment looking up at Anne's smiling face his fighting spirit only knew ease.

Throughout the afternoon the small band of friends and family spent the day relieving themselves of pent up troubles while playing and frolicking in the snow cover. They enjoyed the time they shared with one another even though this time knew only hardships and trouble. Their laughter melting away not only the frosty grip caused by the falling snow outside, but the shivery bleakness that King Paul's rule had laid over Hamilton. The group's enjoyment would only be a brief reprieve from reality when both Russell and Michael began to prepare for their leave this evening after consuming an early supper. The brothers had met with fortune on the yesterday and killed themselves a deer. This allowed for not only a succulent supper but a filling one for the second night in a row.

"Must you leave this night?", disappointedly inquired Lynn wrapping her arms around Russell's waist.

Gazing into her eyes, he spoke softly. "This night we need meet with David." The young man brushing a strand of his love's hair back and behind her ear. "Hence it will also be a good idea to retrieve some more provisions since we will be close to the farms."

"Be safe my love," wished Lynn offering a kiss.

The queen was not the only one to be in the recently built shelter for the horses, Michael also had one who saw him prepare for the journey.

"Keep safe Michael," kindly advised Joan handing him some bread wrapped in a cloth. "In case you hunger later."

"Thank you," he smiled accepting the edible package and tucking it into a saddlebag.

Both women offered up a worried smile as they watched the young men lead the chargers out of their cover and mount up.

"I will return," came Russell before heeling his horse and starting off.

"My ladies," Michael smiled his farewells.

The outlaw queen and her servant watched, as two of their rescuers rode into the white woods and disappeared into the falling snow. This night would be both sleepless and never ending, as Lynn would sit up in the corner worrying. She wouldn't be the only one.

"This be Michael," introduced Russell while they approached David the Beggar out of the snowy darkness. "He be with us."

"The honour be mine."

Neither young man being able to see David's face in the darkness of night or the hood's shadow that hid his face.

"What news do you hold for me?", inquired Russell.

"The happenings get bleaker each day, but there be men who be willing to fight," revealed the man of the city's streets. "Already King Paul's rule be called by many a Reign of Perversion. The wretch turns the wives of those, who struggle to pay taxes into sex slaves. The unfortunate women spend all day and night giving up their bodies as they pleasure not only the king but his men as well."

"How many soldiers have come to town so far?"

"I know not the exact number," replied David. "But by my estimates, there must be at least more than equal to the men who began their service to King Stephen. For there be not enough room for all of them at the castle."

"Where be it they stay?", interjected Michael.

"The ones not at the palace be living amongst the folk. Eating their food and bedding their wives."

"What?", both young men asked simultaneously in disbelief.

"It be true," confirmed the street urchin. "King Paul has decreed that any man who does not share his shelter, his food, nor his wife or daughter with the king's men are to be hung. Already many necks have stretched at the gallows." "I must check on mother and father!", Russell anxiously thought within that instant.

"Do you know of my father?", inquired a worried Michael.

"I am sorry son. I know not."

"Be that all?", questioned Russell.

"One more thing," advised David. "The reward for Queen Lynn be now at five hundred gold coin. It would appear that our corrupt king wishes to find the queen and desires it swiftly."

Clasping the beggar's arm, both Russell and then Michael shook it before sprinting for their mounts. "Watch your back my friend. We will meet in two weeks time from now," hastily blurted Russell as he and his friend disappeared into the darkness of night.

"Be safe lads!", wished the beggar before turning to start for the city. He lifted the blade slightly from its scabbard checking to make sure the frost hadn't caused Sir Timothy's sword to stick. For on this snowy night, it would be easier to sneak back into Hamilton through his secret egress. By now the snowfall should have fully covered the soldier's body that he had placed in the shallow ditch just outside the watch of the wall's guard. A wife somewhere in the countryside would be overjoyed when the man never showed," he thought. David the Beggar, along with his blade, were indifferent either way when it came to Paul's wretches. The man of the streets only wished a meeting with the black knight and the self-proclaimed king to avenge his murdered brother's death.

"Leave her be!", yelled a beaten Robert bound to one of the cottage's wooden chairs witnessing two of King Paul's men attempting to rip his struggling wife's clothes from her body as they held her down on the pallet.

"Unhand me you brute!", cried Nicole to a third of four men, who had been holding and twisting the young woman's arm. Already Nicole's eyes knew tears not only from the pain shooting up her appendage, but also the chaotic scene that had begun to take place a small time ago.

"When we be through with your wife, it be your daughter's turn next," growled the fourth man hovering over Robert.

The soldier's words receiving a spit into his face.

"Insolent bastard!", shouted the soldier followed by a backhand that drove the bound man to the floor as the seat tipped over. Robert's mouth sprayed blood into the air on the way down.

"No! Please!", begged Elizabeth when one of the pawing hands tore her dress open revealing her bare chest and breasts. She soon felt the other man's rough hands on her knees trying to pry her legs open, so he could plunge his manhood into her. In moments, Robert now lying bound in the chair on the cottage's floor heard another tear, and watched as Elizabeth's dress was tossed aside leaving her fully naked to her attackers.

Suddenly a loud bang on the door interrupted the hellish chaos in the room.

"It must be Samuel and Henry," came the fourth soldier watching his comrade sink his manhood into Elizabeth's body. "Prepare the daughter for hers. There be enough hands and dicks here now," he laughed walking out of the room to open the barred door leaving the combining grunts and sobs behind.

Lifting the thick wood beam that secured the door from the inside. The king's man pulled open the portal. "It be about...", his words cut off.

"No!", cried Robert when he witnessed the soldier enter his wife and begin to thrust into her.

The two men holding her down laughed at the woman, who still tried to struggle even though she had already been penetrated. The second man pinning her arms together with one hand while pawing her breasts with the other. Her grunts matching both the growls from the man inside her and his forceful drives.

The third guard started pulling on Nicole's dress even as she tried to fight back and object to the soldier's plans. Suddenly the king's man whom had left to open the door crashed into the entryway of the room. The loud commotion causing all the occupants to start as they took in the sight of two arrows sunk into his neck. His blood sprayed into the air. Within moments, he joined Robert on the floor, but the soldier was dead.

In the doorway stood a young man holding a bow with a notched arrow.

"Christ Almighty!", shouted the man pinning down Elizabeth's arms as he watched the arrow take flight. In seconds it bit into the base of the violator's skull driving him forward and slumping onto the woman. The rapist died without even seeing who was behind him.

"Get em!", the second soldier yelled, as Russell ran from the doorway.

Shoving Nicole to the floor, the third guard followed his comrade out of the cottage and into the snow. The man fortunate enough to catch a glimpse of Russell's leg disappearing into the small, stone barn where the Daniels kept the only horse and flock of sheep.

"That way!", he pointed. The other man following behind.

Cautiously the two men approached the closed portal to the barn while unsheathing their swords. Someone was about to pay a major price for ruining their fun this night.

"Move to the side before I pull the door free in case he be ready with an arrow," reasoned the lead man. "He will miss the shot, and then we will make him pay."

Whipping open the portal both men waited on either side of the door for an arrow to fly out the structure, but nothing came. Waiting a minute, give or take, one of the soldiers peeked in. A bow and quiver of arrows laid on the middle of the floor and a sword lie in front of the one of the pens.

"Looks like the dung pile ditched his bow and lost his sword on his way to hiding," the guard pointing at the blade. "You wait here. I will reveal the want-to-be hero, and then together we can run him through," he shared his plan of attack.

The first man had only taken four steps into the barn before he jumped and spun around when he heard his comrade drop his sword to the ground.

"What be the matter with you idiot?", he growled at the other man in the doorway. "Are you weak of mind or something?", he rasped.

His comrade fell forward into the barn. Two arrow shafts protruding from his back.

Taking a step backwards, the man realized he was the only one left alive of the four king's men that had come to this farm on this night.

Hastily, the soldier turned with all of his intentions to retrieve the missile fire weapon. His eyes meeting the upside down stare of the one that he had originally followed in here. Before he had time to act, the young man who hung inverted from a crossbeam drove a pitch fork into the soldier's chest. Its three points erupting out of the man's back.

"And that be for my mother!", firmly growled Russell watching all the life leave from the surprised invader. The one-time usurper dropped to the floor like a sack of potatoes.

Sitting himself up and grabbing the beam, Russell unlocked his legs hanging over it and jumped down. He went to collect his weapons.

"We have to leave this place," he matter-of-factly pointed out while stepping over the two dead bodies and into the snow. The young, Daniels man ran to the house followed by Michael.

"Watch the door," Russell instructed. "We have no need any more unannounced visitors."

"Thank you son," cried Elizabeth wrapped in one of the bed's blankets. "You saved our lives," added Robert beginning to stand up with aid from Nicole.

"Father can you walk?", the young man inquired.

"Yes son. It looks worse than it be."

"If all can walk, we need to provision the horse and make way to the cottage," advised Russell.

Russell and Michael packed the Daniels horse waiting only a short time for the young man's family to emerge from the cabin. The two rescuers had removed the two dead bodies from the cottage placing them inside one of the empty pens in the barn, along with the other two deceased. Everyone knew that the cold, winter weather would keep the bodies from breaking down and smelling till at least the spring.

It was not long after that that Robert led his mount with Elizabeth and their daughter Nicole into the snow-covered forest heading for the hidden cottage while the young men rode for Michael's father's farm and then the cottage that belonged to Peter and Paul's family. They both knew there would be no sleep, and the only proof of their nocturnal activity was the hoof prints left in the blanket of powder that covered the land. Fortune would favor the two if the snowfall kept up to cover their tracks.

Tonight, Russell and Michael had struck a blow against King Paul's den of serpents. For now four snakes lay dead, but he knew many more adders slithered around Hamilton.

Chapter 49

Everyone in the cottage awoke startled, with the exception of Lynn, when the knock on its door during the middle of the snowy night reverberated through the silence in the room. The young woman sat in the corner she had shared with Russell alone and sleepless filled with fear worrying over her love's welfare. She wished for his safe return as she watched the dancing shadows on the walls and ceiling caused by the fireplace's flickering blaze. Tenseness filled the atmosphere, and all held their breaths when a second rap came from whomever was on the other side of the portal.

The outlaw queen and the other women remained still as they watched the twins reach for their bows and notch an arrow on them. Slowly and quietly, Paul crept across the remaining distance between the chair where he had slept and the door.

"It be late," feigning his aggravation for the disturbance. "Who be waking a man at these wee hours of the morning?"

"It be Robert, along with my family?", the voice responded.

Shooting a questioning look to his brother, who stood at the ready to pull and let loose his nocked arrow, Paul lifted the wooden beam unbarring the door. He opened it ajar to peek out. The twin taken in the sight of Russell's broken and bruised father holding a lead to a packed horse with both his wife and daughter standing beside him.

"Christ Almighty!", the young man shocked waving his hand for Peter to lower his weapon before pulling open the door.

"Peter. Sire Daniels requires assistance."

All in the cottage rose when the Daniels entered the house. Elizabeth began to cry when she was approached by Gwenyth. The Bradford woman already knowing from her own experience what heinousness had taken place.

"Where be Russell?", worriedly queried Lynn. She embraced her childhood friend Nicole. The queen's eyes already watering.

"I know not Lynn," she revealed. "My brother and Michael rescued us from an attack. They killed four of the king's soldiers and then helped us pack the horse. When father said he was alright to walk here, the two said they needed to go and check on Michael's father along with Peter and Paul's family. My brother also mentioned about grabbing some more provisions before returning."

Already Joan and Anne were tending to Russell's wounded father.

For the rest of the morning, no one in the cottage knew sleep. The Daniels had shared their horrific story from last night, while both Peter and Paul took care of unpacking the horse and housing the animal inside the makeshift stable. Paul would eventually go out to scout the woods to make certain that the Daniels had not been followed. The good news was that the snowfall was coming down heavy enough and would eventually cover up any signs of passage left by Russell's family.

When Peter's brother returned to the small hideout in the forest he could not only cut the tension with his dagger, but if he stared hard enough he could see the hope and prayers rising up to the Lord for his friends safe return. Soon his silent words were sent aloft joining the others in the room's air.

Russell and Michael had left their two chargers, along with the horse that Charles had given to him being stabled at the Daniel's farm, in the shadows yards away from the cottage. Stealthily, he and Michael crept towards the stone structure owned by Peter and Paul's parents. The two young men receiving the terrible news that Michael's father had been hung only days ago, and his land seized by an order from the king. The revelation coming from the mouth of one of Paul's soldiers that had arrived in Hamilton only days prior and had taken up residence there with two others. Russell's heart ached for his friend's loss while the tragic news had brought the muscular, young man to his knees.

Stealing a glance left and then right, the young men with bows in hand ran the last twenty feet to a shuttered window with light radiating through the slits. They both scanned the area again for any movement and were relieved that nothing appeared amiss. Eyeballing one another, Russell peered through a crack into the lit room. Inside he witnessed a most unexpected scene.

From his view, the twin's mother and father were sitting at the kitchen table sharing in conversation with what he thought might be a third person. The young man being unsure thanks to a wall hiding the other occupant. Russell pulled his eyes away from the shutter and glanced one way then the other before looking to Michael.

"Looks like Thomas and his wife seem to have a visitor," he quietly informed the other young man.

"Is it one of the king's men?"

"I know not," Russell shrugged before putting his ear closer to the slight opening hoping to better hear.

"Can I get you some stew and a roll Andrew?", Thomas' wife asked. "My husband trapped himself a rabbit earlier this day, and it's been simmering on the fire since supper."

"That would be much appreciated Mrs. Smith," came the unseen voice. "I must offer you folks my sincere gratitude for your hospitality. Without your aid, King Paul would have had my neck stretched like he did the others." "It is nothing," Russell heard her say while pushing her chair from the table and retrieving him a bite to eat. Within minutes, the twin's mother was placing a steaming bowl and a roll in front of the man before returning to her seat. Russell then heard a prayer coming from inside the cottage, and it was coming from the visitor.

"Something is not right here," the peeper stated.

"What be it you mean?", puzzled Michael while remaining ever vigilant.

"Look for yourself."

Rising from his crouching position, the other young man took his first look through the shutter's slit. When he saw and heard what was happening inside, he glanced over to Russell wearing a questioning expression. "What in God's name?"

The unseen man ended the prayer and began to share in a random conversation when Russell and Michael caught a break to their mystery.

"Excuse me Andrew," politely requested Thomas as he rose from his chair. "I need to go and relieve myself."

Soon the two young men witnessed Mr. Smith disappear from sight, and the cottage's door open and shut.

"That be our break," Russell informed Michael. "You stay here and prepare to make haste if we need to. I am going to get a quick word with Thomas."

Michael gave a nod.

The snow fell heavy upon Hamilton this night, and steam both floated in the cold air from Thomas' mouth while it rose from his expelled body fluid. The man was lost in a peaceful thought and a tranquility seemed to take hold of him. If it was the falling powder or the aloneness he felt while relieving himself, he couldn't quite put a finger on it. Feeling himself finally coming to an end, Thomas returned back to the present and gave himself a few shakes. A chill ran through him, but not from the crispness of the air.

"Mr. Smith," the low call drifting through the night like the steam coming from in between his lips.

"Who goes there?", he started.

"It be Russell," the mystery voice answered.

"Russell?", questioned Thomas as he watched the Daniel's son materialize out of the darkness. "I own the notion that you and the boys were at your place hunting."

"We were, but we came upon the royal coach being ambushed."

"Oh my God! Are the twins alright?"

"They are sir," Russell confirmed. "Who be in the house? Is it one of the king's men?", the young man directing the conversation to the main reason of their unplanned meeting.

"Yes, but not one who you may think. His name is Andrew and he was loyal to not only King Matthew but King Stephen as well," explained Thomas. "He was one of the men that found themselves removed from the castle to make room for Paul's own men."

"Why did he not find himself at the end of the hangman's noose?", inquired Russell. "I would own the notion that the traitor would want to rid himself of all the real king's soldiers."

"King Paul has need of bodies to perform tasks that are below the standards of his men, and arrow fodder for the French when he decides to cast us into a self-driven war. Come inside and warm thyself by the fire," invited Thomas.

"Can this man be trusted?"

"What do you mean?"

"The queen is not behind a plot that has King Matthew dead and her in league with the French," Russell explained. "Your sons, Michael, and I came upon the ambush and rescued the queen. King Paul and his black knight orchestrated the treasonous act so he could claim England for himself. It is he who assassinated his uncle and aunt. We harbor and protect Lynn."

"More the reason to come inside and speak with Andrew. There is talk of an uprise against this reign of perversion."

Both young men had one more stop to make this night before returning back to the cottage and the other hideouts waiting on them. The two young men were silent during the ride to reprovision themselves from the dwindling stock pile at the old Bradford's farm, which technically belonged to Russell now. Michael wore a stoic face as he was lost in his thoughts about his deceased father and how he would avenge the man. The hurt replaced by a stewing scheme of vengeance. The two riders instantly recognized that there was something wrong with the place as they approached. A plume of smoke rose from the stone chimney.

Pulling on the reigns, the two stopped and dismounted while scanning their surroundings for anything else that seemed not right. When they were satisfied that they had not walked straight into an ambush, the young men began to slowly and cautiously head for the farm's small barn. Russell led not only his mount, but the extra horse also, while Michael walked his charger toward the rear of the structure. With heads on a swivel, the two knew they would need to be quiet and stealthy to grab the provisions without setting off anything that would alarm the cottage's inhabitants.

Honour

"Who do you ponder be in there?", softly inquired Michael holding the three leads.

"I know not, but I have not the feeling to risk another chance nor any delay to find out," Russell replied. "You remain here and pack. I will go retrieve what we came for."

It be the wee hours of the morning when Russell along with Michael led the three packed horses away from the farm and down the road. The two young men were more than relieved that they had evaded another encounter this night. They had gotten away with their stealthy job pilfering the place with none-the-wiser.

"We will need to cover our tracks and make a lengthy return as not to lead the devil's men straight to us," cautiously informed Russell. "When we have traveled a long enough distance we shall turn into the forest and make our way back."

"It be light within the next few hours," Michael pointed out. "Do you reason the snowfall will aid us in concealing our tracks?"

"We can only hope fortune favors us," replied the young man's friend.

The day's light slowly rose revealing the gray sky above as its clouds still dumped snow on Hamilton. Lynn, along with most of the cottage's occupants, joined her outside. Their eyes pinned to the naked trees in their constant search for Russell and Michael's return. What on the yesterday was a scene of a snowball fight and worry free play had now turned into a place that knew only anxiety and tension.

"I believe I see them!", excitedly admitted Peter pointing out to the bare trees that were now only dressed in fresh snow.

Following his finger, it was Lynn who spotted them fist out of the group.

"I see them!", she happily shouted.

The rest of the gathered group watched and smiled upon their friends' safe return.

"My heart fills with gladness knowing that you are both safe," joyfully came the young woman, as the young men and the three horses approached.

Dismounting, Russell and Lynn simultaneously engulfed each other in a hug.

"This night felt like it be endless," relieved the outlaw queen.

"You speak the truth," agreed her love with a heart-warming smile before looking up to the party of welcomers. "Michael and I have not only brought food, but we have also brought news and rumors."

"I have missed you my love," Russell smiled at Lynn.

"And I love you."

Reaching for his mount's lead and the reigns of the horse carrying more provisions, Russell put his arm around Lynn and started for the makeshift stable. "David be telling me, that the king has raised the reward on you to five hundred gold coins."

"I am worth that much?", she astonished.

"That not be enough," smiled the young man. "There not be a sufficient allotment of gold throughout the whole of England to rival someone who knows beauty the likes of you."

Staring into her true love's eyes, Lynn absorbed every word causing a warmth in both her heart and soul that could not be rivaled by that of even King Paul's coin producing forges.

Unlike the day prior, this day was spent indoors around the fire sharing in food, friendship, and the talk around Hamilton. Russell told about the uprising that the people were talking about, at least those not scared of King Paul. He also shared with the twins the welfare of their parents, and how the Lord had blessed them by putting a loyal guardsman to King Stephen and Matthew in their house. The young man went on to give the details of his conversation with this soldier, Andrew, and everyone found relief when Joan confirmed how Andrew was one of the good guys. Most importantly, the word of the untimely death of Michael's father spread quickly around the small group, and all knew sadness for one of their rescuers. Tears, support, and prayers were offered by everyone, but for now the young man had wished to be alone.

Leaning against a tree trunk and staring towards the overcast sky still dumping snow on Hamilton, Michael's thoughts were lost as memories of the times he had shared with his father played over and over in his mind. His grief was now at the forefront of everything going on around him, and all had given him sometime alone. All but one.

"Michael," called the soft voice.

The muscular, young man taking in the sight of Joan slowly making her way to him in knee deep snow. "May I share words with you?", she inquired.

"You should not be out here my lady," he concerned. "For if you fell, you could bring harm to not only yourself but your unborn child as well."

"I am here to check on your welfare," Joan seemed to brush away Michael's words of concern. "We are all saddened by your loss, but to know sickness be foolish. I did not own the pleasure of meeting your father, but I would think that he would not wish to see you fell to the pneumonia."

"I will be fine once I avenge him," the young man's anger reflecting in the tone of his voice. "He be lost to me, and I can never hope for his return," his agony bringing tears to his eyes.

"I know what it be that your hurt can turn into if you surrender to it," sympathetically spoke Joan. "But know that your friends share in your pain and are here for you. Believe me, for I know what it be that you feel and go through." Reaching up and placing a hand on the side of Michael's face, Joan compassionately continued. "My mother was lost to me when I still be a child," she softly revealed. "If not for King Stephen and Queen Margaret then I myself would have come to know anger and hatred. For my mother was both raped and beaten to death by three men. Like your father, she died knowing only innocence," the woman's eyes filling with tears.

A silence fell between the two, and both Joan and Michael embraced one another.

"I am truly sorry," softly sympathized Michael. His mouth only inches from the woman's ear. Her hug squeezing tighter at his words.

"I call you my friend," sniffled Joan. "I will be here for you."

Leaning back from their shared embrace, she offered a smile to the young man.

"What say you to returning back to the warmth of the cottage and partaking in some food and overdue sleep?"

Michael just nod his affirmative.

Leaning forward the woman placed a small peck on the young man's cheek and slid her hand into his. Michael entwined his fingers locking them into Joan's as they started for the stone structure. It was now Joan who saved her rescuer from not only the weather's coldness, but the frigidness of a lonely heart.

Chapter 50

"Might someone explain to me why the queen has not been found yet!", angrily shouted King Paul annoyed by the guard's report on their lack to produce Queen Lynn so far. His fist slamming into the arm of the throne where he sat staring down from the raised platform at the kneeling soldier in front of him. The young man's raptor-like gaze catching the guard flinch at the enraged blow. The strike's solid pound mixed with that of the woman's groan at the base of the dais on her hands and knees being ridden by Sir Rufus, as her husband and four other guardsmen observed her being plunged into.

"Will someone shut her up!", the king hissed.

In moments one of the onlookers approached the woman and pulled his drawstrings releasing his pants. Grabbing a fist full of her long, black hair, he lowered himself to his knees penetrating her lips with his manhood. The husband witnessing his wife being thrust into from the front and the rear, as her groans became instantly muffled.

"Your majesty! Please!", he pleaded.

"Guards take this man to the dungeon with the rest of the cretins refusing to pay the fair amount of taxes," Paul firmly ordered all the while keeping his eyes fixed on the kneeling soldier.

"Inform me soldier, why the traitorous queen be not meeting my hangman as of yet?"

"We own no success in finding her my lord," confessed the messenger. "Nor any awareness as of where to seek."

"And why not soldier?", inquired the king. "Have your men searched every farmhouse and barn in Hamilton?"

"Not all your majesty," he revealed with a tone of apprehension as he dropped his eyes to the ravishing taken place several feet away from him. The woman's cries quieting as he witnessed her throat work to swallow. The messenger could also tell that Sir Rufus' seed filled her womb.

"Soldier!", shouted King Paul.

"Yes my lord!", he started while raising his eyes back to the throne.

"I sit here not there, and it will serve you well to remember that!" the young royal growled.

"Yes your majesty."

"I will advise the castle's scribe that a new proclamation need to be written on this day. On the morrow you will take some soldiers and tear asunder every cottage in this village until you find out who dares give sanctuary to the queen.", ordered Paul. "For now you be dismissed."

Looking over, Paul waved the guard away who had somewhat silenced the woman during his meeting with the other soldier. "Everyone but Sir Rufus is dismissed," he added waving to the other guards taken in the sight of the farmer's wife lying on her back. The knight had grabbed an ankle in each hand folding the woman almost in half. A foot rested by each of her ears. With her lower back slightly off the floor fully exposing her vagina, Rufus sunk his hugeness all the way into her. The wife opening her eyes almost as wide as her mouth as she pulled a large amount of air.

"How be that?", smugly inquired the royal.

This woman made the twenty first seized wife since King Paul raised the taxes.

"You will be planted and come to know child when I am done," growled Rufus.

"These folk know not that I am a wise king. If you be willing to hang one man then you must replace him to regulate Hamilton's size," he laughed while watching the knight ride another mount. Soon the town's women would be with his men's children causing his army in time to grow and replenish allowing for the invasion of at least both France and Scotland to be written into history. For now, he just opened his robe and placed a hand in his lap while he completely knew joy from overseeing Rufus invade and conquer another woman's womb.

Honour

King Paul sat with one of the royal scribes in the castle's private study dictating to the scholar the new proclamation that would be copied and put into effect on the morrow. His hawk-like stare studied the other man write down some of the king's words, dip his quill in an ink bottle, and look up at the royal for further instructions. When the parchment was finally finished, the scholar read it back out loud.

"Hear ye. Hear ye. By order of King Paul on this sixteenth day of December in the year of our lord fourteen hundred thirty eight, I decree that anyone caught giving sanctuary to Queen Lynn will be arrested and sentenced to death.

Hence, if the outlaw queen is not turned over to the castle's authorities by the first day of January in the upcoming year of our lord fourteen hundred and thirty nine taxes will be raised two fold. If any person does not pay their allotment then he will be hung.

Thenceforth, Queen Lynn's reward shall remain the total of five hundred gold coins if she be brought to justice alive or one hundred gold coins if the queen be dead.

Lastly, all folk in Hamilton, along with the surrounding countryside will be expected to fully surrender to all searches of their cottages, farms, and land by those of the crown's soldiers. If Queen Lynn be found in or on any one of these properties then the owner shall be arrested, charged with lending aid to a fugitive from justice along with treason, and sentenced to death.

This proclamation will be in existence for all till the traitorous queen knows England's justice."

When the scholar was finished reading he looked up. King Paul was gazing into the distance absorbing every word. A devilish smile creased his lips at his own satisfaction with the royal document.

"Enter!", Paul instructed when the knock on the room's door broke him from his own thoughts. He watched as the knight came into the study closing the portal behind him.

"How be the newly acquired wife my greatly endowed friend?"

"When last I departed, the woman seemed to walk as if she had a bow between her legs," laughed the knight.

Returning his attention back to the scribe, the royal ordered the scholar. "Spend the rest of this day and into the night producing copies of the document. For in the morning, I shall send the messengers to deliver my words. You be dismissed," he added waving him away with two fingers.

"Yes your majesty," groveled the scribe on his way out of the chambers with the parchment rolled up under an arm.

"I bring news my lord," revealed Rufus waiting for the door to close shut. "Both Ruth and her mother Sarah show proof they be with child."

"Very well done," confidently smiled King Paul. "Already the future additions to the growth of the conquering army will begin arriving next summer."

"Sir Rufus, retrieve Martha and bring her here to me," he requested speaking of the very first wife he had seized from her husband. "It be feeding time and I would not want her to hunger."

"Yes your majesty," grinned the knight. The image of the woman feasting on her fill of royal meat and gravy throughout the day kept him grinning as he shut the study's door behind him and began down the hallway.

<hr />

"I cannot begin to believe you and I be with child," worriedly remarked Ruth sitting on the chamber's bed speaking with her mother.

"Did you expect different?", inquired her mother. "Rufus and those other men took us over and over."

"What do you ponder King Paul will do with us?"

"We will give birth only to have the king's men plant their seed in us again," Sarah disappointedly revealed.

"How be it you know that?", questioned Ruth.

"I have slept for many nights in Sir Rufus' bed. Do you ponder he has never spoken of the kings plan while he rode me?", Ruth's mother lowered her head and her eyes gazed at her hands locked in her lap. "I can only keep Satan's bastards away from Antionette for so long, but soon even I know she will be mounted and taken." A tear fallen from her mother's eye.

"What be we to do?", queried a hopeless Ruth.

"What can we do? Both you and I be just leaves caught in King Paul's storm winds."

Sitting on the bed and glancing from the baby bump beginning to slowly grow on both her and her mother's body, Ruth partook in knowing that her mother be right again.

The sun was beginning to set behind the horizon this cold winter's day relinquishing the sky to the stars that had just started to reveal themselves in the heavens above. The snow had ceased to fall on this day, but white powder already covered the land and the bare trees. The castle's walls wore both frost and icicles. Two guards stood watch from the gate's battlement breathing smoke on this frigid evening. They were not looking forward to the freezing temperature that the night brought with it.

"Go seek some warmth by the fire," ordered Lieutenant Cobb speaking to one of the guards. "I will take up post here with Adams for a spell."

"Yes sir," saluted the soldier bringing his fist to his chest. Smoke escaped from his lips.

Taking his leave, the man walked by the lieutenant heading for the stone wall where two other soldiers warmed themselves by a small, circular fire.

"I like not what this palace has turned into Adams," disgustedly stated the man in charge. "You would have not fallen witness this perversion if either King Stephen or King Matthew were sitting on the throne."

"I am in accord with you sir, but we must hold our words or find our own necks stretched," worried Adams. "King Paul has turned this into a Den of Sin with all the hangings and fornication with other men's wives."

"I will tell you what it be; a Den of Snakes run by the Devil himself," Cobb hotly opinionated, but he made sure to keep his voice down and control his body language. He could not afford the attention in case any of Paul's men were watching.

The lieutenant leaned against the wall's battlement gazing out into the quickly fading light.

"What do you see sir?", the other watchman inquired.

"Nothing soldier," admitted the man in charge. He paused for a brief moment before continuing. "I own no belief that Queen Lynn is responsible for Matthew's death, if he even be dead at all."

"King Paul said he be."

"I am well aware of what the king spoke," acknowledged Cobb. "Call to memory the night the royal carriage arrived carrying the bodies of Sir Timothy and the other men. Why were King Matthew, Queen Lynn, or even her personal servant's body not with them? Who do you suppose sent us the bodies?"

"You be right sir," agreed Adams.

Cobb only smiled at the man's sudden realization.

"I believe they be out there. Somewhere."

"Do you see something sir?", inquired the other watchman returning from his warm reprieve.

"No soldier. Adams and I were speaking on some desirable spots for hunting," the lieutenant lied.

"I have witnessed both boar and deer in that direction sir," added Adams.

"I pondered you spotted something. If I may return to the fire sir?"

"You still own a few minutes more before you relieve a sentry on the South wall."

"Yes sir," the other man saluted before returning to his seat by the flame.

Making sure they were out of ear shot, Cobb turned back to Adams. "Let us pray that somehow they found shelter from this English weather. Please our Father, protect the king and queen and deliver us from evil."

Chapter 51

Lieutenant Cobb shielded his eyes protecting them from the bright sun's rays beaming down on Hamilton as he stepped out the tavern's door and into the brilliant daylight. He had not been witness to the fiery orb for a few days now thanks in part to the sky's overcast that had threatened to dump more snow on the land. The squinting man's eyes trying to adjust from the dullness of the tavern's interior to the radiance outdoors.

Lowering his eyes, which still be shielded by his hand above them, Cobb glanced from one side to the other before venturing out into the calf-deep snow. He wanted to return to the castle's guard barracks and get some sleep before he would have to return to duty on the city's walls this night. The Lieutenant still knew unease in not only Hamilton's unrest, but also King Paul's enigmatic story that proceeded his seat on the throne.

"From first glance Paul's tale of ambush appeared to be whole, but the more one pondered it many more holes appeared in its truth," reasoned the soldier to himself knowing that he wasn't the only soul who had come to know doubt.

Cobb lost track not only of the number of townsfolk he had passed, but also of the buildings while he remained lost in deep thought. The lieutenant never noticing the man in the upcoming alley opening observing him, as he approached it unaware. The hooded head disappearing into the passageway, as Cobb made his way closer to the intersection.

Suddenly across the weathered street, a girl screamed causing the soldier to turn his back to the alleyway's entrance, as he just took a second step into the intersection of it. She had been struck with two balls of snow from a couple of lads who now tried to flee the scene of the powdered assault. Knowing no warning, a hand clamped over Cobb's mouth while a second arm wrapped around his chest. At the exact moment following the grab, the off duty soldier felt his legs kicked out from under him. He was being dragged into the passageway between buildings. The lieutenant tried to put up a struggle but without his feet under him, Cobb knew no leverage and his attempts at resisting were futile for now. He was dragged around a two-wheeled cart and out of anyone's sight glancing down the alley. Cobb would not receive any aid, for the girl's scream had drawn everyone's attention to the snowy attack.

"If the child be a girl, then I foresee her knowing a beauty rivaling her mother," remarked Michael smiling as his eye's glanced between Joan's face and her swollen belly. "But if it be a boy, then I will teach him to use a bow and hunt for food."

The woman returned the expression. "I be looking forward to that, but take heed in knowing that his interests will not be on catching food but rather crying for it," she laughed.

Michael chuckled at the truth in Joan's words.

"Shall we continue on?", queried the woman with child feeling her breath returning to her. "I take heed in knowing that I need daily movement, but the depth of this snow be encumbering for me."

"We need not walk any further and can return if you wish. The matter be up to your choosing."

"No Michael," she shook her head. "I have made a decision to speak with you on a matter that holds much importance," the woman's expression holding a touch of sadness in her grin. "I query that you not feel ill towards me after I tell you my secret. For I own value in our friendship."

"I know not what it be you mean," puzzled Michael. The young man not owning so much as a thought to what Joan be about to say.

"I know not the one who sired the child growing in my belly," the woman sadly admitted. "I was violated against my will by King Paul and Rufus. The two of them took me over and over night after night."

Her revelation bringing with it both shock and silence to the snow-covered forest.

"I am sorry Joan," the young man sympathized.

"You have been a good friend to me during this short time and have shown me aid on hands and knees," she reached out and took hold of his hand. "I can only wish that your feelings lack any ill towards me," the woman offering a weak smile through watered eyes.

"It be nothing you did!", Michael emphasized the point. "Only those two dogs know fault." The young man bringing his other hand tenderly to the side of Joan's face. "I would be a liar to call myself a man if I held you to blame for their evils. You will never know ill from me."

His gentle smile and words touching Joan's heart. The woman gazed into Michael's eyes searching his soul. Slowly, she leaned forward into him and their lips met one another. For the first time since Matthew, Joan felt something real.

King Paul sat sideways behind his desk in the private study with his left leg up on the piece of wooden furniture. The young man's raptor-like facial features wearing an expression that showed him to be in deep thought. He stared into one of the shelved walls filled with both books and tombs while steadily rolling his fingers drumming the desktop. Kneeling in between his spread legs bobbed Martha, the first wife ever seized by the king and turned into one of the castle's sex slaves. The woman working towards his release and her fill of the royal's body fluid.

"Where you be hiding?", Paul's silent inquiry remaining to himself as he contemplated over his search for the answer. The image of the royal carriage filled with the dead bodies of his cousin's slain personal guards, along with the report that the assassin laid fallen by three arrows protruding from his body and a fourth through his neck had found its way back into his head. These events only began to prove that someone gave aid to not just the queen and her servant, but Matthew as well. The fact that their corpses were missing from the returned coach only reinforced the issue.

King Paul knew that his plan would have more success whether or not Queen Lynn was found, but if his cousin happened to show back up in Hamilton, then he would be the one meeting the acquaintance of the hangman's noose. Matthew's people would rise up in his defense, and even though Paul's soldiers out-numbered his cousin's men at arms, two-to-one, the townsfolk would be enough to switch the favor back the other way.

Paul's face slightly contorted not only at the thought, but also as he began to feed Martha.

"Surely the queen will be found or quickly delivered to me after this day," he thought to himself wearing a devilish smile on his face. "None of Hamilton's townsfolk will be able to hide her thanks to my new proclamation. They will snap like twigs under boot. In the stead of money or their necks being stretched, the people will be ever more willing to turn over the fugitive from justice," King Paul silently laughed to himself. "And only then will I display mercy for all my people to witness by pardoning the queen from the gallows. She will live out the rest of her life knowing seclusion in the castle's tower. Her womb will know only me, and she will produce me an heir wherefore I will sire a child with her every year until her womb knows only barrenness. Then I will have Lynn hung."

Briefly returning from his thoughts, Paul glanced down meeting Martha's eyes looking up from her knees at him.

"Rise Martha," calmly instructed the king while removing his left leg from its resting place on the desk. "Do you still hunger?"

"No my lord," she quietly replied.

Paul patted the desktop in front of him as he rearranged the chair he had sat in.

Martha climbed onto the furniture and sat positioning herself on the desk's edge bracing herself with her arms spread behind her body and her knees bent up. The woman watched Paul sit back down in between her legs and place one on each shoulder. He offered her one of his devilish grins before lowering his face into Martha's nether region.

Soon the thoughts and images over the whereabouts of the queen and his cousin were drowned out by Martha's pleasure-filled moans and groans. The self-made king once again proving that this snake knew more than one way to use his tongue.

"I shall draw my hand from your mouth. Do not call out for any aid," the hooded man's voice placidly instructed from behind the uselessly struggling lieutenant. "Do we own accord?", he followed with the inquiry.

Cobb's muffled yes was accompanied by a nod from his head.

Honour

Honouring his words, the stranger uncovered the off duty soldier's mouth slowly as if waiting for an outburst. None shot forth.

"I will assist you in knowing your footing and release you, but know not the idea to turn on me and release your dagger Lieutenant Cobb!"

"How be it you know my name?", puzzled the paranoid soldier. "Who be you?"

"I be the one who takes heed in knowing that King Paul's reign of perversion does not know any fondness in a man of principal and loyalty to the true king."

"Who be you stranger? For even now this meeting would be enough to offer the both of us a date at the gallows."

"Queen Lynn lives," he plainly stated. The stranger's revelation seeming to remove the air from the off duty soldier's lungs.

"How be it you know that?", shockingly questioned Lieutenant Cobb while taking a step toward the stranger. Just the thought of the true royal's returning to take their rightful place on the throne and ending this perverse reign caused hope to ignite in the man.

"For even now I be in contact with the one who rescued both the king and queen," the hooded stranger revealed.

"King Matthew lives?"

"No Cobb," the stranger's voice filled with sorrow. "Matthew found death defending his queen from an ambush hatched and sprung by Paul. Not an attack that knew of Queen Lynn's conspiring with the French. The new king's words lack that of the truth."

"I knew it!", confirmed Cobb gazing at the snow on the ground. "All the way down to my bones I believed something was amiss when the royal carriage arrived at the gates carrying our dead guards."

"That was a message from the one that led the rescue. He knew that if the king's royal guard showed up dead then it would pressure Paul to bury each man with a proper funeral if he desired his lie to remain concealed."

Lieutenant Cobb was impressed that this rescuer risked their own life to save the king and queen, but had also honoured the fallen soldiers forcing the king to give them a proper burial in the stead of being picked at by wild animals and carrion-feasting birds.

"Will others rise to the defense of Queen Lynn?", inquired the hooded man.

"Those who did would risk much," reasoned Cobb. "Hence I know not even who you be, nor if what you speak holds any truth."

"Fair enough lieutenant." Slowly he pulled back his hood revealing his identity.

Cobb's eyes widened with astonishment. "The beggar!" The lieutenant paused as he tried to mentally work through and comprehend not only who he saw but the words the man of the streets said to him.

"If you see not the truth in my words than I offer you proof of their authenticity with this," David reached for a wrapped item sitting on the cart.

"Lieutenant Cobb hastily took a step back and reached for his dagger while David the Beggar loosened the cloth covering the item. The man of the streets held it up for the off duty soldier to view. In his hand was a scabbard sheathing a sword. A sword that Cobb had laid eyes on many times throughout his years as a castle's guard.

"If not my words then would you rather the dying words of an hononable man?" only spoken full of honour?"

"Where did you procure that sword?", surprisingly asked Cobb. "That be Sir Timothy's blade!"

"I acquired the weapon from the one who not only rescued the queen but now defends her against the devil seated on the throne. The young man brought it to me honouring a brother's dying wish," he added.

"Sir Timothy was your brother?"

"He was," David admitted lowering the sword's scabbard. "And a fine one at that."

"I never knew," confessed the lieutenant. "He never revealed your relations to anyone, or why you to know life on the streets and not in the castle?"

"My bother lived by that which he believed in. He honoured my wishes to be free of the palace's confining walls and held my secret life of the streets until he knew death was upon him. Now I ask, will you believe my words hold truth in them?", questioned David.

"I will," he firmly replied.

"Will others rise for Queen Lynn against King Paul?"

"Inform the queen that all the men who were loyal to King Matthew be hers now to command. We await her orders! It be time for the adders to slither back under that rock they had come from."

Their unexpected meeting coming to an abrupt halt when they heard another yelling in the streets outside the alleyway's entrance.

"Hear Ye! Hear Ye!"

Taking the scabbard under his cloak, the two men made their way to the intersection blending into the gathered crowd as they listened to King Paul's new decree. When the crier had ended, he left after hanging a copy up in the city's square.

Both Cobb and David glanced at one another. What was once a land knowing and living in peace had been turned into a realm that knew only strife and perversion. Hamilton, and soon all of England, was about to know only carnage and chaos. The self-made king's reign would tighten its stranglehold even more. The only chance that England may have in stopping its death and burden on the common folk was the uplifting touch of their loving Queen Lynn and her return back to her rightful place on the throne.

"I will spread your words of revelation on this day," quietly spoke Cobb. "The queen's men at arms will know more spirit now," he added.

"I meet with the queen's rescuer in a week and will inform him of what you have told me. If anything knows change before that time get word to me before we enter a trap waiting to be sprung by Paul," David slipped back down the alley, as Lieutenant Cobb started for the barracks. The man knowing he had a lot of work to accomplish within the next seven days.

No longer would they be planning for a fight with the French. Cobb and the men loyal to King Stephen and King Matthew would need to prepare for a different battle. A civil war between Paul and the royal by marriage Queen Lynn. A small smile came to his face as he knew whose side the townsfolk of Hamilton would be on.

Chapter 52

December 24, 1440

"Must you leave already?", lovingly whimpered Lynn standing in front of Russell and gazing into his face. "It seems like only days ago that you returned with more provisions."

"Not only can we use them, but the mounts need more feed," the young man tried to explain looking into her pleading eyes. "This be the last we can raid from your father's barn."

"You cannot raid from yourself," she pointed out.

"Your words hold truth, but I believe Paul's men have taken up residence there under the assumption that the place has been abandoned by those fleeing the king. Do you recall that we needed to sneak what we took on the last trip there?", it was now Russell who pointed out the fact to the outlaw queen. "This night be the last night for I ponder they are aware of the missing sacks of grain and oats."

"Russell be right Lynn. There be no lack of danger now in our nighttime raids," agreed a mounted Robert.

The young woman casting a disgusted glance towards the snow-filled sky at Sire Daniels and the use of the word "raids."

A smile creased Russell's face. "Not raids my love. My father meant trips. We need go," the young man pointed out. His father and Peter were already mounted on their horses waiting on him.

"Please lack not care this night my dear and may God keep you safe," wished the young woman before embracing her love and sharing a kiss. "Your queen will await your return," she added matter-of-factly.

Russell offered a bow of his head. "We shall return late. For this night I need meet with David."

"Please know care," she pleaded once more.

"You neither Robert," came his wife standing near the doorway with one arm wrapped around her daughter's shoulder.

"Be safe brother. I will see you upon your return," remarked Paul.

Russell swung his leg over his charger and from the saddle reached out to clasp Michael's arm. "Keep them all safe. We will see one another on the morrow."

"On the morrow," smiled his friend.

Russell gave a click with his tongue and a lite tap with his heels on the horse's flanks. His journey began as he started on his way.

Both Peter then Robert followed him.

The small group watched the three mounted members ride into the leaf-less trees that once again was under the siege of snowfall.

"I need check on the horses," Michael softly reasoned. "We can walk after that if you would like."

"Very well," Joan acknowledged accompanied with a smile.

The sun had dropped behind the trees, and considering that the snow fell once again along with the fact there had been no wind throughout the day, the darkness of nightfall was lacking the cold, frigidness of past trips.

"Are we not meeting with David first this evening first?", queried Robert reining his mount to a stop alongside his son.

"Most of the countryside be attending mass on this eve before Christmas," Russell reasoned. We should reprovision before setting out to meet with David."

"Very well thought my son," Sire Daniels voice giving off a slight hint of being impressed.

Giving a click to his mount, Russell started out again.

Both Peter and then Robert followed in a single file. The three remained quiet as they shared no more words throughout the wooded trip.

Robert and his two young companions watched from the safety of their hidden spot behind the small, stone structure with the attached chicken coop, as two of King Paul's soldiers entered the cottage thirty feet away. For a brief moment, the three had observed not only the bright light cutting into the darkness when the door opened, but the sounds of a woman being taken interrupted the silence of the night. All three remained motionless and quiet for the brief time.

"By the looks of the two entering and the sounds coming from inside, they may not be going anywhere anytime soon," pointed out Peter.

"I ponder your words know truth," agreed Robert. "Do you ponder we meet with David first?"

"No father," replied Russell drawing a cross with his fingertips from his forehead to his heart followed from shoulder to shoulder. "The woman gives to us the distraction we require to reprovision quickly and take our leave."

"We be just going to leave her to know ravishing at the hands of those men?", shockingly asked Peter.

"It must be my friend," revealed Robert's son. "The care of the Queen of England be in our hands, and that alone is of more importance. We cannot fail her, for only she can put an end to King Paul's unholy reign."

"I hate to say it but Russell be right Peter," admitted Robert. "We need not chance getting caught and thrown into the dungeons nor killed.

It wasn't long that the three companions formed a small line and had begun to remove the last of the remaining sacks. Already Robert had loaded both his horse and Russell's charger, along with packing half the remaining provisions on Peter's mount.

"Father take both horses that know full packs and begin for the depths of the forest," instructed Russell. "Wait there and we shall meet you."

"All right son but know haste," agreed Robert.

A scream of release broke the silence of the night, as the woman being taken in the cottage voiced her release for a third time. The verbal signal started both Russell and his father. Tenseness filled the air as the three froze in mid-step. Soon silence returned to the night.

Turning around from Peter's horse, where he had just placed another sack on the animal and starting out for the barn's door, Russell pressed up against the stone wall when he witnessed the cottage door open. Light shot forth and a half-naked man walked out into the snow.

"Please Lord. Let father know the safety of the forest!", silently prayed the young man.

Without warning a ringing of bells broke the night's stillness.

Russell helplessly watched the man, who had been relieving himself, quickly look up.

"Stop! Thief!", the soldier ordered. "In the name of the crown, I order you to halt!"

"We need to make haste!", yelled Russell running up and peering into the barn's doorway. The young raider taking in the sight of his friend hanging upside down. A rope with a half a dozen bells ensnared Peter's leg.

"Run Russell! Save yourself!", cried the suspended twin.

Glancing back towards the cottage, which now erupted with four other armed and semi-naked men joining the fifth starting for the barn, Russell ran to Peter's horse. He knew that his sword and bow remained on his mount, which by now was with his father in the trees. The young man slung Peter's quiver of arrows over his shoulder before taking the twin's bow.

"Run!", shouted Russell while slapping the charger on its rear. The horse giving a loud whinny and bolting for the bare forest.

Turning, the young man started back for the structure's doorway, while nocking an arrow and drawing the bow's string. Russell would not leave his friend behind. He loosed the arrow, and with haste lacking retrieved another. He drew back the bow's string.

<hr>

Robert had just made it to the snow-covered tree line when the ringing bells pierced the night's air. Quickly, the man looked in the direction of their origin, but was wise enough to keep leading the two provision-packed horses into the woods.

Robert scanned into the dark seeing the lit corner of the cottage. It was obvious to him that the structure's door had been opened. He also heard a man, lost to his view, cry out. It was then that he made out five silhouettes running from the light's faintness into the darkness.

"Russell and Peter be in trouble!", he momentarily panicked reaching for his sword. "And his bow and blade be on his horse!" The realization striking him like a blow from a knight's lance. Unsheathing his blade, Sire Daniels started out of the woods only stopping when he heard his son shout out "Run!"

Robert's heart sunk remembering the conversation the three had earlier this day before embarking out this night. The fact that it be Russell in trouble made him want to charge straight out of the trees and run to his son's defense, but the young man had made both Peter and Robert swear that if any of them found themselves in trouble this night then the others would do whatever it took for at least one man to escape. Sire Daniels quickly recalled what exactly Russell had said. "Someone needs to protect Lynn! Only the queen could free Hamilton from the siege it faces from Paul's tyranny. England be worth more than one man's life." Tears formed in Robert's eyes as their watery sight took in the third half-packed horse materialize out of the darkness. He also quickly realized that he would need to meet David alone. Hamilton needed rescuing. He would now have to be the way that the outlaw queen could communicate with those still loyal to her.

Sire Daniels knew deep in his heart that his son be right. Reaching out for the third mount's lead and taking hold of it, he lashed its rein to the horse in front of it. Robert sheathed his blade before doing one of the hardest things in his life. Russell's father upheld his sworn word to his son beginning to lead the single file of chargers away into the snow-covered forest. He would have to meet with David, or England could be lost. The burden now fell to Robert.

"Ready yourself!", warned Russell quickly aiming his next shot at the rope that had ensnared his friend around the ankle.

Taking his eyes from his intended target and glancing at the now four onrushing soldiers, while the fifth one lie on the crimson-colored snow with an arrow's shaft protruding from his left leg and screaming profanity at him, Russell knew he would only get one shot at the fibrous cord.

"Ready yourself!", the young man offering his friend one more warning before letting loose the shot. The arrow flying towards and past the rope sailing into a beam supporting the structure's roof. Russell had missed.

Hastily he reached for another arrow, but time had run out. King Paul's men were on him. The soldier in the lead tackled Russell, and the two began to struggle. Both wrestled in the snow until a second off duty soldier used the pommel of his sword to hit the young man in the back of his head. Russell only knew darkness. Peter's friend never hearing the dangling twin scream a warning or his name.

David the Beggar leaned against one of the tree's trunks watching a lone figure materialize out of the darkness and snow flurries.

"David," sadly greeted the other man as he approached.

The man of the streets instantly recognizing the other's voice as Russell's father.

"Robert?"

"We met with trouble this night."

"Where be Russell?"

Casting his gaze on the man while doing his best to keep from choking up, Robert pained. "Russell has fallen into the hands of King Paul, or has come to meet with death at his men's swords."

"What?", shocked David.

"What news for the queen?", straightened up Sire Daniels. His duty to try and orchestrate Lynn's return to the throne was still at the importance. There would be a time to mourn the loss of his son, but now wasn't that time. Robert knew that Russell may not even be dead yet, but the fact that the self-made king would most likely hang him followed on the heels of that hope.

David the Beggar recited that both he and Lieutenant Cobb had met earlier this day. He shared with Robert the fact that according to Cobb those still loyal to the outlaw queen would stand with her against Paul. The man of the streets handed a rolled parchment to Sire Daniels. "This be a copy of King Paul's new decree. It seems that Hamilton will come to know more hangings now then it had in the last hundred years."

Russell's father tucked it away in one of his cloak's inner pockets, and then clasped forearms with David.

"In a fort night?"

"Yes," agreed the beggar.

"I will see what I can do to find Russell if he lives," promised David. "I know sorrow for you and your family, but do not abandon hope for I may know fortune if God wills it."

Chapter 53

"Get in there!", growled the royal jailer while shoving Russell into one of the dungeon's cells and locking the gated door behind him.

The beaten and battered young man staggering from the push before falling against the wall. One eye was swollen shut and his head pounded like a running charger's hooves against the earth.

"Make yourself familiar with your new dwellings," laughed the grungy-looking man with a stomach that protruded a good three feet in front of him. The sneering jailer spit in the new prisoner's direction before walking away from the bars.

Taking a minute to collect himself the best he could considering his head pounded, Russell surveyed his ten by six foot cage. Only a lone, wooden bucket sat in a corner with a urine smell emanating from it. The young man had no problem recognizing what it was used for. The place knew both darkness and dankness with the only light source coming from the hissing torch that remained in its wrought iron sconce located near the locked oak door leading to the cell's corridor. The stuffy air knew only three sounds; groans from others imprisoned here; the snores from those who found sleep in their cells; and the squeaking rats that scurried about the place.

Leaning against the wall, Russell focused on one image; his true love's face.

Peter sat with his bent knees drawn up and into his body with his head resting on them. The young man's right shoulder throbbed from being cut down and landing hard on it. He blamed himself for the situation that both Russell and he found themselves in. Peter felt guilty for not only finding himself here at this lovely inn, but the belief that he had taken one of his best friends down with him only seemed to strengthen his despair. The thought that he would never see his father and brother again also fed the drearyness of his present situation. "Our Father. Who art in Heaven. Hallowed be thy name...", Peter began to recite the Lord's Prayer. The young man taking heed in knowing that only God could rescue him and Russell before King Paul had their necks stretched. If the devil knew haste and beat Him, then only He could offer them life ever-after letting Peter one day to reunite with his family. "Amen," he ended the supplication. With his fingers he drew a cross from his forehead to his heart and then shoulder to shoulder.

"Should we wake the King and inform him that we captured these two thieves at the Bradford cottage?", queried one of the soldiers that had just brought the two young men in from the countryside and thrown them in the dungeon.

"It be rather late, and I wish not to awaken him especially if he finds the matter lacking in importance," pointed out the other soldier.

The two indecisively looking at one another.

Shadows danced and waved across the ceiling and walls in the king's royal bedchambers. Even though winter flurries dumped on Hamilton outside, Paul's room knew warmth, but not just from the fire.

The young man was sitting completely nude on the settee watching as Martha rode his manhood while seated with her back towards him. Already her moans of pleasure were beginning to hang on the air as she felt her release building. The woman's breasts following her motion rising and falling as her pace began to quicken. The two never ceasing their coupling when both heard the knock on the door.

"Who be disturbing me at this time of night?", angrily inquired the king,

"It be Lieutenant Franks your majesty," humbly replied the invader.

"This better be a matter that knows importance! Enter!",

Franks shut the door behind him. The lieutenant taking in the sight of the woman bouncing on the king's lap.

"This better be good!", warned the king.

"Yes my lord. We have arrested two young men for knowing the act of thievery your majesty."

"And you found this matter of importance how?", growled Paul.

"My lord, the thieves were raiding the farm owned by the traitorous queen's sire," he informed. "We believe these two are responsible for the previous thieving of the place."

"And what did they have to say upon your inquiries of them?"

"Due to the farm's previous owner, we knew not if you wished to be present when we begin our inquiries my lord."

"Lieutenant, have you pondered that the two men may be just common thieves?", lackadaisically questioned the king.

"Yes my lord," replied Franks. "but if be only common thieves as your majesty titles them, then why practice their art in the countryside with provisions in-the-stead of here in the city outside of taverns where they could easily separate drunks from their coins?"

Paul thought about the point being presented and with each passing second his suspicion began to grow. "I will join you when you question the prisoners. We may receive some intriguing answers not of our expectations."

"Yes my lord."

Moments later, the royal was throwing on his robe and boots following Lieutenant Franks out the door. "We shall return to our play upon my return Martha," he added before closing the portal behind him.

"Yes my lord," replied the seized wife. Martha really missed her loving husband, but the king was honouring his word. She knew not hunger any longer. Deep inside her slowly becoming perverted mind, already the woman wished for a quick return.

"You lie!", shouted a jailer into Russell's face before connecting with a punch to the young man's chin. The force of the blow causing a spray of blood to shoot in the same direction that the bound up prisoner's head whipped. "You know where the queen be!"

"I know not." The young man had been beaten and interrogated for the last hour. There was not a spot remaining on his body that knew not pain. To accompany the swollen eye and the headache he already had, the interrogator made sure that blood flowed freely from several cuts on his face, along with the good possibility that the young man suffered a couple of broken ribs.

"That be why you and your brother thieved from the farm that originally belonged to the traitor's father? The outlaw sent you both there to retrieve food supplies."

"I know not who the present queen's father be," the prisoner confessed. "My words only know truth! My brother and I only wish to die of old age not hunger! Our father was hung, and our farm occupied by the king's men."

"You are lying!", the man preparing to offer another blow.

"Hold your hand," ordered King Paul standing at the cell's door. "A word.", he used his head to point outside the gated portal.

Giving Russell the evil eyes, the interrogator dropped his hand to his side before turning to take his leave from the cell. "This matter be not over yet," the guard growled walking for the doorway.

"Your majesty?"

King Paul glanced at the beaten, young man lashed to the chair in the center of the dungeon's cell. "The two have given the same accounts for an hour now. I grow tired of this. We are getting nowhere. Release him and his brother from their bonds. Neither will know the charge of "Conspiracy," but they still be thieves. Both will know the hangman's noose when the new year be upon us," instructed the young royal. "Now unless Queen Lynn herself knows my dungeon this night, I shall not be bothered for the remainder of it," Paul giving his subtle warning before starting down the corridor and returning to the fun he was having before this intrusion.

"Be that the king himself ?", slurred the man being escorted by Lieutenant Cobb and another jailer down the same passageway that the royal was heading down.

"Mind your manners street urchin!"

"What be the meaning of this?", angrily questioned King Paul as his gaze fell upon the three men coming towards him.

Dropping to a knee, the drunkard slipped from the jailer and Cobb's clutches. "My lord, might I just say it be my privilege and honor to meet you formally. I be one of your loyal supporters," the drunk belched. "I have come to know the spirits on this Eve of Christmas!"

Grimacing from the stink of ale and horse manure, the king questioned. "What in the name of God is this!"

"I am sorry my lord," apologized the lieutenant. "I knew not to expect you down here at this time of night. This man here be the town's resident beggar, and by his words one of your majesty's supporters."

"David the Beggar, my lord," merrily greeted the man. Beginning to rise, the drunkard lost his balance falling sideways into the wall. The street urchin's eyes glancing at Russell still lashed to the chair in a cell.

"On your feet David," Cobb grabbed the fallen's upper arm.

"What be this man's charge?", inquired Paul with a mixture of disgust and frustration.

"He not be charged with any my lord. I pondered I shall place him here to sleep off his drunkardness and release him on the morrow."

"This be a dungeon not an inn," sneered Paul. "I suggest you leave at once with this, this..."

"David the Beggar of Hamilton your majesty," smiled the drunk with a bow from his head followed by a guttural belch.

An agitated King Paul waved his hand dismissively.

"Lets go David," ordered Cobb. The lieutenant, the jailer, and the street urchin turned back down the corridor away from the cells. On this night, the drunk would know the wetness of the snow to sober him up. Seeing Russell alive had already livened David's spirits more than any ale ever could.

Lynn's eyes quickly opened when she heard the hoot of an owl carry in the air outside. The young woman only knowing a lite sleep thanks in part to her feeling of unease every time Russell had to leave. An instant later she was on her feet at the sound of the second hoot.

Michael and Paul rose to their feet while all of the other women looked to one another.

"I shall go check," came Michael while glancing at Paul. He grabbed his blade before lifting the thick piece of lumber barring the door before slipping out into the darkness of the wee hours.

Paul securing the portal.

Moments later a hoot from Michael signified let the cottage's occupants know the coast be clear and the three had returned.

Paul opened the door and stared into the darkness. The young man's eyes taking in the sight of his muscular friend's silhouette walking beside another leading the horses in a single file line. It wasn't till they got real close that Paul could make out Robert., but where be his brother, and Russell. "Something be amiss. Where be Peter and Russell?", he anxiously queried as he slowly left the cottage's doorway. His words producing angst amongst the others in the room.

Lynn was the first to rush to the open entryway and gaze out into the snow-flurried darkness. Her worried expression taking in the sight of Paul dropping his head into his hands. No one needed to speak. The outlaw queen knew that not only had King Paul taken her husband, her livelihood, her freedom and her father, but now the evil ruler had robbed the young woman of her one true love.

"Noooooo!!!", Lynn hysterically screamed while dropping to her knees. For on this night, the forest and most likely the whole of England heard their outlaw queen's anguish. The feeling of fear and aloneness flooded into her rivaling that like Lynn had known years ago when she had gotten lost in the woods. This time though Russell would not be coming to find her and protect her from the animals that wished her harm.

Chapter 54

December 28, 1440

The two Daniels' women, Elizabeth and Nicole along with Lynn's sister, Anne, sat at the table watching Gwenyth seated near the cottage's only bed. Her oldest daughter laid with her back to the room. Lynn's mother remained vigilant as she slowly rubbed the young woman's upper arm while tenderly speaking to her depressed daughter. "My dear. Come join us at the table and have a bowl of stew."

Several moments passed but a response never came.

"You have to eat," pleaded the heart-broken mother.

Ever since Robert had broken the news that Russell be in the clutches of the self-made king, the young woman had shut down to everyone and everything. Her heart knew only pain and she always wore a blank stare. Lynn who had always been so full of life especially when her true love was around was now just a shell of a person. There would be no hope for Hamilton if the real queen would not snap out of her depression or worse died of a broken heart.

Even Gwenyth's hope seemed to teeter on the brink of disaster. Her daughter was more important than England and she knew that she needed to reignite Lynn's flame of desire to at least carry on. The Bradford woman knowing that everyone has a burden to bear and this amount of loss could be Lynn's cross. Gwenyth bent over and kissed her daughter on the temple.

The act of love brought a sad smile to Elizabeth's face. She knew even though Lynn's heart knew the storm winds of pain from love lost, it was her mother's loving support that weathered the gale forces. Gwenyth was like a mighty, English Oak. She would not easily break.

"I know not what to do," Gwenyth sadly confessed while bringing the chair back to the table and taking a seat at it. "She knows only sadness and despair. Joy seems to have completely abandoned her. Lynn will not even eat," a tear rolling down her cheek.

"Lynn shall know triumph over her hurt with time," reasoned Elizabeth while taking up the other woman's hand in hers. "You be doing all you can."

"It be I, whom should show you sorrow for the loss of your son."

"Nonsense my friend. Even though my heart knows pain, I must believe no matter how hard it may be that our Lord's hands be entwined in this matter. I can only offer prayers to God asking that the Almighty watch over my son," Elizabeth's eyes filling with tears.

Sitting next to her, Nicole leaned into her mother while wrapping an arm around the woman. The girl's eyes knowing tears also.

"Lynn," tenderly called the young man's mother. "Would you join us in a prayer to our Lord in asking to watch over Russell and grant him a safe return to those who deeply love and miss him?"

The young woman's dead stare interrupted by a couple of blinks. The mere mention of her love's name bringing her back from the hell she was lost in. Slowly Lynn tuned over on the pallet. She nodded her affirmation.

Rising from her chair, Elizabeth walked over to the bed and helped the young woman sit up and rise to her feet. "Come on hun. I shall help you," she smiled. The two most important women in Russell's life walked across the floor and joined the others at the table. The Daniels' woman helping Lynn sit in the seat that she had once occupied. Tears flowed freely now from the others.

The five women all joined hands and bowed their heads, as Elizabeth led them in prayer.

"Dear Lord, we thank Thee for the food and shelter You have so graciously provided us. We thank Thee for our loved ones and friends who even now surround us in these times that lack not hardships and know troubles. We also give thanks for the gift of our health and well being.

"We humbly come before Thou's throne and petition Thee to watch over and protect our loved ones, Russell and Peter. For Lord, if not for their aid then we all would know a direness worse than anyone could imagine. Father, we believe they are but a tool in Your mighty hands used to toil Your plan. We hope that it be Thou's will to aid them in the clutches of one of the devil's minions. "Lastly Lord, we pray that Thee will not lose favor with us and will remain ever vigilant over our group. Please protect and guide the whole of us. For this we pray in Thou's name; Amen."

"Amen," the women circled around the table repeated. Their clutches on one another's hands tightened before releasing their grasps.

Elizabeth's prayer aided in more ways than one. Not only did it assist in quelling a bit of hopelessness amongst the women, but it seemed to bring Lynn from the brink of deadly despair.

"Mother," the young woman addressed. "May I partake in that bowl of stew?"

A soft smile grew on Gwenyth. "Yes my dear," Lynn's mother looking over towards the one who had giving the prayer.

"Thanks be to God," Elizabeth smiled.

"Your faith is unwavering like an English Oak," praised Lynn's happy mother.

"What are we to do now?", worriedly perplexed Joan. "I have never been witness to the queen like this!"

"I know not," admitted Michael.

"Will we be caught or die here of starvation?", the woman anxiously queried.

"No!", reasoned the young man embracing the pregnant woman. "We shall hunt for food and remain here as long as we can. Robert and Paul be out in the woods now seeking a deer or a boar." Michael's words attempting to strip Joan of any worry.

"I know fear," she admitted while gazing into his eyes.

The muscular, young man pulling Joan's head to his chest. "All shall be well," he attempted to convincingly confirm, but inside Michael knew not sureness himself.

"I wish your words lack not truth," she hoped tightening her embrace and placing a kiss on his lips. She had grown to know love again, and this time her love would not easily be torn from her clutches.

"Do you ponder that we be able to hunt enough food to remain hidden from King Paul for much longer?", wondered Paul while peering up at Robert kneeling across from him over the freshly killed deer carcass.

"I know not," the man admitted unsheathing his dagger preparing to dress the animal for transport. He knew the more meat they could catch allowed the small group to refrain from consuming some of the stocked provisions that he had returned alone with the other night.

The young man drew his dagger and helped the other hunter gut the carcass.

"Grab that pole and rope," pointed Robert. "We wish not to be wasting time out here this day."

Paul grasped a sturdy, thick, tree branch and handed it to Russell's father. They could lash the kill to it allowing the two to carry this night's supper by an end over their shoulders while the body hung from the pole in between both hunters.

"Do you ponder my brother and Russell still live Sire Daniels?", queried the young man.

"I know not Paul," he grievously replied. "All hope is in the hands of God and David. Lend me your aid with lashing and binding the hooves to the pole."

Sire Daniels used the wet powder to wipe clean his dagger's blade before wiping it dry by running the flat side across his thigh.

Soon both Robert and Paul slung their bows and quivers over their shoulders. Picking up the branch, they began their trudge through the calf-deep snow on their return back to the cottage.

The much needed venison would grace their plates for at least a couple of meals, but for Robert one question lingered in his head. "How much longer would they be favored by fortune during these harsh months before their hunting success in knowing fresh meat would run its course?", he quietly thought.

Lynn had just finished eating her second bowl of stew, and was about to wash the last bite down with a drink of water when she met with misfortune as she reached for the cup on the table. The young woman accidentally spilling its remaining contents on her robe. "Oh my!", she started as Lynn quickly rose from her seat at the table trying to escape the water that even now began to form a dark stain on her garment. .

Retrieving the small, cloth napkin, the young woman began wiping at the wet spot.

"It shall need to be dried by the fire my dear," her mother pointed out. "Remove it and I shall hang it over there."

"My dress be wet too," revealed the young woman while unclasping her robe and handing it to her mother.

"Stand by the door Anne so your sister will know a sense of quick privacy while she changes."

Already Elizabeth had started towards a wooden chest that housed several sets of spare clothing. Opening the lid and retrieving another dress from it, the Daniels' woman turned, stopped dead in mid-step, and joined Gwenyth, Anne, and Nicole staring at the sight of Lynn's nakedness.

"You be with child Lynn!", astonished Russell's mother.

Chapter 55

December 31, 1440

The last day of the year was not only a day that knew a bright, sunny sky with no signs of snow, but one that was not lacking of the cold, frigid air. Puffs of smoke shot forth from the townfolks' mouths and nostrils like a fire-breathing dragon. On this day though, the only biting and nipping that those out and about in the streets of Hamilton knew was not from a winged beast, but in the stead the arctic-like weather of winter.

Opening the door to one of the local taverns, Lieutenant Cobb pulled the hood to his cloak up over his head before fully stepping out into the cold, sunny day. Glancing one way and then the other, the off duty soldier started down the street. He had a very important, secret meeting to attend.

Slowing down his stride several feet from the alleyway's mouth, Cobb cunningly stole a glance over each shoulder making sure that no one watched him. When satisfied the coast was clear, the man quickly ducked down the passage. The footprints he left in the snow blending in with other sets of booted telltales and a pair of straight lines from a cart.

"Lieutenant Cobb," the hooded man of the street softly called out from behind a two-wheeled wagon.

"There you be," the off duty soldier looking one way then the other making sure the two were alone. "Do you own any word from the queen on this day?", he hopefully inquired.

"None at this time."

"Christ Almighty!", tensely carped Cobb. "The queen is aware that the king plans on hanging one folk on the morrow, then two the following day, and up as the dates go?"

"She does."

"Do you ponder she shall act?", curiously Cobb asked.

"I know not surety," admitted David.

"Relay to our queen that all the men loyal to her and Matthew stand-at-the-ready to act in defiance against this imposter," solidified the lieutenant. "What of the other matter?"

"I toil a plan even now, but I shall own one by the morrow," confidently shared the beggar. "We need to know haste before it be too late for the young man."

"How shall I know when you own one or even where to meet you?", Cobb curiously queried.

"Do not trouble your brow my friend for I shall come to you when the time be right."

The two men looking around the area for anyone spying them before ending their secret meeting.

"Until I come to you," David confirmed.

"I shall be waiting." Reaching under his cloak, the off duty soldier handed the man of the streets a full wineskin. "Something to keep you warm on this day that knows not heat and lacks not chill," smiled the lieutenant before turning and walking away.

Watching Cobb head up the alley, David the Beggar smiled to himself while uncorking the skin and taking a pull. Sealing the pouch and reaching into his cloak's pocket, the man of the street felt for another pouch holding some coins. For this night he would help himself, or should it be said his earlier acquired donations would aid him to rent a warm room. David shall know a small bit of comfort and a night's reprieve from the frigid temperature.

One of the many seized wives lie on her back with her feet near her shoulders, as Sir Rufus sunk all of his manhood into her body. The woman's eyes opening as wide as her mouth while taking a large pull of air.

"You know my belly!"

"And you shall know child," he growled quickening his thrusts. The huge knight's final plunge burying his phallus all the way in her. With a loud grunt accompanied by a slight shake, he shot his seed into her womb. Only when the man felt satisfied and his stiffness began to fade did Rufus pull out.

"It be your time now to perform your duty," his statement directed at another while rolling off of the wife and onto his back. Sarah, who already be with child, began to take up her position between the knight's open legs. Moments later lowering her head, she took his manhood between her lips.

Sarah began to bob up and down as she toiled to bring the man a renewed erection. It had been made her duty to the crown. Sarah was already with child, and Paul was not about to have any of his men waste any of their seed in her. Until the birth of the king's new future additions to his army, the woman along with all the seized, pregnant wives would aid their royal and his men in other ways. Sarah's charge here in Rufus' chambers be to keep him at the ready to perform as much planting as he could. In time, the woman's mouth knew the rigidness of the knight's manhood.

"Now it be your turn to be plowed," arrogantly pointed out the knight to the second seized wife that joined the three in the bed. Rufus drawing his fleshy weapon from the clutches of Sarah's oral sheath, and leveling his manhood near the woman's vagina. The second seized wife gasped loudly as she took in Rufus slowly feed her all of his phallus. The farmer happily knowing acceptance with his role planting his germ.

Eventually, Sarah would be at her task again this night. Lowering her head and offering the spent man another set of lips, Sarah returned to her task.

All in the cottage were stunned when it had been revealed to them that Lynn be with child. No one appeared to have expected that news, and not one of them had ever given a thought that she could be. The fugitives' current situation always took precedence over any notion that did not have any concerns with not getting themselves caught and hung.

Finishing their evening's meals Anne and Nicole joined Paul near the fireplace in a game of charades. Lynn's mother sat with Sire Daniels and his wife at the table in a conversation over a cup of tea. Joan and Michael had gone outside, and as for the queen, she went and sat on the bed unrolling the copy of King Paul's proclamation. The young woman had read the royal decree over-and-over since Robert had given it to her a week back, but this time was different. The black-inked words seemed to run into one another, as a blank stare froze her mind. Water slowly formed in the corners of her eyes. Lynn's reading had turned into remembering.

The first memory that entered her mind was of the time when her father had placed her on his shoulders pretending she be a giant. The little girl laughed while chasing the hens around outside their coop. A smile crossing the young woman's face remembering the mock voice of the chickens her father had made crying out their pleas not to be eaten.

That image was replaced by another and another until the young woman could see herself seated behind a log in the woods. Even now she could feel the fear of being lost and alone causing a tear to roll down her cheek. This day and the days past were not unlike that scary day. She had given up all hope of being found and rescued, but then she heard the boy calling out her name. The little, lost girl answered the call. Moments later, she gazed into the brown eyes and soft smile of the one who braved those dark, gloomy woods to come find her and bring her home. That same boy who rescued her that day had protected her through the years from not only other dangers, but from her own self when she risked her own virtues with him. It was his undying love for her since the day in the woods that had caused him to face an assassin and defy a king for her.

Lynn's tears flowed fully as the question to Russell's welfare began to plague her more and more. King Paul had robbed her of every joy in life, and she knew that he would punish Hamilton and drive England into chaos and war. On the morrow this town would know more pain than it ever had and according to Paul's proclamation the outlaw queen be the one responsible.

She thought about how Russell lived by a code. No matter how much he may have feared doing something or the danger in the risk, if it be the right thing to do then he would confront the matter knowing courage, bravery, and honour. Now it was him that be in trouble. Held prisoner and more than likely being hung for protecting his queen and true love. Thinking of everyone at the cottage, Lynn knew the realization that they were all fugitives because of the aid they lent to her. The thought of them hiding in the forest seemed to mirror the same time that she was lost. A boy knowing honour and armed with only a stick had mustered up the courage to come look for her. He had braved the dangers of becoming lost himself or being eaten by an animal for her. Now he was in dire need of rescue.

"I am coming for you Russell!", her softly determined words. No one noticed the internal battle that waged in Lynn or had seen her rise from the bed.

"Sire Daniels," addressed the outlaw queen.

Her firmness not only causing Robert to turn but everyone in the cottage to fall silent. All eyes were on her.

"Russell may still live in the dungeon. Like he has never forsaken me, I shall not him. He would never know surrender if I be in danger and I shall not give up all hope on him. We leave early in the morning for Hamilton," Queen Lynn ordered.

"You shall have my bow!", pledged Paul on his way out of the cottage's door to find Michael and inform him of the decision.

"And my sword!", swore Robert.

On the morrow, Queen Lynn would be walking into Hamilton. The devil king not taking into account that the only thing that could rival the Lord's anger be the wrath of a woman scorned.

"If the king desires a war than he will know a war," she firmly added.

Chapter 56

January 1, 1441

The sun brightly shone down in the clear sky over Hamilton warming the air so that it was a bit warmer than it had been on the day prior. Still the cold of winter held its grip on the land, but there be a lack of smoke exhaled from the townsfolk's mouths and nostrils. For not only had the orb in the heavens defeated the biting and nipping sensation from yesterday's chill, but it helped form a thin crust-like surface upon the compacted snow.

Earlier this morning before dawn had broke the horizon, Sire Daniels had skulked with his horse in tow onto his own farm. He proceeded to hook up the animal to his two-wheeled cart, and stole it right out from under the noses of anyone who still knew slumber inside the cottage. Robert had no idea if the place was occupied but could not afford to risk that the soldiers in the place be loyal to King Paul or had remained faithful to Matthew and Queen Lynn. All he had been focused on was the first part of their plan to free Russell, Peter, and Hamilton. If this robbery didn't know success than there would be no plan.

After the completion of the plan's first part, Robert now found himself traveling into the city with Joan on his side and both Michael and a disguised Lynn seated in the cart's bed. The four giving the impression of a family coming into town to witness the day's events. Behind them rode Paul. The young man acting the part of being by himself. The rest of the women and four chargers that belonged to King Matthew's royal guard remained back at the cottage. If anything should go wrong the others could flee escaping King Paul's clutches for as long as they could.

"Keep moving!", instructed the armoured man at the city's gate to the slowing crowd coming to witness the first hanging of the new year.

"Alms for the poor!", cried out the beggar appearing to be the reason for the snail-like crawl.

"What do we have here?", arrogantly inquired one of the gate's guard surveying the group of four. Instantly Robert knew this man's loyalty lay with Paul. "I do not recall ever seeing you before," the sentry pointed out.

"I ponder you have gazed upon my family and I plenty kind sir," calmly responded Robert. "For on the Sabbath we attend mass services," he convincingly added.

The soldier's eyes scanning the cart while he slowly made his way to the rear.

"Do you harbor any weapons?", the man queried.

"None kind sir," replied Sire Daniels watching the man begin his inspection of the cart.

"Alms for the poor!", the cry growing closer.

Returning his focus back to the soldier, Russell's father became angst as the guard came to a stop in front of Lynn and began to address her.

"And you be?"

"My daughter Nicole," kindly interjected Robert.

"I be speaking to the young woman not you," the sentry's disgustful look matched the tone of his intimidation. The man placing a gloved hand on one of Lynn's knees.

"I be Nicole," the disguised outlaw queen smiled. "May I ask your name kind sir?"

"Name be Stubbs," he began to slowly knead her leg.

Joan remained looking forward. Robert and from his peripheral vision, Michael, took in the sight of the soldier beginning to remove a glove from one of his hands. The bare hand disappearing under Lynn's dress.

"Will we be late for the hanging sir?", inquired Paul desperately hoping to draw the guard's attention away from the outlaw queen.

"Be there a problem here?", sarcastically queried the sentry.

"Alms for the poor!", the shouted request causing Robert to spin around. His eyes meeting those of the hooded ones belonging to David

Honour

the Beggar. Instantly the man of the streets understood Robert's silent request for aid.

"Guardsman Stubbs. Why be it, you make a wretch as myself know toil in the state that I, ..." David's words cutting off as he fell forward into the muddy snow. The beggar falling towards the soldier.

With not a waste of time, Stubbs retracted his bare hand from under Lynn's dress while swiftly jumping back. The man reacting like he would come to know leprosy from the dirty and smelly beggar. "Serves you right drunkard!", he yelled. "You need be locked up in the dungeon for a few weeks and then hung."

"Get moving!", he angrily ordered Robert, who wasted no time slapping the reins signaling the horse to move.

"The next time you try to rush me while doing my job to see a hanging I shall make sure you see one close up," Stubbs snarled at Paul. "Stay out of my sight or it will be your neck stretching."

"Thank you sir," the young man humbled while lightly heeling his mount's flanks. "My deepest of apologies."

"Lieutenant Cobb! The beggar knows drunkeness again. He need be locked up in the dungeon and hung for his constant insolence! "Nuisance," he added placing a boot into David's side.

"Adams!", called Lieutenant Cobb. The soldier had just gotten off duty and was beginning to walk back to the barracks in search of the day's rest.

Turning around, the man took in the sight of his senior officer coming towards him escorting the newly acquired prisoner. The hooded man swaying from side-to-side on unsteady feet. In Adams opinion, the street urchin was drunk again.

"Yes Lieutenant Cobb," he acknowledged with a fist against his heart.

"Know importance and lack of not swiftness of feet!", softly ordered Cobb. "Muster all the men loyal to the queen and inform them to stand-at-the-ready to aid her. She be here! With God's help this day may know the end to the king's reign of mockery. Now be off with you!", he commanded.

"Yes sir!", saluted Guardsmen Adams before making haste as he ran for the barracks. These would be the most important orders that he would ever carry out in service to the crown of England.

"Lead the way lieutenant," came David. "It would appear that we own a date with the castle's dungeon."

"Get a move on it you drunkard!", loudly ordered Cobb.

"Bravo!", the beggar thought. David adding a loud belch.

"Be you well?", worriedly queried Michael glancing over to Lynn. Her body gave a shiver at the thought of where Stubbs had planned to place his hand if not for the timely intrusion.

"I shall be fine," she admitted with a smile.

Robert slowly and cautiously steered the one horse cart through the streets of Hamilton. On more than one occasion, the wagon would come to a standstill due to the throughway being crowded with townsfolk either attempting to peddle some type of goods or make their way themselves to the public hanging.

"I believe this might be as far as we can go by cart," yelled Robert over his shoulder.

"We shall walk," loudly replied the disguised, outlaw queen.

"You there! Boy!", called Sire Daniels while instinctively setting the wheel brake on the cart.

"Yes?", queried the boy.

"How old are you lad?"

"Ten years sir."

"I will be willing to pay one gold coin if you would keep care of the two horses while we partake in viewing the day's royal hanging," ventured Robert.

The boy's eyes slightly opening a bit when Paul offered another gold coin to sweeten the deal. Even the ten year old knew not to look a gift horse in the mouth.

"I will sirs!", excitedly agreed the boy.

"What be your name?", Robert inquired stepping down from the seat.

"Lucas sir."

"Well Lucas, here be the coin I offered you," the man retrieving the gold from a pouch he wore on his belt and placing it into the boy's hand.

A smile stretching ear to ear was Lucas' only response.

Honour

Already Michael had aided Joan from her perch and flipped the cart's bench seat up where a storage area underneath held three swords rolled in fur. Michael took hold of the roll and attempted to conceal it under his cloak.

"You shall receive the other coin upon our return," reasoned Paul.

"I shall not leave even if you pay me now!"

"And how do we know you shall not run after we pay you?", questioned Paul approaching the boy.

"I give you my word of honour," firmly stated Lucas. His oath sounding so much like the ones Robert and Lynn had heard for years from Russell.

"What do you know of honour?", interjected Lynn.

"William the Brave knew honour," he matter-of-factly stated. "So did Sir Timothy and both King Stephen and Queen Margaret, my lady. Even King Matthew and his queen treated us folk with honour."

"And how about the king now?", she further inquired.

"My father tells me that men who use their power or strength to aid others knowing no power or owning no strength have honour, but men who use their power and strength to abuse or oppress those less fortunate lack any honour. King Paul and his men are oppressors. I believe not that Queen Lynn is a traitor, and I pray that God returns her to us. She has honour. I promise my lady, I shall not leave until you return," the boy swore his oath all the while not knowing who he gave his word to.

"That I do doubt not," convinced the disguised queen placing a kiss on his forehead.

When Lucas looked up to smile at her, Paul presented him with the second gold coin.

"Well said lad," complimented Robert. "Well said."

Moments later Lucas witnessed the three men and the two women disappear into the crowd. The boy pondering he recognized the young woman's face he had spoken with, but when he couldn't pinpoint where he thought he had seen her, Lucas let the feeling fade. For on this day little did he know that he need not be a jousting knight to win over a queen's heart.

"I hope that not be him nor his friend," thought Cobb to himself, as both he and David watched as two soldiers led a man by them wearing a black hood completely covering his head and face. Following them with his gaze a bit longer, the lieutenant led a feigning drunk through the open door towards the dungeons.

"I see this one here just does not learn not only how to remain away from those spirits or these cells," sarcastically remarked the rotund jailer. "You know the king does not fancy using this place as an inn. We should consider just hanging this one and being done with him."

Only a groan escaped the rusing beggar, as the man closed and locked the thick wooden door behind them.

"Follow me," the man added while passing the two to take the lead down the corridor.

"Keep it moving," instructed Cobb yanking David's arm as they walked behind the jailer carrying the only torch.

Walking past cells lining both sides of the dank hallway, David snuck a peek into the one he recalled Russell being in.

"Remember this fellow here that came to us on the Eve of Christmas?", the rotund man pointed into the small room.

"I do," recalled the lieutenant.

"This thief and the other one he was with own a date with the hangman on the morrow."

"A fair life knows that of a fair living," Cobb remarked.

The jailer grinned and let out a laugh before starting for the cell that the drunk would be calling home for at least this day.

Walking the rest of the way down the hallway to its final cells on either side, the rotund man placed the hissing torch into the wrought iron wall sconce. He pulled a round, iron key ring from his belt and stepped towards the gated door. Finding the proper one and inserting it into the lock, the cell door opened with a loud; **"click"**.

"Your new home," he sarcastically proclaimed pulling the door open.

With speed rivaling that of a bolt of lightning from the heavens, both David the Beggar and Lieutenant Cobb quickly rushed the jailer. Their forceful shove catching the man off guard and driving him into the wall. He lost his breath as all his air rushed from his lungs. The rotund man bounced off the stone partition and back into a fist thrown by David. The blow landing solid on the jailer's chin sending him crashing to the room's floor with a **"thud"**.

"Key still be in the door," pointed out David. "Lock him in here. The pig has a new pen," grunted the beggar.

"Should we bind and gag him?", anxiously inquired Cobb watching David close and locked the gated door.

"No time," admitted the beggar. "Hence with all the commotion that be about to erupt, I ponder no one will hear him anyways. Be there any weapons down here?"

Already the men being held in some of the other cages were up calling on the new key master for aid in setting them free.

"They have taken our wives!", cried out one prisoner.

"Please give us aid!", shouted another.

"The jailer keeps a small armory down here," replied the lieutenant after taking a moment to ponder.

"Go retrieve some weapons while I open the cells and free the ones we came for lieutenant!"

The two men parting ways in front of the cell holding Russell. Inside the young man beginning to rise to his feet.

"David is that you?"

"It be I young Daniels," the man of the streets searching for the right key for the lock in the dimness. Locating the right one and unlocking the gated portal, the beggar added. "And your queen be here as well," he smiled.

"Lynn! Here?", the bruised, young man surprised.

"Yes my friend. She came for you, and to put an end to King Paul's sick jest."

Minutes later, Cobb returned and dumped a pile of swords and daggers onto the floor.

Soon a beaten Peter was reunited with his old friend, and the four led the freed husbands through the dungeon's corridors and out into the castle. For that day the halls of the palace, which were often filled with sounds of pleasure as of late, now knew only the noise of shouting chaos, ringing swords, and husbands determined to take back their wives. A rebellion had begun.

"Take no prisoners and leave no man standing!", shouted Lieutenant Cobb, as those remaining soldiers still loyal to Matthew and Queen Lynn lent aid to the husbands of Hamilton.

"God save Queen Lynn!", yelled the lieutenant waving his sword.

"We need to take the castle's wall.", loudly advised David engaging in contact with Paul's men.

The crowd of townsfolk watched, as a man wearing a black hood completely covering his head and identity was led by two executioners up the stage's stairs and across the platform. The unknown stranger had his hands secured behind his back, and was directed towards a stool that stood under the gallows. The gathering crowd remained silent for seated on a throne-like chair on the stage sat none other than King Paul. Everyone in attendance knew it would be them up on the platform meeting the hangman personally if one of them dared speak. The hooded stranger stepped up onto the stool, and the hangman slipped the noose over his neck. The king rose surveying the crowd and starting for one of the structure's post.

"Folk of Hamilton! This day be the first day of the new year, but it be not one that knows joy and rejoice," Paul's voice turning to that of disappointment. "In-the-stead this day be one that knows only heartache and sadness. The pain that I feel everyday as I ponder over why my loving people of England not only share my grief in losing a cousin, but in truth hide and harbor the one that is responsible for his murder. Can someone tell me why one of you give shelter to a traitor?", the king pausing after his inquiry waiting for an answer that he knew would never come. His hands clasped behind his back like that of the man ready to hang.

"Very well then. I, knowing mercy shall out of love give you all a brief spell before the first criminal to the crown of England hangs because of the traitor. Taxes will still rise until Queen Lynn be discovered or turned in by one of you," nonchalantly addressed King Paul returning back for his throne. Suddenly he whipped around. "Have I not allotted you all enough of a spell when I issued forth my royal proclamation?" Looking to the hangman, King Paul nod his head. The unspoken signal to begin.

Standing near a small four-wheeled wagon, Queen Lynn watched and listened to the king's twisted and perverted speech. She knew that Paul was going to hang this victim no matter what. The young woman knew her time to act was upon her.

"Michael lend me your aid onto the cart."

The muscular, young man grabbed her hips, as she climbed up and onto the small wagon. He could feel her shaking underneath her garments although one would never know her nervousness by her appearance.

"Hamilton, to know the hangman's noose on this first day of the new year shall be none other than the one responsible for murdering a soldier to the crown and siring the traitor to England!", Paul angrily announced. "The queen's own father Charles Daniels!"

With that the hangman pulled off the hood. Standing on the stool with the rope around his neck and knowing bruises from the repeated beatings he had received was none other than Lynn's father.

"Nooo!", gasped the accused traitor, as she could not get up in the cart's bed quick enough. In moments with Michael's assistance, Lynn found her footing.

Ripping back her hood, the young woman belted out. "Enough Paul! End this mockery now!"

The king couldn't believe his eyes. It actually took him a moment before he comprehended who had yelled out.

For in attendance this day and standing above the crowd's head was none other than the outlaw, Queen Lynn.

A smile formed on his face when one thought entered his mind; he had finally ferreted the rabbit from its burrow. "Seize her!", King Paul shouted the command.

Chapter 57

The crowd of gathered townsfolk turned their heads at the same time as they followed the king's finger pointing towards the woman. As those in attendance came to know realization that it be Queen Lynn standing in a cart's bed before them, loud gasps filled the air.

"I want her alive!", shouted Paul.

The young woman was filled with nervousness for not only her father's life, but from the dilemma that faced her now. Lynn wondering if the people truly believed and held her responsible for Matthew's murder. Scanning the crowd and taking in the sight of a dozen soldiers rushing towards her through the multitudes, the young woman knew she had to fight back. Lynn chose the only weapon she had. She unsheathed the truth.

"Good folk of Hamilton!", the queen called out into the air. "I work not with the French like you have been led to believe, and I knew not of the ambush that murdered King Matthew. A ruler that owned love for his people like that given to him by each and every one of you," Lynn's eyes roaming over the gathered. She could see the king's men approaching, but had also witnessed Sire Daniels and the two young men below unsheathed their blades standing at the ready.

"Paul be the one that should wear the title traitor!", she pointed to the stage. "For he be the one who not only murdered England's true ruler, King Matthew, but had an assassin strike down King Stephen and Queen Margaret!"

Lynn's words causing another loud pull of air from the townsfolk.

"Liar!", yelled Paul. "You dare speak words that know deception!"

"Deception?", the queen could not help but to give a small chuckle. "It be not I, nor my words that know deception. For the devil be a master at speaking deceivingly so he may take hold of what he so wishes and desires. Like that of raising taxes, or knowing the beds of men's wives and daughters. Speak of it as you may. Shroud it with you lies that lack not deception. For under your untruths, your acts be none other than pillaging the good folk of Hamilton with overtaxing and perversion!", anger growing in her words.

Lynn could hear swords clash, as both Michael and Paul engaged two of the king's soldiers. The young woman scanning the crowd only to lay witness to more soldiers arriving. The queens heart sinking further and further into despair at the mounting odds against her, but still she would not waver.

Suddenly the young woman's eyes glanced up to the castle's wall at a commotion going on there. Erupting from one of the towers were armed soldiers and townsmen that by all appearance and actions were loyal to her. Lynn's heart fluttered when she spotted her true love waving a sword above his head leading the new arrivals.

"God save the queen!", shouted one of the armoured men behind the young man on the wall.

Lynn's eye's dropping to where another large group of soldiers entered the courtyard. When she heard the lead guardsmen cry out the command to "Protect the Queen!", the young woman's resolve thickened. Now the feelings of nervousness and despair shook from her body like water from a duck. Stealing a glance downward, the young woman offered aid to Joan as she was assisted up and onto the wagon by Robert.

"Watch for arrows!", warned Sire Daniels before turning to stand at the ready protecting the carts rear. "And remain from the melee!", he added.

Thrusting his sword forward at an upward angle, Russell plunged his blade into one of the king's soldiers who had been blocking the final top three steps inside the wall's tower. The weapon biting into the armoured man's stomach causing him to lean towards the freed prisoner. The soldier's own blade tip knowing contact with the top stone run.

Reaching up with is left arm and taking hold of the guardsman's shoulder, the battered, young man pulled downward as he yanked free his sword and steered the wounded man over the staircase's edge. Russell momentarily watched his adversary fall plummeting to his death. Knowing his fill of adrenaline, the young man charged forward followed by Lieutenant Cobb, David the Beggar, his friend Peter, and a handful of guardsmen, who still remained loyal to the queen. In mere seconds the group erupted out of the tower's entryway into the bright, sunny day. Their eyes beginning to focus at the change in brightness.

"God save the queen!", Cobb's shouting pierced the air.

Russell's sword rang loudly as he brought it across his body blocking the swing of the soldier's blade. Using the momentum that carried him forward, the young man connected the guard with his elbow. His strike opening the man's nose with an explosion of blood. The soldier's arms flailing wide by the blow's force and driving him back two steps. Russell brought his sword swiftly back across his body and dropped the guardsman with a backslash.

The young man saw both the lieutenant and the beggar rush by him to intercept two other men, and he, himself, was looking for a second adversary. Below soldiers loyal to the queen met in melee with those who knew allegiance to the king. A loud cry of anguish robbed the battlement of any other sound. Russell knew that pain-filled scream of horror belonged to his true love, and instinctively he knew she needed him.

King Paul felt no worry even after Queen Lynn's spirit-filled words attempting to sway the townsfolk of Hamilton to her side. The young man's lips sneered in disgust as a commotion broke out on the wall. His ears knew the words being shouted by the newcomers giving aid to the outlaw queen.

"They dare defy me!", disgustedly stated Paul turning to Sir Rufus, who had swiftly taken to his feet. The knight had been sitting on the platform when he witnessed the men burst from the tower.

The courtyard had exploded into chaos, as the two large groups met in combat and the townsfolk screamed and ran for their lives.

"Fear not my king," advised the black knight. "Your men lack not the numbers to defeat the rebels."

"I want the queen and this rebellion broken now!", angered Paul. "Retrieve her and bring her here. For she will know a lack of spirit this night under my thrusts," he sneered.

"Yes my lord," Rufus replied before jumping from the stage. The giant man's hand knowing his sword seconds after his feet hit the ground.

King Paul glanced up. His hawk-like gaze meeting that of the queen's stare.

"I shall not be denied my justice nor my birthright," firmly stated Paul under his breath. "On this day outlaw queen your hands shall know another death caused by them!", he berated Lynn over the crowd before his kick drove the stool that Charles Bradford stood on out from under his feet. The young woman's father plummeting towards the stage only to meet with an instantaneous halt. The helpless man floundering at the end of the fibrous cord as his lungs desperately searched for air.

"Nooo!", Lynn's screams of anguish piercing the air as she stood helpless in the cart's bed over a hundred feet from the stage. The distance covered by men engaged in combat both for and against the young queen.

With no thought to the harm she may suffer, Charles' daughter swiftly began to climb down from the wagon. She had to save the life of the one who had given breath to her.

Turning his attention from attempting to engage an adversary on the battlement to the courtyard below, Russell began to scan the chaotic scene for Lynn. It wasn't long before he spotted Joan and her standing in the bed of a cart. His love's hands covering her mouth. The young man partaking in only a moment before he followed whatever it be she studied. Russell's eyes beholding the sight of his love's father helplessly floundering at the end of a hangman's rope.

"Christ Almighty!". He knew he needed to do something. The young man searching his surroundings. Russell had remembered seeing scattered bows and quivers leaning against the wall.

Fortune favored the young man when he spotted a bow lying near the soldier he had just dispatched. A full quiver leaning against the battlement behind him. Knowing haste, Russell took up the weapon and nocked an arrow. His sight set on the rope that now cut off Sire Bradford's air.

Pulling the bow's string behind his right ear and closing his right eye, Russell took aim. "Speed be the cause of mistake," he remembered his father telling him when he was just a boy learning the weapon. Unfortunately another memory invaded his mind at that time. The remembrance of Peter hanging upside down caught by his ankle in a snare entered into his recollection. He had missed the shot then. The young man's heart raced as he attempted to slow his breathing.

Preparing to fire his shot, the memory of Lynn's pain and tears on that fateful day when he had to reveal to his love that her father be lost to them flooded into his thoughts. The young man feeling for sometime after that his decision was the reason behind Charles' death. Russell knew somehow he had been given another chance to rescue Lynn's father in time. He had to make this shot count, or Charles would be lost twice because of him. The young man not knowing if he could deal with the sight of pain on Lynn's face if he knew failure.

"Look out Russell!", warned Peter who had just run a man through. His eyes taken in one of the king's guardsmen running towards and preparing to land a strike on the young man concentrating on his shot.

It was either save the life of his love's father and leave himself open to a direct hit, or fire the arrow into the charging soldier and risk Charles dying at the gallows. Failure to save his love's father knew not acceptance in his heart. Russell let loose the arrow. The young man bringing his shoulder up to cover his head, as he prepared for a hit that would never come.

"Where be you going?", panicked Joan looking down from the cart's bed at the young woman climbing down.

"My father be hanging and needs aid!", Lynn frightened.

Stealing a glance at the stage, the queen's personal servant took in the sight of the hanging man's thrashing slowing. The woman knowing Sire Bradford's life starting to slip away. Returning her gaze back to the rear of the wagon, Queen Lynn stood there no more. Joan scanning the chaos around her as she attempted to locate the young woman.

"Robert! Robert!", called the pregnant woman atop the cart. "The queen runs now for the platform to rescue her father!"

Finishing just running a soldier through and yanking free his sword, Sire Daniels turned towards the woman crying out. "Where be her now?", he worried. Joan pointing in her direction. "Lynn be there!" Her words sending Robert running the way the young woman went.

The outlaw queen worried not about the dangers to herself as she hastily made her way through the melee. On more than one occasion she had to duck and dodge before a blade knew a meeting with her. The young woman squatted to pick up a sword lying on the ground. She knew she would have to cut her father down.

Taking a hold of the weapon's pommel, Lynn rose and glanced back towards the stage. She now found herself not more than seventy feet away. The young woman's eyes beginning to fill with water at the sight of her helplessly dying father. His daughter knowing she would never reach him in time to save his life. It be then as she prayed and took a step forward that Lynn's silent prayer be answered. The rope began to quickly unravel giving way. Charles' body fell to the stage.

The queen's watery eyes fixated on the sight of the man's mouth working to pull in as much air as he could. Charles' lungs knew breath again. One of the two executioners joined Charles as he lay on the stage. Protruding from his head was an arrow's shaft.

Lynn started when Sire Daniels took hold of her arm. "We need to return to the cart!", he advised.

"I cannot," she explained. "For father needs aid at the gallows before he knows the edge of a blade!"

The two suddenly noticing a commotion when they caught sight of Sir Rufus hacking and slashing his way through the crowd towards them.

"It be King Paul's knight!", frightened the outlaw queen.

"Get behind me!", shouted Robert. Moments later he was the only one between Paul's henchman and the young woman.

"You ponder you can stop me?", laughed Rufus.

"If you desire her. You shall have to go through me first!", Robert gritted his teeth, as the knight began to advance.

Russell winced fully expecting the soldier's strike to slash into his back and shoulder, but his peripheral vision caught a solid object fly past him and over the wall's battlement. His ears knowing the sounds of a blade sinking into meat, punctured steel, and grunts coming from behind him.

Dropping his gaze over the defensive walkway's edge, the young man saw a soldier laying in the snow at the base of the wall. The white powder turning a crimson red. Beside him lay Russell's childhood friend, Peter. A stain beginning to grow around his contorted body. The two men knowing not fortune, as only a couple of feet away was a four-wheeled wagon full of hay.

"Peter!", the young man cried out. The realization that his friend had taken the blow that was meant for him stunned Russell momentarily.

Glancing up to the stage, Russell quickly reached for and nocked another arrow. For even though his first shot had sliced the rope causing it to snap under the weight it knew, a prone Charles was being advanced on. Behind him holding a two-handed, single head axe was one of the executioners.

Pulling the bow's string behind his right ear and aiming his shot, Russell let it loose. The arrow speeding through the air and flying towards the hangman standing over the helpless Sire Bradford.

Raising his axe over his head, the executioner dropped the bladed weapon behind him moments later when the arrow hit its mark. Its shaft protruding from the mouth area of the identity concealing hood. Seconds later the stage knew its third thud, as the second hangman fell dead.

Russell quickly scanned the wall for any of Paul's soldiers rushing to engage him in battle, but when none presented themselves, the young man turned his attention back to the cart where now only Joan stood.

"Where be you Lynn?", he anxiously inquired under his breath while continuing to search the chaotic scene below. He eventually spotted her and his father. In front of the two stood the black knight.

Dropping the bow and reaching for his sword, the young man rose to his feet. Taking a second to calculate his attempt at making the leap from the forty foot wall into the wagon full of hay, Russell jumped from the battlement. The young man's feet kicked freely through the air. Robert's son knowing that he be needed more now on the battlegrounds by his love's side. The one rivaling that of the Bible's Goliath had entered the fray with his sights knowing that of conquest.

Lynn loudly gasped in horror as again she witnessed Sir Rufus land a solid, gauntlet-covered punch to Sire Daniels' chin. The blow causing not only the man's head to rapidly turn, but blood to spray up into the air. The shot's force driving Robert's head backwards while his body reflexively lurched forward exposing his stomach. The man's arms were thrown wide and circled over his head. Robert's grip knew not his sword any longer, as it fell into the snow at his feet. Lacking not haste, the knight thrust his blade into the defender's midsection.

"Oh my God!", she gasped while taking a step back. Her free hand coming to her mouth while her other hand tightened around the sword in it.

The knight offering a growl as he yanked his sword free and booted the wounded man in the snow. Both Rufus and Lynn watched as Robert slid several feet. A crimson trail staining the powder.

"Sire Daniels!", the young woman softly spoke gazing down. The queen's lips quivering in disbelief and shock.

"Run Lynn," his words quiet and alarming as the color in his face already knew change from the man's life beginning to leave his body. "Run."

"Be you sure you desire the hard way?", intimidatingly inquired Sir Rufus taking in the sight of the petite queen raising her sword's point up in his direction.

"I shall fight you!", her words knowing defiance.

"I believe he spoke the same words," smugly laughed the knight pointing with his chin to the fallen man. Lynn swallowed down the fear the best she could. The young woman beginning to know how David must have felt taking in the sight of his mighty adversary Goliath.

King Paul, obstructed from view, watched from behind the stage as his men began to gain the upper hand in the battle for Hamilton. He had quickly leapt from the platform and hid when an arrow felled the second hangman. The young ruler owned no wishes to be the third struck down on count of an archer's shot. King Paul smiled his devilish grin when both the thought of knowing victory on this field of battle, and his manhood thrusting into Queen Lynn later this day, crossed his mind.

"Where be the queen?", shouted Peter's brother Paul climbing into the cart's bed where only Joan stood now worriedly peering into the combat. Blood slowly flowed down the young man's face from the several nicks and cuts while his breath labored a bit from the constant melee he had found before this brief rest. For even now his friend Michael fought at the wagon's base.

"She be there!", hysterically pointed the woman. "And knows only trouble! It be the king's knight that confronts her!" Neither Joan, nor Paul knowing that Robert lay on the snow-covered ground dead.

"Where be Sire Daniels?", perplexed the young man. He felt helplessness because he knew neither he nor Michael would ever make it in time to save her from Sir Rufus. The twin quickly studied the courtyard. Those loyal to the queen were losing this battle, and he realized that if lost, the future knew only darkness for Hamilton and all of England. Somehow. Someway they desperately needed victory. Not just for Lynn and her seat on the throne, but for the people who now desired to know freedom.

"Those of Hamilton!", Paul shouted. His voice carrying in the courtyard's air. "Those of Hamilton!", he yelled out again. The young man's address already causing a quell in the people's panic-stricken cries. Those seeking a spot to hide or fleeing from the combat began to pay heed to him.

"Townspeople of Hamilton. On this day all know a chance. A chance to claim what you have longed for since King Paul has taken his place on the throne. A wish that knows the depths of your souls. The desire to once again know freedom!", the young man's words causing a hush amongst the townsfolk. Only the ringing and clashing of swords hung in the air.

"Behold!", the twin pointing to where Lynn now stood brandishing a sword. Her adversary towering over her. "For even now Queen Lynn takes up arms to fight for you, and for the freedom and peace this kingdom once knew. She fights to separate a murdering, raping tyrant from his seat on the throne that knows no justice. To partake in seeing evil vanquished from this land. When you be needed most, and look fate in its eyes to change not only your destiny, but your future as well, will you not fight for freedom alongside her or shall you run like little mice who know only fear under a hawk's gaze?

"It be Queen Lynn who fights for your freedom!", Paul pointed out. "People of Hamilton, will you not honour King Stephen's visions of freedom and peace and join Queen Lynn now when she needs you most?"

"Take up arms now for Hamilton, and fight to know a future that lacks not freedom from tyranny!"

A large roar erupted from the folk. They had ceased their fleeing.

A smile formed on Joan's face while her eyes witnessed the crowd of men and women rush to join the fray. For at this moment, unknown to the outlaw queen, she knew not aloneness any longer. Those who now fought alongside her outnumbered Paul's men three to one.

"For Hamilton!", a villager shouted.

"For Queen Lynn!" cried out another.

Hiding behind the platform, King Paul stood in awe watching the townsfolk enter the battle. The young ruler only snapping out of his unblinking gaze when his feeling of anger began to rise.

"You will give me an heir," his words coming from behind his teeth.

With that being said, the adder slithered from his spot of concealment and stopped only for a moment to climb the stage's steps. Scanning the crowd the snake located its prey.

Stepping from the place knowing a better vantage point to seek out someone in the rapidly growing chaos, King Paul squatted down to retrieve a lost sword. The young man's hawk-like stare never leaving the rabbit, whom he had ferreted from her burrow. He began to stalk his quarry.

Lynn slowly shifted her weight from side-to-side as she waved the sword's point in front of her staring into the eyes of the mountain of a man standing before her now. The young woman's hearing knowing only vagueness, as the crowd grew silent and someone loudly spoke above the clashing of weapons. In a short time, a loud eruption of shouts and yelling had taken place, but for who or what, she knew not. Behind her laying in the snow, Sire Daniels rested in peace.

"Drop the blade," instructed Rufus while raising his weapon's tip towards the outlaw queen. "It be all over for you."

"I shall never yield to you!", her words knowing more fear than confidence.

The knight beginning to chuckle, but then with a speed unrivaled by Lynn's eyes, the man's blade knocked the young woman's sword out of her hands. The weapon flying through the air before landing and skidding across the snow-covered ground. The startled queen gasping as she jumped back.

"Do not play with me woman!", the large man warned. "Hence, come in ease or know the hard way. For the decision be yours, but take heed in knowing you be going."

"I shall not yield to you or your vile king!"

The knight had finally reached his wits end with the outlaw queen, and took a step forward raising his sword above his head. The menacing look on his face as he started to advance caused Lynn to retreat a step. In her haste, the young woman slipped and in an instant found herself lying near Robert's bloodied body.

Rufus took another step towards her.

Lynn knew the end be near.

Feeling the snow's wetness from her seat on the ground, Lynn started again when she heard a growl of determination and witnessed a blur rush by her. For the young woman knew only amazement, as someone lowered their shoulder and drove it into the knight's gut. The force of the tackle lifting Rufus from the ground and carrying him, along with whomever it be through the air and into the snow.

Honour

Gathering her feet beneath her, Lynn watched, as the two figures separated and had begun to rise. A spark of hope reignited in the young woman when her eyes took in the sight of the one behind the blur. Cautiously backing towards her and away from the head-shaking knight was none other than Russell.

"Be you well?", he worriedly inquired while gazing over his shoulder.

"I am now, Russell," she frightened. For the queen realized her love was about to face off against the greatest rival he had ever known. A knight trained to know war.

Squatting down and retrieving his father's sword from the ground, the young man stood and gazed into the young woman's eyes. "Stay behind me my love, and know that Hamilton fights for you. Take heed black knight," he addressed Rufus as Russell broke away from Lynn's eyes and turned to face his quarry. "You nor your pretend king shall ever know victory over England's rightful queen. So swears her loyal subject."

Growling his madness through his teeth, Sir Rufus charged.

Swords rang, as Russell blocked the knight's swing. The young man feeling the vibration from the strike into his hands while holding the weapons hilt. Both of his feet sliding two inches backward from the force. Lynn's love quickly ducking a left cross and spinning away.

"Where you be off to subject?", angrily queried the man. Swinging for the young man again, Russell ducked another attack and the sword slash over his head.

Springing upward from his evasive move, the young man connected with a punch of his own. The hit landing on his adversaries chin. Russell retreated several steps, taking up a defensive pose.

Eyeballing the young man, the knight roared his anger and attacked with a flurry of strikes. Lynn's love hastily blocking the sword's swings followed by a plunge towards his chest. Attempting to spin from the thrust, the young man felt the edge of the blade bite into his right upper arm, as Sir Rufus swiftly swept it across his foe attempting to dodge. Blood began to stain the cloak he had on.

"It appears I have drawn first blood," sneered the black knight watching his adversary take another defensive posture.

Russell met another slash from Rufus, as the young man again brought his sword across his body. The strike's force so hard it seemed to rattle his teeth. Lynn's love not reacting quick-enough when he caught a front kick in the stomach. The blow sending him flying backwards and landing on the ground. He slid a couple of feet.

Lynn gasped in fear that her love would end up like his father; dead in the snow. For even she knew he was no match for the trained combatant.

Leaping up, Russell decided to take the offensive and attacked Rufus with his own swings. The black knight easily blocking the first blow followed by his sword deflecting a second slash from the young man. Bringing his arm back a bit, Russell thrust forward in an attempt to score a hit, but the man met his sword with a parry. Rufus' blade pointing straight down allowed him to throw an elbow hitting Russell square in the mouth.

The young man's blood spraying through the air. The knight following the blow with a sidekick that struck the man in the stomach. The blow's force lifting him from the ground and causing Lynn's love to land hard in the snow. Her defender losing his grip on his sword.

"Get up Russell!", screamed the young woman watching Rufus making his way over to the prone young man desperately fighting to pull air.

"Be there not one who can rival me in this land?", smugly inquired the knight while switching his grip on his weapon preparing to plunge the blade into his prone foe.

Suddenly knowing the speed of a striking cobra, Russell kicked up landing a shot to the man's groin. The blow sending the stunned man reeling backwards enough for the young man to roll away from the knight's finishing swing and find his feet. Seconds later Russell's hand knew his sword again.

"Russell!", cried out Lynn.

"It not be over yet," defied the young man.

Quickly taking his eyes off his adversary and glancing over in her direction, the queen's love took in the sight of King Paul grabbing her arm and twisting it behind Lynn's back.

"Be done with him Rufus!", sneered the king. "I desire you guarding my bedchamber's door this night while I plant my seed in her womb! The queen will give me an heir!"

Starting in the direction of Paul and his hostage, Russell was cut off by a swing from Rufus' sword. He brought his blade up to block. The ringing of their clashing weapons adding to the sounds of chaos about them.

He heard her scream his name again, as King Paul whisked her away. The cry for help causing the young man to begin a flurry of swings and slashes. All were futile, as Rufus blocked, parried, or dodged from Russell's desperate attacks. The last strike leaving him open to a swing from the knight's blade. The slash cutting across his chest followed by a gauntlet-covered left cross. The combination knocking the young man off his feet. Russell battled the blackness that wished to consume him.

"Be there not one who can rival me in this land?", he yelled into the air while holding his arms and his sword high as he slowly turned in a circle surveying the chaos around him. Sir Rufus laughed at the thought of King Paul riding the bucking mount later. Victory was theirs.

Turning back around preparing to finish off the outlaw queen's loyal subject, the large man's smile disappeared as his eyes met those of a man standing in front of the prone, young man. Sir Rufus taking in sight of a cloaked figure holding a sword.

"The answer be yes knight of no honour," the man stated. "Get up Russell. The queen needs you," his stern words sounding like a command.

"Who be you?", angrily inquired Sir Rufus.

"Do you not know this?", he held the sword up.

"For I be the knight of the road. Brother to one who met death at your murdering hands. A man who knew more honour in his words than one such as you knows of in your whole body."

"On your feet Russell,", the cloaked figure commanded.

The young man slowly, as if automatically, beginning to rise.

"The queen needs your aid."

The words taking root in Russell's mind. His love be in trouble. Just that one thought alone gave him the will he needed to rise up.

"A bow and quiver lie there near your sword. Now go to her while I avenge my brother."

"And you be?", snarled the black knight.

"I be David. Brother to the Knight Sir Timothy," he revealed.

Russell stood on shaky legs at first and retrieved his sword along with the bow and quiver. The young man hearing swords clash in melee and witnessing Sir Rufus' strength and power versus the grace and agility of the man of the streets. He could see both Paul and Lynn in the distance and regaining his stability, he started after them. Russell glancing back at the fight before leaving. The young man would end up missing a man, who fought for his queen; his murdered brother; and the streets he called home, fulfill his vow to avenge a knight of honour. Sir Rufus would eventually take heed in knowing for a moment that his query not go unanswered as death consumed him.

With both the bow and quiver of arrows slung on his back and his fallen father's sword in his hand, Russell gave chase towards the castle. The young man falling to a knee a couple of times as he slipped and slid on the snow underfoot. The slick powder had hampered both King Paul and Lynn enough for him to close the gap between them. Russell trailed the two by only a hundred yards now, but the palace grew even closer.

Dropping down to his knees, and letting the compacted snow-covered ground carry him further, Russell slid while leaning his upper body backwards allowing him to know stability. He grabbed the bow pulling it from his back as he came to a stop. The young man instantly let go of his blade and reached for an arrow. With time only knowing seconds, he nocked it onto the bow's string pulling it back behind his left ear. In the stillness of the aim, Russell could feel his new wounds throbbing in pain. His head pounded from the blows he had received from the black knight. Slowing his breath, the young man heard his father's voice in his thumping head. "Speed be the cause of mistake." He let loose his shot and picked up his sword in his left hand. Rising to his feet, Russell began to give chase again.

Lynn yelled as King Paul yanked on her arm pulling her down with him. His shout of pain breaking in the air. Paul screamed, as something bit into the back of his calf bringing him crashing to the ground. The self-made king losing his grip on his sword and the grasp he had on the queen.

Looking back the way they had come, both the king and the queen beheld the sight of Russell closing the distance.

"Run Lynn!", her love yelled.

"You shall not," sharply rasped Paul reaching out and taking hold of Lynn's ankles.

The young woman attempting to kick free from his clutches, as the two struggled. "Unhand me you beast!", the queen yelled but to no avail Paul was too strong for her.

"If I cannot have you, no one shall!", he yelled releasing a grip on an ankle and taking hold of his sword. "Shut up bitch!", he shouted pointing the blade at her and climbing on top of her. The young man's hawk-like stare gazing down.

In her peripheral vision, Lynn could see her love coming. She knew not if he would make it in time, but she deeply hoped he would. An idea formed in her mind.

"It be over Paul. Hamilton will once again know peace and freedom."

"This land may be saved for now, but an open seat on the throne will surely bring war with it," he pointed out placing both hands on the sword's hilt and raising them over his head. "Tell my cousin I send my greetings."

"Tell him yourself!" Her hand finding the arrow shaft that protruded from his right calf. Seizing it in her grasp the young woman, who lay trapped under the man sitting above her with sword raised, began to violently wiggle the embedded arrow.

"Ahhhhhh!", Paul painfully screamed. He instantly released a hand holding his sword automatically bringing it down to try and stop her thrashing about. The desperate attempt leaving him open to Russell's swing. The devil's hawk-like eyes for a brief moment taken in the sight of the blade's edge seconds before it bit into his neck. The strike separating his head from his body, and launching it into the snow. Paul's body falling to the side from its place atop Lynn.

"Are you well?", worried Russell.

"I am now," she gazed into his eyes. For the first time in months Lynn knew solace.

"You be safe my queen," he smiled down at her.

The young woman knew not doubt in his words. For she always had been with him.

Reaching down with his hand and helping her regain her feet, the two embraced and melted into one another's arms. Their lips coming together.

Breaking their embrace after several minutes, Russell smiled before dropping to a knee and bowing his head. "Your people await you my queen."

"Well it not be honourable to make them wait," Lynn smiled.

Retrieving the king's crown from the snow, the young man handed it to the young woman and they started back to the courtyard.

For on this first day of January in the year fourteen hundred and thirty nine, Hamilton gained back its freedom. The townsfolk fighting not only knowing inspiration from a young queen's act of valor, but a queen knowing unrivaled protection and love from a commoner living his life by a code of honour.

Epilogue

For the first four months of Queen Lynn's seat back on the throne, Hamilton knew not only a rise in the number of women with children, but life had returned back to the village like it had been before the self-made king had ever took his place on the throne. Throughout the countryside, the good folk of this land came to know peacefulness and ease, along with the return of happiness and quietness. But on this night in the wee hours of the morning shouts and cries of pain knowing that of child birthing pierced the air in one of the castle's rooms.

"Push Joan!", instructed Queen Lynn holding onto her friend's hand. The woman squeezing the young royal's grasp as she gritted her teeth and strained to free the unborn from her body's loving protection.

"I lay witness to the child's crown," excitedly informed the castle's midwife. "One more time and the infant will know this world."

"Know one more push my friend," tenderly confirmed the young woman while rubbing Joan's wet, matted hair toward the back of her head.

No longer Lynn's personal servant, the woman gritted her teeth again and bore down deep inside her as she strained to free her little one. A loud guttural scream accompanying the push that released the child from her. In seconds her sounds of pain were replaced by the cries of a child.

"You did it!", smiled Lynn shaking their joined fists in victory. For Joan had won the battle of birthing her first infant.

"He be a boy my lady," happily revealed the midwife still seated at the foot of the bed.

"May I gaze upon my son?", weakly requested his mother.

"Of course Joan. Let me wrap the cherub in a blanket, so he knows not chill," she replied. "The child does appear to have a mark on his upper right leg, but I believe it only be one of birth."

Joan was so tired that she really hadn't understood the midwife's words for a minute or two. "Let my eyes inspect him," she asked when she truly realized what had been said.

"The midwife had just finished wrapping the child in a blanket. Handing the bundled up infant to his new mother, she informed Joan. "He shall want to feed now. For the trip into this world be much toil for him."

The woman's eyes radiating love gazing down upon the newborn, whom had been quieted by the warmth of the blanket. Closely she examined the mark. Minutes passed, as she scrutinized the infant laying peacefully in her arms.

"Are you well Joan?", worried Lynn watching tears beginning to form in the new mother's eyes. The woman's lips beginning to quiver while she began to fully cry.

"She knows exhaustion my lady," reasoned the midwife, and her words held truth. Joan was exhausted, but she sobbed for another reason.

The woman fully believed and had accepted with the whole-of-her-heart that the Lord had turned away from her and forsaken her as Paul and his men used her body. Joan had cried out her pleas to God, as she lacked any clue of understanding as to what sin she had committed that would cause her to know the Lord's wrath.

Taking her free hand, the new mother delicately touched her son's birthmark out of a lack of belief that it be real. The woman couldn't believe that the Lord had protected not only her womb, but her undying love towards the one Joan had known all his life. God had bestowed on her a miracle. It was now more than obvious to the new mother that the seed that had been planted in her womb and had taken root belonged to the one she knew nightly before the rapist.

"Matthew be his father."

Both Lynn and the midwife gasped in shock at the revelation.

Studying the child's facial features, and beholding the birthmark that even the queen had been witnessed to, Lynn pleasantly smiled. For the young woman be happy that her friend birthed a child not out of malice, but knowing that of true love. In these wee hours of morning, the folk of England knew at last a rightful heir to the throne.

The sun burned brightly in the sky allowing Hamilton to know heat on this midsummer's day in July. Russell stood watching the small bird dart through the air and fly toward him like that of a loosed arrow. The sounds of chirps and whistles accompanying it in its flight. The little avian rapidly beating its wings allowing it to hover before gently setting down on top of the stone wall. Crumbs from a fresh, baked roll already littered the meeting spot of the longtime friends.

"Well met Sir Robin," greeted Russell bowing his head while holding an infant wrapped in deerskin.

"I humbly ask your heart to know forgiveness for not meeting with you the last few days," he apologized. "I have known toil throughout them."

The little bird offering his human friend a series of chirps, as it bounced on its perch and seemed to look pass him.

"Yes," he chuckled. "She be there. Lynn wished to pay you a visit also."

Sir Robin directing his attention back to the young man before bouncing his withdrawal when the child Russell was holding began to cry.

A chuckle escaping from his human friend at the avian's chirps and whistles as it appeared to offer consolation to the child. "This be our son, Robert," Russell introduced the red-faced cherub while offering a slight tilt of presentation. Turning towards Lynn seated and leaning against the lone tree with an infant suckling from her breast, he added. "And that hungry lad be his brother, Charles."

As if attempting to flee from the infant's cries, Sir Robin took flight gliding over and finding a new perch on Lynn's shoulder. The little bird's head turning as his eye met the gaze of a feeding Charles.

"Good day to you Sir Robin," happily smiled the young woman. Her greeting followed by a series of chirps from the small inspector.

"Again I offer my apologies my friend for my busying," the young man stated while slightly rocking Robert attempting to console his son. He glanced from the newborn in his arms to Charles and reasoned with a laugh. "And knowing the looks of things, I shall know plenty more busying in the upcoming years." Both Lynn and her love shared a smile. "But take heed in my pledge to you Sir Robin. My visits shall know not lack with you my longtime friend," the young father swore. Like that of his past oaths, Russell would honour his words.

Four Days Later, On The Sabbath

"Thank you my love," softly appreciated Joan in bed leaning against a pillow as she placed a kiss on Michael's lips after he handed her a cloth. Her son Matthew hungrily feeding from one of her breasts.

"You must know fatigue from church earlier," the young man reasoned climbing onto the mattress from the other side of the bed.

"I do my love," she admitted with a tired smile. For on this day, the newly-crowned queen mother not only had her son baptized, but presented him to the townsfolk of Hamilton.

Michael grinned and placed a tender kiss on the side of Joan's head.

Offering her love a smile, the woman looked down and gazed upon her feeding son staring back up at her. "Before you partake in slumber I shall tell you a tale," she lovingly spoke to the infant, who ceased suckling on her breast and offered her a smile. "Your father found fondness with the legend of William the Brave. But not unlike the hero of that story, I shall tell you of a man who not only rescued a queen from an evil king's assassin, but lent the same queen aid in freeing a village held captive by a wicked ruler. A common man known as Russell the Honourable."

About the Author

T.R. Michaud was born in Massachusetts in 1972. He has always been a lover of fantasy, the medieval times, superheroes, football, and hockey. He was introduced to the fantasy game, Dungeon & Dragons, when he was 12 years old, causing his imagination and love to grow. Always finding an interest in architecture, T.R. Michaud worked as a draftsman, and received an Associate Degree in Science for Structural Engineering. He currently works as a Calibration Technician, but his love for fantasy caused him to always want to share his imagination with others. Through his storytelling, T.R. Michaud has introduced us to his first published novel "The Ring of Darkness" in 2017.

Check out: T.R. Michaud-Author on Facebook

CPSIA information can be obtained
at www.ICGtesting.com
Printed in the USA
BVHW031914021019
560043BV00001B/8/P